To
Andy,
Best Wishes
Mike

Thomas E. Lightburn served for twenty-two years in the medical branch of the Royal Navy reaching the rank of Chief Petty Officer. After leaving the service in 1974 he gained a Bachelor of Education Degree (Hons) at Liverpool University and taught for sixteen years. He then volunteered for early retirement and began writing for *The Wirral Journal*, and the *Sea Breezes*, a nation-wide nautical magazine. He interviewed Ian Fraser VC, ex Lieutenant RN, and wrote an account of how he and his crew crippled the Japanese cruiser, *Takao*, in Singapore. Tom is a widower and a member of Wallasey Operatic Society. His lives locally pursuing his favourite hobbies of soccer, naval and military history, the theatre, art and travel.

Books By the same author

The Gates Of Stonehouse (Vanguard Press)
ISBN1843862034

Uncommon Valour (Vanguard Press)
ISBN 9781843863014

The Shield And The Shark (Vanguard Press)
ISBN 9781843863502

The Dark Edge Of The Sea (Vanguard Press)
ISBN 9781843864004

The Ship That Would Not Die (Vanguard Press)
ISBN 9781843864639

THE SUMMER OF '39

Thomas E Lightburn

THE SUMMER OF '39

Vanguard Press

A CIP catalogue record for this title is
available from the British Library.

ISBN 978 1 84386 561 2

*Vanguard Press is an imprint of
Pegasus Elliot MacKenzie Publishers Ltd.*
www.pegasuspublishers.com

First Published in 2009

**Vanguard Press
Sheraton House Castle Park
Cambridge England**

Printed & Bound in Great Britain

Dedication

This novel is dedicated to those sailors and Royal Marines who lost their lives in HMS *Uganda*, and also Robin Seymour, ex 41 Commando RM, and all those that landed in France on D-Day.

Acknowledgments

My gratitude to the following people.

John R. Hailey, MA, Dip Gen, for supplying Photostat copies of 41 Commandos War Diaries for June 1944. To Mrs Gladys Cousins for providing a brief but detailed account of HMS *Uganda's* part in the Salerno landings in 1943. I wish to thank John Dennett, ex AB, RN, for allowing me to read the D Day memorandum issued to him and others after the war and to James Kennedy for his helpful suggestions. Lieutenant Commander G. Storey, RN (Rtd) for his valuable criticism and comments. I appreciate also the help given by Greenwich Library and the British Museum. Also to Mrs Linda Hodgson, Head Librarian at Seacombe Library, Wallasey, for reading my manuscript and offering valuable advice. I wish to thank Linda Sanderson for correcting my computer errors. I am particularly grateful to James Dunning, whose excellent book 'It Had To Be Tough', I have drawn upon. I am also indebted to the late Bill Millin, (Piper to Lord Lovat on D Day), for the use of his delightful and informative book, 'Invasion'. And last but not least to Robin Seymour, ex 41 Commando who landed on Sword Beach, for his eyewitness account of that historic and memorable day.

Thomas E. Lightburn. Wallasey, 2009.

PROLOGUE

I decided to return to France immediately after the injuries I sustained during the war had finally healed. 'Your femur and tibia have knitted almost perfectly, Mr Robertson,' the Orthopaedic Specialist had told me. He was a small, grey-haired man with horn-rimmed glasses. A stethoscope hung loosely from one pocket of his white coat and poking out from the other was the small rubber head of the patella hammer he had used to test the reflexes of my knees. 'And as for the damage to your left calf and thigh,' he went on, 'the muscle wastage is considerable but that will improve in time with physiotherapy, however, I'm afraid your limp will probably stay with you.'

The date was Monday 1st October 1945, sixteen months after I had been badly wounded. But was it wise, I asked myself, to return so soon to France, the country that held so many memories...

When I told my parents I intended leaving in a week's time they were none too happy.

'Must you go, Peter?' mum asked as she came into the dining room from the kitchen. 'You've only been out of hospital a few months, and that last operation must have taken its toll on you. And besides, you haven't arranged anywhere to stay once you get there.'

'There's bound to be a few hotels,' I replied, 'so I shouldn't have any problem finding accommodation.'

I had just finished my breakfast and was sitting at the table. Dad sat opposite me, his broad shoulders and dark brown hair barely visible over a copy of the *Daily Express.*

Dad put down his newspaper and glancing up at mum said, 'We know why you're going, don't we Hilda. It's that lass you met just afore the war started, isn't it?' Before I had time to answer, he continued, 'she could be anywhere by now. And besides, the war's only been over a couple of months and it seems a bit daft traipsing around France, especially after what your mother said about not having a hotel to go to.'

'At least this time he won't be in any danger, Bill,' said mum picking up the teapot and pouring dad a cup of tea.

'Aye, you're right there, Hilda,' answered dad, then looking at me added, 'it was just as well you learnt French at school. At least it will help you to find your way around.'

Mum stood close by staring down at me, her hazel eyes full of concern. Over a plain green dress she wore a red and white polka-dotted apron tied around her ample waist. Like dad she was born locally and at thirty-seven was two years younger than him. A few beads of perspiration ran down the side of her pale, attractive face and her fair hair was kept in place by a red bandana.

'If you remember, your Aunt Matilda moved away. As for your Uncle Claude, well,' she paused and bit her lip, 'what was the name of that town where they lived?'

'Ouistreham, mum,' I said. 'Ouistreham in Normandy.'

'Oh yes,' replied mum, 'that's when you met that young lady wasn't it?'

Before I had time to reply, mum went on, 'As you know Matilda and Claude came to London in 1940 and Claude joined the Free French Army.'

Dad was about to speak when a paroxysm of coughing, a legacy from being gassed in 1917, interrupted him. Using a handkerchief he wiped his mouth and then, with a cautious expression, looked at me and said, 'I only hope you know what you're doing, son.'

'I'll be OK,' I replied confidently. 'I told you what the specialist said, so there's no need to worry.'

Nevertheless, I had to admit dad had a point.

After breakfast the following Monday I prepared to leave. Mum took out her handkerchief, dabbed her eyes and said, 'Are you sure you've got everything? Your passport and francs?'

Yes,' I replied, patting the inside pocket of my jacket.

Mum glanced at the clock on the mantelpiece, 'It's six-thirty love,' she uttered with a sigh, 'your train leaves Lime Street at ten past eight so you'd best put a move on.'

With a wry smile, I reached across and patted her hand. 'I know mum,' I replied, 'and it arrives at Euston at twelve-thirty. You've told me a dozen times. And remember, I have been to France before.'

'I know,' replied mum dabbing her eyes again, 'but I can't help worrying…' Her voice trailed off.

'Come on, Peter,' said dad standing up. Like me he stood well over six feet, although unlike me he had lost most of his hair. 'It's time to get a move on. By the way,' he added with a wry smile, 'I've packed a razor and a few blades in case you need them.'

I stood up and grinned, 'Thanks, dad,' I replied, 'but I doubt if I'll need it.'

Mum helped me on with my overcoat and dad handed me my trilby.

'Cheerio, son,' said mum, reaching up and kissing my cheek, 'there's Spam sandwiches and a flask of tea in the carrier bag. Write as soon as you can, won't you?'

'And keep off that French wine,' said dad shaking my hand, 'as I remember it rots your socks.'

After saying goodbye I caught the bus to Seacombe Ferry and crossed on the ferryboat to Liverpool's Pier Head. The rain was pelting down and after taking a tram to Lime Street I only just made it before the train left.

Sitting opposite me in the compartment were two soldiers and a young lad in the RAF. All three had unbuttoned their tunics, loosened their ties and were smoking. Like typical servicemen they soon struck up a conversation, mainly about the war, their wives and where they were going.

One of the soldiers, a sergeant with dark hair and a sallow complexion lent across and offered me a Woodbine. 'Where yer bound, mate?' he asked.

'France,' I replied, accepting his cigarette.

'Better you than me,' he replied with a laugh, 'saw enough of them Frogs to last me a lifetime. Miserable lot they are.'

Not wishing to get involved in a conversation with him, I simply smiled and said, 'I suppose some of them are.'

An elderly lady with a green coat and a matching small Robin Hood hat who was sat next to me put down her *Woman's Own*.

'I find your remark in very bad taste,' she said haughtily. 'A lot of French people suffered greatly during the war.'

On her left sat a stout man with a round, fleshy face smoking a Meerschaum pipe. He wore an expensive looking blue pinstriped suit and except for a halo of grey hair, was completely bald. Staring at the sergeant with a pair of sharp, brown eyes, he slowly removed his pipe and in a distinct French accent, said, 'Madame is correct, Monsieur. Allied bombs kill civilians as well as the enemy,' and promptly replaced his pipe between his lips, took a quick puff and almost disappeared under a cloud of highly seasoned tobacco smoke.

'Sorry, mate,' replied the sergeant rather contritely, 'didn't mean no 'arm.'

The muggy atmosphere in the compartment was claustrophobic. Warm, tobacco-filled air hovered above like blue fog. Lines of rain splattered outside against the windows making the sound of fine gravel. Small rivers of condensation trickled on the inside making the armrests wet.

Using my fingers I wiped away a circular patch of mist from the window and stared outside. Unlike the first time I had made this journey in 1939, evidence of the war could still be seen. In some towns whole streets had been cleared of rubble while larger buildings stood like steel skeletons. Many villages still had no street lighting and were lit up by lights from within houses.

I opened the parcel of Spam sandwiches mum had packed and offered them around. The three servicemen gladly accepted one, but the others declined.

'To what part of France are you going, Monsieur?' asked the elderly man removing his pipe.

'Ouistreham,' I replied.

'Really, Monsieur,' he answered, raising his greying eyebrows. The man pursed his lips, lit his pipe and was momentarily shrouded in blue smoke. 'My wife visited Ouistreham last month. Of course the area was badly damaged during the war but is slowly recovering.'

'I see,' was my non-committal reply.

The train arrived at Euston on time and after taking the tube to Waterloo I boarded the train to Dover. Clutching my suitcase I bought a return ticket, showed my passport to a weary looking official and boarded the Channel Ferryboat. The first thing that I noticed was the paucity of passengers. In the small lounge several men and women sat around looking tired, drinking coffee and talking. A few men stretched out on the wooden benches sleeping. I found a comfortable chair near a window and ate the remaining sandwiches.

An official voice, speaking first in English and then in French informed everyone the boat would sail in fifteen minutes. The voice also warned the crossing might be rough as the English Channel was choppy and reminded passengers France was one hour ahead of England. The rumbling sound of the gangway being removed echoed around the room. The vibration of the engines quickly followed this. The time was two-thirty.

After drinking the last of the tea from my flask I sat back and closed my eyes. Perhaps my parents were right. Maybe I was wasting my time. Nevertheless I was determined to discover what had happened to the girl whose memory had sustained me throughout the darkest moments of my life. My thoughts drifted back to those carefree, halcyon days before the war…

PART ONE

CHAPTER ONE

A tall, grey-haired figure clad in black academic robes stood behind the highly polished oaken lectern. From under his mortarboard a pair of keen, dark blue eyes scanned the two hundred and twenty fresh faces seated before him. His name was Frederick Leonard Allan, a classical scholar, educated at Cambridge, headmaster of Wallasey Grammar School.

Among the several members of staff seated behind him I easily recognised the pale, thin face of Mr Ratcliffe who taught French. Mr Baldwin, head of English and History, corpulent and as usual sweating profusely, sat next to him. Despite having received the cane several times during the past three years from both, they remained my favourite teachers.

The atmosphere inside the large hall was hot and stuffy. Minute speckles of dust percolated among the rays of the June sun blazing through the high lancet windows bathing everyone in glorious sunshine. My white shirt, saturated in sweat, stuck to me like a second skin.

Like the others, I wore a dark blue blazer with gold piping. On the front of my breast pocket, a blue shield with a diagonal gold band between two lions' heads with red tongues proudly proclaimed the school badge. This was the ancient coat of arms belonging to the Meols family who founded the school, and dating back to medieval times. All blue caps also, with gold piping, were discreetly folded away.

The boys in the first four rows wore long grey trousers while the remainder were clad in shorts denoting their junior status. Several fidgeted uncomfortably waiting for the headmaster's customary address.

Mr Allan pursed his lips then, covering his mouth with his hand, cleared his throat.

With a benign expression on his clear-cut features he stared down at the rows of young faces seated before him.

'I suppose the old boy's going to give us his usual speech,' whispered Gordon Laird who was sat on my right.

'Of course he is, you idiot,' muttered Jim Boughey sitting next to him. 'What do you expect? A chorus of dancing girls?'

I had known Gordon and Jim since junior school. In contrast to Gordon a gangly blue-eyed lad with ginger hair, Jim was small, stocky with a mop of untidy dark hair and cheeky brown eyes full of humour. Both lived opposite the school in Lancaster Avenue.

'Oh do be quiet, you two,' said Stanley Cuthbert-Smyth, who was sitting on my left. 'Or we'll end up outside the head's study when the bell goes.'

Known as CS, Stanley was a tall, rotund lad whose large, horn-rimmed glasses exaggerated his owlish blue eyes.

A sudden hush descended over the hall as Mr Allan began to speak.

'1938 has been a good year for Wallasey Grammar,' he began in a high, resonant voice. 'Our rugby fifteen, cricket and rowing teams were all successful.' He paused and cleared his throat again. Before continuing, a slight frown flickered across his sallow features. 'I am sure most of you will have heard the rumours going around about the dangers of another war. Let me reassure you that, in my opinion, these are ill founded. Despite Germany's incursion into Czechoslovakia I am convinced they mean us no harm. We must all strive to get on with our German friends. War is indeed an evil thing and must be avoided at all cost.' Once again he paused, no doubt hoping what he said would reassure us, then continued. 'To those before me who are leaving today, let me wish God Speed and hope the lessons of sportsmanship, tolerance and understanding you have learnt at Wallasey Grammar will stand you in good stead in the years to come.' He then opened the bible resting on the lectern and in a sombre voice said, 'Let us pray.'

Half an hour later school broke up for the summer recess. Jim, Gordon, CS and myself shook hands with some of the seniors and wished them good luck.

'I hear you're going to France for a holiday, Pete,' said Harry Snape, one of the seniors. He produced a bag of wine gums and offered them around.

'Yes,' I replied, accepting a sweet, 'next Monday.'

'A friend of mine went to Rouen last year. He told me the girls were a bit of all right' and then, with a quick wink, added, 'if you know what I mean.'

'He doesn't need any French tarts, do you Peter?' said Gordon quickly accepting a wine gum, 'Not with that super-looking Maggie Pennington he's been seeing.'

Margaret, or Maggie as she was known, was a statuesque, pretty red-headed girl I met five months ago. She lived in Ashville Road in Seacombe, a stone's throw away from Central Park and very handy for a quick smooch after dark.

'While you're away maybe you could lend her to me?' joked Jim. 'You told us for a bar of Cadbury's chocolate she'll let you…'

'Shut up, you lot,' I replied with mock anger. 'You're only jealous 'cos none of you have girlfriends.'

'That's true,' replied Jim, 'but ask her if she likes Mars bars.'

I grinned but didn't reply. Instead I wielded my brown leather satchel at his mid-drift and missed.

'My parents are taking me in the car on a tour of Scotland,' said CS removing a bottle of lemonade from his satchel. After taking a deep gulp and passing the bottle to myself and the others, he went on, 'Listening to the head saying we ought to be sympathetic to the Germans seemed a bit odd considering he won the Military Cross in the last war.'

'You can hardly blame him,' I replied as we passed the caretaker's cottage and walked towards the main gate. 'My father's the same. They must have seen a lot of killing. And don't forget, the politicians said it was a war to end all others.'

'I hope they're right,' answered CS, 'father was reading *The Times* this morning and I overheard him tell mother that Chamberlain had made some sort of pact with Mussolini to recognise the Italian conquest of Abyssinia. Father said it was a sell out to Fascism.'

'Maybe,' I replied, 'I only hope nothing happens to spoil my holiday in France.'

CS's father was a solicitor with a law firm in Liverpool. CS lived with his parents in a large house in Harrison Drive, an affluent part of Wallasey. Most of the pupils in Wallasey Grammar were fee paying and came from well-to-do families. (£4.10.0d per term for seniors £5.5.0d for juniors). A few, like Jim, Gordon and myself were allowed free admittance due to exceptionally high scholarships grades plus the fact that our parents could not afford the fees.

An air of excitement hung in the air as junior and senior pupils laughed and joked as they streamed out of the main gate into Withens Lane. With a 'See you after the hols,' CS opened a door of a blue Morris Minor, climbed in and was driven away by his father, a dark-haired man with a military moustache.

I then waved a cheery goodbye to Jim and Gordon. Before carrying on, I stopped and looked back at the imposing red-bricked building. Complete with cricket pavilion and wide playing fields it looked like one of many grammar schools dotted all over England. I noticed a few senior pupils walking with their arms around one another, celebrating their newly acquired manhood. I gave a wry smile. In six months I too would be let loose on the world, but what kind of world would it be?

My house was a short walk from the school. After passing Saint Mary's Church I crossed Manor Road and walked passed The Saddle Inn, my dad's local. I then continued further along before turning left into Greenwood Lane. Number 120 where we lived was one of many terraced houses built on a fairly steep hill, which in the winter was ideal for sliding and sledging. My parents moved there in 1920 when dad left the army. Our house was a simple two up and two down with a toilet at the end of long backyard.

Mum was a quiet, down-to-earth woman with a dry sense of humour. Her main concern was looking after the house and dad and me. Dad and myself were keen readers. A few years ago Aunt Matilda, mum's sister, gave him a complete set of Dickens for his thirtieth birthday. He always made a point of reading to mum and myself every night. How well I remember sitting in front of a coal fire on a bitterly cold winter's night with sparks shooting up the chimney listening as dad's deep rich voice brought such characters as Tiny Tim, Mr Pickwick and David Copperfield to life.

It was dad who introduced me to the world of books and insisted I join Earlston Library. On many a night I would curl up in my small bed and fall asleep clutching Alexandre Dumas's *Three Musketeers* or Mark Twain's *Huckleberry Finn*. But it was Victor Hugo's *Hunchback of Notre Dame* that sparked off my interest in France. At first I couldn't understand parts of the dialogue written in French. However, I loved the intonation and lilting sound of the language and with the aid of an Anglo – French dictionary I was able to translate many of the words into English.

However after the First World War times were hard, especially during the Depression. Dad, who was a trained electrician, became a labourer, digging ditches and mum took in washing. After I was born in 1924 mum couldn't have more children due to some sort of internal infection.

In 1936 dad obtained a more lucrative post as hospital electrician at Victoria Central Hospital, Wallasey. As he now received a good wage he insisted mum stopped taking in washing and concentrated on the housework.

I attended Liscard Primary School and in September1935 obtained a scholarship to Wallasey Grammar. Even though the uniform was expensive – the jacket alone cost 17/6d, my parents managed to kit me out.

'By gum,' you look as smart as a guardsman,' I remember dad saying on my first morning before going to my new school. 'Doesn't he Hilda?'

Dad and I were sat down having breakfast.

'He does that,' replied mum stroking my hair, 'only mind you don't slop any of your porridge on those nice new grey trousers.'

Mum poured out the tea while dad studied the headlines in his copy of *The Daily Express.* 'It ses here this feller Mussolini has rejected the League of Nations peace plan and has demanded the Abyssinian army disband their weapons.'

'Weren't the Italians on our side in the last war?' asked mum sitting down and taking a sip of her tea.

'Aye,' replied dad, 'they were that. But if you ask me, this bugger Mussolini seems to be gettin' too big for his boots.'

'Never mind, love,' said mum, 'it'll come to nothing. Nobody's going to fight over some country thousands of miles away full of sand and camels.'

'I expect you're right, Hilda,' answered dad. 'Anymore tea in the pot, love?'

However I was more interested in the headlines telling the country that Malcolm Campbell had broken the 3000mph barrier on Bonnevile Salt Flats in Utah. 'Where's Utah, dad?' I asked munching on a piece of toast.

'Somewhere in America, lad,' replied dad, 'but I bet you a pound to a penny they'll teach you where it is and a lot more at that posh school you're going to.'

How right he was.

After my initial nervousness, I soon settled into the school routine. Jim and Gordon, who also had won scholarships, were in the same class as me.

World events such as Italy's invasion of Abyssinia and Japan's occupation of parts of China went almost unnoticed by us. Gordon, Jim and myself simply carried on with our lives playing cricket and football in Central Park, passing rude remarks at Podger, the portly, red-faced park keeper and flirting with any girls we could find.

People in the streets were more preoccupied with the death of King George V in January 1936 and the accession to the throne of Edward VIII than events on the continent. Winston Churchill's warning to parliament of a Germanic resurgence when Hitler occupied the Rhineland fell on deaf ears.

In August 1936 the Olympic Games, hosted in Berlin, captured the imagination of everyone at school. Mr Radcliffe kept a chart of each event highlighting in colour any medals won by Great Britain. Each day after the final bell I would rush home to the wireless hoping to catch up on the results.

'I see Adolf Hitler snubbed that black runner Jessie Owens,' said dad reading the *Liverpool Echo.*

'How d'you mean, snubbed?' I asked dad.

'Well, this Jessie Owens won the 100 and 200 metres, and Adolf didn't stay to present him with his gold medals. Joseph Goebbels, one of Hitler's henchmen called the American negroes "black mercenaries".'

I shrugged my shoulders. The only black people I had seen were at the pictures. 'What's his being black got to do with it?' I asked.

'From what I read,' answered dad, 'the Jerries seemed to think they are some sort of super white race and don't like the Negroes.'

'Doesn't make sense to me,' I replied, shrugging my shoulders, 'as long as they are good athletes, what's the difference?'

Dad didn't reply. Instead he kept reading his newspaper. Mum, however, was more forthcoming.

'It's not only the blacks Hitler is against,' said mum pouring dad another cup of tea. 'I hear his National Socialist Party doesn't like Jews either.'

'Mmm…'muttered dad, stroking his chin, 'it'll come to no good, mark my words. I wonder what the bugger's up to?'

'Now stop worrying,' replied mum, 'if you hurry up and drink your tea we'll be able to catch the second performance of *Modern Times* on at the Capitol. I love that Charlie Chaplin.'

In America President Roosevelt became the first president to win a second four-year term since Woodrow Wilson in 1916. Meanwhile in Britain, the wireless, newspapers and newsreels were full of King Edward VIII's affair with Mrs Wallace Simpson, an American divorcee.

'I don't know what he sees in her,' commented mum one evening after we had been to the pictures. The Movietone News had shown Edward and Mrs Simpson leaving Claridges in London. 'The poor woman's as thin as a rake.'

Dad gave a laugh and replied, 'Some men like skinny women. And besides maybe she hopes to be Queen one day.'

Mum gave a quick shrug of her shoulders. 'The Queen of England a *Yank,*' exploded mum, 'don't be daft, Bill. Anyway, he's no oil painting.'

On 11 December we listened intently to the wireless as Edward, in sombre mood, announced his abdication.

Afterwards dad stood up, stretched his arms, yawned and then said, 'Best open up a few o' them bottles of Birkenhead Brown Ales, Hilda. Looks like we've got a new king.'

The winter of 1937 was particularly cold. Central Park Lake froze over allowing people to ice skate. Gordon, Jim and I made a wooden sledge out of some orange boxes. Along with a few other lads from the school we rode it down the hills in the park until it collapsed. We then proceeded to pelt Podger with snowballs before gleefully running away feeling as if we had successfully attacked King Kong.

Then on 6 May the Movietone News showed the airship *Hindenburg* bursting into flames as it came to land in New Jersey. Along with the commentator's hysterical voice it was a calamity I'll never forget.

On 12 May the coronation of King George VI and Queen Elizabeth took place at Westminster Abbey. Everyone had the day off school and his family listened to the service on the wireless. Monarchs and dignitaries, from all over the Commonwealth and world, including Neville Chamberlain who had recently become prime minister, attended the ceremony.

'The man on the wireless said it's raining in London,' remarked mum, sipping on a glass of port, 'I hope everyone doesn't get wet and spoil everything.'

'As I recall,' said dad with a mischievous grin, 'it rained on our wedding day, but you didn't seem to mind, did you love?'

'Don't be saucy,' replied mum, nudging him with her elbow, 'and pour me another drop of port. Then give Peter some beer – after all he's passed all his exams this year and he'll soon be fourteen.'

Mum was referring to the end of term results where I had done well in most subjects, especially French, where I came top of my class.

'Aye,' replied dad, ruffling my mop of fair hair, 'and if he carries on growing he'll be able to wear one o' my suits.'

I suppose I really began to take notice of Fascism when I saw the damage inflicted on Guernica during the Spanish Civil War. Franco's air force, aided by Germany's Condor Squadron, laid waste to the city. Photographs in the newspapers, showing the bodies of women and children shocked the world.

'How could they do that to innocent women and children, dad?' I asked one morning.

'Why don't you ask your headmaster, Mr Allan,' replied dad, 'from what I hear he thinks the Germans don't mean any harm.'

Later that day I did just that. During break Jim and I saw the imposing figure of Mr Allan coming along the corridor. His academic robes flapped idly round his legs and in his left hand he carried a bulging briefcase.

Taking my courage in both hands, I nervously said, 'Excuse me, sir.'

Mr Allan stopped, raised his greying eyebrows and in that familiar, resonant voice, asked, 'Yes, boy, what is it?'

'Sorry to bother you, sir, but why are the Fascists killing so many innocent people in Spain?'

My question seemed to take him unawares and for a few seconds he continued to stare at me. Then, his pale features broke into a benign smile.

'Don't worry yourself about such things, young man,' he replied, 'concentrate on your schoolwork,' and continued along the corridor.

'Holy smoke!' exclaimed Jim, 'what was that all about?'

'I'm not sure, ' I answered dryly, 'and I'm not sure he does either.'

'I see Cammell Lairds have launched a new aircraft carrier called the *Ark Royal*,' said dad one evening. 'What with the Japs bombing buggery out of China and Hitler ranting and raving at

Nuremberg, not to mention Chamberlain sucking up to the Jerrys, I don't blame Eden for leaving the government.'

Dad was referring to Foreign Secretary Anthony Eden who, in February 1938, resigned saying the Prime Minister (Neville Chamberlain) was too anxious to please both Hitler and Mussolini, and that was dangerous.

At school, during an assembly, Mr Allan made more than a passing reference to the world situation. 'Most of you will have heard about the fears your parents and others have about the situation abroad. Even though Her Hitler and Mr Mussolini have, according to the newspapers, made what is termed "A Pact of Steel", I want to reassure you all that I very much doubt if anyone wants to go to war.'

'I think Mr Allan's right,' said Jim during break.

'What makes you think that?' asked Gordon, unwrapping a Mars bar.

'Stands to reason, doesn't it,' replied Jim. 'I saw photos of the Duke and Duchess of Windsor shaking hands with Hitler in the paper all friendly like.'

'My mum thinks Mrs Simpson's as thin as a rake,' I said.

'Maybe she should eat a few Mars bars,' laughed Gordon, knocking Jim's hand away.

However when Hitler occupied Austria in March 1938 it only served to confirm dad's suspicions.

'What did I tell you, Hilda,' he said to mum over breakfast, 'that bugger's hell bent on war. Neville Chamberlain and his cronies ought to pay attention to what Winston Churchill is saying about Germany rearming.'

'I do wish you wouldn't go on so,' replied mum spreading dripping on a piece of toast and passing it to me, 'you'll be late for work.'

Dad's pessimistic attitude towards the deepening crisis in Europe was compounded when Great Britain pledged to defend France and Belgium against any unprovoked attack.

'I notice old Neville didn't include Czechoslovakia in the treaty,' said dad after we had listened to the prime minister on the wireless.

'We can't protect every country, dear,' replied mum, 'after all, we're only a little island.'

One evening dad brought home a textbook called *Tidy's Medical and Surgical Nursing.* It was quite a thick book bound with brown leather with many interesting photographs showing patients undergoing treatments. 'Found it lying on the floor after I fixed some wiring in an empty ward,' he said placing it on the table.

That night I took the book to bed and started to read it. At first some of the names of the diseases and drugs were difficult to pronounce. But the more I read about the various surgical techniques and diseases the more interested I became. Each night I read one of the various surgical operations and its after care. I also learned that drugs had two names. One was a fancy complicated one and the other a popular commercial title.

'I bet you don't know what acetyl salicylic acid is?' I asked dad one morning.

'Go on, clever clogs,' replied dad with a sigh, 'I know you're dying to tell us.'

With what must have looked like a supercilious expression on my face, I answered, 'The common Aspirin.'

Dad shook his head, glanced at mum, and said, 'I should never have brought that book home, Hilda.'

However, I became so interested in medicine I decided one day I would be either a male nurse or better still a doctor.

At school the news that Joe Louis had floored the German ex World Champion, Max Schmeling, in one round brought a smile to everyone's faces.

'I see the Eyeties beat Hungary to win the World Cup in Paris,' said Jim one morning on the way to school.

34

'I bet if any of the British teams had entered we'd have slaughtered them,' remarked Gordon who had joined us. '"Dixie" Dean would have got a hat-trick.'

In July Wimbledon the men's singles was won by the American Don Budge. To rub salt into our sporting wounds, his fellow countryperson, Helen Moody, took the woman's title. However things improved when Len Hutton scored 364 runs in 13 hours, beating the Australians in the final Test match at the Oval.

'I say,' gasped C S, running up to Jim and myself as we entered class. 'It's a pity about Don Bradman, isn't it?'

'Why?' I replied, 'what about him?'

'He tripped over during the match and broke his shin bone.'

'Oh. So that's why we won, eh?' remarked Jim. 'Too bad he didn't do it in the first Test.'

'Humf,' muttered CS, 'that's not very sporting of you, old boy.' He walked away.

In September Chamberlain returned from Munich having received assurances from Hitler that he had no designs on the Sudetenland, the principally German-speaking region of Czechoslovakia. Photographs of him waving the white paper containing an Anglo – German accord appeared on the front page of every newspaper and shown in newsreels.

'Peace in our time, be buggered,' said dad on our way back from the *Gaumont* picture house. 'I wouldn't trust that Adolf Hitler with a barge pole.'

A month later dad's fears were confirmed when German forces marched into Czechoslovakia.

CHAPTER TWO

Christmas 1938 was one I would never forget. Wallasey Grammar beat all other schools at rugby and parties were held in every class. Aunt Matilda and her husband Claude came over from France for a three-week visit. Before they arrived we festooned the place with decorations, placed presents at the foot of a glittering Christmas tree, and stocked up with beer and a few bottles of spirits.

Aunt Matilda and Uncle Claude were a few years older than mum and dad. My aunt was small, stout with a round, homely face and, like mum, had short light, brown hair and kindly blue eyes. By contrast, Uncle Claude was tall, sturdily built with jet-black hair that matched his swarthy complexion.

Eager to test my French, I greeted them with. *'Bonjour Aunt Matilda et Uncle Claude. Je m'appelle Peter. Mon pere est Bill, ma mere est Hilda.'* (Hello, Aunt Matilda and Uncle Claude. I am Peter. My father is Bill my mother is Hilda.)

Uncle Claude threw back his head and laughed, displaying a row of perfect white teeth. Aunt Matilda looked at me and smiled. 'Congratulations Peter,' she said, 'your French is coming on very well.'

Our Christmas dinner went on all day. Maggie came around and we gorged ourselves on Christmas pudding and custard. She bought me a fountain pen and I gave a woollen red scarf. By six o'clock Claude and dad were sound asleep on the sofa; mum and Aunt Matilda busied themselves washing up. Maggie and I left and walked through a frost-covered Central Park. Ignoring the icy cold wind we found shelter behind a tree and had a quick snog. Maggie was my first proper girlfriend. I had kissed a few other girls at parties but that was all.

Maggie, however, was different.

We had met the previous summer on Wallasey Promenade when she dropped the lead of her Scottish terrier which she was taking for a walk. Standing a little over five feet six with fiery red hair she immediately caught my attention. The dog galloped towards me, stopped and allowed me to stroke it.

'Bunty, you naughty dog, come here!' I remember her shouting as she ran after the animal. The dark blue blazer with silver piping identified her as belonging to Wallasey High School. As she ran towards me the sun, high in the clear blue sky, shone through the thin material of her pastel coloured dress outlining her thighs and legs. But her main attribute, despite her young age, was her ample bosom that threatened to burst through the fabric of her white blouse.

'Sorry about that,' she gasped, picking up the dog.

'That's all right, I quite like terriers,' I lied, 'no harm done.' Then, as an afterthought, from my blazer pocket I took out a bar of Cadbury's Milk.

Her large amber eyes suddenly lit up. 'Chocolate,' she cried, 'I love chocolate. Can I have a piece?'

That broke the ice. Before she caught the number fourteen bus we arranged to meet the following Saturday at the top of Ashville Road at one o'clock.

So far my only sexual experiences had been fantasising at night about Jean Harlow or Heddy Lamarr.

All that was about to change.

The first time I tried to slide my hand up Maggie's sweater she quickly knocked my hand away. 'Let's have a piece of chocolate first,' she said, 'then maybe…'

Like a magician pulling out a rabbit, I quickly took out a bar of chocolate from my pocket, broke off two pieces and gave them to her. With a sound of a mother cat purring she immediately popped one into her mouth.

Afterwards as I slid my hand over the rough material of her brassier I could hear the blood pounding in my head. By the time my fingers found her warm, rounded nipple I thought my heart would explode. As she stuffed the second piece of chocolate into her mouth I felt the fingers of her free hand slowly undo my flies. Then I really did explode…

After several such mind-boggling episodes my big moment finally came. On a warm, May evening we were lying on the grass in a secluded spot in Central Park. It had gone nine o'clock and the park gates were closed. Hiding from Podger, the park keeper, we managed to remain hidden and had the place to ourselves.

A frantic groping, grinding and kissing session immediately followed this before Maggie pulled me on top of her. As she did so I felt her dress ride up her thighs. In one quick, jerky movement she removed her white knickers. With my heart beating a crescendo, I thought, my God, at last she's going to let me go all the way.

'Do it, Peter,' she gasped, reaching down and unbuttoning my flies, 'do it but be careful…'

Suddenly, like an all-in wrestler she wrapped her legs around my waist and pulled me hard against her body. When I entered her I heard myself gasp – suddenly I felt like a man. She murmured something incoherent and began to move her hips gently up and down. Clearly she wasn't a virgin and was more experienced than me. She must have felt me climaxing and hurriedly pushed me away. After I rolled off her she slipped her knickers back on and pulled down her dress. Then, as cool as a cucumber she smiled at me and said, 'Any more of that chocolate left?'

One evening something occurred that was to have a profound effect on my life.

We were having supper. From the wireless the melodic strains of Stanley Gibbon's Palm Court orchestra echoed around the living room. Claude was about to take a sip of tea when he suddenly stopped, looked at me and said, 'How would you like to come and stay with us during your summer holidays in June, Peter?' Without waiting for an answer, he added, 'It would help you improve your French. Wouldn't it Matilda?'

Aunt Matilda smiled at me and in a loud excited voice, exclaimed, 'Splendid idea! After all he'll be fifteen next December. What do you say, Peter?'

A thrill of excitement suddenly ran through me. So far the only time I'd been out of England was a day trip to Isle of Man. France seemed a world away. I glanced at mum and dad and immediately answered, 'Sounds great to me. Can I go?'

At first dad wasn't too keen on me going. He pursed his lips, looked at mum and said, 'I don't know about you, Hilda, but I think the idea of Peter leaving the country at the moment could be unwise. What if there's a war? Germany has just launched a battleship called the *Bismark.* It's as big as anything we've got. And what if Germany attacks France like the last time?'

With typical Gallic aplomb Claude threw both hands in the air, 'Come on Bill,' he cried, 'they wouldn't dare. France has the Maginot Line and biggest army in Europe.'

'Nevertheless,' answered dad, shaking his head, 'I still feel it could be risky.'

'Well, I think it's a good idea,' interjected mum. 'As Claude says, it will broaden Peter's outlook on life and improve his education.'

And that was that.

Against dad's better judgement he agreed that I could leave on Monday the eighth of June, a week after school broke up for holidays.

'Take the cross channel ferry from Dover to Calais,' said Claude. 'Then go by train to Caen and when you get there, telephone us and we'll come and pick you up.'

Mum said she would write to Aunt Matilda to confirm the details.

During the next few months Neville Chamberlain pledged to defend Poland if that country was attacked, and Hitler and Mussolini visited one another confirming the infamous 'Pact of Steel'. The Spanish Civil War ended with victory for Franco's Nationalist Party. Nearer home more than seventy men died when the submarine HMS *Thetis* sank in Liverpool Bay.

'Poor buggers,' muttered dad reading about the tragedy in the *Liverpool Echo.* 'It says here a hole was cut in the side but only a few men managed to escape. Salvage vessels managed to pass hawsers underneath her but she finally went under.'

The day the school broke up for summer holidays mum and dad bought me a black Box Browning camera.

'It's fully loaded with a role of twelve films,' said dad, 'all you do is place a hand across the top of the aperture to guard against the light, here.' He indicated a small dark square on the top, 'press the shutter and Bob's your uncle. Also remember to turn the handle after each film, and oh yes, make sure the sun is behind you. It gives a better picture.'

Dad passed the camera to me. 'Gosh, thanks, dad,' I replied looking at it, 'these are expensive, are you sure you can…'

'Nonsense,' interrupted mum, 'just make sure you take a photo of Aunt Matilda and Uncle Claude.'

I had never owned a camera. For a while, I practised peering into the aperture and aiming it at various objects. Suddenly my imagination ran amok and I felt like one of those newsreel cameramen taking pictures of famous film stars. I smiled to myself wondering if I would find anyone glamorous to photograph in France.

Two days later I met Maggie at the corner of Ashville and Poulton Road. As soon as I saw her I sensed something was wrong. She wore an old school jacket and her red hair, usually so well groomed, was uncombed. Before I had time to tell her I was going to France, she looked at me furtively and with more than a hint of panic, blurted, 'Mum and dad say I can't see you anymore. My school reports aren't very good and they say it's because of you and me...' She folded her arms and nervously shuffled her feet, then quietly added, 'Sorry Peter.' I was about to reply when she abruptly turned and ran back down the road.

When she had gone I stood somewhat dumbfounded and surprised. Later that day I met Jim and Gordon. Both received the news philosophically.

'Cheer up, Pete,' said Jim placing a consoling arm around my shoulder, 'just think of all the money you'll save on chocolate bars.'

'Jim's right,' added Gordon. He paused, then with a humorous expression in his pale blue eyes winked at Joey and said, 'But I wonder what she'd do for a couple of Mars bars?'

CHAPTER THREE

The night before I left home to go to France I hardly slept. I kept thinking perhaps dad was right. What if war did break out while I was away? Would I be able to return home? And worse still, what might happen if I was interned in one of those concentration camps dad had told mum and myself about.

'Locked up for no other reason than being Jewish,' said dad one evening glancing at us over his *Daily Express.*

'Yes,' added mum with a sigh, 'I heard on the wireless they have to hand in their jewellery or work in the German factories. I don't know what the world's coming to…'

Mum shaking my shoulder abruptly woke me up. I blinked a few times as she placed a mug of tea on my bedside table before drawing the curtains. She wore a pink woollen dressing gown and her hair was in curlers.

'Wake up, sleepy head,' I heard her say, 'it's six o'clock. Remember, your train leaves at eight and you'll need a good breakfast before you go, so don't turn over.'

'No chance of that, mum,' I said reaching for the cup, and then with a spirited cry, added, 'look out France, here I come.'

Mum gave a sad smile, shook her head and left the room.

'Sorry I can't come with you to the station, son,' said dad over breakfast, 'but I have to install lights in the new wards that are opening. Your mother will go with you, won't you, Hilda?'

Mum looked at me and with a half-hearted laugh, replied, 'Of course I will, can't have him getting lost can we?'

'There's no need, mum,' I hastily replied, 'I have been to Liverpool before, you know.'

'Nonsense,' she answered, 'besides, I heard there's a sale on at Blacklers.'

'Oh, and by the way,' said dad shaking my hand, 'your camera is in your suitcase and I've packed a razor and a few blades. You might need it to shave off that bumfluff you have on your upper lip.'

After shaking dad's hand, mum and I left and caught the bus to Seacombe Ferry. In one hand I carried a suitcase and in the unlikely event of the warm weather turning inclement, an overcoat over the other arm. The early morning breeze fanned our faces as we crossed the Mersey in a ferryboat full of commuters on their way to Liverpool. We boarded a tram and arrived at Lime Street fifteen minutes before the LMS (London, Midland and Scottish) train was due to leave.

'Be careful, Peter,' muttered mum, her eyes filling up, 'and send us a postcard when you arrive.'

Suddenly, the sight of mum crying gave me a lump in my throat.

'Don't worry, mum, I'll be all right,' and then, trying to cheer her up, added, 'and don't spend too much at Blacklers, eh?'

Mum tried to smile, then gave me a final hug and a wet kiss.

After changing trains at Crewe and Birmingham I finally arrived at Euston shortly after one o'clock. I then crossed London by tube to Waterloo and caught the train to Dover. The steamship was crowded with holidaymakers but I managed to find a comfortable seat in the lounge.

In less than two hours the ship hove into Calais harbour, where after careful scrutiny of my passport by a keen-eyed official, I made my way to the railway station. The clerk at the ticket office told me my train would arrive at Caen at four o'clock. I then found a telephone booth and contacted Aunt Matilda.

'Bonjour, Pierre,' she cried in her distinctive high-pitched voice, 'I hope you had a good crossing and weren't seasick.'

She then told me to wait outside Caen railway station where she and Claude would pick me up.

'Our car is a small, ghastly red Renault,' she said with a slight laugh. 'Claude chose the colour. You can't miss it. Have a cup of coffee in the café. We'll be about half an hour.'

I felt a surge of excitement run through me. This was my first visit to a foreign land and I had three weeks to see as much of France as possible.

The station was quite big. It consisted of several platforms and waiting rooms covered in grey, slatted roofs separated by black, grimy walls. Porters wearing smart blue and red caps helped passengers with their luggage. Workmen clad in grimy overalls busied themselves unloading goods into warehouses at the end of each platform. The usual caustic smell of billowing steam and grit made the already humid atmosphere unbearably warm and sweaty.

The time by the station clock read five-thirty. I quickly went outside, found a café and ordered a large cup of spicy French coffee. The sky remained blue and cloudless with a faint breeze.

The road nearby was quite congested with green single decker buses and motorcars. Men and women, dressed in cool summer clothes, strolled about, shopping or gesticulating in typical Gallic fashion while engaged in animated conversation. On the opposite side of a busy road ran a variety of shops plus a few hotels badly in need of a coat of paint.

I sipped my drink and watched a group of young Frenchmen wearing blue berets make raucous comments while eyeing up a couple of pretty girls. I immediately remembered what Harry Snape had said at school about French girls and smiled.

Just as I finished my coffee a small red motorcar pulled up near the curb behind a bus. I easily recognised the dark features of Uncle Claude who was driving, and the homely smile of Aunt Matilda sitting next to him. They both got out and greeted me. Aunt Matilda wore a short, pink summer jacket over a floral dress. Claude was dressed casually in an open-necked white shirt and fawn trousers.

'Lovely to see you, Peter,' said Aunt Matilda in English, giving me a kiss on the cheek. 'Good journey?'

'Yes thank you, Auntie,' I replied.

'Good,' she answered, 'and call us Matilda and Claude, aunts and uncles make us sound like old fogies.'

'Welcome to France, Peter,' said Claude, smiling while giving me a warm handshake. 'Now we must speak in French, always. Don't forget we promised your mother and father to widen your education.'

Claude placed my suitcase and overcoat in the boot and I climbed into the back seat.

'How far away is Ouistreham?' I asked, staring out of the window.

'About twelve kilometres,' replied Claude looking around at me. 'We'll be there in no time.'

After driving up a steep road we passed a series of small houses with well-kept gardens. Matilda asked how mum and dad were while Claude concentrated on the narrow, winding road that sneaked out of the city into the wide, undulating countryside dotted with heavily wooded copses.

We passed hamlets full of orchards and farms crammed with poultry along with herds of cattle lazily grazing in the evening sunshine. The windows were wound down allowing the sharp, seasoned smell of the countryside to attack our olfactory senses.

Then came a surprise.

As the car reached the rise of a steep hill the countryside exploded into a pageant of iridescent yellow complemented by the electric blue of the sky. In all directions undulating fields of corn gently swayed in the breeze as if caressed by some unknown force. It reminded me of the scene from *The Wizard of Oz* when Dorothy first sees the Emerald City.

'My goodness, I wish I could take a photo of that!' I exclaimed gazing around. 'I've never seen so much corn in my life.'

Matilda and Claude laughed. 'That's how we get our famous French bread,' said Matilda. Then with a slight girlish giggle, added, 'Don't forget the milk from the cows for our gorgeous Camembert cheese.'

'That's right,' added Claude smacking his lips, 'and the Calvados.'

'What's Calvados?' I asked, still staring outside.

Claude gave a quick glance over his shoulder. 'Apple brandy, very potent,' he said, smacking his lips, 'maybe we'll allow you to taste it before you leave, but don't tell your mother.'

Away to my right on high ground I could see many large buildings and trails of black smoke eddying out of several tall chimneys.

Matilda must have seen me. 'The town over there is called Mondeville-Colombelles,' she said, and with a touch of pride, added, 'that's where they produce most of the steel in France. Claude is the chief engineer there.'

Some distance away on my right I saw a wide stretch of water rippling gently under the warm sunshine.

'Where does that river go to?' I asked with an air of curiosity, 'it looks out of place in the countryside.'

'That's the Caen Canal,' answered Claude without turning his head, 'Ouistreham is a small port and goods are taken up the canal to Caen. You can't see it from here, but the River Orne runs parallel to it.'

We passed a small, picturesque hamlet called Benouville situated near the centre of crossroads. Close by was a steel, arched bridge spanning the canal.

'There's another bridge at Ranville,' said Claude, 'they both cross the river and canal. As you can see,' he added, 'the countryside is fairly flat and good for cycling.'

All of a sudden the road sloped downwards and in the distance the English Channel appeared like a vast expanse of shining blue water. Separating land from sea came a wide curving ribbon of soft yellow sand and the grey stoned buildings of Ouistreham.

'Not far to go, now,' said Matilda, 'I've prepared a nice pan of lamb stew.' She then gave a short laugh. 'Your mother says it's your favourite. I think it's called Scouse.'

Quite abruptly the Macadam became a bumpy cobbled surface as we entered the town square dominated by a church with a tall, pointed bell-tower. Above the arched entrance patterns of Romanesque chevrons told its age. Stout flying buttresses fortified the walls and the multi-coloured glass in lancet and wide mullioned windows reflected the strong sunlight.

The heat of the late afternoon was sultry and rather oppressive; high above, the sun glowed in the sky like a huge yellow orb changing the cobbled stone square from a well-worn grey into a pale shade of mustard.

A mixture of tall and small houses with open wooden shutters and shops selling everything from meat to flowers appeared on the narrow pavements. Men in short sleeves sat outside cafés smoking while women in sombre black shawls gossiped. Children and youngsters thronged around their elders laughing and playing. A passing priest in a brown cassock made a gesture of supplication to some before crossing over the square, opening the heavy doors of a church and going inside.

'That's the church of Saint Samson,' said Matilda, 'built in the eleventh century. It has a magnificent stone vault ceiling. You must see it before you leave.' She then pointed to an imposing building at the far end of the square and added, 'And that's the Hotel de Ville, the town hall, the one that's flying the Tricolour.'

'Is it always this crowded?' I asked.

'The townsfolk do most of their shopping and socialising in the early evening,' replied Matilda, 'and many of the shops are shut in the afternoon, especially in the summer.'

'Siesta time,' I laughed.

'Something like that,' answered Matilda with a smile.

Just then, the ground shook as the melancholy chiming of the church bells rang out. 'My goodness,' cried Matilda glancing at her wristwatch, 'six o'clock already. You must be starving.'

Claude stopped the car outside a large, three-storey, 'gambrel' roofed house on the corner of a wide, dusty road along, which ran a narrow concrete pavement. (This is a symmetrical two-sided roof with two slopes on each side.) In front an iron fence and gate protected a garden ablaze with a mass of multi-coloured roses and a host of other flowers. Behind this, a winding gravelled pathway led up to a set of stone steps and a stout oaken door with a highly polished brass handle.

On the front gable, brown wooden shutters on all the windows were open displaying pink, net curtains. Directly opposite the house, on the other side of the road, was a sign that read, *Avenue Michel Cabieu.*

As I climbed out of the car, Matilda cried a cheerful, 'Bonjour Mademoiselle Rochelle,' to an elderly, grey-haired lady wearing a blue pinafore standing in a garden next door. *'Ca va*, How are your roses?'

The lady smiled, waved a pair of clippers encased in a leather glove, and replied, 'Excellent, I see you have a visitor.'

Matilda nodded and looked at me. 'This is Peter, my nephew,' she replied, 'he's on holiday from England.'

The elderly lady looked at me, her face wrinkling into a gentle smile. 'Welcome to France, young man,' she said in perfect English, 'Normandy is good cycling country, make sure you see lots of it.'

'Thank you very much, mademoiselle,' I replied in French, 'I'll certainly try.'

The elderly lady sighed, as if tired of pruning, placed her clippers in her pinafore pocket, waved again and walked wearily into her house.

For a few seconds I stood and looked around. At the bottom of the road I caught a glimpse of sea and sand. A slight breeze caught the sweet scented smell of flowers; everything looked so tranquil and peaceful. I instinctively knew I would love it here.

Matilda opened the door and I followed Claude along a thickly carpeted hallway into a spacious lounge. A strong odour of garlic and herbs gave the atmosphere a distinctly foreign flavour. Meanwhile Claude disappeared up a winding staircase carrying my suitcase and overcoat.

'Sit down and I'll make us some coffee,' said Matilda, taking off her short jacket.

While she was away I slowly sank down into a comfortable brown Chesterfield settee. To my surprise the style of the room appeared to be typically English with dark, oaken table and chairs – a glass-fronted cabinet housing creamy glazed faience. The floor was covered in a thickly piled carpet and scenes of local beauty hung on the walls decorated with floral patterned wallpaper. Tall, well-stoked bookcases occupied one side of the room and in a corner half-hidden in shade stood an elegant brass lamp stand with a sloping lilac shade trimmed with gold tassels.

A small chandelier hung from the centre of a cream-coloured ceiling. The fawn curtains were drawn aside. This allowed the pale rays of evening sunlight to pour through the wide, bay window making the small glass electric bulbs glitter like diamonds.

In a dark, open fireplace logs lay waiting to be lit. A beautiful green onyx Ormolu clock flanked on either side by framed photographs of my parents rested on a white marble mantelpiece. Above this hung a silver-gilt framed mirror. I stood up and stared into it, frowned, then ran my fingers through my untidy mop of fair hair; I then touched the fury mass of down on my chin and, with a smile, realised I would have to use the razor dad packed after all.

Matilda appeared holding a tray with a silver coffee service and a gorgeous chocolate gateau on a large round Wedgwood plate. The sight of the cake and the aromatic aroma of the coffee made my taste buds come alive.

'Help yourself to cake, dear,' she said placing the tray on a small table. She then poured a cup of coffee, passed it to me and went on, 'When you've eaten, Claude will show you to your room. Then we'll have that Scouse stew I promised.'

While I was eating my second slice of cake Claude came in and sat down and lit a small cheroot.

'When you've unpacked and settled in,' he said, flicking some ash into a silver ashtray, 'we can take a walk around the town.' His swarthy features broke into a wide grin, 'And leave some of that cake for me.'

My room was on the second floor.

'Here we are,' said Claude, opening the door, 'bathroom en-suite and all the comforts of home.'

His last remark was somewhat exaggerated. My bedroom at home didn't have a wide, bay window and certainly didn't overlook a lush green lawn surrounded by bushes of floribunda in full bloom.

The room was cosy and comfortable. I placed my suitcase on the wide patchwork covered bed and unpacked my clothes, neatly placing each item in a chest of drawers. After hanging my jacket and overcoat inside the highly polished wardrobe I sat down on the bed and switched on the small bedside lamp. The famed paintings of the Norman countryside sent a shiver of excitement running through me. Soon, I told myself, I would see the real thing. I lay back, stared up at the shaded electric light hanging from the ceiling, and yawned. It had been a long day and even though I felt tired I had a feeling I wouldn't be able to sleep.

An hour later we were sat in the kitchen at a long well-scrubbed wooden table eating Matilda's delicious lamb stew.

'Is it as good as your mother's?' asked Matilda pouring a glass of red wine and placing it next to my plate.

'Absolutely,' I replied, before breaking off a chunk of bread from a baguette. After wiping the bread around my empty plate I sampled the wine. It tasted bitter. However, not wanting to appear rude, I took a good gulp and washed down my food.

'Do you like the wine?' asked Claude, 'It's made locally, do have some more.'

'Er... no thanks,' I replied, trying to hide my reaction, 'we, err... don't drink much wine at home.'

Matilda rose, and after wiping her hands on her slightly stained white pinafore, took hold of my plate and walked along the stone floor to a wide iron stove at the end of the kitchen. She dipped a long-handled ladle into one of several large aluminium pots, and heaped more stew onto my plate.

'There!' said Claude, smiling at me. 'As your father would say, that'll put hairs on your chest.'

Half an hour later Claude and I left the house.

'Don't be too long, Claude,' said Matilda before closing the front door, 'Peter must be tired.'

51

Matilda was right, I did feel a bit weary, but I was more than anxious to see my new surroundings.

As we left the house I could hear the rasping sound of the sea coming from the end of the road. The sky was a dark, cloudless blue and the earlier warmth of the breeze now held a slight chill.

'The nights can be quite cold,' said Claude, 'that's why I suggested we wore jackets.'

In a few minutes we reached the town square. Electric lighting lit up the church steeple bathing the wide perpendicular windows in a pale, sulphurous light. Once again I was startled as the booming notes of the church bells striking nine reverberated over the cobbled stoned ground.

The shops were still open and the place was still a hive of activity.

We passed a florist with a window packed with a variety of colourful flowers.

'Matilda works there three mornings a week,' said Claude, 'I'm sure she only does it to keep up with the local gossip.'

The people seemed relaxed as they walked around, shopping or standing about, talking, smoking and generally passing the time of day. Many men like myself were stocky built, tall and fair headed – typical of their Norse heritage. Oddly, only a few women had a similar appearance, most being dark and swarthy similar to Claude.

Claude greeted one or two people and stopped to introduce me to an elderly couple sitting outside a café sipping coffee.

'Do not forget to see our wonderful beaches, especially those at Lion-sur-Mer where we live,' said the women whose name was Madam Fevere. She wore a short dark coat and a white, woollen shawl was draped over her shoulders. As we shook hands her pale blue eyes lit up into a kindly smile. The light shining from the café exaggerated the deep wrinkles in her soft, milk-like features. This, plus the strands of grey hair poking from under a coloured headscarf, gave her a kind, homely appearance.

Mr Fever, a small man with a smattering of blond hair plastered over an almost bald head, and a round cherubic face, didn't offer his hand. Instead he lit a Gouloise and lent back in his chair.

'Get the lad a bicycle Claude,' he said, exhaling a cloud of blue tobacco smoke. 'It's flat countryside and easy to get around. As a boy I cycled all around Normandy.' Then showing a set of uneven, yellow teeth, he laughed, 'And don't forget to take a bottle of wine.'

A few narrow lanes led off from the square leading no doubt to other parts of the town. We passed the Hotel de Ville, lit up with the Tricolour hanging limply from above the arched entrance.

'Caen is only twenty kilometres away,' I said noticing a signpost at the corner of a wide, exit road. 'I could easily cycle there.'

Claude gave a short laugh. 'It gets a bit hilly near Caen,' he said, 'as Madam Le Fevre suggested you'd better stick to the beach area. You can borrow my bicycle tomorrow and explore to your heart's content.'

CHAPTER FOUR

The next day, Tuesday 9 June, dawned bright and warm. I awoke to the sound of a motorcar's engine fading away in the distance. A glance at my wristwatch told me the time was half-past seven. The heavy beige curtains were drawn open and through the open bay windows came the melodious chirping of the dawn chorus. I blinked several times, stretched my arms upwards and yawned. For a while I lay, my hands behind my neck, staring at the ceiling. Suddenly, seeing my camera on the dressing table, a surge of excitement ran through me: this was my first day in France and I was determined not to waste a moment of it.

I was about to fling back the bedclothes when a knock came at the door and in came Matilda carrying a cup and saucer. The aromatic smell of coffee instantly filled the room. She wore a spotlessly white pinafore over a floral dress and her hair was in metal curlers similar to those used by my mother.

'Good morning,' she said, placing the cup and saucer on my bedside table. 'Thought you'd like a cup of coffee. Sleep well?'

'Yes, thank you,' I replied sitting up and straightening my pale green cotton pyjama jacket. 'Like a log.'

With a homely smile, Matilda stood back and folded her arms across her ample bosom.

'Before Claude went to work he left his bicycle in the hallway for you,' she said, and then with a shirt laugh, added, 'he says there is a small tool kit in the bag behind the seat in case you break down. Breakfast in half an hour. Eggs and porridge all right?'

'Just the job,' I replied, reaching for the cup, 'and thanks again.'

The coffee was hot, strong and sweet. After drinking it I leapt out of bed and went into the bathroom. For a few minutes I looked at myself in a mirror above the washbasin. Using a finger I removed bits of encrusted sleep from the corners of my blue eyes and blinked several times. My thick fair hair was a tousled mess and after cleaning my teeth, I decided to take dad's advice and shave. Feeling quite grown up, I carefully lathered my face and with the delicacy of a brain surgeon proceeded to remove the fine hairs from my chin and upper lip. I then swished warm water on my face, ran my fingers over the now hairless area, combed my hair and with the air of macho satisfaction dried myself. I then slipped on a pair of grey slacks, tucked in a white, opened neck shirt and drew a slightly tight short-sleeved woollen maroon pullover over my head.

The now familiar pungent smell of coffee filled the air as I walked downstairs. Before entering the kitchen I noticed a sturdy looking Raleigh bicycle leaning against the wall. It was shiny black and had a three-speed gearbox. Attached behind the saddle hung a black leather bag. A quick glance inside showed an assortment of tools.

After breakfast Matilda produced a brown canvas haversack. 'I've packed a slice of Camembert cheese, some wine and bread plus a few apples in case you get hungry,' she said placing the haversack on the floor by my side. 'If you can try and get back by one, Claude will be back and we can have lunch. And oh yes,' she added with a smile, 'I hope you don't need it, but I've included a small medical kit.'

After placing my camera in the haversack I gave Matilda a quick kiss on the cheek, gathered the bicycle and left the house. At the end of a long, gravel-covered road I could clearly see the waters of the English Channel sparkling under the early morning sunlight. A few anaemic looking clouds spoiled what was otherwise an immaculate blue sky and even though it was only a little after nine, I could feel the warmth of the sun on my back.

Cycling down the road I was struck by the individuality of the houses lining each side of the road. Some were half-timbered, others had flat grey, slated roofs. Others with slanting red terracotta tiles reminded me of photographs of those in the Mediterranean, while the tall pointed turrets of many resembled miniature castles. Each was painted in a variety of colours ranging from vivid red to a more conservative dark blue. All had gardens in full bloom protected by wooden fences varying in shapes and sizes.

Graceful elm and ash trees cast early morning shadows on the road along which one or two men and women walked their dogs. Quite a few children, evidence that the schools had broken up for summer recess, laughed while playing hopscotch. One or two older boys and girls on bicycles waved a cheerful *'Bonjour, Monsieur.'*

The Raleigh held the ground well and was easy to handle. In a matter of minutes I arrived at the bottom of the road. Suddenly, with the warn sun fanning my face, the magnificent vista of the Normandy coastline opened up before me.

I stopped cycling and with one foot resting on the ground shielded my eyes. The scene before me was breathtaking. First came the vast stretch of golden sand that ended at the edge of deep green waters of the English Channel. Then, far away in the distance, a white blur lay across the horizon dividing it from a cornucopia of cloudless, cobalt sky.

The bay was horseshoe shaped. Away to my left stood the white-faced lighthouse at the end of the entrance to the River Orne. In the distance the high ground on both sides of curved coastline rose like protective bookends. Undulating sand dunes covered in clumps of sharp-pointed, yellowish-green Sickle gorse swept gently down to the shoreline. Behind, rows of gaily painted summer villas stretched along a wide winding pathway. In front of these, painted in a variety of colours lay rows of trellised bathing chalets. Occasionally a person, swathed in a large coloured towel, would sheepishly emerge from one and make their way onto the beach. Further along, barely visible in the heat haze, I could see the rooftops of a few inland villages. The scene was too idyllic to miss. I immediately removed my camera from the haversack and remembering to keep the sun behind me, quickly clicked the shutter and took my first ever photograph.

Even though it was just after ten o'clock the area was quite crowded. A large sign in red told me I was passing through a village called Riva Bella, an Italian-sounding name that somehow sounded out of place in a French town. Set slightly back from the beach was what appeared to be a holiday park with go-carts, stalls with multi-coloured canopies and an amusement arcade. Then, poking out over a few rooftops I saw the word CASINO painted in white on the side of a large building. Remembering gambling scenes I had watched in the cinema, I wondered if Claude and Matilda ever tried their luck on the roulette wheel. I stopped again and took another photograph.

Several young cyclists passed me in both directions. Children played on the beach, or paddled in the shallow edge of the sea, excitedly kicking and splashing one another under the watchful eyes of adults. Elderly couples strolled arm in arm while others holding onto leashes, walked their dogs. Pretty girls in long summer dresses giggled at one another while shooting cautious glances at boys lounging on the sand. High above, looking like a pack of hungry vultures, seagulls squawked before diving to accept tit-bits from early morning picnickers.

The natural beauty and tranquillity of the scene stretching before me set my pulse racing. Suddenly I felt like an explorer in an unknown land. I took a deep breath, removed my pullover and cycled on.

After giving a friendly wave to a few passers-by I saw a girl wearing a yellow and black polka-dotted flared skirt and a sleeveless white blouse. She was kneeling down in front of her bicycle that was lying on the side of the pathway. A brown carrier bag hung over one of the handlebars. Two lads cycled passed offering help but the girl smiled and shook her head. Then, as I came closer, I heard her cry. Clutching her right hand she quickly stood up. She had her back to me and looked a little over five feet. I immediately stopped, alighted from my bicycle and approached her. As I did so strands of her shoulder-length light brown hair caught the breeze and flew wildly into the air.

'Er... can I help you miss?' I said hoping my French was good enough.

Ignoring the oil stains on her hand she placed an injured finger in her mouth, sucked, then turned and looked at me.

At a glance I guessed she was my age. Her oval-shaped face was slightly flushed, spreading a soft rosy glow over her otherwise slightly tanned features. Under a small but well-shaped nose was a pair of wide sensuous lips that at the moment were curled into a painful grimace. A thin black leather belt with a shiny buckle surrounded a thin waist, and her young figure, evident under the thin material of her blouse was well-developed. She wore a pair of white, flat-soled shoes and ankle-length socks. For a few seconds I stood mesmerised, staring at her. She was undoubtedly the most beautiful girl I had ever met.

Suddenly my heartbeat increased. I felt the blood pulsate inside my head and my stomach contract.

'Thank you,' she replied, removing the injured finger from her mouth. As she did, blood oozed from a small, but deep cut. Tears welled up her velvety brown eyes. 'My bicycle chain came off and while I was trying to put it on I cut my finger on one of the bolts.' Her voice had a husky, beguiling tone that was barely audible over the soft rustling sound of the sea.

'Er... I think I can help you,' I said, remembering the medical kit Matilda had packed.

Straight away I lent my bicycle on the grass verge and opened up my saddlebag. Inside, next to a canvas roll of tools was a small green cardboard box containing a packet of cotton wool, some gauze and plasters.

The girl sat down on the grass while I dabbed her cut and applied a plaster.

'There,' I said, standing back and looking down at her, 'good as new. Now let's see what's wrong with your bike.'

We attracted the attention of several passers-by. One or two offered help but the girl smiled, thanked them and said she was all right.

One of the small nuts on her chain appeared to be loose. Using a spanner I knelt down and tightened it, then turned the pedals, and replaced the chain. With a feeling of gallant satisfaction I smiled and stood up.

'It's all right now,' I said, standing the bicycle upright and pushing it to and fro a few times.

'Thank you,' she replied, offering an uninjured hand, 'my name is Adele Michaud, and you?' As she looked at me I felt an odd sensation in my stomach and once again my heartbeat bounded inside my chest.

'Peter,' I stammered, feeling the colour rise in my cheeks. 'Peter Robertson.'

The palm of her hand and fingers felt pliant and warm. A silver bangle dangled around her wrist and her bare forearm was covered in tiny fair hairs.

'You are English, yes?' she asked, flashing a set of small even white teeth.

I gave a nervous laugh, glanced at my feet and answered, 'Yes, I am.'

'Ah,' she cried, and replied, 'My Knight in shining armour, I study English at college. I speak good, yes?'

'Yes you do,' I replied, passing the bicycle to her, 'I hope you can understand my French.'

'Yes, I can,' she answered pushing her bicycle. 'But we speak English. It is good practice for me. Please, we walk together. I am going home. I live in Lion-sur-Mer.'

'Where's that?' I asked.

'Down there,' she replied, pointing to the far end of the curving coastline. 'The villages you see just along the coast are Collville and La Breche. I live in Lion-sur-Mer about two kilometres from here.'

I told her I was staying with my aunt and uncle.

'For how long are you here?' she asked, glancing across at me. Her eyes as she spoke seemed to have a bewitching effect on me and I found myself trying to avoid her gaze.

'Three weeks,' I answered. 'I arrived last night.'

When we arrived at Collville I told her I had wine and cheese. I suggested we stop and have some.

'Thank you,' she replied, 'but I must not eat. Mama said it will spoil my lunch. But perhaps we can rest.' From her carrier bag she took out a long sleeved thin woollen cardigan. 'To protect against the sun,' she said slipping it on.

We lay our bicycles on the grass and sat down. The high grassy verge sloped down on the beach that by now was quite crowded. As she lay back in the grass a gust of wind blew her skirt up.

'Ooo, la, la,' she laughed and hastily pulled down her dress, but not before I caught a glimpse of smooth white thighs and pink knickers.

She was anxious to know about England.

'Do all the gentleman wear those funny bola hats?' she asked laughingly.

'Not where I live,' I replied. 'Only in London.'

Ten minutes later she decided it was time to leave. 'Mama expects me home for lunch at twelve,' she said, 'we use our cycles, now.'

The pathway curved around the edge of the grassy hills that were quite steep and sloped down onto the beach. On our right the wide ribbon of sands stretched away like a carpet of gold at the edge of breathtaking blue sea that seemed to go on forever.

On our left we passed a small village with an assortment of attractive houses all of which were painted in a variety of pastel colours.

'That's La Breche,' replied Adele, seeing me staring across at it. 'My brother Emile knows a girl there,' she added tossing her hair back and laughing. 'He thinks he's in love with her.'

'And is he?' I replied feeling slightly embarrassed at the mention of love.

She shrugged her shoulders. 'Who knows what love is,' she replied, giving me a coquettish glance.

As we arrived at Lion-sur-Mer my attention was drawn to a tall, imposing house that opened directly onto the front. It had a sloping terracotta roof and embossed into the grey granite wall above the arched entrance were the words HENRI CHALET. 1889.

'What a fine-looking house,' I remarked.

'That's where Monsieur Corbert, the mayor of Lion-sur-Mer lives,' answered Adele.

'Is that his name above the door?' I asked.

'No,' replied Adele, 'that's the name of his grandfather. My house is down the lane you see by the side. It's also a short cut into the main town.'

'If you don't mind, 'I said, 'could we stop while I take a photograph of the house?'

'Oui,' she replied with a smile, 'you photograph me, yes? In front of the house.'

61

We lent our bicycles against the coat wall and I took out my camera. Adele walked up and, with one hand resting on the wrought iron gate in front of the house, smiled and struck a pose. I peered through the lens then clicked the shutter.

'There,' I said with a confident air, 'that's one for posterity.'

More houses came into view and we turned off the path into a wide cobbled street leading into the town. Crowded shops and cafés lined each side. At the end of the street dominating the town square was a church similar in structure to the one at Ouistreham. 'That's the Church of Saint Pierre,' said Adele, 'my parents were married there.' A few passers greeted Adele including one or two young lads who smiled and waved a cheerful 'Bonjour.'

With Adele leading the way we crossed the road and walked down a narrow, cobbled stoned alley.

'When I was little,' she said with a girlish grin, 'I used to sneak down here after dark and play with my friends. You see it's away from the main road.'

We then came to a tall, imposing half-timbered, three-storey house standing on its own at the junction of the two roads. On the opposite corner was a large orchard, its trees heavy with ripe apples.

At each level an open bay window with white curtains and green wooden shutters overlooked the road. The black woodwork contrasted sharply with the cream-coloured brickwork and flat, grey-slated roof. From one of three chimneystacks a trail of black smoke eddied slowly into the air. A wooden fence painted bright green surrounded the house with a swing gate. A gravel pathway led to a wide stone step-way and an arched entrance. Parked close by was a small dust covered black Citroen in need of a wash.

'This is where I live,' she said, stepping out from her bicycle. 'You're welcome to come in and have a coffee or something. Mama and Papa would be pleased to meet you. Papa spent some time in London and speaks very good English.'

'I'd love to,' I replied, 'but my aunt expects me back for lunch.'

Just then a stout woman with dark hair wearing a floral dress appeared at the door.

By her side stood a tall, good-looking young man with tanned features dressed in a bright red short-sleeved shirt. The woman, who looked in her late thirties, smiled and waved. The young man stood with both hands on his hips, smiling

'Lunch in ten minutes, Adele,' shouted the woman, then turned and went inside the house.

'Not another boyfriend,' said the young man throwing back his head and laughing. 'The poor unfortunate fellow doesn't know what he's in for.'

Both spoke French very quickly but I understood what they said.

'That was mama and the other horrible person is Emile, my brother,' replied Adele. 'Pay no attention to him, he's always rude to any boy I speak to.'

Feeling slightly embarrassed, I asked, 'I suppose you have lots of boyfriends?'

'Just a few I know at college,' she replied off-handily, brushing a hair from her eyes. 'Are you sure you won't stay and have coffee?'

Suddenly, the thought of her with other boys sent an acute pang of jealousy running through me. Just as quickly I realised how stupid this was. After all, she was a lovely looking girl and was bound to have lots of admirers even in such a small place as Lion-sur-Mer.

'Er… thank you for the offer,' I said, 'but as I said, my aunt expects me back by one.'

With a slight frown Adele replied, 'What a pity,' and then her eyes widened into a smile. 'This afternoon Mama and I are

63

going to Arromanches to visit my Aunt Marie, but perhaps we could meet tomorrow at the end of that road we came up, the one I used to sneak out to play. You could leave your bike here, we could catch a bus to Caen.'

I could hardly believe my ears. Here I was, my first time abroad and I was being asked by the most gorgeous girl I had ever seen for a date.

'Y…yes.' I finally managed to say, 'that sounds fine. What time?'

'Meet me here at ten,' she answered, 'and in case you get lost, the name of this road is Rue Moulin.' She then smiled and offered her hand, 'Au reviour Pierre,' she added lapsing into French. 'See you tomorrow, then.'

I watched as she pushed her bicycle through the gate and went up the path. Upon reaching the side of the house, she turned, waved, then went inside.

On the way back to Ouistreham I was in a world of my own and nearly collided with pedestrians and fellow cyclists. By the time I arrived at Matilda's house I was out of breath, my shirt was soaked with sweat and I was grinning like a Cheshire cat.

'My goodness,' cried Matilda, 'you look, like the cat that's got the cream.'

'I think I have,' I replied and dashed upstairs to wash my hands.

CHAPTER FIVE

When I told Matilda and Claude about my meeting with Adele they both looked at one another and laughed.

'Mon Dieu!' exclaimed Claude.' It didn't take you long, and I always thought you English were reserved.'

I sat in silence trying not to feel embarrassed.

'Don't tease him so,' replied Matilda, 'they are a lovely Jewish family. I know them quite well. Madeleine and Paul Michaud often come into the florists. Emile her brother and Adele are both at college.'

'Of course,' answered Claude, buttering a piece of toast, 'I remember now, Paul is an engineer. I met him at some function a few months ago. Nice man. Did you meet him, Peter?'

'No,' I replied giving a nervous cough. 'I only saw her mother and brother.'

'Well, you must invite Adele to tea one day,' said Matilda, pouring a cup of coffee and handing it to me. 'Let me know so I can make something special.'

That night I lay awake too excited to sleep. With both hands behind my head I stared up at the shadows on the ceiling. Whenever I thought about Adele a strange, almost painful sensation ran through me. Every time I closed my eyes I saw her smiling at me with those wide, captivating brown eyes and heard the soft mellifluous tones of her voice. Eventually I did fall into a dreamless sleep only to be woken up by the tinkling sound of Matilda carrying a coffee cup into my room.

The thought of my date with Adele excited me so I had difficulty eating breakfast.

'Are you sure you've enough money now, dear?' asked Matilda as I prepare to leave the house. Before I had time to assure her I had ample funds, she gave me a wet kiss on the cheek, stood back, and with a smile, added, 'And don't forget you camera.'

I pushed the cycle down the gravelled path and set off down the road.

A glance at my wristwatch showed nine-thirty. Peddling furiously along the coast road I felt the sea breeze ruin the quiff in my hair that I had taken great pains to perfect.

The early morning sunshine penetrated the thin material of my white open-necked shirt, and my grey slacks secured at each ankle by bicycle clips felt clammy and warm.

When I saw her waiting at the end of the cobbled road my heart rate increased almost to bursting point. She looked absolutely stunning. With one hand resting on leather shoulder bag and the other on her hip, she struck a pose that seemed to highlight every curve in her body. A white sleeveless blouse exaggerated her tanned complexion. I quickened my step and as I approached her, a breeze ruffled her flared, pleated green skirt tantalisingly around her knees. Even the white flat-soled shoes she wore failed to hide her trim ankles and shapely calves. She smiled and waved and as she did so her dark brown hair, tied in a short ponytail, swayed as it had a life of its own.

'You are, 'ow you say, on time, yes?' said Adele glancing at her wristwatch and flashing a welcoming smile. 'The bus leaves in ten minutes from the middle of the town.'

Once more her beauty took my breath away – so much so that I hardly noticed her mother and brother standing behind the gate.

'Fine,' was all I could say before her mother's voice interrupted my thoughts.

'Thank you for helping Adele yesterday,' I heard her say. As we shook hands I managed to smile and mumble, 'Er... it was nothing. I was glad to help.'

'Nevertheless, I wanted to thank you personally,' added her mother. As she spoke, her round, homely face broke into a smile. She wore a pale blue blouse and skirt. A small pair of gold earrings poked out from under a bright yellow headscarf. After a quick glance to the young man next to her, she went on, 'Allow me introduce Emile, Adele's bother.'

Emile's bronzed, handsome features broke into a wide grin. 'Pleased to meet you,' he said as we shook hands, 'I believe you are from England. I hope to go there one day to study your language.' Smiling at Adele, he continued, 'My sister speaks English well, don't you funny face?'

'Oh shut up,' replied Adele, giving Emile a playful punch on the arm, 'and don't call me funny face.'

'Now don't start,' interrupted Adele's mother, 'always fighting these two,' she added, smiling at me. 'Lovely to meet you, Peter. Now if you'll excuse me I must get on and so must you, Emile. Come now or they'll miss the bus.'

Adele kissed her mother on both cheeks, pulled a face at Emile and we said a cheerful *au reviour.*

Walking down one of the narrow cobbled streets that led into the town centre Adele's hand found mine. Her palm felt soft and warm and as her fingers clasped mine I glanced at her and felt a strong surge of emotion run through me.

The town was crowded with shoppers and young people on holiday from school. Several men and women waited at the bus stop outside the church. Adele said a pleasant *bonsiour* to some people she knew and then we settled back to enjoy the journey. The bus, a green single decker, arrived and we found a seat at the back. As the bus pulled away I was conscious of the warmth of Adele's thigh through the thin material of her dress against mine. Once again her hand sneaked into my palm and gave it a squeeze. I turned and, oblivious to everyone and everything, stared into her eyes. In a faltering voice, barely audible over the grinding noise of the engine, I said, 'You know, Adele, when I came to France I never dreamt I'd meet anyone like you.'

'But I'm glad you did,' she replied, tightening her grip on my hand.

The bus arrived at Ouistreham and briefly stopped and picked up more passengers. It then continued up the road leading out of town and up a steady steep gradient. When we reached the summit the rooftops and church spires of Caen became visible through the heat haze of the morning sun.

Away to my left black smoke poured from the tall chimneys of Colombelles, the steel-manufacturing centre Matilda had told me about.

'My Uncle Claude works there,' I said, and with a hint of pride, added, 'he's a head manager.'

'Those who are not farmers also work there,' replied Adele. 'But Caen is really a large market city with railways and roads that takes goods all over Normandy.'

Adele was obviously proud of her Norman heritage. Still holding my hand she proceeded to give me a brief history of Caen.

'Duke William, was the founder of Caen,' she said and with a sly smile added, 'you remember him. He was the one who conquered England in 1066.'

With a half-hearted laugh I replied, 'I did history at school. I do know. I know who William the Conqueror was.'

'It was he who ordered a great castle to be built here in 1050 and city grew around it.' She paused, smiled, and went on, 'There is also two lovely abbeys in Caen. I will take you to them before we return home.'

After passing through Benouville, a peaceful village near the rise, the road dipped and curved to the right and wound through a picturesque hamlet called Blainville. Shortly afterwards we drove by a large town named Herouvillete. The houses in these places were made of the same, limestone, and their whiteness, exaggerated by the glare of the sun, stung my eyes. The road suddenly plunged downwards and below, shimmering in the heat haze, the rooftops and church spires of Caen appeared about five kilometres away.

'That tall spire you can see on the skyline belongs to another church of Saint Peter built in the eleventh century.'

I grinned and said, 'That Saint Peter certainly was popular around here.'

Adele gave me a playful dig in the ribs, 'I suppose you're, 'ow you say? A terrible protestant, yes?' she laughingly asked.

'Yes,' I replied, 'but don't hold it against me, will you?'

She shook her head, smiled and squeezed my hand again.

Caen seemed a large busy, bustling city. Some of the streets were narrow and cobbled with half-timbered medieval-looking buildings with overhanging jetties. Others leading into the centre were wide and covered with tarmac. Shops and stores of all descriptions lined the streets. As we entered the city centre I noticed an open market crammed with people clustered around the many stalls shaded from the sun by gaily coloured canopies.

After a few stops on the outskirts the bus finally came to a halt outside the railway station. The time was shortly after eleven. As we left the bus Adele said *Bonsiour* to the people she had spoken to earlier.

Once more she clasped my hand 'Come,' she said, flashing a warm, beguiling smile. 'I am now going to show you Caen's famous castle, then we'll have a drink of lemonade or something. Yes?'

'Lead on,' I replied with a grin.

We crossed the road and strolled hand in hand through a narrow, cobbled street. Then, shielding our eyes from the sunshine glare, we walked through an iron gate into a vast wide area of parkland. As we entered, a group of children and adults gathered around a stall selling drinks.

Clusters of pink and white bougainvillea lay in well-kept grassy areas. Ash, elm and oak trees dotted the landscape reminding me of home. In the middle, resting on a high grassy hillock, the massive splayed curtain wall and towers of Duke William's castle appeared, looking just as formidable as when it was built all those centuries ago.

On top of one tower the Tricolour hung limply in the warm breeze. From another tower dangled the scarlet standard of Normandy upon which a knight in gold armour wielded a sword while sitting astride a black charger. Set against an eye-scorching blue sky the banner caught a sudden gust of wind and flapped open. The knight appeared to wave his sword as if defending himself against an attacker. Then, just as quick, the wind subsided and the knight crumpled into the folds of the flag.

A wooden drawbridge led over a moat, long since dried up, under an arched portcullis into the outer courtyard. We were not alone. Several people followed on behind glancing around and talking.

'As you can see,' said Adele pointing to a wide area of stone, 'all that is left of the keep are those small towers at each corner.'

Away to our left was an old building with a grey-slated roof and lancet windows. A well-worn stone-flagged pathway led up to a stout, metal-studded door above which was decorated in a series of arched chevron patterns. As I pushed open the door the musty smell of time permeated the surprisingly cool atmosphere.

The hall was rectangular with a high hammer-beamed roof. Shafts of sunlight exaggerated the sheen on a long oaken table in the centre of the room. Slightly cracked black and white tiles lined the floor and faded medieval tapestries hung limply on the walls. Pennants adorned with bleached coats of arms jutted out from each side while in various parts of the room visitors pondered over glass panels containing colourfully decorated books written in Latin.

'Each one of those small flags you see hanging from the walls belonged to William's knights when he invaded England.'

'How do you know all this?' I replied trying to sound interested.

'We learnt about it at school,' she replied with an all-knowing smile.

Together we walked over and looked at them. Bleached by time, the pennants hung from small metal arms. Under each name details were inscribed on a silver plate.

'This one,' said Adele, pointing to a discoloured blue and red flag wrinkled with age, 'belonged to Roger de Montgomerie. He was one of the duke's most trusted knights. For helping the duke, Roger was made earl of Shrewsbury in England. Do you know where that is?'

'Yes,' I answered, 'It's one of the border towns near Wales.'

'That's right,' she cried. 'We were told a part of Wales was named after him and much later, his ancestors moved to some place in Ireland called Donegal. Do you know about this man Montgomerie?'

'Never heard of him,' I replied taking out my camera, 'but I think it would make a nice photograph.'

Little did I realise that in a few years one of Roger de Mongomerie's ancestors, General Bernard Montgomery, would return to Normandy under non-too dissimilar circumstances.

'Come,' said Adele, tugging my arm, 'I think you've had enough history for one day. Let's get a drink and rest.'

I bought two small bottles of lemonade and straws and found a secluded spot between two hilly mounds. The grass was short and warm and as I sat down my shirt, soaked with sweat, stuck to my back. Holding her bottle in one hand, Adele lay back and with the other shielded her eyes from the sun. She looked flushed and a thin trickle of perspiration ran down the side of her face. Under the thin material of her blouse I could see the whiteness of her brassiere. She obviously didn't wear an underskirt because the folds of her dress fell tantalisingly between her legs showing the outline of her shapely thighs and flat stomach. For a few seconds I stared at her unable to grasp how beautiful she was. Suddenly I felt my penis stiffen. I took a long gulp of lemonade, swallowed hard and lay down feeling the warmth of her body close to mine.

'Tell me, Peter,' said Adele, still holding her hand across her eyes. 'Do you have a girlfriend in England?'

'I did have,' I replied, 'but that's finished now.'

'Why was that?' she asked looking at me.

I gave her a brief account of my friendship with Maggie.

Adele took another sip of her drink, placed the bottle by her side and then lent up on one elbow. Her face was so close to mine I could feel and smell the muskiness of her body odour. With a faraway expression in her velvety brown eyes, she replied, 'Foolish girl,' and then, to my surprise she reached across, pulled me to her and we kissed. Her lips felt warm and pliant. I kept my eyes open and caught a fleeting glimpse as she closed hers. The kiss only lasted a few seconds. When we broke apart she kept her arm around my neck and I felt the softness of her body as she pushed herself against me. Suddenly I felt acutely embarrassed. The blood pounded in my head and I moved away; surely, I told myself, she must feel my erection through my trousers.

'Do not feel shy,' she said, once again moving against me, 'this is France not stuffy England. No body minds if people kiss in public.'

By this time my mouth felt like parchment. 'It's not the kissing I'm worried about,' I managed to say moving slightly away.

She threw back her head and with a flirtatious glance, said, 'It's all right. I understand. Come, let's finish our drinks, have a look at the abbeys I told you about.'

'Before we go, can I take a photograph of you?' I asked feeling my ardour subside.

'Of course,' she replied. She then placed both hands behind her head, bent one leg allowing her dress to drift tantalisingly along her leg and smiled seductively into the camera.

Half an hour later we arrived at the magnificent towers and slender, octagonal spires of the Abbaye aux Hommes (Abbey of Men). We joined a queue of people and walked through one of three plain, oaken Romanesque doors and stood in awe at the beauty of the vast nave with its wide rounded arches.

'This was built by William around 1060 and it's where he and his knights met before invading England,' whispered Adele. 'It is said he prostrated himself before the altar and asked God's blessing.'

'God was obviously on his side,' I replied, trying not to sound too impious.

'William's tomb is at the base of the high altar,' added Adele, 'but his remains are not there.'

'Where are they, then?' I asked.

'The Huguenots threw them in the river during the sixteenth century revolution.'

'Poor old William,' I answered trying to conceal a grin.

'Don't be horrible,' replied Adele digging me in the ribs with her elbow. 'Remember he built the Tower of London,' and then with a sarcastic expression on her face, smiled and added, 'so you could keep your crown jewels safe and sound.'

After an exhausting tour lasting half an hour we left the abbey, found a café and had a coffee and croissant.

'I think we've had enough history for one day,' said Adele sipping her drink, 'so I think we'll leave the Abbaye aux Dames for another time. Besides, mama told me she will make us a supper and papa wants to meet you.'

'Good idea,' I replied, spreading a large blob of strawberry jam on my croissant.

We boarded the bus. Without speaking Adele cuddled up against me, and with her head resting on my shoulder, we held hands and fell asleep.

Sometime later the sudden jerking of the bus and the touch of someone gently shaking my shoulder woke me up.

'Wake up you two,' said a throaty female voice. I blinked, looked up and saw the pale, wrinkled face of Madam Fevere, the elderly woman I met at the café in Oiustreham. 'We've arrived at Lion-sur-Mer. This is as far as the bus goes.'

It was still daylight and the time by my wristwatch was a little after six.

Adele opened her eyes and sat upright. 'Oh, it's you, Madam Fevere,' she cried, stifling a yawn with her hand, 'thank you for wakening us.' Adele glanced at me than up at the woman. 'Madam Fevere lives near me. This is Peter. He's on holiday from England.'

'I know,' said Madam Fevere. With a faraway look in her tired eyes, she added, 'my husband fought with the English against the Boch in the last war, let us pray we don't have to do it again.' She then turned and with a feeble wave of her hand walked away.

'Do you think there'll be a war?' asked Adele as we approached her house.

This was the first time either of us had mentioned the threat of war.

'The headmaster of my school, Mr Allan doesn't think so,' I replied, 'but my father isn't too sure.'

'Never mind,' replied Adele, 'we've had such a lovely day, let's not spoil it by talking about such horrible things, eh?'

'You're right,' I answered, feeling her fingers entwined tightly around mine. 'I've really enjoyed myself. Thank you.'

Supper consisted of succulent roast beef and Yorkshire pudding.

'I cooked it just for you,' said Madam Michaud as we entered the dinning room. 'And there is chocolate gateaux for afters.'

During the meal we were joined by Adele's father: a tall, well-built man with a swarthy complexion and straight dark brown hair streaked with grey. We shook hands and Adele introduced us. His eyes, the same deep brown colour as Adele's, wrinkled into a smile, 'Forgive me for being late, work you know.' He sat down, poured himself a glass of red wine then glanced across at me, 'I believe you speak French, Peter?'

'Yes,' I replied.

'I must thank you for coming to the rescue of my daughter?'

I gave a nervous shrug. 'It really was nothing.'

'It's a pity she didn't bang her head,' grinned Emile who was sitting next to me. 'It might have done her some good.'

'Horrible beast,' replied Adele, pulling tongues at him, 'I hope you shoot yourself with that gun you use in the cadets.' After dinner, Adele excused herself, and dashed upstairs. While she was away I asked Emile what he used his gun for.

'It's an old British Lee Enfield from the last war,' answered Emile, 'I'm in the local army cadets. We use it on the rifle range.'

'Just like Gary Cooper, eh?' I replied.

When Adel returned I noticed she wore a touch of rouge and a smear of vivid red lipstick.

'I only hope he doesn't have to use it for real,' said Adele's father frowning. 'In today's newspaper it says all Czech Jews in Berlin are being arrested and sent to concentration camps. Who will be next, I wonder…'

'Enough of this talk,' interrupted Matilda. 'Hitler won't bother us. And if he did, our good friends in England would help us, wouldn't they Peter?'

'I expect we would,' I answered, then licking my lips, added, 'do you think I could have another piece of cake, it's delicious.'

After being allowed to telephone Matilda to say I might be late, Adele's parents were most anxious to know what I thought of Caen.

'It's a lovely old city,' I replied, 'especially the castles and abbeys.'

'You really must see as much of the Normandy coast as possible before you go home,' said Madam Michaud, and then smiling at her daughter added, 'Maybe Adele could show you, couldn't you dear?'

Adele's eyes suddenly sparkled. 'I'd love to,' she replied, then in a somewhat quieter tone, glanced at me and went on, 'what a pity we're all going to Nantes to visit Aunt Marie on Saturday.'

'How long will you be gone?' I asked.

With a sigh, she replied, 'A week. But I could show you around when we come back.'

'What about me?' cried Emile, 'could I come with you?'

'No,' answered Adele giving her brother a scornful glance, 'you can stay here and play with your silly rifle.'

An hour later, after thanking Adele's parents for a lovely evening, I said goodbye. After collecting my bicycle from the side of the house Adele took my hand and we walked down the cobbled street onto the coastal pathway.

We stopped and looked out to sea.

It was shortly after nine o'clock and almost dark. High above, a myriad of twinkling stars decorated the heavens, and the sun, low on the horizon, turned the sea into a carpet of dappled yellow light.

'I won't see you for over a week, then?' I said.

Adele gave a deep sigh, frowned, then glanced at the ground. With a touch of sadness,' she added, 'I don't want to go. I do not like my aunt, and besides, when I come back we'll only have a week together before you go home...' her voice trailed away.

Adele's words made me feel uncomfortable. It was a strange feeling and one I couldn't quite understand. Suddenly the thought of returning home and not seeing her again sent a mixture of dismay and panic running through me. My mouth went dry and for a few seconds I couldn't speak.

Finally I muttered, 'I...I'll miss you, when can we meet...?' Before I had time to finish she looked up, placed a hand on my arm and interrupted me. 'I can't see you tomorrow afternoon,' she said, 'I've promised to see a few friends from college. But if you like we can meet in the evening. Jean Gabin is in a film called *Murder in Montmarte.* It's on in Lion. Afterwards we could have a lemonade, then go for a walk.'

'That sounds fine,' I replied. 'I've never seen a French film. I've heard they're rather... suggestive.'

With a teasing expression in her eyes, she replied, 'Wait and see. Meet you at the bottom of the road at six.' As she finished speaking she reached up, put both arms around me and gave me a long lingering kiss.

Afterwards I watched as she ran up the road, stopping briefly outside her house to wave before opening the gate and going inside.

By the time I arrived at Ouistreham it was dark.

Matilda and Claude were sat in the sitting room drinking coffee.

'Had a nice time, Peter?' asked Matilda.

'Yes, thank you,' I hastily replied.

'Then I suggest you wipe that lipstick off your face before you go to bed,' laughed Claude, and then looking at Matilda, added, 'who said you English were shy.'

CHAPTER SIX

I spent the best part of the following morning at the holiday park at Riva Bella. Even at ten o'clock the place was crowded with children riding on go-carts, crowding around the various stalls or just running about shouting and laughing.

For a while I tried unsuccessfully to win a cuddly toy on the rifle range. I fared no better trying to fit metal rings around small statues. Finally I gave up, bought an ice cream cornet, and sat on a wooden bench and thought of Adele. For the umpteenth time I glanced at my wristwatch. To my dismay it was only half past eleven; only six and a half hours to go, I told myself, then I'd be with her. With a sigh I stood up, squashed the remains of the cornet into my mouth, and made my way back to the house.

In the afternoon I decided to explore the hinterland beyond the coast.

'I've packed you a small apple pie, a nice slice of Camembert, and a bottle of lemonade,' said Aunt Matilda. 'Be a dear and try to be back by five for supper.'

'Don't worry, Matilda,' I replied, once again thinking about Adele, 'I won't be late.'

Once again the sun penetrated through the material my cotton shirt as I cycled along the coastal pathway. The wide expanse of yellow beach was crowded with holidaymakers. White sails of small sailing ships and dinghies littered the silver-crested waves as seagulls swooped down from a cloudless blue sky seeking anything edible they could find.

I found myself riding behind a group of young girls and boys cycling while chattering like magpies. At Le Breche, I turned off the pathway into a narrow road leading out of the town.

The terrain, studded with farms and heavy woodland copses, stretched out before me. Once again I was dazzled by the blinding yellowness of the cornfields as they lazily swayed in the warm breeze.

I continued along the road and reached Hermanville-sur-Mer, a small village with attractive half-timbered houses, an old Romanesque church and a few shops. After I left the village the road began to rise and a few kilometres on I came to a hamlet by the strange name of Plumetot. From here I could clearly see most of the coastline from Ouistreham to Lion-sur-Mer. The roofs of the houses and church spires glinted in the afternoon sun and the English Channel under a dazzling blue sky gleamed like a millpond. The time was just after twelve, my shirt was soaked with sweat and I was tired. A few villagers passed by and gave me a wave and a cheerful *Bonjour.* I returned their greetings, placed my bicycle on a grassy bank and carefully took yet another photograph. Then, after gulping down a long draught of warm lemonade, I sat down and devoured a large slice of Matilda's delicious apple pie.

My return journey was mostly downhill. I arrived at Matilda's shortly after four o'clock, dashed upstairs, washed and changed into a pair of black trousers, cream shirt and grey pullover.

'When are we going to see this young lady of yours?' asked Claude at supper. Hearing Adele referred to as 'my young lady' made me feel slightly embarrassed.

'She and her family are going to some place called Nantes on Saturday,' I replied, 'maybe when she comes back?'

'Fine,' replied Matilda, 'but give me prior warning so I can prepare something special.'

As arranged, Adele was waiting at the bottom of the cobbled road. When she saw me approaching on my bicycle she waved and smiled. With her dark brown hair tied in a short ponytail and wearing a flared green dress and a yellow sweater she reminded me of one of those models on the front of magazines. There was also a trace of rouge on her cheeks and when she smiled her red lipstick exaggerated the whiteness of her teeth.

After the traditional kiss on both cheeks, she said, '*Bonjour Pierre, Ca va?*'

'*Oui,*' I replied, '*Tres bien,*' and then in English, 'you look really nice.'

The picture house was in the centre of town. On the way Adele said a lively *bonjour* to some young people she knew. The girls, seeing Adele and myself holding hands, shot inquisitive glances at one another and giggled.

I hardly noticed the film. Instead I was more than aware of Adele's warm hand resting under mine on my thigh. It was only when Paul Reynaud, the French Prime Minister, spoke on the newsreel that I came to my senses. In a squeaky voice, and gesticulating with both hands, he informed everyone that France would react immediately and with full force to any invader.

'Of course he means Germany,' I overheard someone next to me say.

'Yes,' the person next to him said, 'I hear the Germans are conducting military manoeuvres near the Polish border.'

Adele glanced up at me with an expression of concern etched in her eyes.

'Oh Peter,' she whispered, 'I'm so worried…'

'Don't be,' I replied squeezing her hand. 'Everything will be all right. You'll see.'

The first house showing of the film ended at eight. After a cool glass of lemonade at a nearby café, we strolled hand in hand along the coast. A warm breeze fannèd our faces and far out at sea navigation lights of shipping penetrated the rapidly falling evening dusk. There were not many people around and we found a grassy spot in between the high sand dunes that sloped down from the pathway opposite the house of Henri Chalet.

My nervousness increased and my mouth felt like sandpaper. We found a secluded spot and lay down side by side. Our bodies sank into the sand still warm from the afternoon. For a while neither of us spoke. Our fingers entwined as we both stared up at the stars shining brightly like freshly cut diamonds. I glanced across and saw the sad expression in her eyes. Suddenly she turned to me and cried, 'Oh, Peter, all mama and papa talk about are the Germans. They said the Jews in Germany have lost all their possessions. Some are being sent to special centres. What will we do if there is a war?'

'Same as we did last time, I guess, fight,' I replied placing an arm around her shoulders and pulling her close to me. 'And remember, we did win.'

'Yes,' she muttered, 'but at what cost?'

I removed my hand from hers and reached up and touched her face.

'Let's not talk about war,' I said staring into her eyes, 'you know you really are beautiful. I feel nervous every time I look at you. I don't know what I'll do when you go away on Saturday.'

'No need to feel like that,' she replied. As she spoke I could feel her warm breath on my face. 'I'll soon be back. You can kiss me if you like.'

I didn't need a second invitation.

Her lips as we kissed quivered slightly before pressing hard against mine and I could feel her breasts, soft and pliant, pushing against my chest through the woolly material of her sweater. When, after what seemed like an age, our lips parted, I drew away and what I imagined to be the roaring of the sea was, in fact, the blood pulsating in my head.

'You can touch me there, if you want,' she said, taking hold of my hand and placing it on her breast.

My mouth felt like sawdust. As I nervously placed my hand onto her right breast I felt her nipple harden. At the same time she pressed herself against my groin. For a while I was too nervous to move. I held my breath and thought my lungs would burst. Finally I began to gently caress her. Beads of sweat ran down my face as I plucked up enough courage to allow my hand to slide onto her thigh. Remembering my experience with Maggie, I pressed my hand between her legs.

Suddenly, she drew away and took hold of my hand. 'Not now, *cheri!*' she gasped, 'I have, how you say, "the curse", this week. But when I come back from Nantes...'

Feeling somewhat embarrassed, I replied, 'I... err, understand,' and quickly removed my hand.

However, by this time my passion was aroused to such an extent that nature took its course – luckily stains don't show too clearly on black trousers.

During the week that Adele and her family were away Pierre took time off from work and he and Matilda showed me more of the region. However, even the beauty of Rouen's Notre-Dame cathedral failed to blot Adele from my thoughts and at Bayeux the famous tapestry only served to remind me of Adele's history lesson about William the Conquer.

'Actually the tapestry was made in Kent,' said Matilda with an all-knowing air. 'British embroiderers of course.'

The next few days seemed like an eternity.

When the telephone rang shortly after eleven on Monday morning I instinctively knew it was Adele.

'*Bonjour! Bonjour!*' she cried excitedly. The sound of her voice sent daggers of exhilaration running through me and I almost dropped the receiver. 'How are you?' Before I had time to reply, she added, 'I missed you so.'

'Me too,' I replied, trying to compose myself. 'When can we meet?'

'This evening after supper,' she answered, 'same place at the bottom of the road after supper at seven. Is that all right?'

'You bet,' I hurriedly replied, 'seven it is.'

Later that day at supper Matilda smiled across at Claude, and said, 'Peter looks quite smart in that cream shirt and brown pullover, doesn't he dear?'

Claude's swarthy features broke into a wide grin. 'Yes,' he replied, 'I wonder why?'

I didn't answer. Instead I felt my face redden and helped myself to a piece of chocolate cake.

'Bring her to lunch on Saturday,' said Matilda, reaching across and touching my hand, 'and don't look so worried. About twelve o'clock. All right?'

'I'll...er, ask her,' I replied, glancing at my wristwatch. Then, after dabbing my mouth with a serviette, I stood up.

Matilda smiled, gave a sigh and said, 'Oh what it is to be young and in love.'

As I pushed my bicycle out of the door I pondered on Matilda's words. All I knew about love was what I had seen on the pictures. My feelings for Adele were quite different from those I had felt for Maggie. When I stopped seeing Maggie I wasn't particularly upset. Now, the thought that in six days I might never see Adele again made me feel physically sick.

By the time I saw Adele dusk was falling. The sky was cloudless and a pale yellow moon cast long, lingering shadows on the ground. When she saw me she waved excitedly and jumped up, attracting the attention of a few passers-by. A sudden breeze caught the hem of her button-down red and white polka-dot skirt causing it to flutter around her knees. A woollen cardigan was draped over her shoulders and a bright red headscarf completed a picture that held me spellbound.

I was still standing astride my bicycle when she grabbed one of my hands and cried, 'Oh, Peter, it is so good to see you. I missed you. Did you miss me?' She sounded breathless and when she spoke the moonlight shone in her eyes making them sparkle.

'Yes, I did,' I replied, 'every day.'

She then reached up and kissed me on the mouth.

After parking my bicycle we walked onto the coastal pathway. She told me how she hated her visit to Nantes and I told her about my sightseeing with Matilda and Claude.

'I thought about you all the time, Adele,' I said as we stopped outside the house of Henri Chalet. 'I couldn't seem to get you out of my mind.' I must have sounded very grown-up, but meant every word.

'I know,' she muttered, 'I was, how you say, bored to tears, and I also missed you.'

We strolled onto the beach and once again found ourselves lying in the sand dunes opposite Henri Chalet. In the distance the cry of female laughter told us there were others not too far away. But that didn't bother us. The soothing sound of the sea, the cool breeze and darkness, cloaked us with the kind of anonymity only lovers crave.

Suddenly I was overcome with nerves and when we kissed I felt my body tremble.

'Can I put my hand…?' I murmured.

She gave a muffled cry and said, 'Yes. It's all right now.'

With trembling fingers I unbuttoned the top of her dress and slid my hand onto the warm material of her brassier. She gave a low guttural cry, 'Don't be afraid. I want you to touch me,' she muttered and pressed against my groin.

Her words gave me the confidence to slip my hand onto the soft, warm flesh of her breast and squeeze her nipple. Her hand slipped downwards and over my trousers grasped my erect penis.

The next few moments passed in a blur of fumbling passion. With one hand I lifted up her dress and nervously removed her cotton knickers.

'Please be careful, Peter,' she gasped, pulling me on top of her.

A minute or so after I entered her it was over. I quickly withdrew and with a muted cry, ejaculated onto her stomach.

'Oh, God, I'm sorry,' I pleaded, 'I couldn't help…'

'Do not worry, *Cheri,* there is plenty of time,' said Adele, cuddling into me. 'Mama and papa are out. I don't have to be in till late.'

When we made love again it was more passionate and lasted longer. With each movement of my body against hers I was overcome with a deep-seated feeling of raw emotion that seemed to embrace every fibre of my being; and after it was over we lay, naked and breathless, bathed in each other's sweat.

'Oh Peter,' cried Adele, clinging onto me, 'you'll be gone in six days. What will I do?'

I glanced down and saw a tear trickle down her cheek. 'Don't worry, love,' I said, kissing the top of her head. 'I can always come back and see you.'

'Or I can come to England,' she replied, looking hopefully at me.

'Yes, you could,' I answered. After a pause I added, 'That reminds me, my aunt has invited you to lunch on Saturday. I'll meet you at half past eleven at the bottom of the road. Is that all right?'

'Of course,' she replied, 'now kiss me and hold me tight.'

During the rest of the week we met every evening. Perhaps it was because we were young and couldn't understand our feelings. On one occasion our lovemaking reached such intensity that after it was over we lay in each other's arms and wept. I knew then that after returning home I wouldn't rest until we met again.

Saturday was a typical June day, warm with a clear cloudless blue sky and a sun that threatened to destroy your eye sockets. However, as I cycled to meet Adele these idyllic surroundings failed to dispel the sadness gnawing away inside me.

Adele, carrying a small brown shoulder bag, was dressed in a full-length pale green dress and white, flat-soled shoes. As I parked my bicycle outside her gate she smiled weakly and gave a short wave of her hand.

'Everyone wants to see you before you leave,' said Adele, taking hold of my hand. 'What time will you go tomorrow?'

'My train from to Calais leaves Caen at nine o'clock,' I replied, avoiding her gaze. 'I'll leave at eight. Claude and Matilda are coming with me.'

'Could I come with you?' she asked. The sadness in her lovely brown eyes told me this was going to be a difficult day for both of us. Suddenly, the thought of seeing Adele in tears as the train pulled out was too much for me to bear.

'I... I'd rather you didn't,' I answered dryly. 'It would be too...'

'It's alright, Peter,' she replied, tightening her fingers around mine. 'I understand.'

After a glass of wine I took a photograph of Adele, Emile and her parents standing under the arched entrance to the house. As I said goodbye to them I felt my throat contract wondering if we would ever meet again.

Adele and I collected our bicycles and after a final wave set of for Ouistreham. As we passed the sand dunes opposite Henri Chalet she glanced across at me.

'This place will always be special, Peter,' she said, 'I promise never to go there until we meet again.'

Matilda and Claude greeted us as we arrived.

'I have baked a special apple pie for you both,' said Matilda, ushering us into the living room. 'I've laced it with a spot of Calvados. I've also done a surprise dish. But more of that later.'

'Plenty of Calvados,' grinned Claude, placing Adel's bicycle next to mine in the hallway. 'I made sure of that.'

Claude was right but I found the apple pie, delicious as it was, hard to swallow. Adele and I kept glancing at one another realising this would be our last meal together. By this time I had completely lost my appetite. Matilda appeared with a silver platter covered with a dish. With the flourish of a magician, she removed the dish.

'These are chocolate covered almonds,' she said beaming, 'they're called *Raven's Lames de Jeane,* and are pear-shaped to resemble the tears Joan of Arc cried as she was burned.'

The mention of tears seemed to have an adverse effect on Adele, as she promptly began to cry.

'I'm sorry,' she gasped, taking out a lace handkerchief from a pocket and dabbing her eyes, 'it's just that...' her voice trailed off.

'It's quite all right, my dear,' said Matilda, 'we understand.'

An hour later, after thanking Matilda and Claude for a lovely tea, we started to leave.

'Remember you can come and see us anytime, dear,' said Matilda, kissing Adele on both cheeks.

'Yes,' added Claude, 'and next time we promise not to mention Joan of Arc.'

Adele suggested we push our bikes instead of riding them. The time was shortly after three o'clock and the sun was almost overhead. When we arrived outside Henri Chalet, Adele suddenly stopped.

'Peter,' she said giving me a wistful look, 'there's something I want to give you.'

With an air of curiosity, I asked, 'What's that, then?'

'Let's sit down and I'll show you,' she replied.

We parked the bicycles and found our usual spot strategically placed between two large sand dunes facing the vast expanse of beach and sea.

'Come on then,' I said after we sat down, 'what's this you have for me?'

Adele placed her hand into her shoulder bag and brought out a small silver medallion the size of a shilling (a ten pence piece in modern money) attached to a silver chain.

'This was given to me by my grandmamma before she died,' said Adele, 'she said it would always keep me safe.' She held the medallion up and twisted it around. 'See how it sparkles in the sun. Here,' she added, passing the medallion to me, 'you hold it and see for yourself.'

On one side, embedded in the metal, was a crucifix. The reverse showed the head and shoulders of Christ, one hand raised in supplication.

'It looks like silver,' I said, gathering the chain in my fingers and lifting it up. 'Are you sure you want to give it to me?'

'Yes, Peter,' she quietly answered, 'I am sure.'

Adele was right. The sunlight caused the surface of the medallion to glitter, so much so that it hurt my eyes.

'See what I mean?' laughed Adele. 'Grandma said that whenever the medallion shone in the sun I could make a wish.'

'And did you?' I asked.

'Yes,' she replied. As she spoke, tears suddenly appeared in her eyes. 'I made one now.'

'And what was it?'

'If I tell you it may not come true,' she answered.

'It really is lovely,' I said, feeling how light it was. 'But I thought you and your family were Jewish. Why the crucifix and not the Star of David?'

'Grandma said it didn't matter,' replied Adele dabbing her eyes with a pink lace handkerchief. 'She said everyone worships the same God in different ways.' She paused, then, reaching out and grasping hold of my hand with hers, went on, 'I want you to have this to protect you. Now you hold it up and when it shines make a wish.'

With one hand I held the chain and lifted the medallion up. When it caught the sunlight I twirled the chain making the medallion glitter. Then, looking directly into Adele's tearful eyes, I wished with all my heart we would meet again.

'You have made a wish, yes?' she asked forcing a smile.

Using one hand I gently collapsed the chain and medallion onto my other palm. 'Yes, I have,' I replied. 'And I hope it comes true.'

As if she had read my mind, she answered, 'So do I, Peter, now put it away somewhere safe and kiss me.'

Shortly afterwards we walked hand in hand to her house. Neither of us spoke. We both knew time was short. 'Tonight,' she muttered, 'seven o'clock, same place.'

I nodded and said, 'Yes, seven o'clock.' I then turned and hurried away.

When I arrived at Matilda's house I hurried upstairs and examined the medallion closer. The edges were grooved and inscribed with the date 1870, the start of the Franco-Prussian war.

Later on we sat in the lounge listening to music on the wireless.

I kept glancing at my watch and thinking about Adele while Matilda and Claude discussed the possibility of war.

'I can't see the Boche attacking France,' said Claude, 'I read in *Le Figaro* that we have sixty divisions to Germany's sixteen.' He shrugged his shoulders and went on, 'So you see,' he went on, 'it would be madness. And besides we always have the Maginot Line.' (Named after the French Defence Minister Andre Maginot, this was an elaborate bulwark of French fortifications on the border with Germany constructed between 1920 and 1930.)

'I hope you're right, *Cheri,*' replied Matilda, 'for all our sakes.'

At half-past six I left the house. The realisation that I was on my way to meet Adele for the last time dulled my senses making me feel empty inside. Everything seemed unreal. Dusk was gradually falling and the moon, half hidden behind a cluster of grey clouds, appeared paler than usual. I peddled along the pathway hardly feeling the warm breeze or hearing the ruffle of the long grass coming from the sand dunes. And when I saw her standing in that familiar pale green dress my heart went haywire. Suddenly, the tension inside me became too much. I clambered off my bicycle and ran towards her.

'Bonjour, Peter,' she said hoarsely. Then, as if trying to avoid the solemnity of the occasion went on, 'it is a beautiful evening, yes?'

I nodded and replied, 'Yes, it is.'

She grasped my hand and we strolled down the cobbled street. When we reached the waterfront she stopped. Ignoring a few passers-by she threw her arms around me and cried, 'Oh Peter, I've been dreading this night.'

I swallowed hard and replied, 'So have I. But we both knew one day I would have to…'

'Yes, I know,' murmured Adele, 'but somehow I hoped you might stay a little longer.'

I pulled her against me. 'I wish I could, love,' I answered, and kissed her long and hard.

By now it was quite dark and the lights along the coastal pathway were on. We soon found our secluded spot in the sand dunes. I removed my jacket, placed it on the sand and for a while we lay with our arms around one another.

'You called me "love",' she whispered, 'do you think we are in love?'

'I don't know,' I replied, 'all I know is that I never felt like this before.'

'It is the same with me,' she said, and then with a short laugh added, 'Emile thinks I am behaving like a silly girl. Maybe I am.'

We kissed again and the passion within us grew stronger. Our hands eagerly explored one another and we made love with such intensity I thought I would faint.

Afterwards, lying with our arms around one another, she murmured, 'To me, this has been the most wonderful three weeks. I'll never forget you, Peter.'

Her words sent a surge of sadness running through me. 'And I won't forget you. Honestly I won't,' I replied, feeling my throat tighten.

We did not make love again. Instead we huddled together desperate for time to stand still. Then, as if nature herself was telling us it was time to go, the hitherto warm sea breeze changed abruptly into a cold chill.

'Come,' said Adele, 'It's almost ten. We'd better…'

'Yes,' I replied, 'I suppose so.'

We walked hand in hand not daring to speak. When we reached her house gate our arms immediately went around one another. I looked down and saw tears welling in her eyes.

'Do you have the medallion?' she said, staring up at me.

'Yes,' I replied, patting a trouser pocket, 'it's safe and sound.'

As a tear rolled down her cheek, she asked, 'If there is a war, keep it near you at all times. Promise?'

'I promise,' I replied hugging her, 'but even if there is, I'll come back and find you.'

'Goodbye, Peter,' she sobbed, and after kissing me added, *'Je t' aime,'* then without looking back dashed into the house.

When she was gone I stood for a few minutes staring at the house. A light suddenly appeared in a room upstairs, the curtains were drawn and Adele appeared. She saw me and, after a wave, disappeared. For a moment I imagined her lying on her bed sobbing. The thought brought tears to my eyes.

When I arrived at Matilda's house I reached into my trouser pocket and felt the smoothness of the medallion between my fingers praying there would not be a war. Little did I realise that in less than twelve months German bombs would be raining down on Britain, and Hitler would be master of the European continent.

CHAPTER SEVEN

The first thing I did when I arrived home was to write to Adele. I ended the letter by writing 'Your medallion now has a permanent place hanging around my neck. I will keep it there until we meet again.'

'I hope that's a "thank you" letter to Matilda and Claude,' said mum one evening, 'and remember a stamp to France costs a shilling.'

The correspondence between Adele and I became a weekly occurrence. I wrote in French and she in English. As the weeks passed her letters sounded increasingly concerned with the worsening situation in Europe. 'France has called up the reservists. Papa has been given a commission and ordered to report to an army camp outside Caen. Mama is worried in case Emile is called up and I continue to miss you. Oh *Cheri,* will we ever meet again?'

My letters to her were full of hope, but when each house was ordered to tape up its windows to protect from bomb blast and everyone was issued with gas masks my optimism faded.

'I told you Hilda,' said dad one morning at breakfast, 'it says here in the *Daily Express* the Jerries are smuggling arms and military instructors into Danzig. And remember we've got a treaty with Poland.'

'I must say, dear,' said mum pouring out a cup of tea, 'there seems to be a lot of fuss over this Danzig place. Where exactly is it?'

'It's in Poland, isn't it dad?' I said.

'Quite right, son,' he replied, glancing at me over his newspaper. 'It stands at the mouth of the River Visula. If the Jerries got their hands on it they'd use it as a base to threaten shipping in the Baltic and North Sea. That's why old Chamberlain promised to help the Poles if they were invaded.' He paused and took a long sip of tea, then added, 'Stands to reason doesn't it?'

'I don't understand,' mumbled mum as she walked into the back kitchen, 'what have the Poles ever done for us?'

'Never mind, love,' shouted dad. 'You can always join the RAF. It also says the king has approved the formation of the Women's Auxiliary Air Force (WAAF).'

The day after I returned home I took the photographs I had taken in France to be developed.

'A roll of twelve films,' said a small, stout lady behind the counter at Boots Cash Chemist, 'that'll be three and sixpence. They'll be ready in a week, but I can't guarantee it.'

The next day I went to Lancaster Avenue and called for Gordon and Jim. Much to my surprise CS was with them in Gordon's living room.

'Ah, the intrepid Francophile returns,' said CS peering at me over his horn-rimmed glasses. 'How are you, dear boy?'

'Oh shut up CS,' said Jim, 'Come on, Peter, did you meet any of those French tarts we've heard so much about?'

At first I was tempted to tell them about Adele. But realising they would want to know all the intimate details I thought better of it. Instead I casually replied, 'One or two.'

'Come on,' said Gordon, elbowing me in the ribs, 'did any of 'em like Mars bars. Did you, er…?'

'Pay no attention, to them, Peter,' interrupted CS. 'They probably tossed themselves off blind over the holidays.'

'Hark at him,' laughed Jim, 'and he's the one who wears glasses.'

Much to my surprise the photographs came out well.

'Matilda's put on a bit of weight,' said mum, 'but I expect it's all those cream cakes they eat.'

'That young lass you're standing next to is a smasher,' commented dad. 'Who is she?'

I told them about Adele and her family. As I spoke about Adele my enthusiasm betrayed my feelings for her.

'I think our Peter got it bad, eh, Hilda?' said dad with a twinkle in his eyes.

'Oh shut up,' replied mum. 'You're embarrassing the poor boy.'

I suddenly felt my face redden and left the room. But each night before switching off the light, I would gaze at Adele standing on the beach near Lion-sur-Mer, smiling at me with those captivating brown eyes, touch the medallion and say a silent prayer for her safety.

On the first morning back at school we stood staring at the gymnasium windows covered with rows of grimy-looking sandbags.

'It's the same outside the post office and fire station,' said CS. 'I noticed them yesterday when we came home.'

'That's right,' echoed Jim, strands of untidy dark hair hanging under his cap. 'I watched some workmen painting white rings around trees and lamp posts,' he paused, while passing a bag of gobstoppers around, then added, 'and the edges of the pavements.'

'Why have they done that, then?' asked Gordon. 'So dogs can see to piss in the dark?'

'Clot,' cried CS, pushing Gordon away. 'Don't you listen to the wireless? If war breaks out there's going to be a blackout. No lights in the streets, all windows covered up, nothing. So the white paint is to help us see where we're going.'

'What about lights on cars and buses, then?' I asked. 'They'll need lights to see where they're going, won't they?'

'Father says the lights inside the buses will be dimmed and the headlights all but covered up. We'll even have to put a cardboard cover with a slit in it over our bicycle lamps.'

The deepening crisis in Europe was brought home to us at assembly. Clutching the side of his gown with both hands, the grey-haired figure of Mr Allan peered at us over his spectacles. 'I'm sorry to tell you,' he said in a dull, sombre voice, 'that all our German students will not be joining us. Due to circumstances beyond our control they have been asked to return home.'

'Maybe they've joined that Hitler Youth I saw on the newsreel last week,' remarked CS as we filed out of the assembly room.

'Just as well,' added, Jim, 'the silly sods couldn't play cricket anyway.'

'Quiet,' hissed Gordon, 'I want to hear what the old man has to say, even if you lot don't.'

Mr Allan gave a nervous cough, cleared his throat and continued, 'No doubt you have all noticed the sand bags outside the gym. If hostilities do occur we may well be bombed.' This last remark brought an outbreak of stilted excitement echoing around the hall. Mr Allan raised his hand and went on. 'Should there be an air raid this will be used as an emergency shelter. In each classroom you will find rolls of brown sticky paper. These are to be fixed in a criss-cross pattern to the insides of all windows in order to prevent flying glass should they be damaged.'

Throughout July and August the threat of war gripped the nation. On the evening of 23 August John Snagge announced on the wireless that Germany and Russia had signed a Non-Aggression Pact.

Upon hearing this, dad threw down his *Liverpool Echo* in disgust. 'Christ Almighty!' he exploded. 'This means that if he wants, Hitler can concentrate on the rest of Europe.'

Without glancing up from her knitting, mum said quietly, 'No need to swear, Bill. Anyway, I heard in the Co-op that everything is going to be rationed. Milk has already gone from a penny to two pence a pint.' She then gave an annoying shrug of her shoulders, and added, 'If you ask me it's bloody scandalous.'

'Now look who's swearing,' laughed dad and carried on reading his newspaper.

Sunday 3 September was a bright, sunny day. Tiger, the black Tabby cat from next door was stretched lazily on top of the backyard toilet. I sat outside on the kitchen step cleaning my cricket boots; dad was playing bowls before enjoying a few pints with his cronies, and the smell of mum cooking the roast was making my mouth water.

Consequently, the first thing I knew about war being declared was when dad came bursting into the house, red-faced, breathing beer fumes all over us.

'We're at war, Hilda!' he exploded, 'I knew it were coming,' he added, slumping into his favourite armchair. 'I just knew it.' He lit a cigarette. As he did so I noticed his hands were shaking.

'Calm down, dear,' said mum, wiping her hands on her gravy-stained apron. 'How do you know all this?'

'It were on the wireless,' gasped dad, exhaling a long stream of blue tobacco smoke. 'Switch it on and you'll hear all about it.'

I did as dad said but all we heard was dull chamber music. Still excited, dad went on, 'Old Neville himself said that we hadn't heard that the Jerries would leave Poland and that from eleven o'clock we were now, "in a state of war", as he put it, with Germany.'

Wearing a puzzled expression, mum sat down her hands in her lap. 'Now what?' she asked.

'I don't know about you,' replied dad, flicking his dog end into the empty fire grate. 'But I'm going down to the Nelly again to have another pint. Pity you're not a bit older Peter,' he said ruffling my hair, 'you could have come with me.'

Suddenly I thought of Adele and her family.

'Do you think the Germans will invade France, dad?'

'It wouldn't surprise me,' said dad as he walked out of the room. 'Looks like they're gonna need that bloody Maginot Line of theirs.'

Later that afternoon I was startled to hear a sound that would one day become all too familiar – the undulating wailing sound of the air raid siren. Shortly afterwards the continual low drone of the 'All Clear' followed this. Much to my relief both were merely testing the alarm systems. At nine o'clock in the evening we listened intently as King George VI broadcast to the nation.

'It's all very well for him to tell us "to stand calm and firm and united in this time of trial",' grumbled dad, 'he and the royal family will probably bugger off to America or somewhere safe.'

'William Robertson,' cried mum in disgust, 'you ought to be ashamed of yourself. The king and queen and the princesses will be staying in England. It said so in the paper last week.'

On the way to school the next day the sight of numerous silver barrage balloons hovering in the sky, their pale grey skins flapping in the early morning breeze, fascinated me.

'Fat lot of use they'll be,' said Gordon staring up at the sky as we walked through the school gates, 'the Germans will simply fly a bit higher and bomb us to buggery.'

'That's the general idea, you clot,' remarked Jim, 'and with a bit of luck they'll miss our road.'

However, the expected attack from the air didn't materialise. Instead, what became known as 'The Phoney War' began, a phrase copied from the Americans (the Germans called it 'Sitzkreig'). This so-called peaceful period lasted until November when the first bombs fell on the Shetland Islands causing thirty-two casualties. Until then, many had developed a sense of false security.

'If you ask me all this rationing, identity cards and evacuating kids to the countryside is a waste of time,' grumbled mum a few weeks before Christmas. 'And as for those darn gas masks, they get in the way of my shopping.' (One million, four hundred and seventy-three thousand people, mostly children, were evacuated during the war.)

'Tell that to those poor buggers who went down with that aircraft carrier HMS *Courageous* and the battleship *Royal Oak*,' replied dad, 'not to mention the merchant ships lost bringing that stuff that you get at the Co-op. So stop moaning.'

'All right,' replied mum pulling a face behind his back, 'no need to get shirty.'

When Russia invaded Finland in November mum was even more confused.

'Those poor Finns,' she said ironing a shirt for dad, 'what harm have they done Russia?'

'It's all about fear,' said dad, glancing up from his newspaper, 'it says here the Ruskies want some place called Karelia in Finland. That's close to Russia and they're frightened in case the Jerries attack Leningrad.'

'But I thought the Germans had a Non-Aggression Pact with Russia?' I remarked.

'It sounds crazy to me,' said mum, handing dad his shirt, 'the world's gone mad I tell you.'

Jim, Gordon, and I left school at December having obtained our School Certificates. CS stayed on to gain A Levels in order to go to university.

'It wasn't my idea,' said CS as we shook hands, 'Father wants me to follow him into the legal profession. What will you lot do?'

'I've got an interview with the Mersey Docks and Harbour Board,' said Jim, 'the pays not much but at least it's a job. How about you, Gordon?'

With a bored expression on his face Gordon replied, 'Me mum wants me to become an accountant. Personally I'd rather go on the dole or be a brain surgeon.'

'Well I've got a job as a trainee dispenser at Victoria Central hospital,' I said with an air of superiority. 'Dad had a word with Mr Bowden, the chief dispenser and wangled me a job. I had an interview last week and start after Christmas.'

'You certainly kept that to yourself,' said CS.

Jim grinned at Gordon and gave him a sly wink. 'Great!' he exclaimed, 'He'll be able to get us a few dates with some of those nurses.'

'Don't you ever think of anything else but girls?' asked CS with an air of distain.

'Not really, do we Jim?' replied Gordon.

Jim gave a lecherous grin and shook his head.

The mention of girls immediately made me think of Adele. Her letters continued to arrive regularly. In them she reiterated her love for me and worried about the onset of war. '*Papa is now in the military reserve and looks so smart in his officers' uniform. Emile is jealous but Mama cries every time someone mentions war.*'

Each night, curled up in bed, I read her letters over and over again. With her medallion resting against my chest I would close my eyes and imagine her warm body next to me...

In late December the news of the German pocket battleship, *Graf Spee*, being scuttled at Montevideo cheered everyone up. However, the main thing that made me happy was a lovely Christmas card from Adele.

'Here's to the Royal Navy,' toasted dad on Christmas Day. 'That'll teach old Adolf not to mess with us.'

'These Morrison shelters make good tables,' said mum referring to the box-like metal structure many houses were issued with. Named after Herbert Morrison, the incumbent Home Secretary, they were used as emergency air raid shelters and usually placed in the kitchen.

'A damn sight cleaner and better than those Anderson shelters they have in the next road,' said dad.

'Aye, but you can't grow vegetables on top of them like Jim's dad does on his,' I said.

As rationing was about to be introduced people were encouraged to 'Dig For Victory' and grow their own vegetables in their gardens or indeed anywhere there was spare land.

Mum's Christmas dinner was a feast fit for a king. Laid out on a red and white chequered tablecloth was a delicious smelling roasted turkey on a large dish, surrounded by an assortment of homemade cakes, coloured crackers and paper hats.

A week previously we had fun putting up decorations and hanging trinkets on the Christmas tree. On Christmas morning we gave each other presents. I bought mum a pair of fur-lined slippers from Woolworths and gave dad a Parker pen.

Having told them about my cycling exploits in Normandy mum and dad surprised me by wheeling into the parlour a brand new Hercules bicycle.

'There you are,' said dad, giving the bell a quick tinkle, 'now you can ride to work like a toff.'

'Wow!' I exclaimed running my hands over the black leather saddle, 'Dropped handle bars and all.'

After dinner we retreated into the parlour and roared with laughter listening to Arthur Askey on the wireless in *Hello Playmates*. When the National Anthem was played dad even managed to stagger to his feet, and clutching his glass of beer, stood like mum and myself to attention.

Later while helping mum to wash up a loud knocking came on the front door. I rushed to open it thinking it might be Jim or Gordon only to find a tall figure wearing a dark blue uniform. Her wore a steel helmet and horn-rimmed glasses. He had a gas mask encased in a canvas satchel slung over his shoulder and on his left arm he wore a white arm-band. On it, in bold black lettering, were the words ARP (Air Raid Precaution).

'You've got a chink of light showing from your front window,' he said in an overly officious voice. 'If a Jerry bomber sees that you've 'ad it. Now fix it or your mum and dad'll be fined.'

While adjusting the offending curtains dad laughed and said, 'Those Air Raid Wardens strut around like toy soldiers. If you ask me, this blackout's becoming a bloody nuisance. According to the *Echo* quite a few people have been knocked down due to the dark.'(In the first three months of the war, 2,657 pedestrians were killed on Britain's roads.)

'Don't be so miserable, I think they're doing a worthwhile job. Mrs Hislop's hubby is a part-time warden and gets a pound a week. Anyway,' mum added with a sly giggle, 'I don't suppose the courting couples mind the dark.'

Dad pursed his lips and glanced approvingly at mum. 'A pound a week, eh,' he muttered, before giving the curtain a final tug.

On a bitterly cold January morning I cycled to Victoria Central Hospital to start work. The roads were so slippery with ice I almost came off my bike.

Little did I know 1939–40 would be the coldest winter for forty-five years. The River Thames would freeze over, milk became solidified on the step, cars would become stuck in snowdrifts and villages cut off; and to add to our agony, the rationing finally arrived.

The weekly ration consisted of, tea (2oz), lard (2oz), butter (4oz), margarine (2oz), cheese (2oz), and bacon (4oz). A small loaf cost 2d. In March 1940, meat was also rationed to the value of 1s 10d per person per week. (A year later, all preserves were included in the rationing schedule.)

'How the devil are we expected to live on that?' cried mum one morning frying bacon.

'According to Lord Haw Haw,' said dad, 'the Jerry U Boats will sink all the convoys carrying food to us from abroad and we'll all starve to death.'

Lord Haw Haw's name was given to him by Jonah Barrington of the *Daily Express*. His real name was William Joyce. He was a naturalised US citizen and spoke very 'posh' English. His propaganda programme, *Jairmany calling* broadcast on Radio Hamburg and denigrating the British War effort was tuned in and heard on the BBC. After the war Joyce was convicted of treason and hung.

'Never mind, dad,' I added, wiping my plate clean with a piece of fried bread, 'beer isn't rationed so things can't be all that bad.'

Opened in January 1901, Victoria Central Hospital was a large four-storey red-bricked building accommodating over 500 patients. After parking my bicycle I made my way to the dispensary situated on the top floor reached by a lift. I walked into the dispensary and was immediately greeted by Mr Bowden, a stout, bespectacled man about fifty with a round fleshy face and a shiny baldhead. He wore a white coat with several dark stains on the front. When he saw me he raised his bushy grey eyebrows and smiled, revealing a row of uneven yellow teeth.

'Ah,' he cried, offering his hand, 'our new man. Good morning, lad. When I interviewed you, you told me you were familiar with some drugs. Is that right?'

I swallowed hard and nodded. 'Yes, sir,' I nervously replied, 'I think so.'

'Good,' he replied, still smiling. 'The first thing I want you to do is take an inventory of what we have in the store room.'

'Do you have many drugs, then, Mr Bowden?' I asked.

Detecting my interest, he replied, 'Oh aye, but what you've got to remember, some people are what they call resistant or allergic to certain drugs. My missus, Doreen, can't take Aspirins. They make her sick.'

I wasn't sure what he meant, but trying to sound intelligent, I answered, 'I see. Thank you, I'll remember that.'

Feeling like a proper chemist in my crisp white coat, I began. Half an hour later I dropped a large tin scattering a mass of small white pills over the black and white tiled floor. To my horror Mr Bowden chose that moment to check on my progress. When he saw me on all fours he let out a deep throaty laugh.

'Never mind, my boy,' he said, 'accidents will happen, I'll send Jennifer up to help you,' and left the room.

Earlier I had been introduced to Mrs Jenkins a small elderly lady with short grey hair, and her assistant, Jennifer. With her shoulder-length black hair, and dark complexion Jennifer, immediately made me think of Adele. Then there was Mr Johnson, a tall, dark featured, middle-aged deputy head dispenser. He hardly ever smiled and reminded me of Bella Lugosi.

A few minutes later Jennifer arrived. I guessed she was a few years older than me and the white coat she wore failed to conceal a full figure. As she stood over me I couldn't help but notice how well shaped her legs were. She didn't wear any stockings and wore a pair of soft sandals with high heels.

Her mischievous hazel eyes sparkled into a smile. 'Don't bother to pick them up individually,' she said, they're only Aspirins and we've plenty of them.'

She left and quickly returned holding a small hand brush and pan. She then knelt down and began sweeping up the tablets. As she did so I couldn't help noticing the swell of her breasts under her sweater and the soft fragrance of her perfume.

'Tell me,' she said, flashing a set of small white even teeth, 'I bet a handsome lad like you has lots of girlfriends?'

'Er… no,' I replied, feeling my face redden, 'I don't.'

'My fiancé, Fred, is away in the army,' she replied, 'I don't half miss him,' then with an inviting smile, added, 'especially at night.'

We both stood up and she passed me the pan and brush.

'What a way to start a new job, eh?' I said.

'You ought to be grateful they weren't the condoms on the top shelf,' she added with a seductive smile, 'we couldn't have *them* getting spoiled, could we?'

When I told Jim and Gordon what had happened they both stared at one another and burst out laughing.

'You lucky bugger,' cried Gordon, 'you've got it made.'

'An older women, eh?' grinned Jim, 'I'll bet she could show you a few tricks on the quiet.'

I had to admit the thought of having sex with Jennifer excited me. However, when one of Adele's letters arrived all designs on Jennifer quickly vanished. Nevertheless a week later my loyalty to Adele was about to be severely tested.

It happened one dinner hour when the shop was closed. The rest of the staff were away. I was sat down eating my chicken sandwiches and reading about the imminent capitulation of France in the *Daily Mirror*. With my mind so concentrated on what might be happening to Adele I hardly felt Jennifer's slight tap on my shoulder.

'Catching up on Jane, I see,' she said. (Jane was a cartoon character in the *Daily Mirror* who was always losing her clothes.)

I put down my half-eaten sandwich and looked up. Her sudden appearance startled me. She stood, both hands in her pockets of her open white coat displaying a tight fawn sweater that did little to hide the outline of her well-shaped breasts.

'No,' I hastily replied, folding my newspaper and standing up, 'just catching up on the war.'

'Tell me, Peter,' she said taking a step towards me, 'are you sure you don't have a girlfriend?'

Feeling my mouth suddenly go dry, I replied, 'Er... yes, I haven't.'

'A big handsome lad like you should have,' she answered, patting the side of her hair with a hand. She then took a step closer and placed a hand on my shoulder, 'Don't worry, love,' she said sliding her other down onto my crutch, 'I won't bite, at least, not yet.'

By this time she was so close I could feel her breath on my face and smell her perfume. My heart was at bursting point and the blood was pounding in my head. I felt so nervous my penis remained limp.

'I don't think we should...' I muttered, trying to step back.

A wry smile played around her lips. She stared up into my eyes and said. 'My you are a shy one, aren't you? Why don't you come around to my house this evening? Mum and dad are away at the moment and we could...' her voice trailed away as she rubbed her hand between my legs.

I had to admit Jennifer's offer was tempting. The pressure of Jennifer's finger instantly caused my penis to harden. Suddenly I was wracked with guilt. I closed my eyes and saw Adele's beautiful oval face smiling at me.

'No... no thanks,' I managed to say. 'I... er, have to stay in tonight.' Then, using all my willpower, I managed to push her away.

Jennifer's face turned scarlet. Her eyes narrowed and she flashed me a look of distain. 'I might have known,' she cried, pulling her hand away from my groin, 'I've heard about puffs like you,' then turned angrily and stalked out of the room.

A few weeks later I breathed a sigh of relief when her fiancé came home and Jennifer left to get married. However, it wouldn't be the last time I was to be faced with similar situations…

CHAPTER EIGHT

During the next three months nothing much happened on the home front. The sub-zero temperatures continued; HMS *Cossack* rescued prisoners from the *Graf Spee* who were incarcerated in the German tanker *Altmark;* Denmark and Belgium fell to the Nazi Blitzkrieg; the 85,000 ton liner *Queen Elizabeth* drabbed in dull grey, dodged U-boats while dashing across the Atlantic; and Vivien Leigh won an Oscar for her portrayal of Scarlet O'Hara in *Gone With The Wind.*

However in May, when Winston Churchill superseded Neville Chamberlain to become Prime Minister, dad was overjoyed.

'He'll show the buggers,' said dad as we listened to the strident voice of Alvar Liddell announce the news over the wireless. 'Old Winnie's been warning that lot in Westminster about Hitler for years. Do you know what he said about appeasers, love?'

'No, dear,' replied mum, sipping a cup of tea, 'I don't.'

'An appeaser is someone who feeds a crocodile hoping it will eat him last.'

'That reminds me,' answered mum with a sigh, 'meat has now been rationed. Everyone can only get one and ten pence worth a week. Not much to feed a crocodile, is it?'

By the end of May 1940, Denmark, Norway and Belgium had fallen under the Nazi jackboot. During the first week of June over 300,000 British and French troops were evacuated from the beaches of Dunkirk followed by the capitulation of France.

'Now that the Jerries have bases along the French coast,' said dad one morning at breakfast, 'they'll be within spitting distance of us.'

'What about Aunt Matilda and Uncle Claude?' I asked.

'According to her last letter written last week,' said mum handing me a plate of bacon and eggs, 'Matilda is now in London with friends. Claude has joined the French navy, but she hasn't heard from him.'

'Did she mention anything about Adele and her family?' I asked. 'I haven't heard from Adele for ages. In her last letter she said if Germany invaded many villagers would remain, but sending letters to England would be impossible.'

Dad pursed his lips and glanced at mum, 'I don't think anyone will be getting letters from France from now on, son.'

Suddenly, I lost my appetite.

'What do you think will happen to Adele and her family?' I asked. 'It said on the wireless the Jews were being interned.' I paused and stared at them, 'But she'll be all right, won't she?'

Avoiding my eager gaze, dad muttered, 'Hard to tell, son, hard to tell…'

I pushed my plate away and left the room. That night in bed I fell asleep clutching Adele's medallion and wondering what the future held for both of us.

On June 11 Italy declared war on the Allies. Great Britain now stood alone to face the might of Germany. A week later, on the 125th anniversary of the battle of Waterloo, we sat near the wireless listening to Churchill's famous speech in which he ended by saying, that "if the British Empire and Commonwealth lasts for a thousand years, men will say 'this was their finest hour'." As he spoke his deep resonant voice rolled up and down like a thunderstorm making the hairs on the back of my neck stand on end.

When he had finished no one spoke. We sat in numbed silence staring at the wireless. Then mum stood up, straightened her pinafore, and in her inimitable way, asked, 'Anyone like a cup of tea?'

'Tea be buggered,' replied dad, 'I'm off to the Nelly for a few pints.'

In July came the news that much of the French Fleet in Algiers had refused to surrender and had been sunk.

'I don't understand it, Bill,' mumbled mum washing the dishes, 'the French are on our side. Why are we shooting at them?'

'According to the news,' replied dad, drying a plate with a tea towel. 'The French refused to scuttle their ships, so to stop the Jerries getting hold of them, Churchill ordered the lot to be sunk.'

'Sounds balmy, if you ask me,' replied mum.

Later that month mum came into the kitchen waving a white envelope. Dad and I were eating breakfast.

'A letter from Matilda,' she said with a smile. By this time Aunt Matilda was living in Croydon with friends.

'Great!' I exclaimed excitedly, 'Maybe she'll have some news of Adele.'

However as mum read the letter her cheerful demeanour slowly changed to one of concern. Still holding the letter she looked up and with a blank expression, muttered, 'Claude has been killed.'

'What!' gasped dad, 'How did this happen? When…?'

'Somewhere called Mers El Kebir, in Algiers,' replied mum, tears welling up in her eyes, 'Matilda says he was on a battleship called the *Bretagne.*'

A week later the newspapers reported the loss of 1,297 French sailors killed during the action. In years to come Churchill would admit his decision to attack the French Fleet at Oran and Mers-el-Kebir was the most heart rendering of the war.

On 10 August 1940 Wallasey suffered its first air raid. It was shortly after six o'clock in the evening that we heard the wail of the air raid siren.

'I expect it will be a false alarm, like the others,' said mum who was busy knitting dad a jumper.

But she was wrong. When we felt the ground shake and heard the *clump, clump* of bombs exploding, dad grabbed hold of mum and I and pulled us under the Morrison.

'Some false alarm,' growled dad his arms around mum and me, 'I hope you switched the gas off, Hilda.'

That night there was thirty-two casualties. It was the start of the Blitz that would claim three hundred and twenty lives in Wallasey and many thousands in Liverpool, Coventry, Bristol and especially London.

On a hot August afternoon I called for Jim and Gordon. Both lived in Lancaster Avenue opposite our old school.

'I see Wallasey High was damaged last night,' said Jim as we walked through Central Park.

'I know,' replied Gordon, 'one of the girls I met showed me a huge chunk of a bomb. She told me she was gonna swap it with a friend for a few fags.'

Collecting shrapnel soon became a popular hobby with children. One evening we heard someone banging on the front door yelling, *'All Out, All Out, Unexploded bomb!'*

For a fleeting second we looked at one another, then, hurriedly grabbed our coats. Outside there was pandemonium as people were ushered by ARP wardens and police into lorries. Nearby two St John's Ambulance men were carrying someone into an ambulance.

'Oh my God,' shouted a woman, 'It's Dolly Smith. She must have been hurt.'

'What the hell's happening?' dad asked a pale-faced ARP Warden.

'Apparently a young boy found an unexploded incendiary bomb and took it home,' he said, shaking his head, 'when his mother saw it she had a heart attack. Now the whole street has to be evacuated.'

We were taken by lorries and ushered into the main hall of Egerton Grove Junior School in Liscard. Here, kindly WVS (Women's Voluntary Service) ladies in smart bottle green uniforms and soft felt hats served us with cups of hot tea.

'Not as good as yours love,' said dad winking at mum.

Throughout August what was to become known as the Battle of Britain took place in the clear blue skies above southern England. The air fight sometimes stretched northwards. On one occasion dad and I stood in the backyard and stared up at the swirling, twisting vapour trails as the RAF fought for mastery of the air.

'They're too far up to make out what they are,' said dad, shading his eyes from the glare of the sun, 'but you can bet your bottom dollar they're spitfires and hurricanes.'

Much later I learned that during the war Hurricanes outnumbered Spitfires, but the latter with its slim fuselage and graceful elliptical wing became an icon, epitomising the spirit and courage of the age.

'According to the wireless this morning meat ration is to be reduced from 2s 2d to 1s 2d, 'said mum that evening at supper. 'It's a good job there's plenty of rabbits in the shops or else we'd all go short.'

'Well I for one aren't complaining,' said dad from behind his *Daily Express,* 'I see another convoy got clobbered this week. Those U-boats seemed to picking them off like flies.'

(In the first nine months of the war some 800,000 tons of Allied shipping was lost to a relatively small number of U-boats.) The Battle of the Atlantic was to continue unabated until May 1945.

Meanwhile the Blitz raged on. The centre of Coventry was obliterated, as were parts of Liverpool, Bristol and Sheffield. London suffered most. The East End Docks were razed and over 2,000 lives were lost. By the end of November Wallasey had suffered no fewer than seventeen air raids with over a hundred killed.

'If this goes on much longer,' said dad one evening as we sat under the Morrison shelter listening to the ground shake and the ear-splitting sound of gunfire, 'we might as well just stay in here for the duration.'

'It's all right for you,' I heard mum say, cuddling up to me, 'but it interferes with my knitting.'

One afternoon in late November Jim, Gordon and I stood stony-faced, staring at the damage inflicted on the houses in Erskine Road. The whole area was cordoned off with rope and with each small blast of wind clouds of brown grit flew upwards from the wreckage that had once been someone's home. Pools of water lay around covered in layers of grime. A fire engine was parked close with tired-looking firemen, covered in dust, busily curling up hoses.

Where the house once stood there was a pile of rubble. The protection of the outer walls was peeled away as if some giant tin opener had ripped them apart exposing fireplaces, torn curtains, shreds of wallpaper and broken furniture. A mirror, still intact, stood above a mantelpiece and jagged ziggurats of glass lay everywhere. But the saddest sight of all was a teddy bear, once the guarded property of a child, lying on the ruffled remnants of a small bed.

'Move on there,' came a strident voice. I turned and saw the face of a policeman his ruddy features streaked with sweat. 'There's a danger of gas leaking.'

'Anyone killed, constable?' asked Gordon.

Wiping dust from his face, the policeman looked at us, 'Five of 'em,' he replied grimly, 'the whole Jennings family. One of the girls was only thirteen, poor little beggar.'

That same month Wallasey cheered and lined the streets as King George VI and the Queen visited some of the more devastated areas. Mum, dad and myself stood amongst the crowd and joined in singing the National Anthem.

'By gum, the queen's a good-looking woman,' said dad, standing rigidly to attention.

'I don't know about that,' replied mum digging him in the ribs, 'but I wonder how many coupons her coat cost.'

Just before 25 December I received the perfect Christmas present. I was eating breakfast and, as usual, dad was engrossed reading the morning newspaper.

'Some good news at last,' muttered dad, '30,000 Eyetie troops have been captured in Egypt,' with a laugh adding, 'no moiré spaghetti for them for a while, eh?'

Just then mum came into the kitchen holding a letter. 'I think this is for you,' she said with a smile.

My heart gave a sudden jerk as I recognised Adele's neat handwriting.

'It's from her,' I cried tearing open the letter. 'It's from Adele.'

The letter had a Swiss postage stamp. Still sitting down, my hand shook as I eagerly read its contents. The letter had been smuggled out of France by Mr Duprey, a friend of her family who was a watch dealer. She wrote saying how much she loved and missed me. She went on to say the Germans were everywhere but, so far, she and her family were safe. She also said she would try and write again. Her letter ended, 'What a pity you can't reply. I would give anything in the world to hear from you. I love you and no matter what, one day we will meet again.'

As if hypnotised, I read and re-read the letter over and over again. I would have probably continued doing so had it not been for mum nudging me. 'Come on Peter,' she said placing a cup of tea by my side, 'you're going to be late for work.'

I decided to tell Gordon and Jim about Adele. One chilly afternoon in late December we were sitting in a café in Liscard. Earlier we had been to the Capitol Picture House to see Charlie Chaplain in *The Great Dictator*.

'You've been quiet all afternoon, hasn't he Gordon?' remarked Jim blowing across the top of his scalding hot cup of tea.

'Yeah,' answered Gordon, glancing at me, 'I never heard you laugh once during the picture. What's up? Got the sack or summat?'

I shook my head. 'No,' I slowly replied, 'it's just…' I then opened up and described what had happened in Normandy.

'Bloody hell, mate!' exclaimed Jim. 'You're a dark horse, aren't you?'

'So it's right what they say about the French girls, eh?' said Gordon with a salacious glint in his eyes.

I shot an angry glance at him. '*No,*' I quickly replied. 'It wasn't like that. It was different…'

'Anyway, Pete,' said Gordon. 'What with the war and all, it seems a pretty pointless romance. God knows if you'll ever meet again.'

With a sigh I finished my cup of tea, and feeling my words choke in my throat, answered, 'I know, but this fucking war can't last forever.'

Nineteen forty-one opened on a pessimistic note when British and Commonwealth troops captured Tobruk. Meanwhile the Blitz continued unabated.

In February dad suddenly announced he was joining the ARP.

'What on earth for?' cried mum, 'You did your bit in the last lot. Leave the fighting to the young 'uns.'

'That's just it,' replied dad, 'It's the young 'uns, as you say, that was killed at Dunkirk. Besides,' he went on, 'I'm sick of sitting in that bloody Morrison shelter. One or two of the men at work are joining, and so am I.'

One evening a week later dad walked into the kitchen his six feet plus frame encased in a set of smart blue overalls. On his head a chinstrap held a shiny steel helmet with a large white 'W' painted on the front. From alternative shoulders the canvas straps of a gas mask satchel and first aid kit criss-crossed his chest. Around his left arm was a band on which was written the letters ARP.

'Well,' he beamed, giving his shoulders a quick shrug, 'What do you think? You are now looking at a member of number three ARP group.'

'My goodness,' said mum looking up from her knitting, 'what some men will do for a pound a week. What does this number three group of yours do?'

'Wallasey has eleven ARP groups,' replied dad with a touch of pride. 'My group stretches from Magazine Lane by the promenade to the streets near Peter's old school.'

Trying my best not to laugh, I asked, 'If they give you a rattle, dad, can I borrow it to watch New Brighton play Tranmere Rovers next week?'

'Cheeky sod,' retorted dad, and stormed upstairs.

'I think you've hurt his feelings, Peter,' said mum laughing.

However nobody was laughing when dad was out till all hours during the many air raids that continued non stop throughout the next four months. Shortly after the 'All Clear' sounded he would come home exhausted, covered in dust, his face streaked with sweat and his hands cut and bruised. No mater how late arrived mum would always have a hot meal for him. Sometimes he was too tired to eat and would slowly climb upstairs to bed.

At the end of February I was overjoyed to receive another letter, posted in Switzerland, from Adele. She wrote saying, 'We hear that many Jews in the occupied countries are being sent to what is called concentration camps. If the Germans do come I hope nothing will happen to us,' and added, 'but no matter what, I will always love you.'

It was Gordon's idea to join the Messenger Service. Along with Jim we were in the parlour of Gordon's house in Lancaster Avenue one evening playing gin rummy. The curtains were drawn and I could feel the warmth from the coal fire glowing in the grate. The sound of Ann Shelton's melodious voice singing *Room Five Hundred and Four,* echoed from the wireless. Shortly after six the familiar wail of the air raid siren sounded.

Gordon's mum, a tall, pale-faced woman with her hair tied in a turban, rushed into the room. In one hand she carried a large bag, which we later learnt contained a flask of tea, sandwiches and her knitting. 'Come on you lot,' she cried, 'put those cards away and get into the shelter.'

'Sod it,' moaned Jim, throwing his cards onto the table. 'Just as I was getting a good hand.'

'Won't your mum be concerned about you?' asked Jim's mother ushering us out of the room.

'No,' I replied. 'She knows there's a shelter handy, so she won't worry.'

Together with everyone else in the street we piled into the concrete air raid shelter in the middle of the road. Huddled together on the cold wooden benches we sat and waited. At first there was an ominous silence. People glanced around nervously. The tension was suddenly broken by the sound of a baby crying. Everyone stared around nervously, wondering what the next hour might bring.

Shortly afterwards came the dull throb-throb of the desynchronised German bombers. The sound increased and was immediately followed by the crash of anti-aircraft guns. This was quickly followed by a series of earth-quaking explosions. The pale electric lights flickered and dust fell from the ceiling like confetti.

'Bugger this for a lark,' cried Gordon, glancing at Jim and me, 'I'd rather be one of them messengers the ARP want, than stuck here waiting to be blown to sodden bits.'

'What about them?' I shouted above the din.

'I'll tell yer later,' replied Gordon, ducking his head. 'Bloody hell, that one was close.'

Gordon's mother dug him in the ribs with her elbow. 'Stop swearing our Gordon,' she said, 'if your father was here he'd give you a clip around the ears,' and quietly carried on knitting. Gordon's father was in the army somewhere in North Africa.

Later, back in Gordon's house, he explained about the messenger service.

'All you do is report to the Head Warden at your nearest ARP post,' he said blowing across a hot cup of tea. 'Then, if the telephones are down you take messages to the police or other ARP Wardens.'

'My mum would have a fit,' said Jim. 'She'd never let me do it. Besides,' he added, 'the wheels of me bike are bucked. I crashed into a wall during the blackout last week.'

When I told mum she stopped dusting the mantelpiece and glared at me. 'Over my dead body,' she cried, placing her hands on her hips, 'first your dad, now you. You must be balmy.'

But dad disagreed. 'He'll be all right,' he said glancing over his *Daily Express.* 'Everyone must do their bit. It says here Beaverbrook has called on ten thousand women to volunteer for war work,' he paused and grinned up at mum. 'What do you say, Hilda?'

'You can take a run and jump in the river,' replied mum angrily, 'but Peter is still not going.' She then threw down her duster and stormed out the room.

But between us, dad and I finally got our way. The next evening Gordon and I reported to dad's ARP Post conveniently situated in the main hall of my old school.

'Good lads,' said a stout ARP Warden with a well-waxed military moustache. 'We can do with all the help we can get. Now, make sure your bikes are in good nick. You'll need them.'

During the next two air raids dad and I reported to the headquarters. Along with several others, dad left to patrol his area and help police and ambulance men to rescue people trapped in the rubble of bombed buildings. Meanwhile, much to my disappointment, I remained behind listening to the cacophony of the air raid, drinking tea and trying to keep warm. But all that was soon to change.

Tuesday March 12 was an overcast, miserable day. As I cycled from work the fierce bitterly cold north-westerly wind cut right through my overcoat. By the time I arrived at the home at six o'clock, my face was frozen and the fingers poking out of my mittens were numb. Shortly after six-thirty the sickening sound of the air-raid siren interrupted our supper.

'Bugger,' snorted dad. 'I was hoping to have a quiet snooze then listen to Arthur Askey.'

As usual, an expression of concern became etched on mum's face. 'I'm dead against you two going out like this,' she said, helping me on with my overcoat. 'For God's sake be careful. There'll be some hot soup waiting for you when you get back.'

Dad quickly changed into his overall. We grabbed our steel helmets and gas masks, cycled through the darkening skies to the headquarters.

The streets were deserted and the only sound we heard was the monotonous drone of aircraft approaching from the east. As we entered the main hall of my old school, all hell was let loose. The shockwave from a sudden, ear-splitting explosion sent dad and others, including myself, floundering against chairs and desks.

'Good God Almighty!' cried someone, 'That was too close for comfort.'

At that moment a policeman ran into the hall holding his helmet. He face was red and he was sweating.

'It's Lancaster Road,' he panted, 'the houses and air raid shelter 'ave taken a direct hit. The telephone lines are down. Send a message VCH (Victoria Central Hospital.) Tell them we'll need every available ambulance.'

'Jesus Christ,' cried Gordon. 'That's our road. Me mum and dad...' He didn't finish. Instead he grabbed his bicycle and dashed out of the hall.

I was about to follow Gordon when I felt a hand on my shoulder. I looked around and saw the tall figure of my dad.

'My pal Jim lives there as well, dad,' I said, 'God, I hope he's all right. Maybe I should go with Gordon to see if I can be of any help.'

'You'd best not, son,' replied dad, 'the way things are, you'll be needed to take a message to VCH.'

Straight away I understood what dad meant. After a quick nod from the Head warden, I hurriedly put on my helmet, grabbed my bicycle and left.

The darkness was pierced with searchlight beams criss-crossing the sky like probing fingers. As I sped down the long pathway leading from the school onto the main road I could hear bursts of explosions coming from Lancaster Avenue. The shockwaves made the ground tremble and I almost lost control of my bicycle. Orange flames flickered over the nearby rooftops; clouds of grey smoke mingled with red and yellow sparks rent the air. A halo of pale crimson appeared over the houses casting an orange glow over the grey-slated rooftops. The continual crackle of flames, exploding bombs and the jingle-jangle of fire engines almost made me wished I had listened to mum and stayed at home.

Most of the houses either side of the lower end of Lancaster Avenue were ablaze. The gritty taste of dust caught the back of my throat and stung my eyes. I caught a glimpse of people frantically clawing rubble away from what was once a concrete air raid shelter. Among them I saw Gordon and his parents, who like the others, were bent, scrabbling among the debris. However, there was no sign of Jim. For a fleeting moment I was tempted to go and help them. Instead, I turned down Manor Road and made my way to VCH. As I did so, two fire engines past me, their bells ringing wildly.

I needn't have bothered going to the hospital. The police had already informed the St John Ambulance people. As I arrived two ambulances passed me, no doubt on the way to Lancaster Avenue.

In a weak attempt to make a joke, one of the St John's men said, 'Best get back to headquarters, son, or else they'll send a search party for you.'

I quickly left and was overtaken by another ambulance. With a sigh of relief I heard the constant wail of the 'All Clear'. I leant my bicycle against a wall and walked down Lancaster Avenue. What I saw reminded me of a scene from *Dante's Inferno* that I had read at school. Firemen trained jets of water into the blazing houses. Yellow sparks and smoke billowed high into the night.

'There's people trapped in there!' I heard someone cry.

Men and women joined in helping ARP Wardens, police and firemen remove chunks of concrete from devastated air raid shelter and houses. I eagerly looked around hoping to see dad but he was nowhere in sight.

I watched in horror as a group of St John's men and ARP wardens covered the inert body of a woman with a blanket. Her face was coated with white dust and her dress was in shreds. With the help of four ARP wardens, they placed her on a stretcher and slid her into the back of an ambulance. Several dust-covered policemen managed to keep back people as more bodies, some of which were children, were removed from under the rubble. When the ambulance finally pulled away, sobs coming from the crowd could be heard over the clatter of falling masonry.

'How are you, mate?' I turned and saw the gangly figure of Gordon, his blue eyes were bloodshot and his white shirt torn and smeared in grime.

'OK, I suppose,' I replied. 'Any sign of Jim?'

Gordon glanced down and shook his head. 'As you know he lived near the bottom. Him and his mum didn't stand a chance.'

Without waiting for me to reply, he turned and walked away.

Suddenly, everyone jumped back as one of air raid shelter walls collapsed. A flurry of dust and debris flew into the air like a miniature explosion.

'Jesus!' I heard an ARP warden cry. 'One of our men is in there.'

I joined a few ARP men and policemen, their jackets undone, and began heaving bits of masonry away from what was once a wall. Particles of grime hurt my eyes as I lifted heavy chunks of concrete to one side.

'Here he is,' yelled a policemen,' I can see his legs.'

I watched as two ARP men frantically cleared away bits of rubble and carefully pulled a man out. At first I didn't recognise who it was. Then, to my utter horror I saw the face of my dad. He was unconscious. His hair was matted with blood and his face half-hidden under a fine layer of powdery dust.

'It's my dad, it's my dad!' I heard myself cry and managed to push my way in and kneel by the side of him. I reached down and touched his chest. 'Are you all right, dad?' I cried, but to my dismay, his eyes remained closed and he didn't reply. 'Careful, son,' said one of the ARP men, 'one of his legs is broken and he's hurt his head.'

My head was in a spin and I felt slightly sick. I took hold of one of dad's hands and gently squeezed it. It felt warm, but there was no response. 'Is he…?' I stuttered.

'No, lad,' answered the ARP man, 'he's still breathing.'

With mounting trepidation I watched as a St John's man carefully bound dad's legs together with bandages while another put a dressing around his head. Dad was then placed on a stretcher and covered with a blanket.

'Can I come with you to the hospital?' I cried, staring at dad's inert figure.

'All right,' replied a tired-looking St John's man. 'But what about your mum?'

'I'll let her know,' said a small stocky ARP warden, his red face streaked with sweat and dirt, 'Bill's a pal of mine and I know his missus.'

On the way to hospital I sat on the floor, holding dad's hand. Opposite, completely covered with a grey blanket, was the body of one of the victims. Every time the ambulance jolted it wobbled gently as if still alive.

Four orderlies, their white coats stained with blotches of blood, took dad into the emergency ward. I waited outside, hoping and praying he would be all right.

Mum arrived, clutching her coat around herself like a protective cloak. She wore a pair of old slippers and metal hair curlers poked out from under a yellow headscarf. Her face was pale and drawn and when she saw me, she bit her lip.

'How is he Peter?' she cried as we hugged one another. 'Please God, is he all right?'

Just then, a doctor, tall, thin-faced and badly in need of a shave, with a stethoscope hanging around his neck, came out of the ward. A small nurse with dark hair followed him. For a few seconds mum and I watched out of earshot while they spoke to one another. Then, the doctor shook his head, turned and walked towards mum.

'Oh my God,' pleaded mum, her eyes wide with pain, 'he's not, he's not...' Her voice trailed away as she collapsed into my arms.

Thirty people, including women and children, were killed in the Lancaster Avenue shelter. Three days late a baby's cry was heard coming from within the rubble. A rescue party found a baby a few months old. The child's mother and father were killed – their bodies had protected the child who was taken to VCH and recovered.

CHAPTER NINE

'Your husband is alive, Mrs Robertson,' said the doctor kneeling down in front of mum. 'He's regained consciousness, but he has a nasty fracture of his right shinbone. He also has a deep cut in his scalp.'

I was sitting on a chair next to mum. She sat with her head in both hands. I had an arm around mum's shoulders and felt every movement as she sobbed her heart out.

The doctor's words made mum and I look up. Mum quickly removed her hands. Her face was streaked with tears and her eyes were red. 'Oh thank God,' she cried, 'is he... is he all right?'

I helped mum to her feet. Dabbing her eyes with a pink handkerchief, she said, 'Can I see him?'

The doctor stood up and glanced across at the nurse. His brown eyes wrinkled into a tired smile. 'Only for a few minutes before he goes to X-ray.' He gave me a reassuring glance, then turned and walked down the corridor.

Dad was lying on a bed. The arched bulge of a bed cradle under a blue coverlet protected his right leg and his head was bandaged. His first words when he saw mum and me were, 'Bloody hell, love, I could do with a smoke.'

Mum cried and kissed dad. I laughed and winked at the nurse.

Two weeks later dad was discharged from hospital. He had a plaster cast on his leg and hobbled into the house on crutches.

'All I need is an eye patch and a parrot and I'd look like Long John Silver,' he joked, flopping onto the settee.

Gordon and I attended the funeral of Jim and his parents. Afterwards we felt so depressed that Gordon and I, despite being underage, went into the Wellington in Liscard and got drunk.

On 4 February I received another letter from Adele. The envelope was badly wrinkled and dirty. In it she said her father was now a prisoner-of-war. She went on to write, 'Some of mother's relatives in Rouen have been taken away by the Germans. Emile is going to try and come to England and join the Free French army and I have finished at college.' She ended by writing, 'Monsieur Durprey, who smuggles the letters into Switzerland tells me his business will fold. We hear England is being badly bombed. I worry and love you so…'

Adele was right to be worried about the bombing. From February onwards hundreds were killed on Merseyside. Parts of London were razed; Bath, Bristol, Plymouth and Portsmouth were severely damaged. Coventry was also bombed but worse was to come the following year when the city centre was almost obliterated.

From March to May 412 British, Allied and neutral ships were lost at sea, mainly as a result of U-boat attacks. After the shock sinking of HMS *Hood,* her nemesis, *Bismark,* was finally sent to the bottom of the Atlantic. Germany broke her pledge and invaded Russia; our prize aircraft carrier *Ark Royal* was sunk and the American destroyer, *Reuben James* was torpedoed by a U-boat with the loss of 70 lives.

President Roosevelt announced 'Lend Lease' and delivered fifty World War One destroyers to boost Britain's depleted naval strength. However, after Japan's surprise attack on Pearl Harbour on December 7 1941 Germany declared war on America.

'It says here on the front page of the *Daily Express*,' said dad one morning at breakfast, 'that over two thousand sailors were killed at Pearl Harbour.'

'The poor lads,' answered mum with a sigh, 'more telegrams for grieving mothers.'

'Aye, you're right there, Hilda,' replied dad, 'but now that the Yanks are with us, we'll give 'em what for.'

A week before I celebrated my seventeenth birthday, mum presented me with a pair of woollen gloves she had knitted and dad gave me a new wristwatch.

'Got it in the Nelly,' said dad with a sly wink, 'it fell off a lorry.'

Christmas was a rather muted affair. As usual mum worked miracles with the dinner. Using a walking stick, dad managed to hobble to the Nelson. Gordon and I visited CS in his posh house on Harrison Drive. Much to our surprise CS had lost much of his puppy fat. He no longer wore those hideous spectacles and was now quite slim.

'I say, do you realise, we'll all be eighteen next year?' said CS as he passed Gordon and I a large glass of red wine. 'I don't know about you lot,' he added, 'but I'm going to join the RAF and be a pilot.'

'What about your eyesight?' I replied.

'Don't need the old specs anymore,' he replied, filling up our glasses. Then with a loud laugh, added, 'Lots of carrots you see, old boy. What about you two?'

'Dunno,' I replied shrugging my shoulders.

'Foreign Legion for me,' laughed Gordon, seeing off his drink, 'belly dancers in Baghdad. 'He then passed his empty glass to CS and with a grimace, added, 'Got any beer, this blinkin' wine you toffs drink is too sour for me.'

Nineteen forty-two began badly for the Allies. In February Singapore and Hong Kong fell to the Japanese. In Burma, Rangoon was evacuated, the tiny island of Malta, a constant thorn in Rommel's supply route to North Africa, became the most bombed place on earth. Despite this, the RAF struck back by dropping their new 4,000-pound bombs on the ship building yards at Lubeck and the Krupp factory at Essen. It was reported that during a speech, Josef Goebbels, the Nazi propaganda boss, used the term 'final solution' for the first time. He went on to say, 'The eleven million Jews living in Europe must be dealt with...'

On a lighter note the Board of Trade announced that, due to the shortage of cloth, the hemlines of ladies' skirts would be raised.

'Whatever next,' cried mum. 'It's all right for you men. You can use ordinary soap to shave and plaster your hair with water. Make-up for us poor women is so scarce we have to use soot mixed grease for eye make-up.'

Dad replied with a deep-throated laugh. 'Give over,' he replied, 'you don't complain when I help you paint your legs with that brown stuff then draw a stocking line up your leg.'

'Yeah,' I said, digging dad in the ribs, 'and it all comes off when I use the bath when she's finished. The six inches of water we are told to use is a right mess, I can tell you.'

One morning after delivering some dressings to the busy admitting ward I found myself helping two tired-looking nurses to lift an injured man onto a bed. He had a bloodstained bandage around his head and was unconscious.

'What's he done?' I asked one of the nurses.

'Serious head injury,' she replied, 'not too sure.'

Shortly afterwards, a stout doctor with a greying walrus moustache arrived. From a pocket in his white coat he took out a small torch. Then, gently lifting up each eyelid, he shone a light into the man's eyes.

'Better get him to X-ray,' he said replacing the torch. He glanced across at one of the nurses, ran a hand over his unshaven chin and added, 'Unequal pupils, probable fractured skull.

Whenever I wasn't busy I would leave the store and go onto the ward. The wards were always busy and short staffed. On one occasion, after washing my hands, I held a tray while a nurse changed a dressing on a boy's leg.

'You'd make a good male nurse,' said a pretty dark-haired girl smiling at me. 'Now pass me one of those bandages.'

Little did I realise how prophetic her words were.

In May, Britain signed a twenty-year pact with Russia.

'Those Ruskies change sides more often than I change my socks,' said dad one morning. 'One minute they're with the Jerries, the next minute they're with us.'

'I think it's great,' I replied, 'If I was old Adolf, now that the Yanks are in the war, I'd be more than worried.'

'You have a point, there, son,' replied dad. 'On the news this morning I heard that some General called Eisenhower was now in charge of all American forces in Europe. And the Yanks have sunk a lot of Jap ships at some place in the Pacific called Midway.'

'All very well,' said mum, picking up the breakfast dishes and walking into the back kitchen, 'but thank goodness the bombing seems to have stopped.'

It had now been almost six months since the last air raid on Merseyside.

'Don't count your chickens before they're hatched,' replied dad. 'I'd trust Hitler only as far as I could throw him.'

In July Air Marshal Sir Arthur Harris made a speech over the wireless promising to attack Germany day and night. He went on to say, 'Our new Avro Lancaster bomber has a range of three thousand miles, flies at three hundred miles an hour, is armed with ten guns and carries a bomb load of eight tons. Together with our American Allies we will bomb the Hun into submission.'

'Bloody great!' exclaimed dad. 'Now we'll get our own back for Coventry.'

'And Wallasey,' chimed in mum, 'don't forget Wallasey.'

(320 men, women and children were killed in Wallasey during the Blitz, including twelve air raid wardens.)

Following the news of the heavy casualties during the raid on Dieppe, the country was heartened by hearing of General Montgomery's victory over Rommel at El Alamein. Churchill immediately ordered all church bells to be rung.

'That reminds me,' said mum, as we listened as the dull ding dong of the local church bells echoing around, 'I'd like to go and see *The Hunchback of Notre Dam,* it's on at the Capitol.'

'Please yourself, love,' said dad, winking at me. 'I'm going to the Nelson to have a few pints.'

On August 14 a convoy, battered and bruised, brought badly needed material to Malta enabling that brave island to survive, and in November the Russians finally routed the Germans outside the gates of Stalingrad.

It had now been over a year since I had heard from Adele. At night I would re-read her letters. Sometimes I would wake up in the morning still holding her photograph, hoping that a letter might arrive. Each morning when I heard the clatter of the letterbox my heart pounded. I would leap out of bed and race to the vestibule hoping to see a wrinkled envelope with Adele's neat handwriting. And each morning I would stand and stare in despair at dad's copy of the *Daily Express* lying on the doormat.

My behaviour didn't go unnoticed.

'It's the war, love,' said mum. 'Letters from the troops aren't even arriving. Mrs Johnson down the road hasn't heard from her Bernard for months.'

'In the trenches during the last lot,' said dad, 'some of our lads in the Cheshires couldn't write home for ages. No one to collect the letters you see.'

However, their words failed to comfort me. On the wireless one evening it was reported that Anthony Eden, the Foreign Secretary, had given a speech in the House of Commons, condemning the atrocities committed against the Jews. This plus further news of deportations from France and elsewhere in Europe of Jews to concentration camps only served to increase my concern for Adele's safety.

'Why are they doing this?' I cried after listening to the broadcast. 'What kind of people are they?'

'Only the good Lord knows the answer to that, son,' was mum's sober reply.

'Then I wish he'd tell me,' I muttered and walked upstairs to bed.

On December 17 I was eighteen. Mum and dad, CS, and Gordon and I went to the Nelson and celebrated. Among the several servicemen was two matelots. The sleeves of their tight-fitting uniform were rolled up and their round caps perched precariously on the backs of their heads

'Never mind, mate,' said one of them, a tall lad with weather-beaten features and bleary blue eyes. 'You'll be getting yer papers soon.'

'Aye,' blurted his pal, a short, stocky, dark featured sailor with a tattoo of a dancing girl on his forearm. 'Join the Grey Funnel Line and see plenty o' boozers, that's wot I say.'(The Grey Funnel Line was the nickname for the Royal Navy.)

Suddenly an expression of concern came into mum's eyes. 'They won't call you up so soon, will they, Peter?' she asked.

I shrugged my shoulders, 'I don't know.' I turned and looked at CS and Gordon. 'You two are just eighteen and you haven't heard anything, have you?'

'Not yet, old boy,' replied CS, before taking a long gulp of beer. 'But one or two chaps where I live have received their papers.'

'Pity poor Jim isn't with us,' said Gordon staring into his glass, 'if I get in the army, I'll get one of them Nazis for him, believe you me.'

Dad saw off his pint and looked at mum. 'It's always the young 'uns, ain't it Hilda?'

'You ought to know,' replied mum, placing a loving arm around his waist. 'You were eighteen when you joined in 1914.'

'Never mind,' I said, trying to cheer her up. 'Maybe they'll forget about the lot of us.'

Two weeks later on 14 January 1943, the same day American forces landed on Guadalcanal, Gordon, CS and myself received our call-up papers.

PART TWO

CHAPTER TEN

'Cheer up, Gordon, old son,' said CS with a grin, 'maybe you'll fail the medical. Then you can join the Salvation Army.'

Along with several others, CS, Gordon and I were sitting on a cold bench in Wallasey Town Hall waiting to be medically examined. In front of us sat a stout, grey-haired sergeant in the Territorial Army. His sparse grey hair was plastered over an almost bald shiny scalp. A pair of wire-rimmed spectacles balanced on the end of his bulbous red nose and on the upper left side of his baggy khaki battledress was a row of faded medal ribbons from the First World War. Behind him was a closed door. When a man came out the sergeant called out a name and that person would be told to enter. However, before this happened each man was interviewed by the sergeant. When it came my turn the sergeant's rheumy blue eyes stared at me over his spectacles.

'Ses on yer papers you worked in VCH,' he muttered gruffly. 'And you want to join the navy. Right?'

'Yes, sir,' I replied feeling my mouth suddenly become dry.

'Mmm,' mused the sergeant. 'We'll see about that.'

The door opened and out came a tall, gangly lad with a mop of fair hair. 'Bloody pervert that quack is,' he said glancing around. 'Watch out when he tells you to bend over.'

'*Really!*' exclaimed someone sitting behind me. I turned around and saw a pale-faced man wearing a black homburg. 'I can hardly wait,' he said, squirming in his seat.

Gordon looked at me then at CS. 'D' you think they'd take me in the Sally Army?'

Gordon needn't have worried. The three of us passed our medicals.

A week later I received another buff envelope with a one-way travel warrant and a letter ordering me to report to the Royal Naval Barracks at Plymouth. CS got his ambition and was accepted to train as a pilot and Gordon had to report to Aldershot.

'I'm going train to be what they call a sick berth attendant,' I cried.

'Plymouth took a terrible pasting during the Blitz,' said dad shaking his head. 'The city centre was flattened in 1941.'

'When do you have to go, son?' asked mum, tears welling up in her eyes.

'In two weeks,' I replied putting my arms around her. 'Monday the 28th.'

'I shouldn't worry, Hilda,' said dad trying to sound cheerful. 'He'll probably spend the rest of the war in the dispensary, won't you Peter?'

'More than likely,' I answered, little realising how wrong dad's sentiments were to become.

On a bitterly cold January morning mum, dad CS and Gordon came to Lime Street to see me off. The platforms were crowded with personnel from the three services. Some soldiers carried bulky canvas kitbags with rifles, gas mask satchels and steel helmets slung over their shoulders. Many like myself were being seen off by friends and loved ones. The astringent smell of trains billowing clouds of steam seemed to add to an atmosphere heavy with the finality of goodbyes.

'Cheer up, Peter, old son,' said Gordon, handing me a bottle of Birkenhead Nut Brown Ale. 'It'll be our turn next to catch this train.'

'Speak for yourself, old boy,' added CS shaking my hand. 'My father intends driving me to the RAF base at Cardington in the Bentley.'

With tears in her eyes mum sobbed, 'Write as soon as you can, love. We'll all be so worried about you.'

'Aye,' added dad. 'And take my advice, son, never volunteer for anything.'

After a final hug from mum and dad, I grasped my small suitcase containing a flask of tea and Spam sandwiches and climbed onboard the train.

The journey to Plymouth took ten long, tedious hours. The train was packed with servicemen and women. In some compartments the overhead nets were used as hammocks. Others sat on cases in the corridor while groups sat on the floor and formed card schools outside the toilets. I shared a compartment with three soldiers, a stout matelot who stank of beer, two pallid-faced lads in the RAF and an attractive girl in the ATS (Auxiliary Territorial Service). Before leaving the train at Birmingham the ATS girl, ignoring a chorus of wolf-whistles from the soldiers, smiled, pulled out her tongue and slammed the carriage door.

With a cheery goodbye, the soldiers left the train at Bristol. By the time we arrived at North Road Station, Plymouth, the matelot was wide-awake and I felt exhausted.

'Does it always take this long from Liverpool?' I asked the matelot.

'This was a good trip,' he replied, pulling his dark blue blouse over his portly waist and adjusting his collar. 'Last time I came down the line we was bombed to buggery. Took best part of a day, so it did. Where are you bound?'

I told him.

'Best report to the RTO (Rail Transport Officer). You'll find his caboose at the end of the platform.'

He then wished me luck, slung his gas mask and steel helmet over his shoulder, grabbed a small brown suitcase and left.

A group of tired looking recruits carrying suitcases stood outside the RTO. A tall, gaunt, officer holding a clipboard greeted us. He wore a smart navy blue uniform and his well-creased trousers were neatly tucked into a pair of white gaiters. On his left arm were three gold stripes. On the other arm was a pair of crossed guns and across his left breast rested a single row of medal ribbons.

'Me name's Petty Officer Carloff,' he said. He spoke with a distinct Cockney accent and his small, beady black eyes peered at us under a shiny peaked cap. 'Spelt wiv a "C" and not "K".' (Boris Karloff was a well-known film star who usually portrayed a vampire.)

Next to me stood a small lad with bright ginger hair, humorous blue eyes and a pale, slightly pockmarked complexion. He carried a battered old pale green suitcase on the side of which was a shamrock painted in bright gold. 'Be Jebbus, he could 'ave fooled me,' he muttered, digging me with his elbow. 'I wonder if he's got fanged teeth?'

This immediately brought forth a quiet chorus of giggles. Needless to say the PO was immediately christened 'Boris'.

'So you fink it's funny, eh, Paddy?' said the petty officer. 'Well, I'm your DI (Drill Instructor). We'll see how funny you lot feel after two weeks on the parade ground. Now, outside there's a lorry. Sling your gear in the back, climb inside and pipe down.'

As we climbed into the lorry, a stocky built lad with dark, curly hair remarked, 'I dinna think the bugger likes us.'

'To be sure, yer not wrong, there, Jock,' replied Paddy. 'I don't even think he even likes 'imself.'

Royal Marines armed with rifles guarded the high barrack gates.

'Och mon,' cried Jock, his brown eyes staring wildly. 'Why does that sign say HMS *Drake?* I thought this was the naval barracks.'

'Besides 'avin' an official moniker, shore bases also are named after famous ships or sailors,' shouted the PO from the front. 'You *do* know who Drake was, I suppose?'

'Played bowls or summat, didn't he?'

'Ignorant Haggis yaffler,' replied the PO in disgust.

Paddy's blue eyes wrinkled into a grin. 'To be sure,' he whispered to Jock, 'you've upset old Boris again.'

Consisting of a long rectangular room, our mess was on the fourth floor of a large grey granite building. A blue haze of tobacco smoke almost blotted out the pale overhead electric lighting. On each side were double metal bunks and lockers. Two enclosed coal fires heated the room. The blackout was still adhered to and dark curtains were drawn across the windows.

Several sailors wearing blue jerseys sat at a wooden table. Some were engrossed writing letters, others played cards. A few lay on their bunks reading and smoking.

One of them, swarthy, broad shouldered, able seaman with an untidy mop of black wavy hair, looked up, shrugged his shoulders and grinned. 'More one day wonders,' he remarked to his mate and carried on writing.

I felt tired and was in no mood for sarcasm. I threw my suitcase onto my bunk and shot a sharp glance at the speaker. 'Bollocks,' I grunted, 'I didn't ask to come here, so shit in it.'

The swarthy matelot stood up. Like myself he was well over six feet tall.

'Who the 'ell are you telling to shit in it?' he hissed. He spoke with a pronounced Yorkshire accent. His dark eyes narrowed as he walked slowly towards me. Suddenly the room was filled with tension.

'You,' I replied returning his stare. 'D' you want to make anything out of it?'

141

'Yeah,' he growled. With one hand he pushed me in the chest and was about to draw back the other when Boris came into the room. The PO immediately saw what was happening and cried, 'Right you lot pack it in and stow yer gear.' He then looked at the swarthy faced sailor and added, 'If yer feeling frisky Yorky, maybe you'd like to go and help the chef wash up a few hundred dishes?'

Yorky gave a short laugh, glared at me and sat down.

Boris told us to choose a bunk, and stow what little belongings we had in the lockers. 'The keys are in the locks,' he snapped. 'Eatin' irons and a mug are on the bedding. Make up yer beds then fall in outside in ten minutes for supper.'

'What the blazes is that?' asked Paddy pointing to a round aluminium dish in the middle of the linoleum-covered floor.

'That, my son,' replied Boris, placing his hands on both hips, 'is what is where you throw yer dog-ends and rubbish. Savvy?'

'Looks more like one of them spittoons they have in the cowboy films,' replied Paddy using his fingers to draw an imaginary gun from his side.

'If you try that on, my son,' answered Boris bayoneting Paddy with an icy glare, 'you'll find yerself scrubbing the fuckin' thing till it gleams.' The PO then did a smart about turn and left the room.

'Now then, yer daft bugger,' said Jock throwing a pillow at Paddy. 'Who has upset who, now?'

After Boris had gone, Yorky stood up, glared at me and said, 'Anytime you're ready pretty boy, so am I.'

'You don't scare me, pal,' I replied. 'Where I come from we eat big bastards like you for breakfast. Now fuck off.'

We were about to square up again when Jock intervened. 'For Chrissake, mon,' cried Jock angrily, 'why don't you two save your fighting for the Jerries?'

Yorky gave a short sarcastic laugh. 'I'll be seeing you, make no mistake,' he grunted and left the mess.

Paddy and I shared a bunk, he on top, me on the bottom. His surname was O'Malley and he hailed from Londonderry.

'Where they sell the best Porter in all Ireland,' he said taking my hand.

Jock grabbed the lower berth opposite us.

'Me mane's Davy Weir,' he said.

After shaking hands I had to flex each finger. 'You've got mitts like an all-in wrestler,' I said introducing myself.

He replied with a wide, yellow-toothed grin, 'Och yer right their Peter m' boy. I done wee bit in me time.'

Jock was from Glasgow. He was twenty-four having been a Bevan Boy and deferred from call-up. On each forearm he had a pair of dancing girls in grass skirts tattooed that he was only too proud to show us. (In 1943, due to the shortage of mine workers Ernest Bevin, Minister of Labour conscripted men under twenty-five to either go down the mines or serve in the armed forces. Those who chose the former were called Bevan Boys. They were later allowed to join up.)

'I can make 'em dance fer yer if yer like.' He promptly tensed up the muscles in his arm making the girls sway their hips. 'Lovely aren't they? I calls them Maggie and Maud after me missus and daughter.'

Occupying the bunk above Jock was a small, fresh-faced lad with round spectacles that exaggerated his large sleepy brown eyes.

'Nice to meet you,' he said reaching down from his bunk. He spoke like a BBC announcer and reminded me of CS. He turned out to be the quiet studious type and always had his head buried in a book. His name was John Hailey and we nicknamed him 'the Prof'.

All four of us were hoping to be medics.

During the next fortnight we were kitted out with blue serge uniforms that didn't fit, inoculated and vaccinated against diseases I had never heard of and given hair cuts that would have made our mothers weep.

'Good God!' exclaimed the Prof, running his fingers through what was once a head of thick dark hair. 'I look like a damn Apache Indian.'

'That's nowt,' cried Paddy after we underwent our medical examinations. 'When that young quack grabbed me goolies I thought he was gonna give me a wank.'

'Aye, I ken what yer mean,' replied Jock, 'it's a pity they dunna have women doctors in the navy.'

Boris's early prediction was right – after two weeks square bashing none of us saw the funny side of things.

'Och ma bloody feet are killin' me,' growled Jock dragging his boots off. We were in the mess after an exhausting morning on the parade ground. 'If we keep up this drillin' I'll end up bowlegged.'

'I didn't think they did this much marching in the navy,' I replied throwing myself onto my bunk.

'To be sure,' grumbled Paddy. 'It's not the bloody marchin' I mind. It's that rifle drill that gets me. No bugger told me about that. Maybe I shudda joined the army.'

However, much to our amazement, our class of twenty recruits soon discovered our right foot from our left. Under the experienced eyes of Boris we even mastered the art of slinging a hammock.

'Just remember,' said Boris, pulling a tight seventh turn around the sausage-shaped bundle of canvas. 'Done properly, this should keep you afloat if you have to abandon ship. It can also be used for shoring up holes in a ship. Believe you me I know. I've used it for both.'

The day before the completion of our basic training we were allowed leave. Shortly after secure at 1600 our class was lined up outside the mess.

'Be back onboard by twenty three fifty nine (11:59pm) or you'll be in the rattle,' said Boris. 'And keep away from those partys in the Standard, the Antelope and the Long Bar in Union Street. They'll suck you in and blow you out in bubbles.' (The term 'partys' we later learnt were a colloquial expression for girls.)

'Sounds like paradise, so it does,' said Paddy nudging me in the side with his elbow. 'I wonder how much they charge?'

Payment was on a fortnightly basis and earlier that day each of us had received the grand sum of two pound ten shillings.

From the corner of my mouth I replied, 'They're probably poxed up to the hilt so forget it.'

'I don't bloody care,' answered Paddy. 'If there's an air raid I might get blown up.'

'On your head be it, old boy,' said the Prof who was standing on the other side of Paddy. 'If you want your John Thomas injected like we saw in that film on VD, go right ahead. Anyway the Blitz is over and they haven't had a raid for ages.'

The danger of invasion had receded. Churchill had ordered that church bells could now be rung each Sunday and on any other special occasions.

'Well,' argued Paddy, 'I might have a heart attack so I...'

'You'll get more than a soddin' heart attack if yer don't pipe down,' interrupted Boris. 'And don't forget to salute the quarterdeck as you go ashore.' (The term 'going ashore' is always used when leaving a ship or shore establishment.) Tomorrow you'll be told which hospital you'll sent to do your medical training, so don't be adrift.'

The quarterdeck was a round, immaculately kept lawn near the main gate from which the white ensign fluttered from a tall mast. Anyone caught by the eagle-eyed Master-at-Arms, forgetting to salute ended up doubling around the parade ground holding a rifle above his head.

'I've often noticed ye wear a wee trinket around yer neck,' said Jock. We were in the bathroom. Jock, the others and myself were striped to the waist shaving. 'Is it a lucky charm or something?'

'You could say that, Jock,' I replied looking at the medallion in the mirror. 'It was given to me by a close friend.'

'I see,' answered Jock. 'I hope it brings yer luck, then, laddie.'

I hadn't heard from Adele for ages. The headlines in the newspapers of atrocities, especially in Poland, only served to increase my anxiety about her. I still kept her photograph in my wallet and at night, away from prying eyes, I would take it out and stare at the face I missed so much. I gently fingered the medallion wondering where she was...

Feeling like Dutch admirals in our single-breasted blue serge uniforms (known as fore-and-aft rig) we piled into the Naval Arms opposite the barracks. The place was smoke-filled and crowded. The melodious voice of Vera Lynn was barely audible over the raucous chatter, so after a pint of Watneys, Paddy suggested we leave.

'Drop us off at Union Street, love,' said Paddy as we climbed onboard a bus.

The female clippy, a blonde buxom woman, smiled. 'Noisy lot,' she said looking at our new Burberrys, caps and boots. 'I bet this is your first night out.'

'Right, first time, so yer are me darlin'' answered Paddy giving her a cheeky grin. 'So what time does yer lovely self finish work, then?'

The clippy threw back her head and laughed. 'Randy bugger,' she said. 'I'm fed up not hard up. That'll be tuppence each please.'

We left the bus at the top of the street.

'I say, you lot,' said the Prof, peering owl-like over his spectacles, 'There's a sign over there pointing to the Royal Naval Hospital, Stonehouse. It must be just up that road.'

'Och, I expect we'll find out soon enough,' replied Jock.

'To be sure, I hope we'll be drafted here,' added Paddy, 'it's right handy for a run ashore.'

As we walked along I caught a glimpse of the entrance to the hospital. It had a wide main gate flanked by a high, grey-granite wall.

'Looks more like a bloody prison than a hospital,' I muttered.

Union Street was a straight, busy, bustling road leading into the heart of Plymouth city centre.

'Bugger me,' said Jock, gazing around. 'There's more pubs here than the whole of Sauchiehall Street.'

'Aye, yer right there, Jock,' replied Paddy, 'and more women, I bet.'

'Can't you think of anything else but tarts,' said the Prof. Then, pointing to a large, red-bricked theatre on the other side of the road, added, 'Look at the stunning Baroque architecture of that building.'

Paddy ignored him. Instead he gave a low wolf whistle at two Wrens walking in front of us (WRNS – Women's Royal Naval Service). We had seen a few groups of Wrens being drilled in the barracks. They looked smart in their dark blue serge uniforms, pancake caps and white blouses. One of them, a pretty blonde, turned and with laugh, said, 'Bugger off. We don't associate with "ODs".' (OD is a colloquial term for newcomers in the service.) Then, with a toss of her head, she and her mate crossed the road.

'Come on, Clark Gable,' said Jock. 'I dinna ken about you but I could do with a wee dram or two.'

Thus began our first pub-crawl in the navy. In the Standard we downed a couple of pints, then walked across the road into a large drinking den called the Long Bar. The atmosphere reeked with the smell of beer and tobacco smoke. Servicemen leaned against a curved bar that stretched around the room. Others sat at tables with underdressed women with thick make-up. On a small stage an oversize, heavily rouged women wearing a low-cut red dress, played a piano while trying to sing *Come to Me My Melancholy Baby.*

'Blimey,' I said looking around. 'The whole fleet seems to be here.'

'I can't understand why,' remarked the Prof with an air of indifference. 'It certainly isn't the music that's attracted them. Anyway, she ought to have that piano tuned.'

Just then a tall, willowy brunette, one hand on her hip, sashayed up to the Prof. She wore a black, low cut dress, ruby red lips and eye lashes the size of bat's wings.

'Hello, my 'andsome,' she cooed in a thick West Country drawl. 'Buy a thirsty girl a drink?'

With an air of detached aloofness the Prof replied, 'My good woman, how dare you proposition me. Please go away and pester someone else.'

'How about pesterin' me, darlin'?' asked Paddy staring down the front of her dress. 'How much?'

'For you, m' bird,' replied the girl, slipping an arm around Paddy's waist, 'ten bob, short time.'

Paddy raised his eyebrows and backed away from her. 'Ten bob!' he exploded. 'I only want to borrow the thing, not buy it.'

'Bleedin' cheapskate,' said the women who promptly turned away and made for two drunken sailors leaning against the bar.

Shortly after nine o'clock we staggered into a pub called the Antelope. This consisted of a small overcrowded bar polluted with the usual blue haze of tobacco smoke and a few tables occupied by tarts and sailors.

By this time I was feeling somewhat tired and more than a bit drunk. Prof had already vomited into the gutter and looked like death warmed up. Jock and Paddy, no doubt used to riotous living, appeared quite normal.

'A few more then let's get big eats from that café we passed,' said Jock.

'Please don't mention food,' moaned the Prof, 'I think I'll be glad to get back to my dear old bunk.'

The Prof leant pathetically against a small space at the bar while Paddy attempted to chat up the buxom barmaid who had arms as big as Tarzan. Jock was about to order a round of drinks when a loud voice sounded out behind us. 'Well if it ain't that big mouth Scouser who fancies his chances.'

I turned and saw the swarthy features of Yorky. On the left arm of his blue bellbottomed uniform were two gold stripes (called badges) signifying at least eight years' service. On his other arm he wore crossed guns. Behind him stood two other ratings, both of whom wore a badge.

'Oh, Christ, look what the cat dragged,' I moaned. 'I still fancy my chances, now why don't you and your mates piss off.'

Yorky moved close to me, his dark brown eyes blazing. 'Why don't you make me,' he snarled, shoving me in the chest. I reacted by grabbing Yorky's collar and butting him on the bridge of his nose. Yorky let out a harsh, animal cry and fell onto a table scattering glasses onto the floor.

Suddenly all hell broke loose.

Two girls sitting at the table leapt up screaming. Yorky staggered to his feet knocking over another table. Blood oozed from between Yorky's fingers and ran down his hand onto his arm. A crowd of girls and servicemen gathered around.

'Kick 'im in the balls,' yelled one of the girls to no one in particular.

With his face smeared with blood he aimed a punch at me that narrowly missed.

'Try again,' I shouted, keeping my guard up.

He tried and missed again. This only served to infuriate him. 'You bastard,' he cried, throwing a wild swing. 'I'm gonna 'ave you.'

Meanwhile Yorky's two pals moved closer to Paddy and Jock. One of them, a tall, mean-looking sailor with a pockmarked face threw a punch at Paddy sending him crashing against a table. This was quickly followed by more screams as glasses and bottles crashed to the floor.

At that moment I felt a sharp pain run through my head as I was hit on the side of the face by the third sailor, a stocky, dark, curly-headed man. I reeled back against the bar and took a wild swing at curly who promptly ducked. The next thing I remember was hitting my head on the bar, seeing stars and blacking out. When I came too I felt fresh air on my face and a pair of arms on either side of me dragging me along the road. I opened my eyes and saw a mist of dim lights and heard the noise of car engines.

'W… what happened?' I gasped, trying to steady myself. 'Where are we?' I opened my eyes and saw Jock and the Prof. I felt their arms around me as they half carried me along the road. I shook my head and noticed the small figure of Paddy in front carrying my cap.

Paddy turned around and with a wide grin, said, 'When the landlord sent for the patrol we thought it best to make a quick exit, so to speak.'

'Take it easy, old boy,' I heard the Prof say, then added, 'Jock and I have got you. We're in Union Street. With a bit of luck we'll catch a bus back to the barracks.'

'Christ Almighty,' I moaned, 'my head feels like it's gonna burst.'

We stopped and I caught my breath. 'What happened to that bastard, Yorky?' I asked, accepting a cigarette from Paddy and lighting it.

'A patient in the naval hospital, I hope,' replied Jock. 'I popped him one and the last I saw of him he was lying on the deck. One of his oppos was fighting with a bootneck (slang for Royal Marine). As for the other one, the barmaid had him in a half nelson and was choking him to death.'

'What happened to you, Prof?' I asked.

'Nothing, old boy,' he replied nonchalantly, 'I don't get involved in that sort of thing.'

CHAPTER ELEVEN

'*Barrow Gurney*!' I exclaimed. 'Where the hell's that PO?'

The date was Monday 10 February 1943. We had finished our basic training and were fallen in outside the mess. The bitterly cold wind swept in from the River Tamar making my eyes run and smarting my cheeks. And even though I wore a greatcoat my body felt chilled to the bone.

From a clipboard the tall figure of Boris stood reading out names of those going on draft. Some were being sent to the naval hospitals in Plymouth, Chatham or Portsmouth. Much to our surprise Jock, the Prof, Paddy and I were being posted to The Royal Naval Auxillary Hospital, Barrow Gurney, a place none of us had heard off.

'Pipe down,' cried Boris. 'The other three bone yards are full. Barrow Gurney is in Somerset near Bristol. It was taken over by the navy to train you lot to be Sick Berth Attendants (SBAs), so stop moaning. Collect your railway warrant and be on the twelve hundred train from North Road. A lorry will be waiting outside the mess at eleven hundred. Don't be adrift.'

'Well,' I said with a sigh of resignation, 'At least the four of us'll be together.'

'Do they 'ave nurses there, PO?' asked Paddy.

'No,' answered Boris with a smirk on his face, 'only some VADs (Voluntary Aid Detachment). If they've any sense, they won't have anything to do with you riff-raff.'

The train slowly shunted into Bristol Temple Meads at two-thirty. After reporting to the RTO we were met by a thickset SBA with a fresh-faced complexion whose name was Gordon Scott. 'Scotty to me friends,' he said in a thick West Country accent. 'Lorry's outside.'

We piled our kitbags and suitcases in the back of the lorry and climbed inside.

'What's this place like, Scotty?' I asked.

'Not too bad, my 'andsome,' Scotty replied. 'The hospital has a few mental patients as well as the usual cases?'

'Bloody hell!' exclaimed Paddy. 'You mean we've been sent to a nut-house?'

'It's not actually a loony-bin,' replied Scotty, 'the patients have suffered badly during the war. Most have amnesia and shell-shock and the likes.'

'Poor blighters,' said Prof, 'will we have much to do with them?'

'Not really,' answered Scotty, 'only if you meet them walking in the grounds. You'll mostly be doing practical work on the medical and surgical wards.'

We left the outskirts of Bristol and continued along a bumpy secondary road flanked on either side by grazing cattle and farms. In the distance on the slopes of a steep valley I could see a scattering of small hamlets.

'The village you see away to your right is Long Ashton. That'll probably be your only run ashore. They sometimes hold dances in the main hall. The local partys come from near and far. Randy lot they are too. The river you can see is the Avon. It separates Somerset from Gloucestershire.'

'Partys!' exclaimed Paddy rubbing his hands together. 'Bergorra that'll suit me just fine, so it will.'

The village Scotty was referring to was fairly large. Lining each side of a narrow cobbled road I saw a mixture of thatched cottages, shops and older, Victorian houses. To complete what was a picturesque setting a Romanesque bell tower of a church could be seen dominating the grey skyline. It was a peaceful sight far removed from the ravages of the war torn cities.

'Och mon,' cried Jock. Like the rest of us, he was staring out of the end of the lorry. 'It's like one o' those villages on a biscuit tin.'

'I only hope they've got a pub down there, so I do,' said Paddy licking his lips.

'They have two,' answered Scotty, 'The Gardeners Arms and The Angel dating back to 1495.'

'The cider they make around here should be well and truly fermented then,' joked the Prof.

We arrived at a wide area surrounded by a wall topped up with barbed wire. A petty officer waved us through a set of open gates.

Directly ahead I could see rows of red-bricked Victorian buildings with blue slanted slate roofs. Some distance away were several smaller, buildings looking like expensive villas. Clusters of yellow and pink Bougainvillea bushes lay near the edge of a gravelled path that led around a large circular field. Oak, elm and ash tree dotted the landscape and in front of the main building a white ensign fluttered from a tall flagpole.

'Who lives in those?' I asked pointing to several Nissen huts grouped together on the field. Each had a thin trail of black smoke eddying upwards from a squat chimney.

'That's where you'll be billeted,' answered Scotty. 'There's about a hundred and fifty probationers here. I expect you'll join a class starting lectures tomorrow.'

'Bloody hell, mon,' exclaimed Jock, 'this place looks like, one o' them new fangled holiday camps.'

'Don't be fooled,' replied Scotty with a sly grin, 'wait till you meet Billy Bligh.'

Jock, Paddy, Prof and I looked at one another, eyes raised in disbelief.

'Billy *who*?' gasped Jock.

'Billy Blight,' replied Scotty grinning like a Cheshire cat. 'He's the officer in charge of us lot. We don't pronounce the *t*, except when he can't hear us.'

'Any relation to the one off the *Bounty*?' I asked.

'That one wasn't spelt with a *t* but it wouldn't surprise me in the least, mate,' answered Scotty, his shoulders shaking with laughter.

Just as the lorry pulled up on the edge of the field the high-pitched sound of a bugle rent the air.

'What the blazes is that?' cried Prof. 'Don't tell me there's pongoes here as well.' (Pongoes is a derisory term given to the army.)

The lorry stopped near the edge of the field, close to one of the huts. 'You'll get used to it,' said Scotty, 'that's Reg Moss. Before the war he used to be in the Boys brigade. When Billy Bligh found out Reg could play the bugle he ordered him to play at certain times of the day. It's now 1600. That call is for secure.'

'Och away wee ye,' cried Jock, 'in the morning as well?'

'Especially in the morning,' replied Scotty helping us with our gear, 'dead on 0600.'

'It must drive the patients balmy,' I said, picking up my kit bag.

Everyone looked at one another and burst out laughing.

Our Nissen hut was immaculate. The sharp smell of mansion polish permeated the air along with the faint smell of disinfectant. From a series of thick celluloid windows, shafts of light made the highly polished brown linoleum floor shine like glass. In the centre, leading from a black grid fire, a stove-pipe led upwards through the roof. On either side of the fire was a well-scrubbed wooden table and chairs and a round aluminium basin ready for used cigarette ends.

Beds covered with a blue coverlet embroidered with a ship's anchor lay in perfect rows either side of the room. Next to each bed was a metal locker upon which rested clean ashtrays and an occasional framed photograph. Coats and Burberrys, folded neatly, hung behind each bed.

'By all the Holy Saints,' cried Paddy as we looked around. 'You could eat your dinner off the deck. Who does the cleaning?'

'You do,' answered Scotty, 'every morning and evening. Billy and the duty PO do rounds every night. And woe betide any mess if there's as much as a bed out of line.'

Scotty told us to leave our gear by an unoccupied bed then follow him. 'Ted Weeks, the regulating chief, wants to see the four of you. Then I expect he'll take you before our lord and master.'

As we followed Scotty outside a crowd of Probationary Sick Berth Attendants (PSBAs) dressed in single-breasted blue serge uniforms and caps, met us. All of them carried small brown leather suitcases which I later learnt contained medical manuals and exercise books.

'Thank goodness you've finally got here, lovely boys,' said a lad in a thick Geordie accent. He was tall, slightly built with light brown, curly hair. 'I expect you lot'll be in our class. We start lectures tomorrow.'

'Too bloody true,' added a small, ginger-headed lad with a bad case of acne. 'The sooner we get out of this soddin' concentration camp the better. I've only been 'ere a week and that bastard Bligh has already picked me up for a haircut.'

'And a slack hammock, Ginger, my son,' added Geordie. 'You're lucky he didn't run you in for that.' ('Slack hammock' was a term used for an untidy bed or a badly lashed hammock.)

Ginger glowered at Geordie, his eyes dark with anger, 'I'll swing fer the bugger one day, so 'elp me.'

Ted Weeks was a well-groomed chief petty officer with a pale complexion and light brown hair, greying at each temple. He sat behind a desk cluttered with papers and files. Directly behind him was a closed door with a varnished sign written in gold lettering that read *Wardmaster Lieutenant W.G. Blight. MBE. RN.*

Nearby sat a stout, buxom Wren busily typing. On the walls hung a large ordnance map, a colour-coded watch bill, signals and lists of personnel. Both of them looked up as we entered. The Wren smiled and carried on typing.

'Right,' said the chief putting down a sheaf of papers, 'you'll be here for ten weeks. Do your joining routine and be ready to start work in the morning. Any questions?'

'Aye,' said Jock. 'When do we get our rum ration, chief?'

With a slight smirk the chief replied. 'There's no rum during training or in hospitals.' He stood up, flicked a speck of dust of his sleeve, and then added, 'Mr Blight will see you now.'

As we entered the office 'Our Lord and master' as Scotty put it, was standing at the side of a wide oaken desk. On it rested a leather-bound blotting pad, sheaves of official-looking papers and folders. Close by was a telephone. Behind, on the wall, was a large framed photograph of King George VI and Queen Elizabeth. The four of us lined up in front of his desk.

The officer was medium height with well-groomed light brown hair, a fair complexion and sharp, clear-cut features. The edge of a cufflinked shirt poked out from the end of each sleeve around which were two gold rings. A white handkerchief protruded out of his breast pocket above which rested a row of medal ribbons. The creases in his trousers would have done justice to a Guardsman. With his black shoes glistening like patented leather, he looked the epitome of a naval officer.

'Come properly to attention,' he snapped. 'You're standing like a load of old women.' The resonance in his voice exaggerated his pronounced West Country accent.

Like the others I immediately pulled in my stomach and braced my shoulders back.

After pursing his lips, he looked at Chief Weeks then at me. 'This man is improperly dressed, chief.'

Straight away the chief looked me up and down.

'Yes, sir,' replied the chief. 'One of his buttons is undone.'

I glanced down and saw a button on my jacket was loose and quickly fastened it.

'Don't you ever let me see you in such a state again, young man,' said the officer, 'do you understand?'

Feeling my face redden, I replied, 'Yes, sir.'

Lieutenant Blight opened a drawer and took out a pair of brown leather gloves. 'Now, all of you hold out your hands palm down,' he snapped.

He then proceeded to inspect our fingernails. After doing so he tapped each of us on the shoulder with his gloves, and with an expression of disgust retorted, 'Filthy, get them cut before the morning. See to it chief.' He then turned and sat down, and in a stern voice, said, 'I will not tolerate untidiness, drunkenness or slack behaviour.' Surprisingly, his dark blue eyes that had glared menacingly at us suddenly softened. 'You may find the training regime here hard. However, do your best and I'm sure you'll all successfully complete the course. Carry on, chief.'

'*Phew*!' exclaimed Jock when we were outside, 'Now we know why they don't pronounce the *t* at the end o' his name.'

As Scotty said we were woken up the next morning by the shrill sound of a bugle.

I opened my eyes and saw the springs of the bed above me bulge. 'Bugger me,' I heard Jock yawn, 'I wonder who wakes that sod up. Only miners get up at this hour.'

'It's still bloody dark outside, I tell yer,' Paddy moaned from the bunk next to ours.

'Oh stop complaining,' came the voice of the Prof. 'Just think of all that fresh air and clean living you got to look forward to.'

'That's what I'm afraid of,' snorted Paddy as he slowly rose and sat on the edge of his bunk.

Just then a six-foot plus, athletically built, petty officer came into the mess. His thick ginger hair plastered down with Brylcreem, stood out against his white vest. He wore a pair of creased blue shorts and a pair of white plimsolls.

'Right, you lot,' he cried walking past each bed, 'outside in ten minutes. Chop chop.'

'Is he serious, Geordie?' I asked Geordie, one of the lads we met the previous day.

'He is that,' he replied pulling on his vest. 'That's Jack Watson. In civvy street he was an actor. Now he's a PT Instructor. We go fer a run around the camp every morning. The other thirty-fives remain behind and clean the mess. Now if you know what's good fer yer, I'd hurry up.' (After the war Jack Watson featured in many films, usually as a tough sergeant or police officer.)

Shivering like jellies in our flimsy PT gear along with two other classes of twenty, we followed PO Watson out of the grounds.

'Be Jebbus, Scotty,' gasped Paddy, 'do we do this every mornin'?'

'Oh, no,' replied Scotty breathing hard, 'we have a lie in till six thirty on Sundays.'

By the time we returned to the mess we were puffing like steam engines and soaked in sweat.

Half an hour later as we were getting changed into our uniforms in came a short, stocky chief petty officer. He had small dark penetrating eyes and the pallid feature of someone recently discharged from prison.

'Divisions as usual after breakfast,' he cried in a thick Lancashire voice. 'And don't be adrift.' (Divisions was a term used meaning inspection.)

'Who's he?' I asked Geordie.

'That's Chief Pearce,' answered Geordie. 'He is our divisional chief. Recently recovered from appendicitis. Used to be an all-in wrestler before the war. Strong as an ox he is.'

'How many more are there?' I asked, fastening my tie.

'Let me see now,' replied Geordie. 'There's Chief Alsop and Dinnage, quite a few petty officers and a killick called Griffiths.'

'Don't forget Sister Stapleton Atkins, boyo,' added a corpulent PSBA with a mop of wavy fair hair. 'She a right smasher, so she is?'

'Shaggin',' said Geordie, 'that's all you bloody Welshmen can think of.'

'That's quite all right, old boy,' interrupted the Prof, 'we have a mad Irishman who's the same.'

As usual after breakfast we had Divisions. The tall figure of Reg Moss stood smartly to attention facing the Nissen huts, his pink cheeks puffed out blowing a clarion call on his bugle. We fell in two deep. (Two separate lines.) I found myself standing next to Ginger.

Billy Blight, holding his leather gloves, walked between the lines. Ted Weeks, holding a notebook, and Chief Pearce followed closely behind. Billy Blight slowly moved along carefully looking each man up and down. When he came to Ginger, he suddenly stopped. From the corner of my eye I saw Billy move close and stare directly into Ginger's face.

'Take this man's name, chief,' snapped Billy. 'He hasn't shaved this morning. Put him on a charge.'

'I bloody well have,' cried Ginger. 'You've got it in fer me, you 'ave, you…'

Before anyone had time to speak I saw Ginger move forward. 'I've 'ad enough of you, so I 'ave.' He then drew back his arm and was about to strike Billy. Fortunately Chief Pearce reacted quickly and grabbed Ginger's arm. In one quick movement he quickly pinned Ginger's arms behind his back. Ted Weeks dropped his notebook and hurriedly placed a restraining arm around Ginger's shoulders.

For a few seconds nobody spoke. Struggling with his captors Ginger yelled, 'You can fuck off, the lot of yer. I've 'ad enough of you an' this soddin' place.'

Billy calmly stared at Ginger. Then, in a quiet but stern voice, said, 'Put him under close arrest in the guardroom.'

The incident seemed to affect everyone. After Divisions no one spoke as we quietly returned to our messes. 'That's the last we'll see of old Ginger,' said the Prof. 'Attempting to strike a senior officer is a serious offence. He'll probably get SNLR (Services No Longer Required) and end up in DQs (Detention Quarters.)

'Or in the soddin' army,' added Jock.

But they were both wrong. To everyone's surprise Ginger returned two weeks later, full of the joys of spring.

Throwing his gear onto his old bed, Ginger, grinning like a Cheshire Cat, looked at us, 'Believe it or not,' he said, 'Billy Blight recommended I come back. He said everyone deserves a second chance and put me in charge of the sports store.'

From that moment Ginger was a model student and eventually passed out with high marks.

As Billy Blight said, the regime was hard but highly effective. Lectures started at 0800 everyday and finished at 1600. Sister Stapleton-Atkins, a tall, willowy blue-eyed blonde that every PSBA lusted after, and the diminutive Sister Morrisey, lectured us on medical and surgical procedures. Then there was Surgeon Captain Lambert Rogers Royal Navy Volunteer Reserve, a stocky, grey-haired Professor of Surgery, gave us informative talks on his subject. From him and Surgeon Captain V.D. Allison, a tall, man with humorous blue eyes, we learned how to suture a wound and to differentiate between a case of acute gastritis and appendicitis. There was even a mock-up sick bay similar to one onboard a warship that lent authenticity to our surroundings. The Officer-in-Charge was Surgeon Rear Admiral St. Clair Colson, a stocky silver-haired man whom we didn't see much of.

During the week we sat our final examinations. Luckily all of us passed. That evening we celebrated in the NAAFI. (Navy, Army, Air Force Institute.)

'How you managed to get ninety per cent in your nursing and drug papers beats me,' said Ginger, 'most of us just scraped through.'

'Pure genius, Ging,' I replied breathing on my fingernails, 'some of us have it and some of us, well…'

One morning, doing a few knee bends, Paddy muttered, 'You know what they say. Fit men make good lovers.'

'Aye,' replied Jock, 'that's all very well, but where are the lassies?'

'Oh, I don't know,' replied Paddy, 'that dark-haired VAD (Voluntary Aid Detachment) whose always givin' Peter the eye is a bit of all right.'

The girl Paddy was referring to was a small, attractive brunette. We met one morning in the NAAFI. She was standing in front of me queuing up for tea. Her dark brown eyes and fresh complexion reminded me of Adele.

'My goodness,' she said, looking up at me, 'you're a big lad, where are you from?'

When I told her she smiled, touched my arm and added, 'I'm from Blackburn. Me name's Pamela. Pamela Watkins. What's yours?'

I told her and after buying our tea, she smiled and said, 'See you at lectures,' and joined her fellow VADs.

'I think she fancies you, laddie,' remarked Jock. 'Why not give her a try?'

'I think our lad from Scouseland is spoken for,' interjected the Prof. 'Isn't that so, Peter?'

'I suppose so,' I replied giving the Prof a sheepish grin.

One evening after a few pints of beer in the canteen, I had broken down and told them about Adele. After all, they were my closest friends and it was hard to keep a secret in such confined company.

'Your French lassie sounds a wee bit o' all right, Peter,' remarked Jock. 'I hope yer both meet up one day.'

'So do I mate,' I quietly replied. 'So do I...'

Five weeks into training we were finally allowed to work in the wards. One Saturday morning Pamela and I were sent to M1, a ward dealing with patients suffering from pneumonia and chest complaints. Her smart red-cross uniform and sexy black stockings contrasted sharply with my drab, ill-fitting white operating gown.

'Is this your first time on the wards, Peter?' she asked as we walked down a wide corridor.

'Not really,' I replied. 'I helped out a bit in the hospital at home.'

'Good,' she answered, squeezing my arm. 'Maybe they'll give us something interesting to do.'

The ward was full. SBAs and VADs busied themselves attending to patients behind portable white screens. Other members of the staff tidied beds while the sister, in her smart blue and white uniform talked quietly to patients while handing out medication.

Pamela and I were detailed to give a patient a bed-bath.

'So much for getting something interesting,' she muttered from the side of her mouth.

The patient was an able seaman named Perkins. He was thickly set with broad shoulders and arms like a navvy. He had a pallid complexion and a chest full of curly black hair, some of which poked out from between the buttons of his blue striped hospital pyjamas. Pamela carried towels, a basin of warm water and soap while I drew the screen around the patient's bed.

'Aye, aye,' said Perkins, giving Pamela a lecherous grin. 'My luck must be in. Usually one of them hard-handed SBAs do me.'

'Just lie back and let us get on with it,' replied Pamela in a no-nonsense voice. She then drew back the bedclothes. As she did so, the shiny bulbous end of a long, circumcised penis flopped through Perkin's fly. Pamela giggled and I felt my face redden.

'Sorry about that,' grinned the sailor, slowly adjusting his clothing, 'it just popped out, so to speak.'

I shot a quick glance at Pamela. She pursed her lips and tilted her head to one side. 'Don't worry, love,' she said quietly with a bored expression, 'I've seen bigger ones than that.'

Afterwards in the heads I looked at her and laughed. 'Have you really seen a bigger one than he had?' I asked, pouring the dirty water down the sluice.

Her eyes lit up. 'Maybe,' she said, seductively running her tongue along her lips, 'but I haven't seen yours… yet.'

During the first week in April we sat our finals and everyone passed. Afterwards we celebrated in the NAFFI canteen.

'Och away, Peter,' cried Jock taking a deep gulp of beer. 'I heard nobody has ever got full marks for drugs and nursing. How the hell did yer manage that? I barely got forty per cent.'

'Remember, Peter worked in a chemist before the war,' interrupted the Prof, 'now drink your beer and shut up.'

The next morning a list of our future postings had been promulgated on the main notice board. Myself, Paddy and Jock were being sent to the Royal Naval Hospital, Stonehouse in

Plymouth but the Prof was off to Haslar, the naval hospital Portsmouth.

'Bloody great, mon!' exclaimed Jock after reading the notice board. 'We'll be right in the centre of the city. Bags of beer and partys.'

'Aye, you're right there, Jock,' replied Paddy, then looking at the Prof, added, 'pit you're not coming with us. But we'll give yer regards to that party that fancied you in the Long Bar.'

'I shouldn't bother if I were you,' replied the Prof. 'If memory serves me right, Peter said Stonehouse looked more like a prison than a hospital,' he paused, stared at the ground and in a quiet, sober manner continued, 'but I must say, I've become used to your ugly faces...' He didn't finish, but we knew what he meant.

The night before we left a dance was held in the main hall of the hospital. Everyone attended, including the SRA and the nursing sisters. A ten-piece orchestra organised by Jack Watson played on a wide stage behind which hung a large, framed photograph of the king and queen. Black curtains were drawn on the windows and the electric lighting highlighted the coloured bunting decorating the walls. In one corner Jack Watson stood behind a makeshift bar keeping a watchful eye on proceedings.

'Don't want you lads getting drunk, now do we?' he said as Jock, Paddy, Prof and I waited patiently for our bottles of beer. 'Remember you're all goin' on draft in the morning.'

Earlier a few of the lads from our mess had been into Long Ashton and smuggled in several bottles of Scumpy (apple cider) bought at the Gardeners Arms. Before the dance the bottles were passed round and by the time we entered the hall my head was spinning.

The floor was crowded. Many stood around smoking, laughing, making the most of what was a rare occasion.

The orchestra was playing *When You Grow Too Old To Dream*. Suddenly, Jock plucked up enough courage to have a dance. 'It's a waltz,' he muttered to me, 'the only one I canny do,' and promptly asked an attractive Wren standing next to him to dance. Paddy also decided this was his big night and had his arms around a corpulent VAD. As they passed he gave me a lecherous grin and slid a hand onto the girl's ample buttocks. I laughed as she immediately reached down and gave his hand a playful slap before and pulling it up around her waist. Meanwhile the Prof was engaged in a deep conversation with one of the doctors – something about a new drug called Penicillin. Just then I felt a tap on my shoulder. I turned around and saw Pamela. Looking very attractive in her single-breasted blue VAD uniform and white shirt and black tie, she smiled and said, 'Put down that glass of beer and dance. If you don't I'll let out a scream and say you tried to get fresh with me.'

'OK,' I replied, 'but I warn you. I'm no Fred Astaire.'

'And I'm no Ginger Rogers,' she replied, taking the glass from my hand and placing it on a table.

We had no sooner started to move than the music stopped. 'Never mind,' said Pamela, 'There'll be another one. They come in threes, you know.'

She was right. To the tune of *Blue Moon,* I attempted to do a fox trot. After kicking her a few times, she said, 'Just move in time with the music. Let me do the rest.'

The rest, as she called it, included pressing herself against me and placing her head against my chest. Whether or not it was the drink, or the fact that she reminded me of Adele, I don't know, but I felt myself respond. She looked up at me and said, 'My, my. You've been cooped up here far too long.'

I felt my face redden and tried to move away.

'Oh no you don't,' she said, pulling me even closer. 'I'm enjoying this.'

With that she began to gently gyrate her pelvic bone against my groin.

Beads of sweat poured down my face. 'Bloody hell, Pamela,' I gasped, 'if you keep that up I'll…'

She gave a throaty laugh and said, 'You'll what?'

Thankfully the music stopped. She took my hand and as we left the floor my shirt was clinging to me and I was shaking like a leaf.

'Come on, love,' she said laughing, 'let's go out for a smoke before you collapse.'

As we pushed our way towards the door, I heard the unmistakable voice of Paddy ring out, 'Glory be, he's human after all.'

Outside a warm breeze rustled the leaves in the trees while high above a full moon moved imperceptibly in and out of grey clouds. We walked, hand in hand, in silence and found ourselves on a secluded area of grass behind a Nissen hut.

As soon as we sat down our arms encircled one another. My heart began to pound against my ribs and when we kissed I thought it would explode. With a trembling hand I unbuttoned her jacket and felt her nipple harden under my touch. She then grabbed my other hand and slid it under her skirt. With mounting excitement I moved my hand over the smoothness of her stockings, passed the tiny button clips of her suspenders and onto the softness of her knickers. As I did so, her legs opened and I explored further…

'Oh my God,' I heard her cry, 'Touch me there, hard.' Her hand quickly undid my fly buttons and grasped my aching penis. 'Do it Peter, now,' she gasped and drew me on top of her.

When it was over, we lay panting staring up at the sky. A few minutes later she sat up, buttoned her jacket and straightened her skirt. With a girlish giggle, she turned to me and said, 'I told you I'd find out if yours was the biggest I've seen.'

'And is it?' I asked fastening my fly buttons.

'Now that would be telling,' she coyly replied. She then took out a packet of cigarettes from her handbag and after offering me one, added, 'Oh, and by the way, my name's Pamela, not Adele.'

PART THREE

CHAPTER TWELVE

Paddy, Jock and myself left Barrow Gurney early on 8 April and arrived at North Road Station, Plymouth shortly after 1300. We gathered our gear and joined the crowds of service personnel lazily disgorging from the train.

After glancing at our draft orders, the RTO, a tired-looking three-badge petty officer directed us to tilly (an abbreviated name for a naval van called a Utillican) waiting outside the station. 'You can't miss it,' he said in a thick Yorkshire accent. 'It's the one near the sealed off bomb crater.'

'I thought the air raids were finished,' I said, picking up my Pusser's green suitcase. (Everything belonging to the navy is referred to as 'Pusser'.)

'They 'ave, son,' replied the PO, 'the city centre was badly bombed in 1941 and they're still clearing up.'

Outside the station we were met with a cold blustery wind and grey skies. We easily found the tilly and with the help of a small, stout SBA, threw our gear in the back of the blue van and clambered onboard.

The journey to the hospital took roughly five minutes. On the way we drove along a high grey granite wall. 'I told you it looked like a prison, didn't I?' I remarked to nobody in particular, then added, 'I wonder how old it is?'

The SBA, whose name we learned was Harry (Dicky) Bird was sat up front with the driver. In a thick North Country accent, he turned and said, 'Laid down in 1758. Same year Nelson was born, so it were. Rumour has it during the Napoleonic Wars some Frenchies were held prisoner here.'

'There,' I replied flatly, 'what did I tell you?'

We entered the hospital through a set of wide, wrought iron gates.

'The Receiving Room on your left,' said the Dicky, 'and those ruins you see by the flagpole used to belong to the Senior Wardmaster and Pharmacist before they were bombed.'

'Was the hospital badly damaged, then?' asked Jock as we peered out the back window.

'Not 'arf,' answered Dicky, 'I and J blocks copped it. Twenty-four bombs fell on the place. Two of our lads were killed, so they were.'

'To be sure,' replied Paddy. 'It's a good job we left fer Barrow Gurney when we did.'

We continued up a slight gradient passing three massive storey wards connected by an arched colonnade. Like the other blocks I could see across a wide grassy square, they were built in what was now familiar grey granite stone.

'That's G, H and I blocks,' said Dicky, 'medical wards. The smaller ones in between are called pavilions. The first one is the Victualling Store and the other between G and H blocks is where some of the Chuffs and Puffs (slang for chief and petty officers) live. The wards you can see on the other side are A, B, C and D blocks. They're mainly orthopaedic and surgical. The big building with a clock and cupola is Trafalgar block. That's where the CDO (Central Duty Office) and regulating office is.'

'What's that big yellow bricked building?' I asked looking to my right.

Dicky's dark blue eyes lit up, 'That, me old cocka,' he answered with a smile, 'is the Training Division. Used to house lunatics in the old days.'

Jock, Paddy and myself turned and looked and laughed.

'Here we go again,' cried Paddy. 'From one nuthouse to another.'

As the tilly continued on a group of nurses wearing dark blue capes passed by.

'Holy Mother of God!' exclaimed Paddy leering out the window, 'D' you see what I see? Nurses, and a sight fer sore eyes they are too.'

One of them saw Paddy waving, smiled and returned the favour.

'I think I'm gonna love it here,' sighed Paddy sitting back in his seat. 'Where do the nurses live?'

'At the end of the staff quarters,' replied Dicky, 'strictly out of bounds to you and me, matey.'

'Just as if...' replied Paddy, rubbing his hands together.

The staff quarters was a large building built of similar stone to that of the Training Division. The tilly stopped outside an arched entrance and we unloaded our gear. Opposite, on a slight rise, stood a church surrounded by scaffolding.

'A bit of renovation going on, I see,' I remarked.

'That's the Church of the Good Shepherd,' replied Dicky taking hold of a suitcase. 'It was bombed as well.'

Inside the staff quarters a warm, mouth-watering smell of cooking greeted us.

'I don't know about you lot,' I said, 'but I'm starving.'

'The galley, dining room and some messes are upstairs,' said Dicky. 'I expect they've saved some scran for you.'

Several members of staff passed us and walked up a winding staircase that led onto the upper floor. One, a tall SBA built like a scrum half with dark, wavy hair looked at us and laughed. 'More lambs for the slaughter, boyo,' he said in a voice straight from the Welsh valleys.

'Bloody sheep shagger,' growled Jock as we went upstairs.

The messes, overlooking a playing field, were light and spacious with individual beds and lockers. By the time we had

173

eaten and stowed our gear it was four-thirty. A tall petty officer with spectacles told us to settle in and report to the regulating office in the morning. 'Be there at 0800,' he added, stifling a yawn, 'and don't be adrift.'

After supper Jock, Paddy and I found the bar and got into a conversation with a few SBAs. One was the powerful looking Welshman we had met earlier.

'Taffy Wilson,' he said as we shook hands, 'from Cardiff.'

'What's it like on the wards, Taff?' I asked, offering him a cigarette and lighting it.

'The busiest is A1,' he replied, 'acute surgical, bullet and shrapnel wounds and the like.'

'He's right,' added a small, freckled face lad with spectacles who introduced himself as Knocker White. 'That's where they're using that new Penicillin stuff. And by all accounts it's working wonders.'

'What about the nurses?' asked Paddy. As he spoke his eyes creased into a wide grin, 'I hear they live in the building.'

Taffy's dark features and brown eyes lit up. 'So they do,' he replied, 'and a lovely lot they are too. As a matter of fact boyo I have a date with one this evening. Her names Mavis O'Toole and she's a real smasher.'

'Now that's a good Irish name if ever there was one,' replied Paddy. 'Has she got a friend?'

'Yes,' growled Taffy, staring at Paddy, 'me!'

Just before eight the next morning the three of us made our way to Trafalgar block. Upon leaving the staff quarters several SBAs and nurses hurried passed on their way to the wards. One SBA, a small lad with spectacles, grinned at us and in a sing-song voice, chimed, 'You'll be sorree.' The others laughed and disappeared down one of the colonnades.

As we entered the regulating office a chief petty officer with dark hair and the ruddy complexion of a dedicated bass drinker, looked up from his desk. In one hand he held a cigarette and the front of his jacket was speckled with ash. Behind him sat a sallow-faced SBA pounding an old Imperial typewriter.

'Ah,' grunted the chief, staring at us with a pair of bloodshot eyes, 'you must be the three from Barrow Gurney. Right?' I immediately recognised his accent and wondered which part of Merseyside he was from. Without waiting for a reply, he continued, 'Me name's Chief Petty Officer Oakey.' He then paused, took a deep drag of his cigarette, and allowing a stream of blue smoke to trickle from each nostril, went on, 'You and Robertson will be on A1. Weir, you'll go to B1. Any questions?'

'What's B1, chief?' asked Jock.

'Orthopaedic,' replied the chief. 'And by the way, you'll all be in red watch, which means you're on duty this weekend.' He then stood up, stubbed his cigarette out in an ashtray, fumbled in a pocket, took out a packet of Woodbines and with shaking fingers lit another. 'Oh, and yes,' he added as an afterthought, 'you lot'd best make out an allotment to Cooper's Naval Tailors and get measured up for a number one doeskin uniform. They visit here every Saturday morning. Now bugger off.' With a tired expression on his face he slumped down into his chair. As he did so the ash on his jacket filtered down onto his desk like a miniature snowstorm.

A block was situated at the bottom of the far colonnade opposite B block. As Taffy said it was indeed a busy ward. A small, thin-faced woman with grey eyes and strands of fair hair poking out from under her cap introduced herself as Sister Clark. She in turn called over a tall, stocky rating with a swarthy complexion and an untidy mop of black hair. Like the other male members he wore a loose-fitting white operating gown over his uniform.

'I'm Taff Morgan, killick of the ward,' he said without shaking hands. 'Make yourselves useful. You'll find OT gowns outside in the linen cupboard. Put one on and help the nurses put those beds back.' His dark blue eyes then broke into a grin. 'And when you've done that I have a special job for you both.'

For the next hour Paddy and I found ourselves helping two nurses to pull into the middle of the ward beds and lockers allowing an SBA to brush behind. Then, having rubbed in polish with a brush, another SBA proceeded to swing a bumper from side to side until the wooden deck gleamed like silver. We then pushed them back and pulled out the next row of beds. This process was repeated until the area behind all the beds had been attended to. Then the centre of the ward was cleaned and polished.

By this time, Paddy, who like myself was out of breath and sweating profusely, turned to a pretty blonde nurse, and gasped, 'Bejebbas, darlin'. How often do you do this?'

Her blue eyes wrinkled into a warm smile. 'Every morin',' she replied. 'It's Medical Officers rounds at nine-thirty and the place has to be spic and span.'

Paddy, recognising her distinct Irish brogue smiled and said, 'And what might yer name be then?'

'Mary O'Toole,' she replied, 'from dear old 'Derry, and you?'

With a slight bow, Paddy answered, 'Patrick O'Malley, from County Antrim, at yer service.'

'You'll be on yer way back there if you don't watch out,' came a voice from behind us. Paddy and I turned around and saw Taff Morgan staring at us.

The nurse glared at Taff then walked away. Taff then turned to Paddy, 'Just keep away from her,' he said in a threatening manner, 'if yer know what's good for you.'

'Just passin' the time o' day,' he replied, shrugging his shoulders. 'Now what was that special job you had fer us?'

For the next hour Paddy and I mopped, cleaned and polished every part of the ward heads. (Bathroom and toilet.)

'Some bloody special job, I must say,' muttered Paddy wiping the insides of the sluice. 'No bugger told us about this in Barrow Gurney.' Just then Nurse O' Toole came in carrying a bedpan covered with a piece of brown jaconet. Suddenly the smell of faeces was overpowering.

'Sorry about this, lads,' she said, wrinkling her nose. She removed the jaconet and quickly tipped the contents of the bedpan down Paddy's highly polished sluice and pulled the flush lever.

'All me bloody hard work down the drain,' growled Paddy, holding his nose.

With a smile Nurse O'Toole looked at us and said, 'Aye, I suppose you could say that,' pushed open the door and left.

After changing our gowns Paddy and I joined the medical officer, sister and staff on the doctor's daily ward round. A nurse pushed a trolley with shelves containing patients' bed tickets X-rays and an examination tray. Paddy and I followed on behind pulling a set of white screens. Before examining a wound or operation incision, Paddy and I would hastily place the screen around the patient's bed. Like the rest our noses and mouths were covered with an operating mask. Most of the patients were young servicemen suffering from wounds or recovering from operations. They lay in bed, some with their heads swathed in bandages, others with cradles bulging under bedclothes protecting lower limbs.

One of these was a young royal marine who had a deep shrapnel wound in his right thigh and lay quietly in bed. I gently pushed past Taffy and two nurses to see what was happening. The marine had black rings under his eyes and his face was ashen. Even to my untrained eye I could tell he was very ill.

The medical officer, wearing a white coat, was a medium-sized young doctor badly in need of a haircut. After undoing the dressing and examining the wound, he stood up and out of earshot of the patient, whispered, 'Notice how red the wound is and also the green pus oozing from inside. His temperature is high and many of his glands are enlarged.' He glanced around, raised his eyebrows and looked at me, 'What does that tell us, young man?'

My mouth suddenly dried up. I nervously glanced at Paddy, then at the doctor and answered, 'Infection, sir.'

'Good man,' replied the doctor. 'And what do you think we should do about it?'

I could hardly believe what was happening. Here I was, an OD (naval slang for a raw recruit) discussing the treatment of a patient with a doctor. I glanced around again and noticed everyone looking at me.

'Er...' I stuttered, 'Maybe that new Penicillin stuff, sir. I hear it's very good.'

A tired smile spread over the doctor's face. 'He's been given that for the past five days, hasn't he sister?'

Sister Clark stood next to the doctor. She quickly opened the patient's bed ticket looked at the doctor and replied, 'Yes, 100,000 units of Procaine Penicillin bd (medical term for twice a day.')

Just then I remembered something Mr Bowden, my old boss told me. 'Maybe he's resistant to it, sir,' I said.

'*Resistant*,' replied the doctor, raising his eyebrows, 'what do you know about that?'

'I worked for a chemist before joining up, sir,' I replied.

'Did you indeed.' He then stared at the marine and with one hand thoughtfully rubbed his chin. Then, glancing at Sister Clark, said, 'He could be right you know. Continue Boric Acid fomentations, stop the Penicillin and continue with Sulpha powder, tds (three times a day). What is your name, young man?'

I told him.

'Mmm, I see,' he muttered.

'Bloody know all,' whispered Paddy as we moved on. 'I expect you'll be a surgeon rear admiral next week.'

'More than likely,' I replied giving him a sly dig in the ribs.

The marine's condition improved. His wound began to heal. A red recommend was placed on my service documents and three weeks later, after intensive physiotherapy, the marine was discharged to light duties.

Meanwhile the RAF continued to attack Germany. On the 21 April they dropped their 8,000 Blockbuster bombs on Berlin to mark Hitler's 54th birthday.

'Pity they didn't hit old Adolf,' remarked Paddy, 'then we could all go home.'

The following day I received a letter from mum. I opened it thinking it would contain the same old news telling me everyone was all right now that the bombing had stopped.

As I unfolded mum's letter, another, written on pink paper fell out. My insides gave a sudden lurch. The letter was from Adele. As I read its contents the faint aroma of her perfume attacked my nostrils. I caught my breath. Suddenly, its intoxicating fragrance reminded me of balmy nights, soft sands and the sensual touch of her body. Written in French, my eyes devoured every word. As I did so, I instinctively fingered her medallion under the thin material of my shirt.

Her letter contained startling news. She told me Emile, her brother, had joined the Free French Army and had escaped to England. 'Before we said goodbye I gave him this letter and your address hoping he could deliver it to your parents.' I read on and felt the blood drain from my face, as she added, 'I am sick with worry. Father is now a prisoner of war and the Gestapo have taken mother and some of our relatives away. They came in the middle of the night and broke down the front door. Poor mama, all she had on was her nightgown. I can still hear her screams as they dragged her away. However, I managed to hide in our wine cellar. Please darling, do not be alarmed I am now safe with friends. I hope this letter reaches you and that you are safe. How I would love to hear from you. Always remember, especially if you are in danger, my prayers are with you. I will love you forever.'

By the time I finished reading my hands were shaking. Where was she now, I asked myself? Who were these friends she was with? Where was she living and what was she doing? And most important of all, was she in danger? According to the news all Jews were being rounded up and sent to concentration camps. Stories of atrocities committed against them and others had been reported in the press. The thought that she might be in the hands of the Gestapo sent shivers of fear down my spine. Still holding the letters I slumped into a chair and stared at the floor.

Paddy's voice interrupted my thoughts. 'Are you all right, Peter my son? Not bad news I 'ope.'

I glanced up at him and shook my head, 'No mate,' I replied, slowly folding the letters, 'everything's OK.'

As soon as we could we decided to go ashore.

'Och aye,' said Jock, 'the three quid we've just been paid is burnin'a hole in me pocket.'

Payment in the navy was on a fortnightly basis and for the first time since we arrived, we felt like Barons. (Naval slang for feeling well off.)

'First, we'll down a few in the staff bar,' said Paddy, 'I hear the whisky's only three pence a shot. Then go to the Hospital Inn, so we will.' He was standing in the mess front of the mirror admiring himself while running a comb through his bright ginger hair, 'Tis a lovely looking lad I am, the partys will tink I'm Clark Gable.'

'I dunna ken about that, laddie,' replied Jock giving his new jacket a quick brush. As Chief Reed suggested we had recently acquired smart doeskin uniforms. Jock abruptly stopped what he was doing, turned and with a twitch of his nose sniffed the air.

'But whatever soap yer usin'," he said with a grin, 'yer smell more like Betty Grable.'

The few drinks Paddy suggested turned out to be large whiskies with beer chasers. By the time I left the staff bar the world appeared a little brighter even though my head was spinning like a top.

The Hospital Inn, conveniently situated just outside the main gate, was a favourite watering hole for the medical staff. Consisting of a small bar and an even smaller recess and dartboard it always appeared crowded.

It was shortly after eight when we entered. Everyone seemed to be smoking and a fog of blue smoke swirled around the electric lighting. Medical staff of all ranks bunched against the bar. Squashed in a corner sat a few elderly locals chatting to a group of VADs and nurses. A darts match was in progress and on the wireless, Vera Lynn singing *I'll See You Again* was barely audible over raucous laughter and noisy conversation.

'Well I'll be a monkey's uncle,' cried Paddy, 'D'yer see who's over there?'

I looked to the end of the bar and saw the petite figure of Mary O'Toole, the girl who worked on A1. Like the other nurses she wore a blue Wren uniform with a round flat cap.

'My round, lads,' I cried, and elbowed my way to the bar. As I did so I saw Paddy make a beeline for Mary.

'Och, mon,' burbled Jock, watching Paddy push his way through a group of SBAs. 'One 'o these day his dick's gonna get 'im into trouble, mark my words.'

An attractive young barmaid with short dark hair passed me three pints of Bents best bitter ale. 'Haven't see you in 'ere before my 'andsome,' she said, flashing me a radiant smile. 'I'm rather partial to tall men with fair hair. Anymore at 'ome like you, then?'

I was just about to reply when above the noise I heard someone yell, 'I bloody well told you to keep away from her, you Irish bastard.'

I turned and saw the burly figure of Taff Morgan. What happened next took a few minutes but seemed longer. Taff had grabbed Paddy by the lapels and pulled him close to him. Paddy was quite small and for a second or two was forced to stand on tiptoe staring into Taff's brooding dark eyes. At that moment Paddy reached down between Taff's legs and grabbed hold of his testicles. Taff's face suddenly became contorted with pain. He let out an animal-like scream and quickly removed his hands from Paddy's lapels and tried to pull Paddy's hands away from his crutch. The two toppled over, hit a table and in the process knocked glasses of drinks over Mary O'Toole and her friends. Then, still clutching one another, they tumbled onto the floor. Male and female personnel leapt up from chairs or stood back as the pair of them rolled over the floor. Taff's cries seemed even louder as he fought to loosen Paddy's grip on his genitals. Everyone, including those playing darts, stopped what they were doing. 'Who's an Irish bastard now?' I heard Paddy cry.

At that moment Mary O'Toole bent over and struggled to pull them apart. 'Leave him alone,' she cried, although exactly whom she was referring to wasn't clear. Unfortunately she received a blow from a flawing hand for her efforts. She screamed, and holding her face, staggered back into another Wren SBA.

'Kill the bugger,' yelled someone.

'Yank his balls off,' cried the barmaid.

Jock immediately went to Paddy's aid. Using both hands Jock managed to pry Paddy's fingers away from Taff's testicles. Taff lay back on the floor moaning. His face, bathed in sweat, remained creased in agony. He lay on his left side with both knees drawn up and both hands tucked between his legs. Meanwhile I had both arms around Paddy.

'Come on, you mad Irish bugger,' I cried, yanking him clear of Taff's almost inert body.

The landlord, a small, thin-faced man in need of a shave appeared. 'Pack it in, you two,' he cried, 'or I'll call the naval patrol.'

'Oh don't do that, love,' cried a pale-faced SBA, licking his lips. Then, smiling sweetly at Mary, he placed a hand on his hip and said, 'I'll take care of dear Taffy. The poor boy will need the touch of an expert.'

'Or admission to the Luton Girls' Choir,' added another, which brought a chorus of laughter.

Mary didn't reply. Instead she put two fingers up at pale face, picked up her cap, turned and said, 'Thank God I won't be seeing either of you for a while. I'm going on leave tomorrow.' She then turned and with a few other nurses pushed past a group of ratings, pulled open the door and stormed out.

By this time things had quietened down. Taff, his once swarthy features now the colour of milk, had been helped into a chair and was sipping a small glass of spirits. Paddy was slumped against the bar, his ginger hair a tousled mess, gulping down his pint. Both their uniforms were dishevelled and covered in dust.

'That was a terrible thing to do to a man,' said the barmaid fluttering her baby blue eyes at Paddy. 'He'll be no good to any girl for ages after that.'

'That, me darlin' girl,' he replied, with a grin, 'was the general idea.'

The next day Paddy appeared on the ward, with an ugly large bruise on the side of his face. Taff came in sporting an angry looking black eye and was walking gingerly. For a few seconds they stood and stared at one another.

'Surely to Jesus they're not gonna start again,' said Jock.

Jock needn't have worried. Paddy shrugged his shoulders, held out his hand and said, 'I don't suppose there's any chance of yer givin' us a song, is there?'

'Bugger off yer Irish bogtrotter,' muttered Taff and walked away.

During the next month Paddy, Jock and myself went ashore as often as possible.

Evidence of recovery from the Blitz was evident by the sound of pneumatic drills coming from workmen high above on steel girders. A forest of scaffolding surrounded several buildings. Badly damaged structures were in the process of being demolished. Halfway up the road on our right the walls of a cathedral was under repair while convoys of trucks took away mountains of rubble.

'The poor buggers must be working day and night,' said Jock as we walked down Union Street.

'By the Saints, it looks thirsty work, so it does,' added Paddy, licking his lips. 'So I suggest we wet our whistles for them.'

(As early as September 1943 the City Engineer James Paton Watson designed a plan to rebuild Plymouth. By April 1944 this was approved and a new and vibrant city slowly emerged.)

Meanwhile, on A1 ward I learned what real nursing was about. Along with senior staff I helped to dress wounds, remove sutures, recognise various abdominal complaints and head injuries. Then there was the bleaker side trying to comfort a next of kin when a loved one died.

On the morning of Monday 12 June, Paddy and I were busy making beds when Jock appeared.

'Chief Oakey wants you in the Reg office, Peter,' he said, 'you'd best get over there chop chop. He didn't sound too happy.'

'Probably still pissed from last night,' added Paddy, 'or else yer in the rattle.'

Paddy was wrong but I was in for the shock of my life.

CHAPTER THIRTEEN

'But that's impossible, chief!' I exclaimed. 'I've not long qualified as an SBA, now you're telling me I'm being sent to a cruiser. It doesn't make sense.'

I was standing in the regulating office facing Chief Oakey. He was sat back in his chair. As usual a half-smoked cigarette dangled from one corner of his mouth.

'Don't blame me, my lad,' he said, removing the cigarette and stubbing it out in an ashtray overflowing with dog ends. 'One of the staff, a young SBA named Pearce, a Chatham rating has died and you're his relief.' He paused took out a packet of Senior Service and lit one. 'Anyway. Think yerself lucky. You'll be given yer hook and that means a pay rise.'

Being rated up to leading hand was indeed a piece of luck. Nevertheless the thought of going to sea came as a jolt to my system. The only sea time I had experienced so far was crossing the River Mersey on the ferryboat. I suddenly conjured up a picture of myself clinging to a guardrail in a howling gale vomiting my guts over the side.

'W… what type of ship is it?' I asked.

'HMS *Uganda* is a colony class cruiser,' answered the chief, 'and a little bird tells me she's going to sea shortly after you join her.'

Having seen warships sail in and out of the Mersey, like all inquisitive schoolboys I soon learned to identify the various parts of the ships, especially the gun turrets, gun director platforms and the secondary armament.

'A colony cruiser,' I repeated, raising my voice, 'they have six inch guns as well as torpedoes. Where's she going to?'

'You'll find out soon enough,' answered the chief.

Placing both hands on his desk I leant forward. 'Is there any chance of me getting out of it?' I pleaded.

The chief's bloodshot eyes stared up at me. 'No chance, my boy,' he replied. 'You'll be given a week's leave then join her on 25 June in Portsmouth. Pack your kit bag and it'll be sent to the ship. Oh, and make sure you've got your tropical gear. You might need it.'

'Tropical clothing, chief, where's the ship going?'

'How the hell do I know?' replied the chief angrily. 'Could be anywhere.'

'When am I going on leave?' I asked.

A sly smile slowly flickered over the chief's rubicund features. 'First thing in the morning,' he replied.

'Blimey,' I gasped. 'I won't even have time to tell me mum and dad I'm coming home.'

'Be grateful it's not a Pier Head jump, at least you'll get some leave,' replied the chief. 'Now bugger off and do your leaving routine, then report back and collect your railway warrant.' (A Pier Head jump is a naval term for an immediate draft to a ship without leave.) The chief continued, 'And remember, on yer way back from Liverpool, you have to go to Euston in London. Then report to the RTO and they'll show you how to get to Waterloo where you'll catch the train to Pompey. So don't get lost.'

When I told Jock and Paddy they too were amazed.

'Och, it's yer own bloody fault, laddie,' said Jock, shaking his head in disbelief. 'If yer hadn't got all those high marks in yer exam they'd 'ave sent a good fightn' man like me instead.'

'Aye, that's right,' replied Paddy, 'All brawn and no brains.'

That night we had a farewell drink in the staff bar.

'Pity it isn't this Irish bogtrotter,' said Taff passing me a pint and digging Paddy in the ribs with his elbow. 'It would keep him away from Mary.'

'To be sure I bet the poor girl's in Ireland missin' me at this very moment,' answered Paddy.

'Aye, and pigs might fly,' grinned Taff.

The freckled-faced figure of Knocker White chimed in, 'Just think Peter,' he said, peering at me over his spectacles, 'you'll be able to draw your tot.'

'Och, now we know the truth,' laughed Jock passing me a pint of beer. 'He probably volunteered to go to sea.'

After breakfast next morning Paddy and Jock walked outside the staff quarters where a tilly was waiting to take me to North Road Station. After the previous night's drinking my head was aching and I felt slightly nauseous. As we shook hands I felt my throat contract. It was sad leaving them. We had become close friends and now we were saying goodbye.

'Och, laddie,' said Jock, 'mind yer take care o'yersell and drop us a line.'

'Aye,' added Paddy, 'and I hope you find that party you told us about. Look after yourself mate.'

I climbed into the tilly and, as it sped up the slight gradient, I turned and gave them a final wave wondering if we would ever meet again.

Carrying my green Pusser's suitcase, gas mask satchel and steel helmet I climbed into a compartment. Sitting on one side were two elderly gentlemen. Both were dressed in blue pinstriped suits and each was reading a copy of *The Times.*

'I see Stalin's still demanding a second front,' said one of them glancing at his companion.

'Yes, so I believe,' replied his friend from behind the newspaper. 'Harry, my boy who's in the Royal Marines, thinks we'll invade Sardinia.'

'Mmm…' muttered his companion. 'Even Sicily, who knows…'

I ignored them and as the train pulled out my thoughts turned to Emile's visit to mum and dad. I hoped Emile might have left a message telling me where Adele was and what she was doing. Her letter tucked inside my wallet had renewed my determination to find her when the war was over.

I also began to think about HMS *Uganda.* The prospect of going to sea filled me with a mixture of excitement and apprehension. A dozen questions filled my head. What would the sick bay on board be like? What would the staff be like? As a newly promoted leading hand how would I fit in? Would I see action? The sight of blood-splattered surgeons conducting emergency operations sent a shiver running through me.

I finally fell asleep and dreamt of raging seas, blinding blizzards and the roar of gunfire. With a start, the sudden lurching of the train woke me up. I opened my eyes. The train had arrived at Crewe. The two elderly gentlemen stood up and each carrying a black briefcase opened the compartment door and left. The time was just after three o'clock. In a few hours I would be home.

'Your money's no good,' cried the grey-haired clippy as I boarded the tram outside Lime Street. 'My lad's in your lot,' he added, 'put it in yer pocket, son.'

A thrill ran though me as I saw the twin cormorants on top of the Liver Buildings and the familiar landmarks I knew so well. The journey across the Mersey on the ferryboat to Wallasey seemed to take ages. This was my first leave and I couldn't wait to get home.

Needless to say mum and dad were overjoyed when they saw me. Then came the inevitable question.

'How long are you home for, son?' asked mum.

'Just a week, ' I replied giving her a hug.

'You should have told us,' she said, wiping a tear from her eye. 'We could have met you.'

'That's right, son,' added dad, grinning wildly while shaking my hand. 'And yer mum could have made yer a pan of Scouse.'

Still holding my suitcase in my one hand, I asked, 'Tell me about Emile's visit. Did he say where Adele was?'

'No, love,' replied mum. 'His dad is a prisoner of war and his poor mother is in a concentration camp.' She paused and took a sip of tea before going on. 'He did say Adele was with some of his friends, but didn't say exactly who they were, isn't that right, Bill?'

'Yes,' answered dad, 'said he couldn't stay long as he had to get back to his unit. A fine looking lad, stood over six feet. Said he was in the Free French commandos under someone called Commandant Keiffer.'

With a sigh I put down my suitcase. 'Pity,' I sighed, 'I was hoping…'

'Come on, son,' interrupted mum, 'let's get you settled in. Then you can tell us all about what you've been up to.'

Later, over a welcome cup of tea, I told them about my draft to HMS *Uganda.* 'She's one of those big cruisers with huge guns,' I said.

Mum was sat next to dad on the settee. With a teacup poised in her hand, she glanced apprehensively at me. 'I expect you'll be off to sea then?' she asked.

'I expect I will,' I replied.

'Any idea where you'll be going, son?' asked dad.

'Dunno, ' I replied, 'maybe the Atlantic. Who knows.'

'Oh God,' said mum, 'so many ships have been lost there. I do hope you'll be all right.'

Dad put down his cup and placed an arm around her. 'Now don't take on so, Hilda,' he said giving her a hug. 'The navy's getting to grips with those bloody U-boats. I read in the *Express* that we now have a new radar system and Asdic sets that help to find the beggars. And what's more,' he added, giving mum another hug, 'last month we sunk seventeen of them.'

'Dad's right, mum,' I added, 'And I bet the *Uganda's* well equipped to deal with anything old Adolf can throw at her.'

Mum reached across and tenderly squeezed my hand. 'I hope you're right, Peter, love,' she said. But the look in her eyes told me she wasn't convinced.

That evening mum, dad and I celebrated my homecoming in the Nelson. As usual the place was crowded. Several old friends insisted on buying me drinks and, long before closing time at ten o'clock, I was well and truly drunk. The next morning I had a welcome surprise. Mum woke me up at around ten o'clock.

'Wake up, lazy bones,' she cried, holding a cup of tea. 'Gordon and your friend that speaks posh are downstairs.'

I forgot about the tea and quickly dressed. Tucking my shirt in my trousers I hurried downstairs.

CS and Gordon were sat in the kitchen drinking tea. As I entered both of them grinned and stood up.

'Ha Ha,' cried Gordon, as we shook hands, 'if it isn't Jolly Jack Tar himself?' Gordon's usual mop of ginger hair was now short and his baggy battledress hung on his lean frame like a badly clothed scarecrow. On each shoulder he wore the insignia of the South Lancashire Regiment.

By contrast CS, whose once portly frame was now quite slim, looked immaculate in his pale blue RAF uniform. His greeting was more poetic. 'Great to see you Peter,' he said extending his hand, 'Home is the sailor, home from the sea and all that.'

'Not yet, CS,' I said, shaking his hand. 'Congratulations. I see they gave you your wings, then.'

'Yes, dear boy,' he replied. 'You are now addressing Pilot Officer Cuthbert-Smyth and I'm stationed a few miles away at West Kirby.'

'Lucky bugger,' quipped Gordon. 'But if you think I'm gonna salute you,' quipped Gordon, 'you know what you can do…'

'As a rich officer,' I said, placing an arm around CS's shoulders, 'I think he should buy the first round, what d' you say, Gord?'

'Good idea,' answered Gordon, 'and to think Peter here is miles away in Portsmouth, I'm stationed at Aldershot, while you're up home every night. Make mine a large whiskey.'

Mum and dad were sat on the settee. Dad's head was hidden behind his *Daily Express* and mum was sipping a cup of tea.

'That's if the Yanks haven't drunk it all,' dad said, poking his head over his newspaper. 'One of them even beat me at darts, would you believe.'

'There were a few American warships in Plymouth,' I said. 'But I didn't realise they were up here as well.'

'There's a large base opened at Burton Wood, near Warrington,' added CS. 'We sometimes go there for a jolly. They seemed to have an unending supply of everything.' He grinned, gave me a playful nudge, and went on, 'Including popsies.'

'*Popsies!*' I exclaimed, 'What the hell are those?'

Once again dad's slightly muffled voice came from behind his newspaper, 'That's posh talk fer girls, you daft article,' he said. 'Don't you sailors know anything?'

'And you told me you'd led a sheltered life,' quipped mum, while pouring out cups of tea.

Dad didn't answer. Instead he gave a quick wink at mum and continued reading.

'Talking of girls,' said Gordon, looking at me. 'I met Maggie yesterday in Liscard. She's told me she was engaged to a marine.'

'Is that the red-headed one that likes Mars bars?' asked CS with a twinkle in his eyes.

Gordon and I looked at CS and burst out laughing. Dad, who suddenly cottoned on to what CS meant, lowered his newspaper and joined in. Mum stood up, shook her head and walked into the back kitchen muttering something incoherent.

The week passed in an alcoholic haze of drinks, laughter and song.

On the night before my leave was over we piled into the Nelson. The usual smoky crowd were there. A few American soldiers wearing brown pointed forage caps and smart uniforms swapped jokes with the locals while playing darts. Someone began playing a mouth organ and the place immediately erupted into a boozy chorus of *Bless 'Em All.*

Remembering our pal Jim Boughey and his parents who were killed in the Blitz, CS lifted his pint, and in a solemn voice, said, 'To absent friends.'

'Aye,' added Gordon. 'We're the lucky ones.'

Their voices, barely audible over the singing, made me think what lay ahead for us. I looked at CS, his posh demeanour momentarily forgotten, singing his head off; then at Gordon, his humorous brown eyes sparkling with laughter. So much had happened to the three of us since we left school. As we clinked glasses our eyes met and I wondered when or if we would meet again.

.

CHAPTER FOURTEEN

The journey to London was long and tiresome. I found myself slumped on my suitcase in a congested corridor. Groups of service personnel leant against the sides of the corridor smoking. Some like me sat uncomfortably on their upturned suitcases. Others simply stared out of the grimy windows no doubt wishing they were still at home. A brief stop at Crewe resulted in a stampede to the tea trolleys waiting on the platform. The train rumbled on and finally arrived at Euston at one o'clock.

Remembering Chief Reed's instructions I reported to the RTO, a stern-faced three-badge petty officer, who directed me to the Northern Line. 'Seven stops or else you'll end up in Morden,' he said in a sharp, cockney voice.

The train to Portsmouth was crammed with various ranks of naval personnel. I climbed into a compartment reeking with stale sweat and alcohol and heaved my suitcase onto the net rack. I then managed to find room between a stout, fleshy-faced chief cook and a stocky, able seaman with a large bruise around his left eye. When I took off my Burberry the AB noticed my Red Cross.

'Can yer do anything fer this, Doc,' he asked gingerly touching his eye.

'Sorry, mate,' I replied shaking my head, 'maybe the chief cook here has a raw steak handy.'

'How did you manage that, Jacko?' asked the chief cook.

'Had a run in with a Yank,' replied Jacko. 'Knutsford's full of the buggers. They think they own the place. One of them tried to tap my party up, so I let 'im 'ave it.'

On the seat opposite sat three other matelots, their white topped round caps perched precariously on the back of their heads.

'How was yer leave, Knocker?' asked one of them, a good-looking, dark-featured able seaman. 'Did yer get a bit, then?' His question was directed to a small, pasty-faced matelot with freckles.

'A bit fuckin' older more's the like, Digger,' replied Knocker. 'Me missus had the rags up. Silly cow.' Knocker glanced at the third sailor, a ruddy-faced three badge able seaman with grey sideboards. 'What's up with you, Sharky,' he said, digging his pal in the ribs. 'You look a bit pissed off.'

'So would you,' growled Sharky, a well-built able seaman with dark, brooding eyes, 'if your old girl had taken the kids and fucked off with some slimy spiv.' He then brought out a bottle of beer, took a deep swig and passed it to his two mates. 'If I ever get my hands on 'im I'll swing fer the bugger, so 'elp me.'

'How about you, Slim?' asked Digger looking at the chief cook. 'Don't tell me your missus kept you in the galley all week.'

The chief's florid face broke into a grimace. 'With four mouths to feed,' he said, lighting a Senior Service and passing the packet around, 'I did little else. Personally I'll be glad to get onboard the *Ganda.*'

Suddenly my ears pricked up.

'*Ganda,*' I asked excitedly. 'You lot wouldn't be from the *Uganda* by any chance?'

'Careful, Doc,' replied Slim, touching the end of his nose with his fore finger, 'careless talk and all that. But yes, we are.'

'Blimey!' I exclaimed. 'That's where I'm going. I'm joining her today.'

'Your first ship?' asked Knocker, passing me a cigarette.

'Yes,' I replied.

'Then you'd best 'ave a wet of this,' said Sharky passing me the beer, 'the buzz is we're sailing tomorrow.'

Portsmouth harbour was crowded with warships of all shapes and sizes. As the train slowly pulled into the station I strained my eyes hoping to see the *Uganda*.

'Which one is…?'

The chief quickly interrupted me. 'She lying alongside Troopship Wharf,' he said. 'You can just see her masts poking up over Semaphore Towers. That's the huge red-bricked building with the tower on top. And the three main masts you can see away to your right belong to the *Victory.*'

Sure enough there, high in the clear blue sky, were the masts and yardarms of the two ships including those belonging to Nelson's famous flagship. Suddenly, I felt a surge of excitement run through me – at last I was in the real navy.

'My God!' I gasped shifting my gaze to a harbour crowded with warships. 'There must be most of the Home Fleet out there.'

'Aye,' replied Knocker. 'There's summat in the wind all right.'

'The station seems very close to the dockyard,' I remarked.

'Aye, it is that,' replied Knocker. 'Handy for a quick run ashore it is.'

'What's it like onboard?' I asked nobody in particular.

'Not bad,' answered Digger, 'the captain's a real gent, but watch out fer The Jimmy. He can be a bit of a bastard.'(The term Jimmy-the-One, or simply The Jimmy, dates back to James 1st and refers to the First Lieutenant who is responsible for the discipline of the ship.)

'Your boss is a two-and-a-half ringer doc,' said Knocker reaching up for his suitcase.

'And you've got a surgeon lieutenant,' added Jacko, 'nice feller. Cured me chinky toe rot, so he did.'

'Do they have a big sick bay, then?' I asked, putting on my Burberry and collecting my suitcase.

'Keen bugger, isn't he lads?' answered Sharky looking at the others.

'He'll soon learn,' said Knocker, 'come on Doc, you'd best follow us.'

After leaving the train along with a crowd of other sailors we walked a short distance, flashed our pay books to an eagle-eyed policeman and entered the dockyard. As we did so my teeth were set on edge by the harsh staccato of workmen using pneumatic drills on a destroyer lying in a nearby dry dock. On the upper deck of another warship a team of engineers using acetylene torches sent sparks cascading in the air like incandescent Roman Candles. Both vessels were kept in place by stout supports wedged between their respective hulls and the dockyard wall. The superstructures of both vessels were covered in splotches of red lead, evidence of recent damage, and in the distance above a row of massive red-bricked buildings I could see a forest of masts and yardarms. This, I told myself as I walked along the cobble-stoned road, was my new world – a world fraught with danger, death and destruction.

'My God!' I exclaimed, 'She's looks bigger than the *TITANIC.*' I was standing on a long jetty staring up at the biggest warship I had ever seen. In the past I had often watched ships of all descriptions sail down the Mersey. From a distance they had looked quite big but none compared with this floating fortress towering in front of me.

'The *Ganda's* only just under 9,00 tons,' said Slim. 'If you think that's big you should have seen the KGV (King George V battleship), she was 41,000 tons. I did a commission onboard her in 1939. It took me a week before I got me bearings.'

Set against a clear blue sky, *Uganda*'s hull was painted in a camouflaged grey and green zig-zag pattern. At various intervals wires and thick lines of hemp connected her to dockside bollards. A huge anchor was barely visible, firmly secured into the starboard eye close to the end of her sharp bows. (There are two anchors situated on either side of the bows. The eyes are apertures on either side into which each anchor is secured.)

A thin line of black smoke eddied upwards from her two tall funnels. And behind her enclosed bridge stood the gun director platform and a mainmast that seemed to reach up to the heavens. My eyes swept down to the imposing barrels of her triple 6-inch armament protruding ominously from A and B's massive gun turrets. I took in the superbly flared fo'c'sle ending in sharply raked bows from which fluttered a huge Union Flag.

Further along came the ship's secondary armament. This consisted of 20mm Oerlikons, pom-poms, AA (Anti-aircraft guns) and two sets of triple torpedo tubes. Passed these I could just see the bent arm of a small crane. Next to this were whalers secured to davits, rows of Carley floats, and finally right aft were the long barrels of X turrets 6-inch guns barely visible on the quarterdeck.

'By God,' I gasped, 'she's armed to the teeth all right.'

'That's right,' replied Slim as we arrived at the bottom of a wide gangway. 'The *Ganda* was only commissioned early this year. When we first met the Luftwaffe as we crossed the Bay of Biscay we were attacked but managed to zig zag our way out of trouble.' He paused and gave me a reassuring glance. 'She's a lucky ship, so she is.'

'We could all do with a bit of luck,' I replied touching Adele's medallion under the thin material of my shirt.

From a lighter (a barge carrying stores and such like) on the starboard side I noticed metal boxes being hoisted onboard.

'What's happening Jacko?' I asked gazing around.

'Ammunitioning ship,' he replied.

'You know what, Doc,' I heard Slim mutter. 'I have a feeling those bloody six-inchers will fire in earnest sooner than we think.'

I followed behind Slim and the others up a steep brow that led onto the quarterdeck. Waiting at the top was a short, barrel-chested Master-at-Arms. Standing next to him stood a tall, fresh-faced sub lieutenant with a telescope under his left armpit. Behind him was the duty quartermaster, a thick set, two-badge matelot. Around his neck was a boson's whistle attached to chain. A group of sailors, their blue overalls rolled up and caps flat-a-back, occupied themselves scrubbing the quarterdeck with long handled hard brushes.

'Aye, aye,' shouted one of them, a tall, gangly sailor with a cheeky grin, 'good leave, Digger?'

'How's yer missus and the kids?' asked another sailor, his overalls tied around his waist displaying a sweaty mound of corpulent white flesh.

Digger, who was in front of me, looked up and growled, 'Piss off, the lot of youse.'

As I arrived at the top of the brow the long tapering snouts of Yguns triple barrels poking menacingly from their huge turrets looked even more intimidating. I stepped down onto a metal plate in the deck into which the ship's name was embedded.

Following the example of Slim and the others I saluted the quarterdeck before reporting to the MAA who, with sharp, steely eyes looked us up and down.

'Carry on, chief,' said the MAA in a gruff West Country accent.

Slim turned to me, 'When you've settled in, come round for a wet, Doc,' he said before disappearing through an open hatchway into the citadel. (The citadel is the main upper section of the ship.) The other four waited before being dismissed. Then after a quick cheerio, they picked up their suitcases and took the same route as the Slim.

'I suppose you're Robertson, the new SBA?' grunted the MAA.

'Yes, Master,' I nervously replied.

With a hint of a smile on his leathery features, he said, 'No need to stand to attention, my 'andsome, this ain't RNB (Royal Naval Barracks).'

Just then the young sub lieutenant yawned and in a plumy, schoolboy accent, asked, 'Where are you joining from, SBA?'

'Plymouth, sir,' I replied, 'Naval hospital, Stonehouse.'

Stifling another yawn, the officer answered, 'Jolly fine hospital, had my appendix out there last year.'

'Ahem!' interrupted the MAA, then turning to the QM, said. 'Take the Doc down to his mess and no stopping for sippers.' (Sippers and gulpers of rum were given for favours.)

'Just as if...' grinned the QM who nodded at me and said, 'follow me, Doc,' and then with a painful grimace added, 'me name's Jimmy Parker, Nosey to you. Maybe you could do summat for me piles.'

The first thing I heard as I followed Nosey through a hatchway into the citadel was a constant throb of generators. To this was added the musty smell of oil paint and polish. Clusters of pipes and wires ran under the deck head like railway lines; neon lighting spread an even yellow light below on a deck covered in shiny brown linoleum.

Along a wide passageway we passed several ratings making a token gesture at polishing brass work. Others simply leaned on their brushes talking and laughing. One of them, a tall, lean sailor with fair hair, looked at me, and in a broad Geordie voice exclaimed, 'Ha, another flamin' bloodsucker! I hope yer better at usin' those needles than the others, Bonnie Lad.'

I grinned at him then carried on behind Nosey.

'That's the chippy's workshop,' said Nosey, indicating a large room in which a group of shipwrights were working, 'and the mail office is in front.' We stopped at the top of an open hatchway. 'You'll be in the S and S mess down here. Watch yer step it's two sets down.' (The S and S stands for the Supply and Secretariat branch, i.e. cooks, stewards, stores assistants and medics.)

Just then came the sharp click of the tannoy. 'Ammunitioning complete. Secure. Hands to tea,' sounded an impersonal voice. 'Duty watch muster on the fo'c'sle. Leave to the first part of starboard and second of port till 2330. Mail will close onboard at 2200. The ship is under sailing orders.'

'Sailing orders,' I gasped,' does that mean we're going to sea?'

'That's right, Doc,' replied Nosey, 'at 0600 tomorrow. Now watch yer head as yer go down these ladders.'

To my surprise I found the mess much bigger than I imagined. Shafts of light from four open portholes on the starboard side exaggerated the shine on the metal lockers lining three sides. Ventilation trunking fitted with punkah-louvres (small compartments adjustable for the flow of air) ran around the underside of the deck head.

Over a dozen lashed up hammocks swayed eerily from steel crossbars. A few with bedding hanging over the edges were occupied. A couple of spare hammocks lay in a small caged off area.

Adjacent to where we were was another mess. Clipped to the front of each locker on coat hangers hung the unmistakable dark blue uniforms of the Royal Marines, complete with gleaming brass buttons and gold epaulets. Lined up on a table I saw the smart white pith helmets worn only on ceremonial occasions. Several royal marines sat around polishing their boots while others carefully blancoed webbing.

One of them, a short, stocky lad with close-cropped dark hair took out a shiny silver trombone from its case, placed the mouthpiece to his lips and produced a resounding blast that startled his fellow mess-mates.

The marines plus those from my mess stopped what they were doing and looked at him.

'Give over, Jock,' cried one of them, 'I've still got a head like Birkenhead from last night's run ashore.'

'Shove it up yer arse,' cried Nosey.

'If he did that,' laughed one of the marines, 'he'd still be able to play it.'

Jock stopped playing his instrument. His humorous blue eyes wrinkled as his fleshy features broke into a wide grin. 'Och dinna be like that,' he replied, 'have ta make sure instrument's in tune fer the lassies when they wave us off.'

'I know what I'd like to wave at them,' said another marine grabbing his crutch.

'I wouldn't bother, if I were you, Sticks,' cried a marine flexing his little finger, 'I've seen you in the shower.' (Sticks is the nickname for drummers).

To me it was odd seeing Royal Marines serving in a warship.

'What are they doing onboard, Nosey?' I asked raising my eyebrows.

'That's the bootneck's (royal marines) mess,' replied Nosey. 'They man the ship's six-inchers, and AA guns,' answered Nosey. He paused, then rolling up his eyes added, 'Not to mention the soddin' bugler who wakes us up every morning.'

'How many of them are there?'

'About a couple of dozen,' answered Nosey. 'When they're not playin', the musicians work in the after-transmitting room.'

In the mess I was joining several ratings in shirtsleeves sitting at a long, well-scrubbed wooden table. Two were playing cards, some were writing letters, others sat reading newspapers while another clad only in underpants and flip flops stood by an ironing board pressing a pair of uniform trousers. All were smoking, adding to a blue haze that swirled lazily around the pale neon lighting.

Everyone looked up as Nosey and I entered.

'New Doc, just joining,' said Nosey to a thickset lad with fair hair who was sitting at the end of the table. Licking his lips, Nosey added, 'I don't suppose you've got one in the bottle Scribes?'

Scribes (nickname for a Writer) stood up, his six feet plus framed towering over Nosey, 'Piss off, you horrible little rum rat,' he said, 'you still owe me sippers from last week.' Scribes then turned to me, 'Dutchy Holland, killick of the mess, welcome onboard, Doc.' As we shook hands his dark blue eyes wrinkled into a smile. 'Pay no attention to Nosey, he's the ship's drunk.'

'Bollocks,' replied Nosey indignantly, then looking at me, added, 'just because he's a leading writer and looks after our pay, he think's he's a tin God.'

'You can still piss off,' said Dutchy.

'Miserable sod,' muttered Nosey, before drawing back the curtains and leaving.

'This ugly bugger here is one of your lot,' said Dutchy. He introduced me to a sturdily built lad with a pockmarked face and dark hair and humorous grey eyes.

'Peter Robertson,' I said, shaking hands with him.

'Hello, there, Scouse O'Malley's me name,' he said as we shook hands. His accent was straight from Scotland Road. 'I 'ope youse has yer sea legs 'cos were sailin' tomorrow.'

'So I've been told,' I replied.

'Where are youse from?' he asked cocking his head to one side.

'Wallasey,' I replied.

'Not another bloody Scouser in the mess,' cried one of the lads at the table.

'Don't be daft,' replied Scouse O'Malley, 'they're not proper Scousers in Wallasey. They're all posh like, with indoor lavs.'

'Well, we'd best call him Pete,' said another rating, 'one nutter from Liverpool in the mess is enough.'

Nodding towards a corner locker, Dutchy said, 'That's a spare. Unpack your kit and Scouse'll show you where the sick bay is. You can help yourself to a hammock.'

'Here,' said Scouse, handing me a small medicine bottle half full of brown liquid. 'Take a shot of Nelson's blood, it'll warm the cockles of yer heart.'

My first drink of navy rum slowly burnt its way into my stomach before spreading a warm feeling throughout my body.

'My God!' I exclaimed. 'D' you mean to say we get that everyday?'

'Not really,' replied Scouse. 'That were a drop of neaters given to me by the Jack Dusty (Stores Assistant). Good tack aint it?'

'You bet,' I gasped.

Ten minutes later, feeling a warm glow inside me, I followed Scouse up the ladders.

'This is the starboard passageway,' said Scouse, 'the port passageway runs is on the opposite side to where we are.'

We passed a large main galley and bakery manned by an army of cooks engaged in a myriad of tasks. Some, their faces flecked with flour, stood at long wooden tables pounding large lumps of sticky brown dough. Several were engaged slicing masses of vegetables while others were bent over huge metal vats steadily stirring its contents.

From an anti-room came the grinding sound as peeled potatoes spewed out from the spout of a round tub into baskets being held by men in wet overalls.

'Chips again!' yelled Scouse over the noise.

'Fuck off,' came a curt answer from a sweaty-faced cook with a black beard.

'We 'ave wot is called broadside messing onboard,' said Scouse as he passed the galley. 'The duty mess cook collects the scran each mealtime in large trays. He brings it to the mess, dishes it out and afterwards returns the trays to the galley.'

As we continued along the passageway blasts of warm air fanned our faces from two open hatchways. 'That's A and B boiler and engine rooms,' said Scouse. 'There's four of each in four separate cross-connected watertight compartments. At the moment they'll be flashin' up ready to go to sea.'

Just as we came to a closed door marked 'Senior Rates' a voice over the tannoy blasted out, 'Liberty men fall in portside of the well deck.'

The sick bay was situated on the starboard side of the passageway. Next to it was a door with a sign that read Surgeon Lieutenant (D) Watts. RNVR. Suddenly the nerve-jangling sound of a drill echoed from inside.

'No need to tell you what that is,' remarked Scouse, pulling a face.

Next was the PMO's office. 'The Principal Medical Officer is Surgeon Lieutenant Commander Davenport,' said Scouse, 'and next door is Surgeon Lieutenant Alford's surgery.'

'What are they like?' I asked tentatively.

'Bloody good doctors, matey, I can tell yer,' came Scouse's firm reply.

We stopped outside another door marked 'Sick Bay Regulating Office'. Without knocking, Scouse opened the door and we went inside. The office was quite small with a solitary open porthole. The deck was covered with the ubiquitous brown linoleum, and in one corner, next to a folding steel sink, was a green metal filing cabinet. Papers and forms attached to clip boards hung on a bulkhead next to a large coloured map of the world. On another bulkhead was a wall chart with colour-coded cards poking from tiny slots.

A heavy built man in his shirt-sleeves stood behind a desk littered with papers. He was medium height, slightly round-shouldered with a bald patch surrounded by greying dark hair. A jacket with red crosses on each lapel, a row of medal ribbons and three brass buttons on either sleeve hung on a chair behind his desk. As we entered, he turned and stared at me.

'Who the hell are you?' he rasped in a thick North Country accent. When he spoke his rheumy brown eyes narrowed exaggerating the wrinkles in his walnut features.

'SBA Robertson, chief,' I replied, 'just joined today.'

The chief sat down, took out a Packet of Senior Service, lit one and lent back in his chair. 'And about time too, m'lad,' he said allowing a cloud of tobacco smoke to escape from his mouth. 'You do know we sail tomorrow?'

'Yes, chief,' I replied. 'I heard the pipe.'

'Good,' answered the chief, his cigarette moving up and down as he spoke, 'my name's Chief Sampson. Besides you and O'Malley here, there are two other SBAs, Miller and Ellias, plus Petty Officer Shone.' He paused and removed the cigarette and after flicking ash into a small brass tray, continued, 'According to the signal I received you are to be rated up leading hand so put in a request and you'll see the PMO. You'll be in red watch. O'Malley here will show you the ropes. Any questions?'

'Er... any idea where we're going, chief?' I asked tentatively.

'No bloody idea, son,' he replied. 'But judging by the amount of stores we've taken on in the last two weeks, we'll be gone for some time. Now bugger off, I've got work to do.'

'What's eating him, Scouse?' I asked once we were outside.

'Nowt really,' replied Scouse. 'He was in the last lot and is pissed off because he was recalled. Can't say I blame 'im, really.'

The sick bay was next to the chief's office. On the door was a sign painted red and white stating the times of treatment. As I entered the familiar stringent smell of antiseptic assailed my nostrils. I was immediately met by a very tall, broad-shouldered petty officer with light brown wavy hair and a pallid complexion.

'Welcome,' said the petty officer as we shook hands, 'Derek Shone.' He paused and his pale blue eyes wrinkled into a smile. 'But for some reason these miserable sods call me Lofty. Hope you've packed your tropical gear 'cos the buzz is we're going to the med.'

With a half-hearted laugh, I replied, 'At least it'll be warm.'

The place where I was to spend most of my time looked like a miniature hospital. The bulkheads and deck heads were painted pale green. Tubes of neon lighting shed an even sheen on the corticene deck. On the starboard side were three open portholes and opposite side, through a glass panel, was a small sluice. Next to this was a door marked 'heads' and attached to the bulkhead were four shiny metal lockers used for the patients' belongings. In one corner rested a leather examination couch, a dressing trolley in what I assumed to be the treatment area. However, what really caught my eye was a section, close to the dispensary, cordoned off by a green curtain.

'That's the OT,' said Lofty Shone. 'Have a look inside. There's nowt going on at the moment.'

The first thing I saw when I drew back the curtain was an operating table. Secured to the deck head directly above, was a set of electric lights attached to a circular metal frame. A Boyle's anaesthetic trolley complete with dials, rubber masks and tubes lay close by. Not too far away were two tall, oxygen cylinders identifiable by black and white markings and a portable X-ray unit. In the corner were a stainless steel sink and steriliser. Next to this was a glass cabinet with shelves full of surgical instruments.

'Blimey!' I exclaimed looking around. 'Has the MO ever done any operations?'

With a note of caution, Lofty replied, 'Not yet, but there's plenty of time, believe you me.'

Two SBA's were busy changing the bedding on one of the two sets of metal-framed cots in the far side of the sick bay. Both wore OT gowns. One was small and stocky with dark hair, the other, fair and slightly built.

The smaller of the two gave me a quick grin. 'I hope you're "G" boyo,' he said in a deep-throated Welsh accent.

'What does that mean?' I asked the Welshman.

Taff's dark brown eyes lit up. '"A" stands for Grog,' he

replied, 'and...'

The tall SBA quickly interrupted him. 'Pay no attention to him,' he said in a thick Lancashire dialect. 'It all began,' he went on with a wide grin, 'in 1655 when we captured Jamaica from the French. The Jamaicans were so glad to get rid of the Frogs they granted rum to the navy.' The SBA paused and started to laugh. 'Needless to say Jolly Jack tars became continually pissed and couldn't work. So in 1740 Admiral Vernon ordered rum to be watered down. The sailors were so disgusted they nicknamed the admiral, "Old Grog", so now you know. By the way, me name's Dusty Miller and this poison dwarf,' nodding towards the Welshman, 'is Taff Ellias.'

'Dusty's right,' added Scouse, 'it's stamped in yer paybooks. If yer don't drink yer calssified as "T" and get three pence a day extra. Those under eighteen are known as "UA".'

'All I can say is that bugger Vernon has a lot to answer for,' moaned Taff.

Dusty slowly shook his head. 'If he had his way everyone would spend the war pissed as arseholes.'

'Now that you lot have got that settled,' said PO Shone, looking at me, 'you'd better come and meet the boss.'

CHAPTER FIFTEEN

Surgeon Lieutenant Commander Edward Davenport sat behind a highly polished desk reading a document. Dark hair, greying at each temple, exaggerated his finely chiselled features. He was well-built and the two and a half gold rings interlaced with scarlet indicated his profession and rank. (Officers in all but the Executive branch had different colours between their gold rings. The electrical branch had green, supply, white and dental, maroon.) The tip of a white handkerchief poked over his breast pocket and his uniform looked as if it had been tailored in Saville Row. As I closed the door my hands brushed against an overcoat hanging from a hook along with a steel helmet and gas mask.

For a few moments PO Shone and myself stood in silence. With a nervous glance I quickly looked around.

The bulkheads were the same colour as the sick bay and the only hint of luxury was a small plain green carpet on which we stood. A tray containing a stethoscope and various medical instruments rested on one side of the desk. Behind this, screwed to the bulkhead, was a framed photograph of the king and queen and a glass cabinet lined with medical books. In one corner below a mirror a folding washbasin fitted snugly into the bulkhead. On the opposite side shafts of sunlight shining through an open porthole exaggerated the sheen on a brown leather examination couch.

'What's the problem, PO?' said the doctor looking up. A frown crossed his face, and as he spoke his sharp brown eyes stared directly at us. 'I'm rather busy at the moment.'

Lofty quickly introduced me.

The PMO slowly sat back in his chair and smiled. 'Ah yes, Robertson,' he said displaying a row of even white teeth. 'We've been expecting you.' He paused, reached into his pocket, took out a packet of Senior Service, lit one and after exhaling a steady stream of tobacco smoke, went on, 'Make sure you read my standing orders. Any problems come and see me.' He then leant forward picked up a document and without looking up said, 'Thank you. Carry on PO.'

'He seems OK,' I remarked when we were outside the PMO surgery.

'Damn fine surgeon,' replied Lofty, 'amputated someone's leg on his last ship.'

'What's the other doc like?' I asked as we entered the sick bay.

'Surgeon Lieutenant Alford?' answered Lofty, pursing his lips. 'He's R.N.V.R. Hostilities Only, but he's all right. He's ashore with his party. You'll meet him in the morning.'

For the next few hours Scouse volunteered to show me around the ship.

'Forget the engine room, bridge an' all that,' said Scouse, sniffing the air. 'This 'ere,' nodding towards a door marked 'Provision Room', 'is the most important place in the ship.'

We paused outside a large steel door marked 'Victualling Store'.

'This is where the rum ration is prepared for each mess,' said Scouse. 'We take it in turns to collect the rum,' adding with a cheeky wink, 'keeps everyone 'appy like.'

Further along, from the open shutters of the NAFFI shop a small, grey-haired man was busy serving a long queue of sailors.

'Found a new friend, Scouse?' he said with a grin.

'Bugger off and count yer fags,' replied Scouse with a grin. 'That's Pongo Waring the canteen manager,' said Scouse as we continued along the passageway. 'He's in the first aid party so you'll be seeing lots of 'im.'

We passed a group of sailors lazily polishing brass work.

'Don't bend down in the shower bonnie lad,' yelled one of them, 'these Scouser's will fuck anything.'

'Yer right, there, Geordie,' replied Scouse with a laugh, 'that's wot yer missus told me last night.'

Pausing outside a door marked 'Instruction Office' Scouse informed me this was instructor lieutenant's room. 'During action stations,' said Scouse, 'it's used as an emergency medical station.'

Scouse stopped outside an open door marked 'Master-at-Arms'. I immediately recognised the portly chief petty officer sitting at a desk drinking from a large yellow mug. His barrel chest threatened to bust the buttons of his jacket and a pair of wire-framed spectacles decorated his leathery features. What little dark, greying hair he had was parted neatly in the centre. With a tired expression he put down his mug and looked at us.

'What d' you two want?' he grunted.

'Nowt, Master,' replied Scouse. 'Just showin' the new doc around.'

'We've already met when he came onboard,' the Master surly replied. 'Now piss off I'm busy.'

We left and continued along the passageway. 'The Master's name is Pusser Hill,' said Scouse. 'And if I were you, I'd keep out of his way.'

Finally we arrived at a massive barbette (the circular steel section that forms part of a gun turret.) In the surrounding area lashed up hammocks secured to steel bars swung lazily. Attached to the side of the bulkhead were a series of square metal lockers. Several sailors in various stares of undress sat at a table smoking, playing cards or talking. Our presence provoked a few more ribald comments.

'If it's more blood donors yer after,' shouted a stout sailor with an untidy mop of ginger hair, 'yer can bugger off. After givin' the last lot I was too weak to shag me missus.'

A couple of sailors looked at each other and burst out laughing

'I'm no surprised,' said one of them in a sharp Scottish accent. 'I've seen yer missus and I wouldna touch her wi a coalminer's prick.'

'Bloody rabble,' snorted the stout sailor and lit a cigarette.

We were about to turn away when suddenly from behind a hammock I heard a harsh, familiar voice. 'Well, well, look who's here,' came a cry, 'if it isn't the arse bandit from Plymouth.'

I looked across the mess and saw the swarthy features of Yorky. Except for a pair of white underpants he was naked. His chest was matted with black curly hairs and his tattooed arms looked like tree trunks. A faint smile flickered over his face. 'You and me 'ave unfinished business, don't we?'

'What's up, Yorky?' said a sailor, sitting close by. 'Does he owe you a fiver or summat?'

'More than that,' replied Yorky, staring at me with those dark eyes I remembered so well. 'And I'll collect, mark my words.'

Staring back at him, I replied, 'How's your nose? If you want it putting out of shape again, you know where I am. Now bugger off.'

Scouse tugged my arm and led me away. 'What the 'ell was all that about, Pete?' he asked as we came to an open hatchway.

'We had a slight difference of opinion in Guzz,' I replied. (Guzz is a nickname for Plymouth. It was a wartime signal given by warships entering the port.)

212

'That Yorky's a nasty bugger, so I'd watch out if I were you,' said Scouse, then added, 'that was the seamen's mess. It's used as the for'd first aid station. The stokers and some of the senior ratings messes are below that one. And those ladders you see there,' he added, pointing to an open hatchway, 'leads to A and B gun's magazine rooms. They're the same as Y gun aft.'

Our next port of call gave me the surprise of my life. After clambering up a set of metal ladders we entered a large hangar.

'My God!' I exclaimed, 'What's a hangar and an aeroplane doing onboard a ship?'

In front of me, secured by wires and cables, lay one of the most ungainly looking aircraft I have ever seen. With wings folded snugly into the fuselage it looked like a brooding pigeon. A huge round radial engine was housed over an enclosed cockpit and at each side of the tail arose a high fin. Mechanics in dirty blue overalls busied themselves under the fuselage. One sailor, his face smeared with oil, looked across and gave us a wave.

'Fancy a trip around the harbour, Doc,' he yelled. 'Cost yer a week's tot.'

'You Wafus give me the shits,' replied Scouse. 'You know what you can with yer soddin' Shagbats.'(Wafu is an acronym for Wet And Fucking Useless and is a the nickname for a member of the Fleet Air Arm. They in turn call sailors Fish-heads.)

'That's our one and only Supermarine Walrus,' replied Scouse, 'it's used mainly for reconnaissance, but they can carry a few bombs and depth charges as well. We used to have another one in the hangar next to this one, but it was transferred to another ship. It's launched from the catapult outside and retrieved by the crane.' After leaving the hangar Scouse nodded towards another set of ladders. 'Up there leads to the bridge and the heavy gun director control tower. Incidentally, the captain allows us to use his bathroom for medical emergencies.'

'That's decent of him,' I replied. 'What's he like?'

'Captain Andrews is a four-ringed skipper,' replied Scouse. 'He's all right I guess but we don't see much of him, only on divisions.'

'And the Jimmy?'

Suddenly, Scouse stopped and grabbed me by the sleeve. 'Bloody hell, Pete,' he gasped, 'here he comes.'

Walking towards us was a tall thick-set lieutenant commander and an equally tall chief petty officer. The chief and the officer were engrossed in a conversation. The officer said something causing the chief's hawk-like weather beaten features to break into a wry smile.

'Afternoon sir,' said Scouse as we came near.

The officer nodded but didn't reply. However, the chief stared at me with a pair of dark, sharp eyes. 'Who are you, lad?' he snapped in a voice suggesting he gargled with gravel.

'SBA Robertson, just joining the ship, chief,' I replied.

'Hmm... I see,' muttered the chief, then with a sly grin added, 'don't let this Scouser lead you astray.'

The officer didn't speak. Instead he gave a weak smile and looked me up and down. Then he and the chief continued along the passageway.

'That was the Jimmy, Lieutenant Commander Newham,' said Scouse. 'And the other one was the Knocker White, the Chief GI.'

We retraced our steps and continued aft along the port passageway passing the ship's laundry, mail office and night heads. Finally we stopped outside the wardroom situated in the after deckhouse.

'The wardroom is also used as an Emergency Medical Station,' said Scouse, with a short laugh he continued, 'we won't bother goin' in there.'

Slightly out of breath I followed Scouse up two sets of ladders into a large compartment. A dull red light outlined eleven royal marines in half-blues sitting in front of sets of illuminated dials. Five wore earphones while the others appeared to be checking instruments. Bending over them was a young sub lieutenant. Standing next to him was a tall, fair-skinned royal marine corporal.

'This is the Transmitting Room, and above is the HACP (High Angle Central Position),' whispered Scouse. 'It's from there and the Director that the after guns are controlled.'

'You said earlier this place was manned by Bandsmen,' I replied, 'why them?'

Scouse shrugged his shoulders. 'I dunno,' he answered, 'maybe it's because they're used to twiddling knobs on their instruments.'

Just then the corporal bayoneted us with a pair of sharp, brown eyes. 'What the 'ell are you two doin' here?' he rasped, 'on a Cook's tour or summat?'

'Keep yer 'air on Harry,' replied Scouse, 'just showin' the new doc around.'

'Harry Tate,' said the corporal as we shook hands. Then turning to Scouse, added, 'This'll cost both of you sippers.' The corporal grinned and looked at the officer. 'Don't worry, sir,' he said jokingly, 'you can come around for a wet as well.'

The officer laughed and turned away.

From a platform outside the Director, the tall after mainmast looked like a black phalanx against the blueness of the sky. Then, looking towards the quarterdeck, the barrels of the 40mm pom-poms and those of the triple gun barrels of Y gun glinted menacingly in the late afternoon sun.

By this time my legs were aching and my shirt was sticking to my back like a second skin.

'Come on, Doc,' said Scouse, wiping his brow with the back of his hand. 'I don't know about you but I'm knackered. The officers' cabins are further aft, but I'm sure yer don't wanna see them just yet. And as fer the boiler and engine rooms, the chief stoker and his lads won't welcome us as they'll be too busy flashing up steam.'

The mess was more crowded and noisier than earlier. Off duty cooks sat around in whites talking and smoking. A few ratings with towels wrapped around their waists clutching toilet gear passed us on the way to the heads. In the adjacent mess I noticed several royal marines busy polishing their boots while another, using an electric iron attached to a cable, busily pressed a pair of service trousers.

'Keen lot aren't they, Scouse,' I said looking across at them. 'I thought they'd finish doing that earlier on.'

'Typical Boot necks,' answered Scouse, shaking his head. 'If one of them was marooned on a desert island and only had a glass of water, he'd use it to blancoe his webbing. They're a good lot though.'

Just then a small, slightly built lad with an anaemic face wearing spectacles greeted us. His jacket was undone and he was smoking a cigarette.

'I heard you were onboard,' he said, removing the cigarette. 'I'm Cyril White, the dental SBA.'

As we shook hands Taff Ellias arrived.

'Thought you two 'ad got lost, boyo,' he said to me. As he spoke his large brown eyes wrinkled into a grin. 'And me with a small tincture to welcome you with.' He opened his locker and brought out a green-fluted medicine bottle.

At that moment a fit-looking marine with his dark hair gleaming and smelling of Brylcreem appeared. 'Ah!' he exclaimed, raising his eyes in mock surprise. 'Just in time I see.'

'Watch yourself, Peter,' said Taff, 'this ugly bugger,' nodding towards the marine, 'is Bagsy Baker.'

Three other marines appeared. The first one, a small dark, thick set lad with freckles whose name was Harry (Wacker) Payne came close, and like a bloodhound, closed his eyes and sniffed Taff's bottle. 'Nectar, I tell you,' he cried, licking his lips, 'sheer nectar.'

'Bugger off Wacker,' cried Taff, 'You still owe me sippers from last time.'

The second marine was built like a rugby scrum half. He had pale blue eyes and an untidy mass of ginger hair. With a handshake that left my fingers feeling numb, he introduced himself as Bud Abbot, 'I hope yer better with a needle than the other bloodsuckers,' he said in a rich Lancashire accent, 'me arms still sore from the last lot they gave me.'

By this time quite a crowd had gathered around us.

The last of the three was a tall, gangly lad with short brown hair and a thin face. He shook my hand. 'Joe Ward,' he said with a smile, 'nice to meet you Pete.' He then lent forward, narrowed his blue eyes and stared Taff full in the face. 'Play you uckers for a week's tot, Taffy, me old mate?'

With a look of sheer defiance, Taffy straightened up. 'Yer on Sharky m'laddo,' he cried, slapping the marine on the back. (Anyone named Ward, was nicknamed 'Sharky'.) 'And even though yer brother's an SBA with 45 Commando, it won't do yer any good.'

Someone produced the uckers board and everyone including the marines gathered around while Sharky and Taff sat down and took it in turns rolling the dice. When Sharky rolled a six, the marines cheered. When Taff got lucky myself and the others did the same. There was very little in it. At the end both needed to roll a six to get home. Sharky stood up and with the air of a Las Vegas gambler, slowly placed the dice in the small Bakelite cup, rattled it close to his right ear, then with a flick of his wrist threw the dice onto the board.

'Six, I win,' he cried, jumping to his feet.

The marines cheered as if they had won first prize in a lottery. 'Pass it round,' shouted one of them, 'then we can all have a wet.'

Sharky took a quick swig and passed the bottle to me. 'Never let it be said a royal marine was selfish. After all our Jim is one of yours.'

As I lifted the bottle to my mouth everyone gave a loud cheer.

'See it off, Doc,' yelled someone – and I did.

That evening I found myself standing next to Sharky in the NAAFI queue.

'How come your brother's with the marines?' I asked him.

'He volunteered,' answered Sharky. 'He told me an AFO (Admiralty Fleet Order) was circulated asking for medics to join Special Forces so he put in a request. Judging by his last letter he's playing silly buggers somewhere in Scotland.'

'Better him than me,' I replied.

That night lying cocooned in my hammock I began to think about Adele. With all the excitement of joining the ship I hadn't given her a thought. I closed my eyes, caressed her medallion hanging loosely around my neck and prayed she was safe. Then, with the soporific throbbing of the generators invading my senses I finally fell asleep wondering what the following days would bring.

CHAPTER SIXTEEN

'*Close all water tight doors and scuttles. Hands to stations for leaving harbour.*' The metallic click and impersonal voice of the tannoy system echoed around the sick bay.

The time was shortly after eight-thirty on Tuesday 26 June. Two hours earlier the sudden blast of the bugle followed by the shrill sound of the bosun's pipe had woken me up. This was followed by the grating voice of the QM bellowing, ''Eave ho, 'eave ho, cooks to the galley. Lash up and stow (a term referring to securing the hammocks).'

After breakfast Scouse and I reported for duty. On the far side of the sick bay Dusty was screwing down the butterfly nuts on the scuttles while Taff stood in the treatment room bandaging a rating's hand. The chief was in his office and through a glass partition I saw Lofty Shone standing in the dispensary carefully pouring dark liquid from a large bottle into a smaller one.

'Do we have to fall in, Scouse?' I asked.

'No,' he replied. His pockmarked features breaking into a wide grin. 'It's far too chilly up top for us delicate medics. Besides, there's a line of lead swingers waiting outside the MO's office.'

At that moment the door opened and in came a tired looking surgeon lieutenant. He was well over six feet tall, big boned with well-groomed fair hair. Dark rings surrounded his slightly bloodshot, brown eyes.

Stifling a yawn, he asked, 'How many this morning, O'Malley?'

'Quite a few, sir,' answered Scouse. Then nodding towards me, continued, 'This is SBA Robertson, sir. He joined yesterday.'

'Good,' replied the doctor staring wearily at me. 'We could do with all the help we can get. Let's get cracking, then.' There was no smile or handshake and I immediately sensed something was wrong.

When the doctor left the sick bay, I turned to Scouse, 'He seems jumpy,' I said, 'is anything wrong with him?'

'Doc Alford's all right,' replied Scouse. 'It's that judy of his. I think she's a nympho.'

'All right for some,' I answered with a grin.

'Yeah, I suppose so,' replied Scouse, then nodding towards the door, added, 'c'mon, we'd best get weavin'. I'll show you the routine when anyone reports sick. I've already got the documents out for those waiting to see the MO.'

Half an hour later I felt the deck vibrate as the ship got under way. Even though the scuttles were closed from the quarterdeck I could hear the vibrant strains of the Royal Marine band playing *Rule Britannia.*

'Do they always play us out?' I asked Scouse.

'Come hail, rain or shine,' replied Scouse, 'and the odd Jerry bomb.'

For the next hour I stood in the doctor's surgery as ratings reported with every conceivable ailment ranging from piles to headaches that seemed to occur just as work parties fell in.

When the last patient had left, Doctor Alford sat back in his chair, and with a bored expression, sighed, 'Not much to enrich medical science there, eh, O'Malley?'

'No, sir,' replied Scouse, picking up a stack of treatment cards. 'But let's not tempt fate.'

The doctor placed his fountain pen in his top pocket, stood up, yawned again, and then, rubbing both eyes, said, 'If you want me, I'll be on the upper deck catching a breath of fresh air.'

As he spoke I felt the deck shudder violently as the ship increased speed. 'Maybe not,' said the doctor, 'Perhaps I'll have a lie down instead.' He then put on his cap and left.

As soon as the ship had cleared the harbour Lofty gave me permission to go on the upper deck.

His youthful features broke into a wide grin. 'It'll help you get your sea legs,' he added, 'but if you spew your ring up, make sure the wind's behind you.'

I found a spot on the portside of the hangar and lent on the guardrail. High above cumulous-nimbus clouds rising like miniature explosions raced across a pale blue sky. Away to port the thin white line of the Hampshire coastline was quickly fading away. I glanced aft and saw the frothy bow waves of two destroyers bounding through the calm, greeny-blue sea.

For a few seconds I closed my eyes, allowing the fresh wind to attack my face, flap against my trousers and play havoc with my hair. I inhaled deeply while watching the yardarms of the after mast sway drunkenly from side to side. The vibrations of the engines sent small shivers running through my shoes as with each slight pitch and roll the ship cruised down the English Channel.

Strangely enough, the motion of the ship didn't have any affect on me. I cupped my hand around a cigarette, struck a match and carefully lit it. With their overalls rolled up to their knees sailors washed down the decks. Ratings busied themselves checking the three sets 4-inch guns situated along the portside. Under the keen eyes of a petty officer whalers were secured while other sailors ensured the awning covering the captain's barge was firmly in position.

I was just about to take a deep drag of my cigarette when I heard the ubiquitous click of the tannoy.

'First Lieutenant speaking,' came a crisp well-modulated voice. 'I'm sure you'll all be anxious to know where we're going. In company with the destroyers *Exmoor* and *Eskimo* we are to proceed to Algiers. Here we will embark Admiral Cunningham and his staff for transit to Malta. Our destination after we leave Malta will be told to you when we are at sea.' The officer paused, cleared his throat and went on. 'Reports have been received informing us that U-boats have been withdrawn from the Atlantic and are now operating in the Mediterranean. Lookouts will be doubled and action stations will be exercised without warning. That is all.'

My God, I thought, action stations-U-boats. Suddenly, as I stepped inside the hatchway, I felt a cold shiver run down my spine.

In the treatment area of the sick bay Taff was syringing the ear of Nosey Parker, the able seaman I met when I joined the ship.

'Careful wot yer doin' with that thing,' muttered Nosey glaring at Taff who was holding a large bulbous syringe. 'All I wanted was a pill fer me 'eadache.'

'Keep still, boyo,' said Taff, 'and hold that dish under your ear.'

Taff inserted the nozzle into Nosey's ear, pushed the plunger and squirted water. Almost immediately a plug of foul smelling wax oozed out into the kidney dish.

'There, 'said Taff, with a grimace, 'now you'll be able to hear the bugler sound action stations.'

'That reminds me, Taff,' I said. 'I looked through the PMO's Standing Orders last night but couldn't find my action station.'

'You'll be up for'd with a couple of stewards and Duchy Holland,' replied Taff, 'but don't worry, the *Ganda* is a lucky ship. Dusty and me'll help you out if need be.'

'That's where I am, too,' said Nosey removing a wet towel from his shoulder. 'Me and the lads from for'd mess are in A gun magazine.'

A voice over the tannoy suddenly piped, '*Up Spirits. Cooks to the galley.*'

'Ah,' gasped Nosey, 'me favourite time o' the day,' and he grabbed his cap and hurried away.

The mess was crowded. Those ratings off duty were lined up in front of a table on which rested a large aluminium pot (called a rum fanny). Each man was smoking, and the sound of laughter and loud conversation reverberated around the room. As I entered the room the unmistakable aromatic smell of rum attacked my taste buds making me salivate with anticipation.

The duty rum bosun was a small, stout cook with a round, pale fleshy face. As each rating approached he dipped a Bakelite cup into the fanny, drew it up and poured its contents into a glass tumbler. He then handed it to whoever was next in line.

'See it off in one,' said the cook, laughing. 'If yer leaves any I'll have it.'

'No chance,' replied the recipient, a tall ginger-headed steward. 'Here's to a vicious run ashore down The Gut when we get to Malta,' and promptly downed the amber liquid in one go. (Strait Street in Malta, otherwise known as The Gut, was notorious for its bar and prostitutes.)

'I'll drink to that,' cried Scouse, then pensively stroking his chin, added, 'I wonder if Slack Alice is still working in the Jippo (Egyptian) Queen.'

During this cherished ritual, sippers or gulpers were given, usually for favours rendered. As newcomer all of the lads gave me sippers and by the time I sat down to dinner my head was spinning.

Early next morning I was suddenly woken up the ear splitting strains of a bugle call. This was quickly followed by, '*Hands to action stations. Close all screen doors and scuttles. Red Alert! Red Alert!*' booming over the tannoy.

Like Jack-in-the-Boxes, ratings leapt out of their hammocks, grabbed tin hats and what clothing they could and hurried out of the mess. The clatter of boots vibrated from the deck above as ratings hurried to their stations.

'Come on, Pete,' yelled Scouse, who slept next to me, 'chop chop and don't forget your anti-flash gear and yer first aid bag.' (Anti-flash clothing consisted of a pair of long-handed gloves and a hood made of thick cotton impregnated with asbestos. It was extremely irritable but was effective at preventing burns.)

'What's Red Alert?' I asked Scouse, reaching for my clothes.

'Air attack,' he replied, 'We're pretty close to the French coast where the Jerries 'ave air bases, so it might be one of those Focke-Wulf Condors.'

'They're the spotter planes, aren't they Scouse?' asked little Cyril White.

'That they are, boyo,' said Taff, 'and it'll mean a big raid later, mark my words.'

'Fuckin' Krauts,' I heard Dusty yell as he dashed out of the mess, 'maybe it's a bloody false alarm.'

But it wasn't.

Just then the deafening sound of gunfire rent the air. The deck quivered slightly. The red nightlights flickered followed by a flurry of dust cascading from the deck head. I suddenly felt the blood drain from my face. I had often heard the noise of ack-ack fire during the Blitz but this time the closeness and immediacy of the noise was personal. For a fleeting moment I imagined the bulkheads caving in consigning me to a watery grave. The faces of my parents and that of Adele flashed through my mind. By the time I arrived at the for'd mess deck I was trembling and my legs felt weak.

Dutch Holland, the two stewards Tomo Thomas and Nutty Slack were already closed up at action station. The expression on my face must have told its own story.

'Don't worry, Pete,' said Dutch forcing a grin, 'that was the 4-inch AA guns. The big boys are used mainly for bombardment. When they open up the whole ship shakes.'

'Any idea what's up?' I asked, adjusting my anti-flash hood around my face.

Nutty Slack, a skinny, pale-faced lad was about to speak when he was interrupted by another retort of gunfire. Everyone instinctively cowered down and covered their ears with both hands.

Just then the ship heeled to port. The mess deck, bulkheads and everything leant imperceptibly to the left. Everyone including myself grabbed hold of the mess table. Lockers rattled, tin mugs bounced across the deck and unmade hammocks swayed as if pushed by an unseen hand.

'My God,' I cried hysterically, 'surely we're not capsizing…'

'Calm down, Pete,' said Dutch, 'the ship's zig-zagging.'

'That means the buggers are bombing us,' cried Tomo, a small, overweight steward suffering from a bad case of acne. 'And we've only left Pompey two days ago.'

The ship suddenly changed course, turning abruptly to starboard altering the angle of everything. Once again we held on grimly.

'Never mind, Tomo,' said Dutch, 'we'll be in Gib the day after tomorrow. Maybe we'll get a run ashore. What d' yer think?'

'No chance,' answered Tomo, 'the buzz in the wardroom is that we're not even stopping to re-fuel.'

Tomo had no sooner spoken then the ship righted its self and slowed down. This was quickly followed by the bugler blaring 'Stand Down'. The First Lieutenant then announced himself over the tannoy. 'Ourselves, *Eskimo* and *Exmoor* have successfully beaten off an attack by enemy aircraft,' he said in his usual strident manner. 'Well done the gunnery department. I think you frightened the life out of them.'

'Thank fuck for that,' sighed Dutch, passing his cigarettes around. 'Now we can all get some scran.'

Just before Stand Easy Taff and I were cleaning up the treatment area after morning surgery. Dusty was polishing the deck with an electric bumper, Scouse was in the dispensary and Lofty and Chief Sampson were by the OT talking to one another.

Suddenly the door opened and without knocking two officers came into the sick bay. The smaller of the two was the First Lieutenant. The four gold rings on the sleeves of the taller one immediately told me he was the captain. Both kept their caps on. The captain's weather-beaten features were well defined and his grey-haired sideboards suggested he was in his late thirties. His sharp, but tired-looking brown eyes quickly looked around then concentrated on Chief Sampson.

'The First Lieutenant and I are just having a walk around,' said the captain. His manner was crisp and he spoke in a sharp, but well-modulated voice. 'Everything all right?'

'Yes, sir,' replied the chief. 'No problems.'

By this time everyone had stopped what they were doing. Dusty switched off the bumper, Lofty turned and looked towards the door, Taff was fumbling with a kidney dish and I froze. Meanwhile Scouse was in the small dispensary adjacent to the main area. Looking through the glass partition I saw him quickly sit down pretending to be examining something under a microscope.

'Good,' replied the captain. 'Please carry on chief.'

The First Lieutenant covered his mouth with a hand and gave a cough, then said, 'I noticed the for'd first aid post wasn't reported as closed up when we went to action stations. Make sure it doesn't happen again, chief.'

'It won't, sir,' replied the chief shooting a withering glance at me.

With a quick nod of his head, the captain followed by the First Lieutenant turned and left the sick bay.

On the night of 30 June *Uganda* and her escorts sailed through the Straits of Gibraltar into Mussolini's *Mare Nostrum.* The sky was a cloudless umbrella of dazzling blue, the sea calm and the sun seemed hotter than usual. Daily Orders (bulletins promulgated around the ship every day) ordered a change into tropical whites and for the first time since I was a boy I wore shorts.

During the next two days our small armada suffered several air attacks by enemy bombers. Although closed up at action stations we heard and felt the shockwaves as near misses exploded nearby. On each such occasion I wished I were back in the sanctuary of Barrow Gurney.

We arrived at Algiers early on the morning of 3 July. At 0900 Admiral Cunningham and his staff were piped onboard and the ship quickly put to sea.

'You can bet your bottom dollar summat big's in the wind,' remarked Dutch Holland at tot time. 'The C in C isn't going to Malta for a joy ride.'

'It's almost as if the Jerries and Eyeties knew old ABC (Admiral Bruce Cunningham) was onboard,' cried Dusty.

'I wonder why they're going to Malta,' I said accepting my tot from Scouse who was duty rum bosun. 'No bugger tells us anything.'

CHAPTER SEVENTEEN

To the strains of the royal marine band playing *Hearts of Oak* and *All The Nice Girls Love a Sailor,* HMS *Uganda* arrived in Malta on the morning of 5 July 1943. Before entering Grand Harbour our two escorts had left to go to Silema Creek, a large anchorage on the other side of the island.

Along with the off-duty members of the mess I was fallen in on the port waist. The sky was cloudless and the sea, covered in a steamy heat haze, shone like glass.

As the ship nosed its way past the breakwater Valetta with its rising mass of terracotta houses, church spires and huge walls opened up before me.

'Bloody hell!' I exclaimed, nudging Scouse who was standing next to me. 'Look at all those ships in Grand Harbour. There must be the whole of the Mediterranean fleet anchored there.'

As far as I could see there were aircraft carriers, battleships, cruisers and even several civilian liners camouflaged green and grey.

'I'll be buggered,' I gasped pointing to one of the liners. 'That's the *Rena del Pacifico,* I've often seen her in Liverpool. I wonder what she's doing here?'

'She isn't on a cruise, I'll bet,' replied Scouse, 'not with all those troops onboard anyway.'

The guardrails and decks of the liner were crowded with soldiers, some of whom gave us a cheerful wave.

'We're gonna invade some place,' said Cyril White next to Scouse, 'stands to reason don't it?'

'That wouldn't surprise me, in the least, boyo,' added Taff who was next to Cyril. 'But I wonder where…'

'Keep silent there,' came the officious voice of Bud Abbot, the Chief GI, 'and stand still.'

Uganda continued her way into the port. Almost within touching distance, a massive, medieval-looking fortress jutted out into the harbour. Its stout, crenulated walls swept majestically downwards onto a bed of rocks. A small forest of gun barrels could be seen poking over the battlements and from a square tower a white ensign flew on top of a tall, flagpole.

'That's Fort St Angelo,' said Scouse, 'the C in C used to have his headquarters there, but it's been moved to Lascaris over in Valetta.'

'How do you know all this?' I asked him.

'I was here a year ago on the *Urchin*,' replied Scouse. 'Stick with me and I'll show yer the sights.'

Just then came the shrill sound of the bosun's call. '*Attention on the upper deck,*' came the pipe, '*face the port.*'

Under the eagle eye of the chief GI, everyone immediately snapped to attention. This was a ritual salute to other ships and was accompanied by the dipping of the ensign from the jack on the quarterdeck.

The evidence of Malta's defiance of Hitler's Luftwaffe was everywhere. Wharfs and dry docks still bore the scars of countless air raids. When we were ordered to stand easy Scouse nudged me again.

'That string of bombed buildings you see on your left,' he said, 'are called the three cities, Vittoriosa, Seneglea and Cospicua. Being so close to the dockyard they caught the worst of the air raids.'

'According to the newspapers at home Malta was supposed to be the most bombed place on earth,' chimed in Cyril.

'Maybe that's why the king awarded them the George Cross last May,' added Dutch, 'if Malta had fallen Rommel would have been able to supply his army in Egypt.'

Uganda tied up outboard of the HMS *Newfoundland,* who in turn lay outboard of the cruisers *Mauritius* and *Orion.*

'Bloody hell,' I said to Scouse, staring across at *Newfoundland.* 'She looks identical to us.'

'She ought to,' replied Scouse, 'she's our sister ship.'

Shielding my eyes from the sun I saw an armada of small gaily coloured gondoliers. Like the pictures of those I'd seen in Venice each was propelled through the water by a man standing at the back, manipulating a single oar.

'What are those, Scouse?' I asked.

'They're called dghajas (pronounced "dicoes"),' replied Scouse. 'They'll take you ashore or bring you back. But remember to haggle or else the sods will rob yer.'

Dressed in Number 4s (white open-necked shirts and blue trousers and caps) Taff and myself and a few dozen other liberty men fell in on the starboard waist. The Officer of the Day was a tall lieutenant with startling blue eyes and hawk-like features. Next to him stood the barrel-chested figure of Pusser Hill, the Master-at-Arms.

With a telescope firmly tucked under his left armpit, the lieutenant slowly walked down the ranks inspecting each of us.

'What's that hanging around your neck?' he snapped, stopping in front of me.

'It's a medallion, sir, given to me by, err... my mother,' I lied, not wanting to feel embarrassed.

The lieutenant pursed his lips, 'Your mother, eh,' he mused, raising and then carrying on down the line.

'Who's that?' I asked Taff as we climbed down into the liberty boat.

'Lieutenant Reed,' replied Taff. 'He's the DCO (Damage Control Officer). Keen as mustard he is. Always doing exercises and thinking up different ways of shoring up holes in the ship. Drives Percy Bradley, the chief chippy (shipwright) crazy.'

I later learned the chief shipwright was responsible for providing timber for such emergencies.

Along with many motor vessels carrying men from other ships we arrived ashore at a landing called Custom House Steps.

'Famous place this is,' said Scouse as we clambered onto the cobblestone jetty. 'Nelson's lads used to come ashore here.' At that moment one of his shoes squelched into a small pile of foul smelling dog faeces.

'Looks like they left summat behind, boyo,' laughed Taff.

The town centre was awash with servicemen. French sailors with red bobbins on their blue caps, mingled with Americans wearing their familiar crumpled pork pie hats. There was even a splattering of the RAF's Brylcreem boys clad in tropical pale blue. Groups of bleary-eyed Highlanders in colourful swaying kilts swapped banter with Royal Marines; but the bulk of the bustling crowd wore the round and peaked caps of the Royal Navy.

After passing the ruins that was once the island's Opera House, we pushed our way into a stretch of wide road called Kingsway. We then turned left and continued along until we came to a crowded narrow street packed with humanity. The street stretched downhill and was lined on each side by a variety and of bars, above which gallery balconies jutted out from high walls. Open wooden shutters provided ventilation for the room inside. Carpets were draped over iron verandas, and washing lines, festooned with clothing hung limply in the warm evening air. Old women dressed in traditional black rocked gently on chairs, arms folded over ample bosoms, soberly viewing a scene they had witnessed countless times.

'This,' announced Scouse, motioning with his hand, 'is the famous Gut.'

'Aye,' added Taff, 'so keep yer hand on yer wallet and the other on yer balls.'

The Gut sloped downwards, disappearing into a mass of dimly lit bars. Each bar we passed looked the same: whitewashed walls, dingy lighting with heavily rouged women in a tight-fitting dresses lounging outside.

'Ah, the dear old place,' cried Scouse looking around, 'hasn't changed a bit. I suggest we have big eats at Ben Marls. Ben makes the best spaghetti on the island.'

Ben Marl turned out to be a fat, swarthy man with a round fleshy unshaven face, large bulbous blue eyes and a grin as wide as the Mersey Tunnel. He wore an off-white apron splattered with brown gravy stains and carried a red and white polka-dotted towel over one arm.

'Come in boys,' he cried, displaying a row of uneven yellow teeth. 'I give you good price.' Gesticulating wildly he showed us to a table. I couldn't help but laugh. Even though the restaurant was almost full he greeted us like long lost relatives.

After the bland naval food onboard, the spaghetti bolognese, washed down with a couple of bottles of Marslala wine, tasted wonderful.

'OK, you lot,' said Scouse, wiping his mouth with the back of his hand, 'it's time I introduced you lot to Slack Alice.' He paused and finished off the remains of his wine and with a grin, added, 'That's if she's still working at the Jippo Queen.'

We passed such colloquial named places as the Blue Peter, Harry's Bar, the Texas Bar and finally arrived at the Egyptian Queen situated halfway down the street.

As I pushed through the western-style swing doors I was met with a blast of warm air, raucous laughter, music and the smell of cheap perfume.

The place was full. A blue hue of tobacco smoke hung under a low ceiling and music blared out from gramophone records behind the bar. Several lads from the *Uganda* sat at a table along with two peroxide blondes and a dark-skinned girl with ruby red lips and long black hair. Among them I recognised the rubicund face of Nosey Parker.

'Hope you've got plenty of that new Penicillin stuff, Doc,' cried Nosey. He leant across the table and gave a stoker a playful push. 'This randy bugger's already had his five bob's worth from Sweaty Betty.'

'Less of the Sweaty Betty rubbish,' replied one of the peroxide blondes indignantly. 'My fuckin' name is Elizabeth, named after one of your queens. And he,' she added glaring at the stoker, 'only gave me two shillings, bloody English cheapskate.'

Scouse pushed his way to the bar and returned with three bottles of Blue Label. He had just handed them to Taff and me when a tall, coffee-coloured woman wearing a short red dress came and stood behind Scouse. With a defiant expression on her face she drew back her arm and hit him across the head with her red handbag.

'Liverpool Scouse bastard!' she screamed. 'Lousy crook. You still owe me ten shillings for all nighters I gave you when you on *Urchin.*'

Scouse's hand shot to his head. 'What the hell?' he yelled and quickly turned around.

'Alice, me darlin',' he cried, rubbing the back of his head. 'I was wondering where you were.'

'Don't you darlin' me,' she yelled. As she did so, her dark, bloodshot eyes narrowed. 'Give me my money or I'll fill you in.'

'But, Alice,' replied Scouse, backing away, 'that was last year.'

'I know,' replied Alice, 'what ship you on now?'

'Careful, Alice,' replied Scouse wagging a finger. 'Careless talk costs lives.'

'Fuckin' rubbish,' she answered, 'everyone on island knows there's gonna be an invasion somewhere, maybe Sicily,

233

maybe Italy or even Sardinia, who fuckin' knows. We know all the names of all the ships. Now buy me a fuckin' drink.'

'Still port and lemon?' he asked, winking at Taff and me. He then turned and pushed his way to the bar.

'So you're Alice?' I asked, trying to be sociable.

With a lecherous glint in her eyes she slowly looked me up and down.

'That's me,' she replied, displaying a row of uneven yellow teeth. 'And I love big fair-skinned sailors like you.' She came so close I could smell the sickly aroma of her sweat. As she stared at me she reached down and gently squeezed my testicles and penis. 'Mmm…' she muttered, 'you are a big boy. For you I give special price.'

Taff gave a laugh, 'Indeed to goodness, lovely lady,' he said, staring down her cleavage, 'he's spoken for but I'm not.'

Alice removed her hands from my crutch then gave Taff a sly look, 'Dirty Welsh sheep shagger,' she replied, 'for you I charge full price.'

I was about to laugh when out of the corner of my eye I saw the burly figure of Yorky. He was on the far side of the room laughing and joking with a group of American and British sailors. When he looked across and saw me the expression on his face immediately changed from one of joviality to anger. With a smirk on his swarthy features he pushed his way through a crowd of soldiers and stood in front of me.

'What the hell do want, Yorky?' I asked, just as Scouse arrived with Alice's drink.

'You,' retorted Yorky, breathing beer fumes into my face. As he did so he saw Adele's medallion hanging around my neck. Using one hand he flicked it outside my shirt. 'Just as I thought,' he burbled, 'all queers wear jewellery.'

I felt anger rise from deep within me. 'If you touch that again,' I snarled, clenching my fists,' I'll fuckin' kill you.'

'Come on Pete,' said Scouse, taking hold of my arm. 'We don't want bother. The naval patrol's all over the place.'

'He's right,' added Taff, 'besides. I haven't finished me beer.'

I hardly heard them. Instead Yorky and I continued to glare at one another. At that moment Alice stepped in between us.

'No fightin' in here,' she said, glancing at Yorky then at me. 'It's bad for business.'

'Piss off, you slut,' cried Yorky and pushed Alice away.

'Who are you callin' a slut?' she cried falling backwards onto the floor.

At that precise moment a small, stocky American sailor bumped into Yorky and spilt beer down Yorky's white front. Yorky's anger was suddenly transferred to the American. 'You stupid Yank bastard,' yelled Yorky, stepping back. 'Why don't you bugger off back to the states?'

'Say, feller,' drawled another American sailor standing behind his stocky counterpart, 'you can't talk to my buddy like that,' and shoved Yorky so hard he stumbled back knocking Sweaty Betty's glass out of her hand.

'Yorky bastard,' she cried as Scouse helped her to her feet.

Suddenly pandemonium broke loose. Yorky threw a punch at the big American and missed. One of Yorky's pals hit the stocky American full in the face. Blood splattered everywhere. Another American appeared from nowhere and grabbed me around the neck, my cap flew off and we tumbled to the floor. As we did so, I caught a glimpse of Yorky grappling wildly with the big American. Meanwhile Taff and Scouse were swapping punches with two more American sailors. They also had lost their caps. The music stopped. Tables crashed over. Beer, from broken glasses, stained the sawdust on the floor. Girls screamed as servicemen of every description joined in the melee. I managed to land a telling blow on my adversary's jaw and watched him roll over. I staggered to my feet and witnessed a scene that would have done justice to a barroom brawl in a western film.

Then, from somewhere, I heard the shrill blast of a whistle.

'Come on, Pete,' yelled Scouse, who was standing next to Taff. Both their trousers were covered in dust and Taff's shirt was torn. 'That sounds like the patrol, we'd better piss off outta here, sharpish.'

Taff grabbed my arm and avoiding those still fighting, the three of us pushed our way to the swing doors. The last thing I saw were Sweaty Betty, Slack Alice and some other girls cowering behind upturned tables, screaming like wild banshees. Finally, panting like racehorses, we ran in to the warm night air and up the street.

'The fight's in the Jippo bar, mate,' yelled Scouse to a group of RN and American patrolmen as they hurried passed us. 'Throw the lot in cells if I were you.'

'Shut up you crazy sod,' cried Taff. 'Our best bet is to get back onboard. Don't forget we sail tomorrow.'

Sometime later, along with other members of the ship's company, we wearily climbed from the liberty boat onto *Uganda's* upper deck.

'Where's your caps,' snapped Pusser Hill, 'you're improperly dressed, so you are.'

With a contrite expression on his face, Scouse replied, 'Some tarts stole them. Master.'

'That's right, Master,' added Taff, 'they snatched them and ran away.'

'Get below and report to me in the morning with new caps,' replied the Master-at-Arms. 'And pipe down.'

However, my cap wasn't the only thing I lost. When I got undressed I discovered Adele's chain and medallion was missing.

CHAPTER EIGHTEEN

Despite a frantic search around the area of my hammock and the upper deck the medallion was nowhere to be found.

'Never mind, Pete,' said Scouse, who along with Taff and the others had helped in the search, 'maybe yer judy will send yer another one.'

I hadn't told any of them about Adele – only that the medallion was a present from a girl back home.

'Yeah, I suppose so,' was my disconsolate reply as I climbed into my hammock.

That night I couldn't sleep. The sickening emptiness I felt inside was compounded by the unfamiliar nakedness around my neck. Four years had passed since that balmy evening in Normandy when she gave me the medallion. Four years of war, worry, suffering and death. I hadn't heard any news of Adele for ages; for all I knew she might be dead or dying. The thought sent a sudden shiver down my spine. I closed my eyes; suddenly, her words hoping the medallion would protect me echoed around my mind. Now it was gone, and soon we would be sailing to face the enemy.

Next morning the news of my promotion failed to lift my inner gloom. Dusty and I were in the treatment area. He was bandaging a sailor with a sprained ankle and I was sterilising surgical instruments. Suddenly Chief Sampson appeared.

'You're being rated up,' he said with a grin. 'Put in your request this morning. It'll be routinely granted, then see the Jack Dusty and he'll issue you with your hooks.'

'Just think, Peter me boy,' said Dusty, shaking my hand. 'This time tomorrow you'll be a leader of men.'

However, my thoughts were elsewhere. I gave him a sickly grin and carried on working.

A little after 0900, '*Special Sea Duty men fall in. Hands to sea stations Close all Screen Doors and Scuttles,*' was piped. An hour later the First Lieutenant's voice came over the tannoy. Everyone in the sick bay stopped what they were doing and listened.

'As Daily Orders informed you, we are sailing in company with the cruisers *Newfoundland, Orion and Mauritius.* We will shortly be joined by the destroyers *Eskimo, Nubian, Tartar, Loforey, Loyal* and *Lookout.*'

'Bloody hell!' exclaimed Dusty. 'That's some escort. I wonder where we're ...'

'Pipe down, will you,' interrupted the chief, 'and maybe you'll find out.'

The First Lieutenant continued, 'We will be under the command of Rear Admiral Harcourt and be known as Force K. Now the news you've all been waiting for.'

I glanced around. Everyone was silent. Tension filled the air. Even the chief, who, as a junior, had seen action in the First World War at Jutland wore an anxious expression on his gnarled features.

The First Lieutenant went on. 'Together with our American Allies we are going to invade Sicily under the code name Operation Husky.'

Gasps of surprise suddenly went around the sick bay.

'Bugger me,' cried Scouse, 'Slack Alice was right after all.'

After giving a nervous cough, the First Lieutenant continued speaking. 'We will be part of the Eastern Task Force under the command of Admiral Sir Bertram Ramsey. Our job will be to give close support to the troops landing in the area around Syracuse near the western tip of Sicily. The Americans, commanded by Vice-Admiral Hewitt, will land on the Eastern side of the island. D-Day will be in two days' time on 9 July. This will be the first step in wrestling Europe from the grip of the Nazis. We are therefore making history. I will keep you informed. That is all.'

The throaty voice of the PMO, who without anyone noticing had joined us, was the first to break the silence.

'Check all first aid posts and stretchers, chief,' he said. 'And make sure all officers are issued with morphine.' His sudden intervention startled everyone.

'Yes, sir,' replied the chief turning around. After a quick, serious glance the PMO turned and left the sick bay.

The chief looked at us and frowned. 'Right, you lot,' he said taking a deep breath, 'pay attention. From now on it'll be red alert and action stations around the clock. Believe you me, I know. So be on your toes.'

Shortly after hands secured from sea stations Stand Easy was piped Scouse suggested we went up onto the boat deck for a smoke. When we arrived the scene that met my eyes was one I'll never forget. The sea was calm with a few white clouds dotted against a cerulean sky. Forming a protective barrier a forest of silver barrage balloons suspended from the ship's cables glittered in the morning sun. As well as those in our squadron there were battleships, cruisers, minesweepers and the unmistakable flat-topped aircraft carriers. Sleek destroyers, guarding against U-boat attack, cut through the sea sending up huge foamy bow waves.

'Jesus Christ!' I exclaimed handing Scouse a cigarette, 'look at them. They're all in perfect line ahead with battleships leading the way. I've never seen so many ships in my life. There's even a few hospital ships.' (It would take over 3,000 sea-going craft of all kinds to ferry the invasion force to Sicily.)

'You're right, there, lad,' replied Scouse. Cupping his hand against the warm breeze he lit our cigarettes. 'The brass must be expecting a lot of casualties. The biggest hospital ship is called the *Talamba.*'

Much to my dismay the bulky figure of Yorky came out of the hatchway and leant on the guardrail next to me. He wore blue overalls and a cigarette dangled from the corner of his mouth. A large bruise almost closed his left eye and his nose looked swollen and slightly out of shape.

'You look as if you should be in sick bay?' I grunted glancing at him. 'Don't tell me you want to carry on from last night?'

'Funny bugger,' he replied sarcastically. He paused and lit a cigarette. 'I heard you lost summat last night,' he added, exhaling a stream of tobacco smoke that was immediately whipped away in the breeze. 'I overheard the Lieutenant Reed tell the Jossman (nickname for a MAA), that your old girl gave it to you.'

'So what?' I replied, without looking at him.

He then dug a hand into a side pocket. In his oil-stained palm, curled up in a small shiny bundle, lay Adele's medallion and chain. 'I think this is yours. I was gonna keep it but...' he paused, his voice hardly audible over the stiff breeze, 'y'see, my mum was killed in the Blitz and...' His voice trailed away as he handed the medallion to me.

For a few seconds I could hardly believe my eyes. 'My God!' I exclaimed, 'where... how did you find it?'

He gave a quick shrug of his shoulders. 'I didn't,' he replied, 'you can thank Slack Alice. After the crushers (naval patrol) left, she found it on the floor and gave it to me.'

The relief I felt as I looked at the medallion was indescribable.

'I don't know what to say, Yorky,' I stuttered. 'I... I can't thank you enough.'

I held the medallion up, turning the delicate chain between my fingers. With a lump as big as a football in my throat I watched how the sun made it shine like silver. At that moment I was sure Adele and I would meet again.

'Thanks again, Yorky,' I said shaking his hand. 'You'd better come around at tot time. That's the least I can do for you.'

'By the way, Yorky,' said Scouse, 'what happened in the Jippo Bar after we did a bunk?'

Yorky shrugged dismissively. 'Nowt much,' he replied. 'There were too many of us to be arrested so the patrol buggered off.' He paused briefly and grinned. 'But the Yanks ended up in Bighi.' (The Royal Naval Hospital in Malta.)

The next morning I came out onto the upper deck and was met by a gust of cold wind that nearly blew my cap off. Grey cumuli-nimbus clouds hung in the sky like angry explosions and what had previously been a placid, calm sea was now an angry mass of white-topped waves. I tightened my grip on the guardrail as *Uganda* pitched and rolled. Glancing aft I saw the mast and yardarm swaying drunkenly, and above the howl of the wind the rigging rattled like the bones of a skeleton. I watched as the other ships plunged in and out of the sea sending mountains of spray in the air and wondered if the landings would be postponed.

As if reading my thoughts a voice behind me said, 'I doubt if they'll be able to land in this weather.' I turned and saw the tall, gangly figure of Sharky Ward. He was capless and wore a dark brown duffel coat over his half blues.

'Maybe it'll calm down by tomorrow,' I replied, trying to light a cigarette.

At first Sharky didn't speak. Instead he lent against the guardrail and peered out to sea. Then, in a sombre voice barely audible over the howling wind, muttered, 'I hope our kid's safe. I wonder if he'll be landing with the commandos tomorrow?' Without waiting for me to reply, he turned and with a worried frown etched on his face went inboard.

However, the landings weren't postponed.

At 0245 on 10 July the crew went to action stations. The First Lieutenant announced Force K would be bombarding enemy shore batteries north of Syracuse. In a somewhat subdued manner he went on to say, 'Those whose action station is on the AA and Oerlikons will have seen many gliders carrying airborne troops ditch in the sea. Apparently they were released too early from their tow-ropes. The airborne landings have therefore failed. That is all.'

Shortly after this I thought my head would burst as *Uganda*'s heavy armament opened up.

'I told you the AA stuff was nowt compared with this, didn't I?' I heard Dutch yell, who, like Tomo, Wacker and myself were huddled under the mess table hands clutching our ears. With each ear-splitting salvo the whole ship shook. At one point the noise was so deafening I thought my head would sink into my body. Finally, the firing stopped. When I removed my hands my ears were ringing and I could hardly hear myself think.

The chief suddenly arrived looking tired and drawn. 'The hospital ship *Talamba* has been sunk,' he said grimly. 'Several of the survivors have been picked up by *Newfoundland* and *Mauritius*, but most of *Talamba*'s patients have been lost. Two of you lot go and get some tea and scran then relieve the others.'

The worst part of being closed up was not knowing what was happening outside. On several occasions the ship heeled over as shockwaves from bursting bombs bounced against the ship. The thunderous recoil of the gun barrels plus explosions from nearby bombs exploding added to the deafening cacophony. With each detonation I felt the bulkhead might suddenly implode crushing me to death. Even during the Blitz waiting and praying for the All Clear, I hadn't been so scared.

'Don't worry,' said the chief on one of his frequent visits. 'After a while you get used to it.'

But I didn't. This fear and claustrophobia remained with me during the next three weeks by which time my nerves were so bad I could hardly hold a cup.

'Hey, Pete, watch you don't spill that,' said Scouse at one of our rare tot issues. 'Anyone would think you had DTs (delirium tremors) or summat.'

I gave a cynical smile and drank my tea.

Throughout July the crew were constantly closed up at action stations. On numerous occasions *Uganda* was forced to take evasive action from the bombs of the Luftwaffe. Force K continued to assist the Eighth Army and the Canadians as they advanced inland. At the end of July *Uganda* was able to use the ports of Syracuse and Augusta.

'I don't suppose there's a chance of a run ashore, is there chief?' asked Scouse.

We were in the sick bay. As hostilities were still in progress everyone was at Defence Stations.

'Pigs might fly,' replied the chief. 'Anyway, you'd only catch the boat up.' (A colloquial expression for contracting venereal disease.)

An hour later the pipe, '*Mail is ready for collection,*' obliterated any thoughts of steamy nights ashore.

'About soddin' time too,' added Cyril, 'the last time we had mail was before we left Malta four weeks ago.'

Five letters, all from mum, awaited me in the mess. One by one I ripped them open hoping they might contain news of Adele. However, reading her last letter stunned me – CS, my old school pal had been killed. 'His Spitfire was shot down over the English Channel,' she wrote, 'I read it in the *Wallasey News* and have enclosed a clipping.'

The excited comments from others reading their letters faded away as I slumped down onto the wooden bench by the mess table. 'CS dead,' I muttered to myself. I could hardly believe it. The clipping contained a small photograph of him with the stupid owlish grin I remembered so well. As I read details of his death I felt my throat contract.

'What's up, Peter?' asked Dusty, 'Not bad news I hope?'

I didn't reply. Instead I placed the clipping in my wallet next to Adele's photograph and left the mess.

Force K remained in Malta for two weeks. During this time we played soccer, Housey-Housey, went ashore and got drunk. We even held a rowing regatta in Grand Harbour and cheered as the royal marine bandsmen came second to *Newfoundland.* Later in the mess we rewarded Sharky, Bud Abbot, Harry Tate and the others with a well-earned drop of rum.

With a slight grimace, Sharky gingerly touched his backside, 'Got anything for blisters on the arse, Peter?' he asked.

'Don't bend down behind him.' said Harry Tate, giving me a playful push. 'You never know with these medics.'

'Watch it, 'arry,' replied Sharky, 'remember our kid's an SBA with the commandos.'

On 16 August it was announced Sicily was finally in Allied hands although we learnt later that much equipment and many German troops escaped across Straights of Messina to Italy.

Force K sailed on 1 September to take part in the invasion of Italy. Shortly after sailing the First Lieutenant informed the crew that Italy had surrendered and her fleet would sail to Malta and be interned.

'Bloody hell, what kind of war is this!' exclaimed Scouse. 'Those Eyetie bastards'll be fuckin' Slack Alice and Sweaty Betty while we're being bombed to buggery by the Jerries.'

'Think yourself lucky,' said Lofty, 'I've just stained five slides from the lads in the stoker's mess. They've all caught a dose from the partys in the Jippo Queen.'

'Great,' replied Scouse. 'I hope they all get Syph.'

Dusty and Taff looked at Scouse and laughed. 'What about you, Scouse?' asked Dusty. 'I hear you had all-nighters with Alice.'

'All lies,' retorted Scouse and stormed out the sick bay.

A week after we sailed he was seen creeping out of Doctor Alford's surgery with a bright red face.

Over the tannoy the First Lieutenant announced *Uganda* would, along with the rest of Force K, assist the landing of the U.S. Fifth Army at Salerno. 'The British Tenth Corps will land to the north and the American Six Corp will do so in the south. This major undertaking is called Operation Avalanche,' said the officer. '*Uganda* will lie off some distance and give artillery support to those ashore.' He paused for a few seconds before going on. 'I am informed that the Salerno bridgehead has been sealed off by the German Tenth Army commanded by General Von Vutingoff, so we can expect a warm welcome from the enemy batteries and the Lufwaffe. Everyone on station keep a sharp lookout.'

'Blimey Pete,' gasped Scouse, 'more action stations and bully beef sarnies. I wonder how long this lot will last.'

'I dunno,' I replied soberly, 'but if you ask me it doesn't sound too good.'

However, on 11 September disaster struck the ship. While closed up at action stations a tremendous detonation some distance on our port beam rocked the ship.

'What the hell was that!' exclaimed Dutch, staring at me wide-eyed.

'Search me,' I gasped, 'but whatever it was I'm glad it missed us.'

'Relax,' cried Scouse, 'I told yer the *Ganda's* a lucky ship.'

But *Uganda*'s luck was about to run out.

CHAPTER NINETEEN

On the morning of 13 September *Uganda* was lying about three miles off shore bombarding the Italian coast. The calm sea was a deep transparent blue and visibility was good. The coastline around Salerno Bay was cloaked in dense clouds of grey smoke as ships sent salvo after salvo raining down on them.

Dutch, Nutty Slack, Tomo and myself were closed up at action stations. As usual with every recoil the deck shook as A and B guns opened fire.

'I'll never get used to this,' yelled Nutty, who like the rest of us was cowering under a table holding both hands over his ears.

I knew exactly how he felt. Even though we had been bombarding the Italian mainland for days on end, each report made me flinch making me wish I was anywhere but banged up in a floating metal box that might one day be my coffin.

Around midday the bombardment ceased and the bugler sounded Defence Stations. This meant half of those closed up could take it in turns to go for food and drink, but had to remain closed up.

'Thank fuck for that,' cried Dutch, rubbing his hands together, 'I'm bloody starving.'

Tiny beads of sweat trickled down the side of Nutty's pale face. 'I expect we'll be on corn dog sarnies as usual,' he muttered, 'when this soddin' war's over I never want to see another cow again.'

'Bugger the scran,' said Tomo, running his hand through his untidy ginger hair, 'I'll settle for me tot.'

Dutch and myself left while Nutty and Tomo remained closed up. Scouse, Dusty and a few stewards from the other first aid parties were the only ones in the mess.

Taff, who was rum bosun, appeared carrying the fanny.

'Come and get it you rum rats,' he cried, placing the large aluminium container on the table. 'And be bloody quick about it.'

'Where are all the boot necks, Taff?' I asked, glancing across at the empty Royal Marines mess deck.

'The bandsmen are still be closed up in the Transmitting Room,' he replied, handing me my tot, 'the others are still on duty. The cooks will take their meals to them and they'll get their tot later.'

Dutch and I downed our rum, grabbed a handful of corn beef sandwiches and hurried back to relieve Nutty and the others. Just as I arrived Red Alert was sounded over the tannoy.

'Bastard,' cried Nutty, 'there goes me tot.'

For the next hour *Uganda* and the rest of the fleet beat off several air attacks. Shortly after 1430 there was a lull in the action.

'Great, come on Tomo,' cried Nutty, 'maybe we can get our tot. That's if any of those buggers have left...'

Nutty was suddenly cut short as the most deafening explosion I have ever heard rocked the ship. A shockwave shuddered through the ship like a miniature earthquake. The lights flickered then went out. The cables and fitting in the deck head rattled. A flurry of dust and debris filtered onto everything. I lost my balance and grabbed hold of Dutch as we both crashed on the deck. With startled cries Tomo and Nutty fell alongside us in a crumpled heap.

'We've been hit!' screamed Nutty. 'We've been fuckin' hit, I tell yer.'

'Stop yelling and get off my face,' I heard Tomo cry.

For a few seconds I lay still feeling the swaying motion of the ship. Then, almost imperceptibly the ship gently took on a slight list to starboard.

Feeling a surge of panic I cried, 'Christ All mighty, Dutch, we're sinking!'

'Take it easy, Pete,' replied Dutch reassuringly, 'it'll take more than a few shells to sink this ship.'

For a few seconds I lay bathed in sweat, my heart racing, thinking my last moment had arrived. Just then the voice of the First Lieutenant came over the tannoy.

'The ship has been hit by a bomb aft,' he said, 'damage control and first aid parties report at the double.'

'Come on Pete,' he said helping me to my feet. 'That means us.' Looking down at Nutty and Tomo he added, 'You two better stay here in case you're needed. And keep your life belts at the ready, just in case.'

'Thanks a lot,' replied Nutty. 'You two bugger off and leave Tomo and me to drown, eh?'

Dutch shook his head and ignored him.

Clutching my first aid valise and still shaken, I followed Dutch along the starboard passageway to the sick bay. On the way we were passed by several ratings hurrying towards the after section of the ship. Among them were Lieutenant Reed, Percy Bradley the chief shipwright, and his damage control party.

By the time we reached the sick bay the dull red emergency lighting was on. Chief Sampson, Lofty and Surgeon Lieutenant Alford met us.

'This way,' yelled Chief Sampson hurrying aft. 'That must have been some bloody bomb,' he added, 'the explosion has buggered the X-ray machine and the dental chair is bust.'

The after deckhouse was a mess of tangled metal. The First Lieutenant and the PMO were already there directing operations.

'How badly are we damaged?' Doctor Alford asked the PMO.

'As you can see,' said the PMO glancing around, 'a bomb has penetrated the Director. The Oerlikon guns crews are dead and the Transmitting Room is badly damaged and flooding. As far as we know the bomb has gone straight through seven decks including the engine room before penetrating the bottom starboard bulkhead and exploding some distance away from the ship.'

'My God,' replied the doctor, 'if it had gone off inside the ship we'd have been blown out of the water.'

Oddly enough nobody seemed to panic. The caustic smell of cordite permeated the dusty atmosphere. Meanwhile orders came thick and fast. Everyone, irrespective of rank, helped dazed men up from below into the arms of the first aid parties. Under the eagle eye of Bill Cousins, the Chief Engineer, sailors attached hoses to emergency engines and ran them below in an attempt to suck water from flooding compartments.

Meanwhile, Lieutenant Reed and his damage control parties could be heard below decks shoring up leaks in the cracked bulkhead.

'First aid party over here,' yelled the chief GI beckoning Dusty and myself.

Slumped on the deck outside the wardroom lay three sailors in blue overalls, their anti-flash gear a wrinkled mess around their necks. One of them was Yorky. Blood was pouring down the side of his oil-stained face and his eyes were closed. The other two were awake their faces ashen and eyes glazed with shock. One of them reached out and tried to speak.

'Easy mate,' said Dusty, 'where are you hurt?'

The sailor pointed to his chest and as he coughed his face became contorted in pain.

'Don't worry,' replied Dusty, 'just lie still and we'll have you fixed up in no time.'

I concentrated on Yorky. He had a large open gash on the left side of his head.

'How d' you feel mate?' I asked while applying a shell dressing to his wound. He didn't answer. Instead his head lolled to one side and blood began to trickle from each of his nostrils.

'Yorky!' I cried catching him as he fell to one side. Just then Chief Sampson appeared and knelt by my side. 'Leave him, son.' said the chief checking Yorky's pulse, 'no bugger can help him now. He's had it.'

'Dead! Dead!' I cried unable to comprehend what had happened. *'How can he be…?'*

Over the cacophony I heard the chief shout, 'Pull yourself together man. There's a lot of injured men and they all need our help.'

I tore my gaze away from Yorky and stood up. Men from the gunroom flat below with bloody faces were being helped up by Lofty and a first aid party. Surgeon Lieutenant Alford, Pongo Waring the canteen manager and Scouse were busy attending to several badly injured men lying in the passageway. Among them were Able Seamen Digger Barnes and Nosey Parker. Digger sat holding his left arm and Nosey's left leg lay at an acute angle. Both were conscious but the expressions on their pale faces showed they were in considerable pain.

'There's three men in Y gun turret,' I heard someone cry. 'They're alive but can't get out.'

Glancing up I heard the Chief GI yell, 'Someone get down there with the damage control party and see what you can do.'

Immediately a young sub lieutenant along with two royal marines scrambled down Y turret hatchway. We later learned the trapped sailors were fed soup through the voice pipes and after twenty-four hours were eventually rescued.

'There's men trapped below in the High Angle Central Position and it's flooding,' I heard an excited voice cry from an open hatchway leading below decks.

Lieutenant Reed and his team moved quickly. His white overalls, unbuttoned to the waist, were stained with oil, and lines of perspiration ran down the side of his sharp features. His eyes looked tired and bloodshot. Behind him stood Bill Cousins, the Chief Engineer.

'You'd better come with us, Doc,' said Bill glancing at me. 'We'll probably need you.'

I followed them down a set of steel ladders onto a small confined space. The large round hatchway leading into the HACP was open. I looked down and saw the faces of two men clawing their way upward. The chief and I knelt down and helped them out.

'There's more down there in the Transmitting Room,' spluttered one of the rescued men, 'but the water...' his voice tailed off as he vomited black liquid over my shoes.

'He's right, sir,' said Bill Cousins, his voice strained and nervous. 'And if the hatchway isn't closed the water could enter the after deckhouse.'

Lieutenant Reed glanced around with a frantic expression. 'But the men down there, they'll all...' He didn't finish. Instead he clenched both fists and shook his head and cried, 'I... I can't do it, Chief. I can't send those men to their death.'

'You've got to do it, sir,' yelled Bill, 'or else the after part of the ship will flood.'

'I... I can't,' gasped the officer, 'I can't...'

'Then I'll do it,' the chief bellowed and made to grab the hatchway lid.

'No, no, Chief,' shouted Lieutenant Reed, 'it's my responsibility,' and knocked the chief's hands away.

Suddenly the dank seawater bubbled up to the brim of the hatchway. With the expression in his eyes of a man about to face the gallows, the officer slammed the steel lid shut. With the help of the chief the screws around the hatchway were tightened.

After it was firmly secured the officer slumped back against the bulkhead, holding his head in both hands.

At that moment Captain Hale, Royal Marines, arrived. I had only met him once when the marines invited him to their mess for sippers. He was young, fresh-faced and relatively inexperienced. The sight of him made me suddenly remember that the Transmitting Station was the action station of the bandsmen.

The realisation that by now they were all dead hit me like a hammer blow. The faces of Sharky Ward, Bud Abbot and Corporal Harry Tate and others flashed before my eyes. My stomach churned over. I felt slightly nauseous and hardly heard the captain's panic-stricken voice ringing in my ears.

'My bandsmen,' he cried, 'they're all down there. Can't you do something?'

With tears in his tired eyes, Lieutenant Reed glanced up at him and slowly shook his head and muttered, 'May God have mercy on their souls and mine.'

Despite being distressed we later learned Lieutenant Reed and his damage control parties worked non-stop throughout the night shoring up (i.e. strengthening) bulkheads and plugging holes. We later learned the bomb that hit the ship was a radio-controlled PC. One thousand four hundred kilograms type Fritz-X missile. This new type of bomb carried 600 lbs of Amatol in its warhead. One also hit the USS *Savannah* damaging the American cruiser severely.

In all there were thirty-one casualties – three killed outright. Eleven, including three stokers in the engine room, were trapped below presumed dead, nine seriously wounded and eight minor injuries. The serious casualties were taken to the sick bay. Those with minor injuries were treated for shock and kept on camp beds in the schoolroom.

Throughout the day and during the night all the staff tended to them. The PMO gave Nosey an intravenous injection of

Sodium Pentothal and with the assistance of Surgeon Lieutenant Alford managed to set Nosey's fractured tibia. True to form when he regained consciousness the first thing he asked for was his tot.

At 0200 I was giving a sip of water to an able seaman who had been hit in the chest with a metal splinter, when the ship was once again rocked by a series of explosions.

'Christ Almighty,' muttered the seaman, wincing with pain, 'don't tell me the buggers have returned to finish us off.'

The seaman needn't have worried. Over the tannoy the First Lieutenant told us *Uganda* would be moving a few miles southward out of range of the enemy batteries. He added, 'However the ship can still make nine and a half knots. As a precautionary measure the USS tug *Narragansett* has passed us tow wires. Tomorrow (14 September) in company with *Exmoor, Erebus* and *Niad* we will proceed to Malta.'

Yorky and the three seamen killed were buried at sea. I was on duty in the sick bay and didn't attend the ceremony held on the quarterdeck. Meanwhile the bodies of the eight bandsmen and three sailors remained below.

Rum issues that day and for many days after were muted affairs. In particular everyone felt the loss of the bandsmen. Living in such close proximity, friendships were inevitable. Now all that was left to remind us were instrument cases stowed neatly in an alcove and a few blue uniforms hanging in front of lockers. No longer would we enjoy the usual jovial cross-mess banter. Instead in sombre mood we accepted our tot, downed it in one then quietly ate our dinner.

Uganda and her escorts arrived in Malta at 1720 on 15 September 1943.

In the sick bay the staff were busy preparing to transfer the seriously wounded ashore.

'Just think of all those nurses in sexy black stockings,' I said to Nosey as Scouse and I lifted him onto a stretcher.

Nosey grinned and tapped his plaster cast, 'How the 'ell can I get me leg over with this fuckin' thing in the way?' he moaned. 'It weighs a ton.'

All of the duty watch and a host of volunteers helped us to carry the men ashore into a small fleet of ambulances waiting on the wharf.

'Next stop, RNH Bighi (the naval hospital in Malta),' said one lad with a fractured pelvis as we carried him down the gangway.

'Not 'arf,' shouted someone behind, 'and maybe a ticket to Blighty t' boot.'

A week later the hatches of the after engine room were opened and the bodies of the stokers were removed. The duty watch and volunteers, helped by a generous tot of rum, did this grisly task. Oil fuel was pumped out from compartments below; holes and damage were plated over.

Meanwhile during a run ashore Dusty and Taff were evicted from the Vernon Club, Scouse was given a shiner from Slack Alice and I received six letters from mum. Sadly none contained news about Adele.

At 0930 on 28 September *Uganda,* along with several destroyers, escorted a convoy en route for England via Gibraltar where we would remain for three weeks. The day before we sailed, the HCAP was opened and volunteers were requested to go down and bring up the bodies of the bandsmen. Scouse, Taff, Dusty and myself stood by, as one by one, the bodies encased in Neil Robertson stretchers were hoisted up. Each one bloated almost beyond recognition was a sight that would remain in my mind forever.

We then carried each one to the spare hangar, undid the stretcher harnesses and covered them up with a sheet. It was then the painful task of Captain Hale to try to identify each one. Afterwards he was seen vomiting over the side.

As soon as the ship left harbour the bandsmen were prepared for burial at sea.

The grim task of stitching them in their hammocks and weighing the bodies with a heavy 6-inch shell was undertaken by the Chief GI and the Master-At-Arms. The ship's bell was wrung. The crew fell in on the quarterdeck and with heads bowed we listened to almost inaudible prayers of the ship's padre, the Reverend Paine. Each body, covered with a white ensign, lay on a stretcher held steady on the guardrail by four marines. Captain Hale, looking pale and drawn, stood to attention alongside most of the other officers. With bugler sounding the melancholy strains of the last post each one splashed into the sea. Suddenly I realised that somehow I had to get off the ship. The thought that I might have to go through this again made me feel physically sick.

That night I lay in my hammock wondering what excuse I could give for leaving the ship. Desertion, of course, was unthinkable. Complaining of nervous exhaustion or shell shock crossed my mind. Perhaps I could even plead insanity!

I couldn't help thinking about the bandsmen. Every time I closed my eyes I saw their faces. Suddenly I gave a start and opened my eyes. Of course, Sharky Ward! I inwardly gasped. I remembered him telling me his brother who was an SBA had volunteered to join the commandos. That was it. At least I'd be given a weapon and wouldn't be enclosed in a metal box waiting to be blown to kingdom come.

That night I hardly slept. Next morning, without telling anyone, I wrote out a request to be transferred to a commando unit and left it on the chief's desk. When he saw it he burst out laughing.

'You must be bloody crazy,' he cried, holding my request and staring up at me. 'They're always first to land on the beaches. You do remember Dieppe, don't you?'

'Yes, chief,' I replied, 'I do.'

With a sigh the chief slowly shook his head and with a paternal glint in his eyes, asked, 'Are you sure you know what you're doing, lad?'

I told him I did. 'Right,' he replied flatly. 'I'll put your request through the normal channels, but I expect the PMO will go up the wall.'

Needless to say everyone was just as surprised as the chief.

'Bootnecks don't get a rum issue,' said Dusty with a grin. 'So you won't get your tot, Peter, my son.'

'Our kid's a pongo,' added Scouse. 'And he says khaki itches like fuck.'

'Ah, but I hears they does their tranin' somewheres in Scotland,' said Taff, 'and them Scottish lassies take it up the back so they do.'

'How would you know that?' interrupted Derek.

''Cos I married one,' answered Taff.

Two weeks after arriving in Gibraltar the PMO sent for me and told me my request had been granted. 'Tomorrow,' he said leaning forward on his desk, 'you'll be flying from Gibraltar to Lee-on-Solent for an interview with a royal marine officer. I'll be sorry to see you go, but I'm sure you'll do well. The chief has all your flight documents.' He then stood up and as we shook hands he added, 'Good luck and God speed.'

The next morning after saying goodbye to Scouse and the others, I climbed into a tilly waiting on the wharf. As we drove out of the dockyard a lump as big as the Rock came into my throat. I looked back at *Uganda's* two tall grey funnels and offered a silent prayer for the future safety of the ship and all the lads I left behind.

CHAPTER TWENTY

This was the first time I had been near an aircraft let alone flown in one. For a few moments I stood and gazed at the dark green, cigar-shaped Dakota, the multi-purpose aircraft of the armed forces that was to fly me over a thousand miles to England.

'You look a bit pale, mate,' quipped an RAF private stowing my suitcase in an open compartment under the aircraft's belly. 'The vomit bags are inside.'

I shot him a weak smile and looked up at this long, snub-nosed aircraft camouflaged a dull green and grey.

'It's not the flyin' that bothers me,' I replied, feeling my throat seize up, 'it's the crashin' I don't go much on.'

As I climbed inside the sharp smell of aviation fuel, dust and aircraft 'dope' played around my nostrils. Inside was a long wooden bench either side of the plane. I nervously sat down and stowed my gas mask satchel between my legs. Two long leather straps with large silver buckles attached to the bulkhead dangled by my side. Next to each strap hung a brown paper bag. I looked up and saw a long cable with hooks attached stretching the length of the plane.

Among the passengers were several high ranking army and naval officers, a group of nurses and a scruffy-looking soldier handcuffed to two sturdy military policemen. An anonymous voice informed us we would miss Europe and fly out into the Atlantic before turning for England. 'Just to avoid meeting any would-be inquisitors, you understand.'

During the bumpy take-off I began to sweat and my heart bounded against my ribcage. My knuckles turned white as I gripped the edge of the bench and for a fleeting second wished I were back onboard *Uganda*. Gradually the plane levelled off, the tone of the engine seemed to change from a loud roar to a dull throb and that same impartial voice told us we could now unbuckle our straps.

An hour later, the same cheery RAF private I met earlier passed plates of corned beef sandwiches and flasks of tea around. Then, under the dull red lighting the soporific droning of the engines slowly lulled me to sleep. Some time later that same anonymous voice woke me up.

'Landing in half an hour,' it said, 'fasten your safety belts.'

The plane touched down at Lee-on-Solent at 1600 GMT. The date was 30 October 1943.

The nurses were allowed to leave first, followed by the senior officers, then myself. Last came the military policemen who bundled their prisoner into a lorry that quickly drove away. In stark contrast to the warmth of the Mediterranean, the sky was overcast and even though I wore an overcoat over my doeskin uniform the chilly north-easterly wind seemed to go right through me.

As I left the plane the ubiquitous RAF private appeared.

'Enjoy the trip, mate?' he asked, handing me my suitcase.

'No problem,' I replied with the air of an experienced flyer, 'and you know what you can do with your vomit bags.'

A tilly was waiting to take me to HMS *Bellerophon,* the Royal Naval Barrack at Portsmouth. When we arrived, the duty petty officer at the guardroom checked my name on a list.

'It ses here,' said the PO, 'that you are to report to the main admin office at 0900 tomorrow,' he paused, then added, 'and you won't be doin' a joinin' routine. Got it?' He then detailed off a sallow-faced, two badge matelot to show me where to go.

'Yes, PO,' I replied, picked up my suitcase and followed the matelot.

As we crossed the wide parade ground the matelot nodded towards a large red-bricked building. 'That's the admin block and the dining hall is next to it. Yer eatin' irons and bedding will be on yer bunk.'

Just before 0900 next day I managed to find my way to the administrative building and reported to a pale-faced petty officer badly in need of a shave.

'Oh yes, Robertson,' he yawned, displaying a row of uneven, yellow teeth. 'You'll be seein' some bigwig marine officer at 0930. Apparently he's come all the way from Deal to interview you.' (Deal was a RM barracks in Kent.)

The bigwig officer turned out to be a stern-faced royal marine major with dark brown hair, and a row of medals over the left pocket of his battledress. In front on his desk lay a green beret attached to which was a small silver Globe and Laurel badge. On each shoulder was the insignia of the Royal Marine Commandos, Combined Operations. (Red anchor and crossed rifle.) Close by was a yellow wooden swagger stick. As the petty officer ushered me inside, the officer penetrated me with a pair of steely grey eyes.

He didn't return my salute. Instead he came straight to the point. 'Stand easy,' he snapped in a crisp, clear voice. 'My name is Major Dunning. Now what makes you think you can pass the commando course?'

I immediately felt my mouth go dry. 'Well,' I nervously replied, 'you managed to do it, didn't you, sir?'

A wry smile flickered across his handsome, suntanned features. 'Cheeky blighter, aren't you?' he said sitting back in his chair and steepling his fingers on his chest.

I was about to reply when he narrowed his eyes and said, 'I see you served in *Uganda.* Why do you want to join the commandos?'

259

Without hesitating I returned his stare, clenched my teeth and replied, 'To get back at those bastards, sir.'

'You realise, don't you,' he said, releasing his fingers and sitting forward, 'as a medic the weapon you'll be given will be to protect your patients?'

I gave a quick shrug of my shoulders and grinned. 'Then it'll be too bad if any Krauts get in the way, won't it, sir?'

The officer pursed his lips, placed both hands palms down on the desk, and said, 'Right, Robertson, carry on and wait outside.'

I saluted and did a sharp about turn and left the room. In the office outside two Wrens were busy typing.

'Och yer no bein' sent to "DQs" (Detention Quarters), are you, love?' asked one of them, a blonde girl with a distinctive Scottish accent.

I shot her a week grin and replied, 'God knows where I'll end up.'

I soon found out.

Five minutes later the petty officer emerged followed by the major, who, fitting his green beret on his head, strode out of the building.

The petty officer looked at me and grinned. 'Well, Doc,' he said, 'you've passed muster. You're to have a medical and if you pass that, you are to take two weeks' survivors leave then travel to a place called Achnacarry.'

'Achnacarry!' I exclaimed. 'Where the hell's that?'

'It's the commando school in Bonnie Scotland,' interrupted the blonde Wren. 'On the banks o' the river Arkaig, close to Ben Nevis.' She paused looked up and sighed, 'I went oot we one o' them marines once. He was lovely…'

I was still non the wiser and said, 'When do I go on leave, PO?'

'Straight away after your medical,' he answered. 'When that's over come back and collect your railway warrant, leave pass and draft note. The train for Smoke leaves every hour from Pompey Harbour station. Go to Euston on the tube and catch the train for Liverpool. Any questions?'

'No chance of a tot is there, PO?'

'Bugger off,' came his gruff reply.

Before I left the office, the blonde Wren smiled at me and with a mischievous glint in her big blue eyes, said, 'Pity you're going so soon, love, I could hae taught you the highland fling.'

The elderly surgeon lieutenant in the sick bay gave me a thorough going over.

'Have you ever suffered from flat feet?' he asked, testing my knee reflexes.

I told him I hadn't.

He gave me a wry smile. 'Well where you're going, young man,' he said, 'you may end up with them.'

An hour later I caught the train from Portsmouth to London and arrived at Lime Street shortly after five o'clock. Outside the station dusk was falling and dark grey clouds threatened rain. I managed to catch a tram to the Pier Head. The female clippie refused my fare.

'Me old feller's in your lot,' she said flashing me a friendly smile, ''aven't seen the silly old bugger fer over a year now.'

Scars of the Blitz abounded. Lewis's store and the surrounding buildings remained pathetic looking skeletons of their formers selves. Workmen were busy restoring the cobblestoned façade outside the neo-classical St George's Hall while Merseysiders, hunched up against the bitter north-westerly wind hurried down Lord Street seemingly oblivious to the devastation on either side of them.

The Liverpool docks sprawled along the north bank of the River Mersey was crammed with ships. Sleek destroyers, corvettes and a few minesweepers were moored alongside Princess Pier and beyond. Further down in Trafalgar Dock I could just see the twin funnels and guns of a battle cruiser, and as spots of rain splattered against my face I thought about Dusty and the lads onboard *Uganda*.

When mum opened the front door the shock of seeing me almost made her drop the teapot she was holding.

'It's our Peter, Bill,' she cried, throwing her free arm around my neck. As she gave me a slobbery kiss on the cheek I saw tears in her eyes and smelt her musky body aroma I remembered so well from childhood. Dad shirt-sleeved and beaming appeared. He walked with a slight limp, a legacy of his injury during the Blitz.

'Bloody hell, son,' he laughed taking hold of my suitcase, 'you don't give folks much warning, do yer?'

Then mum asked the inevitable question.

'How long are you home for, son?' she asked giving me a hug.

'Two weeks, mum,' I replied, 'then...'

Before I had time to finish dad interrupted. 'Bloody marvellous,' he cried, 'now I can really hammer yer at darts in the Nelly.'

With our arms around each other we went into the kitchen. Nothing had changed. The warmth from the coal fire caressed my face; the criss-crossed white tape on the window was peeling but the furniture, carpet and rug was the same. The smell of stale frying filled the cosy atmosphere and the small, oaken encased clock on the mantelpiece ticked silently away. So much had happened since my last leave. I had seen good men killed and witnessed the horrors of war. I took a deep breath and thought, my God it's great to be home.

An hour or so later after a plate of rabbit stew and dumplings we sat listening to the voice of Alan Adell reading the eight o'clock news. In Europe the Red Army had crossed the River Dneiper and broke through the German 1,300 defence line. The Allies were inching their way up the boot of Italy and were being held at Monte Cassino. He went on to say, 'Despite commando raids around the area the Nazis are dug in around rugged Apennine Mountains and winter is closing in.'

'Poor buggers,' muttered dad, pouring out a generous measure of Higson's Ale into a glass. 'Those commandos won't take any prisoners believe you me. They're a tough lot so I hear.'

Now, I thought, is the perfect time to tell them. 'I expect they are, dad,' I replied, 'because I'm going to join them.'

With a startled expression in his eyes dad suddenly stared at me. 'What do yer mean, son?' he asked, his glass poised half way to his lips. 'You're in the navy aren't you. How can you join that lot?'

Mum stopped knitting and looked at me. 'Your dad's right,' she said, 'what do you mean, love?'

As best I could I told them what happened in the *Uganda* – about Sharky and the others and how I had to get off the ship. As I spoke mum and dad sat in stunned silence. When I had finished they looked at each other in surprise. After a few seconds dad shook his head. 'I hope you know what you're doin' Peter,' he said. 'It sounds a might dangerous to me, doesn't it Hilda?'

Mum sighed, put down her knitting and stood up. 'Yes, dear,' she said brushing her skirt with her hand, 'but at least they'll give him a gun to protect himself. And that young man, Adele's brother, Emile was a commando and he seemed happy enough.'

I gave mum a hopeful glance and said, 'I don't suppose there's been any news of Adele has there?'

'I'm afraid not, son,' she replied. 'Now let's forget about the war and have a cuppa tea.'

A week later my mate Gordon Laird appeared at the front door wearing a wide grin and a set of corporal's stripes on each arm of his battledress.

'Holy Hell!' I exclaimed pumping his hand. 'I see they've made you a general.'

'And you've become an admiral,' he said glancing at my hook.

Fifteen minutes later after he had said hello to mum and dad we were sat in the Nelson having a pint. When I told him about the commandos his jaw dropped and he stared at me in disbelief.

'They're like the paras,' he said, 'they jump out of perfectly good planes and the commandos are the first on the beaches. They're both fuckin' crazy, I tell yer.'

'Sad about CS,' I said, taking a sip of beer. Suddenly our joviality changed and for a few seconds we sat in silence. Then, lifting his glass, Gordon quietly said, 'Aye, here's to him and Jim.'

PART FOUR

CHAPTER TWENTY-ONE

'I was told in Pompey that Achnacarry was somewhere near Ben Nevis but God knows where it is,' I said to Gordon. 'I checked in my old school atlas but couldn't find it anywhere.'

'I think Ben Nevis is in the highlands, mate,' replied Gordon, 'you'll need plenty of warm gear up there, I'll bet.'

It was midday and Gordon and I we having a pint in the Nelson. Except for Harry the bald-headed barman and three young American soldiers standing at the bar next to us the place was empty. Each stood over six feet and their shoulder insignia read '82nd Airborne'.

Just then one of the Americans, a sharp-featured lad with fair hair, turned to Gordon. 'Say bud,' he said in a slow drawl reminiscent of John Wayne, 'did I hear you say Achnacarry?'

Gordon looked at me, then at the American. 'Yeah,' replied Gordon. 'My mate here is going there.'

'Did yer hear that fellas,' said the American turning to his two pals. 'There's a guy here's goin' to Achnacarry.'

The two other Americans looked at me with guarded expressions.

'Better you than me, buddy,' said a dark-haired American. 'Some of our guys went there to do the commando course. They said it's a right ball breaker of a place.'

The third American, a fresh-faced lad with freckles, glanced at his pal. 'Sure thing, Dutch,' he added, 'Elmer and Dixie said it was tougher than a longhorn's hide.'

'Yes, but did your mates say where Achnacarry is?' I asked.

'Sure did,' replied Dutch, 'Dixie said it wuz near someplace called Spean Bridge, wherever that is.'

'Watch it you lot,' said Harry, leaning over the bar, 'careless talk costs lives an' all that.'

'Too damn right,' said Dutch, slapping me on the back. 'Let's have a round of that Higsons beer. It tastes just like the stuff back home in Boysie Indiana.'

We introduced ourselves and by the time the pub closed at three o'clock and we said goodbye, Gordon and I had cemented Anglo-American relations to such an extent I had to help Gordon home, but I still didn't know where Achnacarry was.

I left home early on the morning of Thursday 1 November.

'I've packed some woollen socks and a few jumpers,' said mum giving me a tearful kiss and a hug. 'Make sure you wrap up well now.'

After I had said goodbye to mum, dad walked me to the bus stop. The sky was overcast and a harsh easterly wind almost blew my cap off.

'I've put a small bottle of whisky with the sandwiches your mother packed for you,' said dad shaking my hand. 'It's a long journey to Scotland and I expect it'll be a might cold,' then with tears in his eyes, added, 'look after yourself Peter and drop us a line when you can.'

The train journey en route to Glasgow via Liverpool took an endless eight hours. In my compartment were two young Royal Marines, two matelots, a young RAF lad and a soldier wearing the blue shoulder flashes of the Cameron Highlanders.

No sooner had the train left Lime Street than the cards came out. A case was used as a table.

'Gin rummy all right, lads, five fags a game,' said one of the matelots, a two-badge stoker with a five o'clock shadow.

Everyone nodded in agreement. Someone passed around the cigarettes and the muggy atmosphere became thick with tobacco smoke; the windows fogged up and lines of condensation trickled down onto the armrest; then, to complete a gloomy picture it started to pour down. Lancets of rain splattered against the outsides of the window obliterating the view.

'Joining a ship, Doc,' asked the two-badger, taking a card from the top of the deck and sliding it among those in his hand.

'Not really,' I replied, 'A shore base in Scotland.'

'Hello, hello,' laughed one of the marines, a small stocky lad with short brown hair. 'Whereabouts in nicky-knocky-noo land are yer going, then, Doc?' His Cockney accent sounded like Max Miller and as he spoke his pale blue eyes narrowed into a cheeky grin.

'Hey, you there,' grunted the soldier, shooting a wary glance at the matelot, 'watch yersell, the noo. That's God's own country yer talking aboot.'

'No offence, Jock,' replied the marine, 'only Porky and me are on our way to do the commando course at Achnacarry, aren't we mate?' he added looking at the other marine.

The name Achnacarry gave me a start. I was about to say something when the Scottish soldier interrupted me. 'You must be bloody crazy, mon,' he said staring at us. 'I hear Achnacarry is fer hard knocks only.'

'That's us, ain't it Porky, hard knocks?' replied the other marine straightening up. 'So watch yer step, Jock.'

Porky, a thin-faced lad with dark hair slapped a card onto the case looked at his mate, and replied, 'Yeah, you're right there, Spider, but anything's better than doin' fuck all in Deal.'

'I'm going to Achnacarry as well,' I blurted.

A look of surprise came over Spider's face. 'You a doc?' he cried. 'Are you going there to patch us up, or what?'

'No,' I answered, 'I'm gonna do the commando course. Me name's Peter Robertson and I'll be attached to you lot.'

'Well I'll be buggered,' laughed Spider. 'I'm Robin Seymour, Spider to me mates. And this long streak of piss is Porky Saunders.' He paused, grinned and went on, 'We best be good to the Doc here, or he'll stick a needle up our arses.'

So far the RAF lad had spoken very little. His dark brown eyes suddenly looked up from his cards and in a timid voice, said, 'I read in newspaper those commandos are a lot of thugs and gangsters.'

'Bullshit, laddie,' retorted the stoker, 'tell that to those poor buggers killed at Dieppe.'

'Personally, I don't care one way or the other,' chimed Porky. 'At least we'll get extra pay and 'ave it away with the girls.'

The soldier looked at Porky and gave out a loud guffaw. 'Where you're goin', son, I dinna think you'll find many lassies.'

'By the way, lads,' I said, laying my cards down, 'that'll be Gin. You lot owe me five fags each.'

After a shake of hands the soldier and the RAF lad left the train at Carlisle. When we arrived at Glasgow the stoker left leaving me with no sandwiches and an empty whisky bottle. Shortly afterwards the compartment door was drawn open and in came a tall, broad-shouldered royal marine. His weather-beaten features suggested he had spent a lot of time outdoors. Beads of sweat ran down the sides of his face and his bull neck threatened to burst the collar of his shirt. He wore a green beret with a silver badge of the Coldstream Guards and three stripes on either arm. On each shoulder of his battledress, written in small red lettering on a dark blue background was the word COMMANDO. Above his left pocket was a row of campaign ribbons. As he entered the compartment he surveyed us with a pair of sharp grey eyes.

'What are you lot staring at?' he asked in a stern North Country accent. Without waiting for a reply he threw his holdall up in to the rack, plopped himself into the seat, lit a cigarette and said, 'Any of you fer Achnacarry, then?'

'That we are, sarg,' replied Porky, 'is that where you're goin' as well?'

The sergeant unbuttoned his battledress top, loosened his tie and sat back. 'That's better,' he sighed. He then smiled displaying a set of uneven, tobacco-stained teeth. 'Yes, I am,' he said. 'Me name's Sergeant Bellringer,' he paused, then added, 'needless to say the buggers call me Ding-Dong.'

This, of course, brought a chorus of laughter from everyone, including the sergeant.

Spider passed around his cigarettes and we settled down.

'How come you volunteered for this Doc?' asked Ding-Dong. 'We usually have army medics.'

I didn't feel like telling him about Sharky Ward and his brother, so I simply replied, 'The AFO asked for naval personnel for Special Duties, so here I am.'

'Just where exactly is the commando school, sarg?' I asked.

'It's roughly seventeen miles from Fort William,' he replied. 'We get off at a place called Spean Bridge.'

'Tell us about it, sarg,' said Porky leaning forward, 'is it really as tough as I've heard?'

Ding-Dong's upper body shook as he gave out a loud guffaw. 'You bet,' he replied, 'and if you don't measure up, it's RTU (Return To Unit) for orders.'

'Someone told me it's in a castle or summat,' said Spider. 'Is that right?'

'The camp is in the grounds of Achnacarry Castle,' answered Ding-Dong sending a stream of cigarette smoke into the already polluted atmosphere. 'It belongs to the head of the Clan Cameron, Sir Donald Cameron of Lochiel. He and his family left it to us and went to live on his estate in Clunes.'

I suddenly remembered something Mr Baldwin my history teacher said. 'Wasn't it near there the Duke of Cumberland's troops nearly captured Bonnie Prince Charlie during the Jacobite Rising in 1745?'

My outburst of knowledge surprised everyone.

'Hark at him,' cried Spider, 'a regular bloody know-all, so he is.'

'Shows he went to a proper school,' replied Porky. 'Not soddin' Borstal like you.'

Ding-Dong ignored them and said, 'You could be right. They say old Charlie's ghost haunts the hills around the camp.'

'Best not to get lost then,' laughed Spider.

The harsh rain had turned to a fine drizzle. I wiped the cloudy condensation from the window and saw the dark shapes of the Grampians shrouded in mist. Then, stretched out before my eyes was a vast lake with mountains sweeping down to their very edge. The water lay still, glistening like silver. It was a scene of such utter serenity that took my breath away.

Ding-Dong noticed me staring out the window. 'What you can see there is Loch and Ben Lomand,' he said, 'and we'll soon be passing through Crianlarch and Tyndrum. And that miserable looking land you see stretching away in the distance is Rannoch Moor.'

The rest of the lads heard him and crowded against the window.

'You tak the high road and I'll tak the low road,' sang Spider.

'Bloody-hell, Spider,' said Porky, 'if Van Gogh had heard you sing he'd 'ave cut off his other ear.'

'Whose this Van Gogh feller?' asked Spider. 'Don't tell me he's at Achnacarry.'

Everyone except me laughed. I was too busy staring out the window.

'God those mountains are beautiful!' I exclaimed. 'They've got nothing like that in Cheshire.'

Ding-Dong gave a wry smile and said, 'Maybe you won't be so impressed when you've climbed up a few of them.'

After a brief stop at Fort William the train continued through a valley steeped on either side by rugged mountainous ranges covered in dense fir trees. Away to the right I saw a huge mountain peak blanketed by dark grey clouds.

'Is that Ben Nevis, sarg?' I asked.

'That's right,' he replied, looking out the window. 'It's 4,406 feet high, the biggest in Great Britain,' he paused, turned his head and with a wry smile, added, 'take a good look. It's eighteen miles away from the camp and one day you'll have to climb up her.'

'Blimey!' exclaimed Spider. 'What do they think we are, fuckin' mountain goats?'

'You will be afore you leave Achnacarry,' replied Ding-Dong.

Bellowing steam, the train slowly shunted to a stop at a small hamlet.

'Here we are you lucky lads, Spean Bridge,' cried Ding-Dong. He pushed his large frame up, straightened his tie, buttoned his blouse and put on his beret. 'And I think you may have a welcoming committee.'

Spider and Porky took their 303 rifles down off the rack, put on their blue berets and prepared to leave the train.

Standing on the platform was a tall, stocky, stern-faced RSM (Regimental Sergeant Major). He had a well-waxed moustache and a complexion like tanned leather. Next to him stood two sergeants. All three wore Denison smocks (camouflaged 'jumping jackets') and the coveted green berets.

A biting, bitterly cold wind attacked my face as I left the train. I shuddered and turned up the collar of my greatcoat. Dark, foreboding, low-lying clouds raced angrily across the sky. The time was two-thirty and I was slowly freezing my bollocks off.

I glanced around and saw men clambering onto the platform clutching rifles and kit bags. Each wore badges from almost every regiment in the British Army. (I later learned they would keep the parent badges when awarded their green berets.)

There was also a large contingent of royal marines and several American Rangers. Suddenly, I felt self-conscious; not only was I without a rifle I was also the only one in a naval uniform.

All at once the heavens opened up and I felt rain splatter onto my cap.

'Does it always rain like this?' Spider asked Ding-Dong.

'Always,' came Ding-Dong's curt reply. 'So you'd better get used to it.' He then walked across to the RSM; both looked up at the sky and laughed. Ding-Dong then strode out of the station into a waiting jeep.

Despite wearing overcoats everyone stood around slowly getting soaked, smoking and talking. My overcoat was saturated and hung on me like a lead weight.

The RSM removed his pace-stick from under his arm, tapped it against his thigh and glared at us.

'Fall in single file and face me,' he bellowed, 'and put those cigarettes out.' As he spoke his moustache twitched from side to side.

Everyone immediately shuffled into a line that stretched the length of the platform.

Spider who was standing next to me flicked his soggy dog-end onto the railway track. 'Where's the bloody transport then,' he muttered. 'If we stay here much fuckin' longer we'll all go down with pneumonia.'

Spider's question was soon answered.

'Your training starts now,' bawled the RSM. 'Achnacarry Camp is seven miles away, so shoulder arms, pick up yer gear and follow me.' With a quick reflex action he replaced the pace stick under his arm, did a quick about turn, and marched towards the station exit.

I led the way. Behind me was Porky and Spider. Ignoring the rain, one of the sergeants, a small, wiry man with razor sharp eyes cried, 'Right you lot, you 'eard wot he said, now let's go. *Left right, left right.*'

Just then someone began to sing *Pack Up Your Troubles In your Old Kit Bag.* Everyone joined in except the Americans who probably thought we were crazy.

With streams of breath issuing from mouths and nostrils we wound out of the station. On either side of the village the peaks of desolate mountains disappeared under a blanket of grey, swirling mist. The sharp crunch of boots on tarmac echoed around as we marched past several thatched cottages and a small, whitewashed post office. Despite the weather, a few locals gave us a welcome wave that was cheerily reciprocated.

As soon as the singing petered out the small, wiry sergeant struck up another song.

'Come on, lads, only five miles to go,' he yelled, before breaking into *It's a Long Way to Tipperary.*

'I don't know about fuckin' Tipperary,' I heard Porky grunt, 'it's along way to this bloody castle.'

Pretty soon I was sweating like a pig and out of breath. I glanced behind and saw Spider, red-faced and gasping. 'Five soddin' miles,' he groaned, streams of vapour pouring from his mouth and nostrils, 'me legs'll give way well before then.'

Porky, turned around. His young face was saturated with sweat and he looked like he had run a marathon. 'If we keep this up much bloody longer,' he gasped, 'we'll wear our soddin' legs out.'

Both sergeants continually marched up and down the line chivvying up stragglers and shouting encouragement. 'Keep going Bonnie lads,' yelled one of them, a short, barrel-chested man with a Geordie accent. 'Only four miles to go.'

On the surrounding hillside the bracken and heather glistened with rain and near a clump of fir trees a beautiful stag, its spiky antlers dripping wet, gazed innocently down at us.

'D' yer think that beast knows summat we don't?' gasped Spider. 'It's given us a funny look.'

'Maybe it fancies you,' grunted Porky.

With a rumble of boots we crossed a small wooden bridge spanning a wide expanse of clear water.

'That's the Gairlochy,' shouted the Geordie sergeant, 'you'll be seein' more of that when yer do yer boat work.'

'Boat work,' I muttered to myself – maybe I should have stayed with the navy.

We slowly made our way up a long steep hill. When we reached the summit a buzz of excitement echoed around. In the distance, lying close to the banks of yet another large lake, loomed an imposing, irregular shaped edifice. Flanked on each side by small round crenulated towers it looked more like a fairy tale castle than the baronial seat of Scottish Laird.

'Be Jebbus,' some Irishman cried, 'is that Achnacarry castle I can see, sarg?'

'That it is Paddy,' replied the Geordie sergeant, 'and the loch yer see is Lake Arkraig.'

'Thank the Holy Mother fer that,' I heard the Irishman reply. 'Me feet are droppin' off, so they are.'

Suddenly the skirl of bagpipes could be heard coming from the camp. The melodious whine filtered through the rain and hung in the wind as if conducted by an invisible hand. At the bottom of the hill stood a solitary piper standing rigidly to attention, blowing into his chanter. From the pipe bag firmly tucked under his left arm, three drone pipes wavered in the air. He wore a green beret, Denison smock, boots and puttees, grey stockings and a dark blue and green checked tartan kilt. (I learned later this was the tartan belonging to Cameron of Lochiel.)

As the column approached, the piper began to walk towards us. With each step his kilt and sporran swayed rhythmically from side to side. When he was about fifteen yards away he did a slow about turn. The tune he was playing changed as he marched ahead of the RSM.

'That's my pal Bill Millin,' said the wiry sergeant. 'He's Lord Lovat's piper and the tune he's playin' is his boss's favourite, *Highland Laddie.*'

About half a mile away I saw a Union Jack hanging limply from a tall flagpole. Then the guardroom and curved tops of several steel Nissen huts came into view. The time was just after four-thirty and dusk was falling.

'Straighten up, you lot,' bellowed the RSM, 'Colonel Vaughan'll be waitn' to give yer the once over.'

His words had an immediate effect on me. I increased the grip on my suitcase, and pulled back my shoulders.

As we reached the guardroom the RSM barked, 'Eyes left.'

With parade ground precision I snapped my head to the left. The piper stopped playing, saluted, then marched smartly ahead into a nearby hut.

Standing outside the guardroom was a thickset, medium-sized officer. His appearance was striking, upright but rather portly. His round, fleshy face was heavily bronzed and on the front of his green beret he wore the badge of the Coldstream Guards. Under his left arm he held a swagger stick and above the left pocket of his battledress was a row of campaign medals. His right hand came up palm outwards in a quivering salute, while scanning us with a pair of sharp, dark eyes. This was the commanding officer, Lieutenant Colonel Charlie Vaughan M.B.E.

CHAPTER TWENTY-TWO

The Commando Basic Training Centre (CBC) lay within the shadow of Achnacarry Castle. On either side of the camp a grey swirling mist blotted out the surrounding mountainous peak adding to the scene a touch of sinister unreality. Barely visible in the gloom, pale lights flickered from within the numerous Nissen huts sighted around the edge of the large drill square. On the far side a large Nissen hut lay in the shadow of a giant Douglas fir tree. This, we were later told, was called 'Iris hut', used for a multitude of purposes in wet weather.

It was a cheerless, depressing sight but what I saw next frightened the life out of me. Just passed the guardroom on the left side of a grassy verge was a row of well-kept graves with wooden crosses.

'Bloody hell,' I heard Spider cry, 'what the 'ell are those?'

On one was written, 'This man failed to keep his rifle clean.' On another, 'This man stood in the skyline,' and so on.

'Good God, sarg!' I exploded. 'They don't mess about here, do they?'

The Geordie sergeant ignored my question, gave a hearty laugh and carried on marching. (We were later told the 'graves' were there to impress upon everyone that carelessness can cost you your life.)

The RSM brought the column to a halt outside the huts. 'The dining halls, if yer like to call 'em that, and the NAAFI canteen are over on you left,' he yelled, 'and the ablutions is next to it. As it's always pissin' down, the duckboards you see are to stop you disappearing in the mud. The first twenty-five will occupy the hut in front of you. The remainder can sort yerselves out in the other two. Dismiss.'

With Spider, Porky and the others hard on my heels I opened the wooden door and went into the hut. The rain beat a steady staccato on the roof. For a few seconds I stood soaked to the skin and as I looked around my heart sank.

On each side were beds consisting of well-scrubbed wooden planks supported on red bricks. A thick lining of coconut matting provided a mattress. The floor was made of concrete and the windows were slits of thick cellophane. Lighting was in the form of two electric bulbs and in the centre of the room a conduit from an unlit cast-iron stove disappeared through the roof.

Sergeant Bellringer came in grinning like a Cheshire cat. 'Here you are, me lucky lads,' he rasped, 'yer cosy 'ome from 'ome. Grab a bed. Use yer pack fer a pillow.' He paused and kicked a nearby bucket. 'And this here is to piss in at night.' As an afterthought, he continued, 'Oh, and this aint the Ritz, there's no hot water.'

'Jesus Christ,' cried a marine, his distinct Liverpool accent echoing around the place. 'They live better than this in Walton Prison.'

Ding-Dong slowly walked up to the marine. 'If yer don't approve of the accommodation, my son,' he said with a wry smile, 'you can always be RTU'd.'

'No ta sarg,' grinned the marine, throwing his kitbag on a bed, 'at least it's better than the foxhole I 'add at Dunkirk.'

'I wouldn't be too sure of that,' replied Ding-Dong. 'Fall in outside at 0630 tomorrow. The CO will give yer a talk after breakfast.'

'What aboot our wet gear, sarg?' asked another marine.

The sergeant walked to the door then turned around. 'You won't need 'em,' he said, 'because later on you'll be issued with denims.'

Someone found a few pieces of wood, opened the stove and started a fire. Vapours of steam rose from uniforms as everyone crowded around the stove eagerly rubbing their hands together.

'Jesus,' said Spider, shivering like a leaf, 'if any of us get pneumonia we'll end up in one of them graves by the guardroom.'

The dining hall, next to the galley, was equally Spartan consisting of a dozen so long wooden tables and benches.

After a welcome feast of rabbit stew and spotted dick we were ushered to the quartermaster store. The quartermaster, a small heavily built man issued everyone with a FSMO (Full Service Marching Order) kit. This consisted of Denison smocks, two sets of denims, puttees, two blankets, a cap comforter and a pair of black hobnailed boots. In addition we were given a waterproof ground sheet, a fleece-lined sleeping bag, a trenching spade and a couple of shell dressings. All this was packed into a large camouflaged Bergen rucksack. He then asked what cap size we wore.

'For yer green berets,' he said, making a note on a form, 'if and when you pass the course.'

'Funny bugger, eh?' replied Spider, 'we ain't come all this way fer a picnic yer know.'

The corporal didn't reply. Instead he looked at me. 'You're gonna need a BD (Battledress) uniform before you leave here.' He looked me up and down and muttered, 'Large size chest, long leg,' and jotted this down on the form.

He then turned and unlocked a rack containing a row of .303 Lee Enfield Rifles, took one out and handed it to me.

'Treat it better than yer missus,' said the corporal, 'and yer won't go far wrong. And seein' as yer a doc, later on you'll be issued with a Colt 45 pistol. To protect the injured, mind, not to kill Jerries,' he then gave a short laugh and added, 'an' if you believe that, you'll believe anything.'

Up till now the only rifle I had fired was at clay toys in the fairground at New Brighton. I raised the rifle to eye level, placed the butt firmly into my right shoulder and swung it around.

'Jesus!' exclaimed Porky, 'Fer fuck's sake don't point that thing at anyone. It could be loaded.'

'Bugger me,' cried Spider who was next to me. 'He thinks he's Buffalo Bill.'

'Any ammo, corps?' I asked tongue in cheek.

'You'll get plenty of that soon enough,' replied the corporal.

After supper everyone, wearing denim battledress, boots and cap comforters made their way over the soggy duckboards into Iris hut. A bright full moon dodged in between black clouds and although the rain had stopped a bitterly cold wind stung my face.

Lieutenant Colonel 'Charlie' Vaughan stood at the end of the hut flanked by a tall, fresh-faced young officer, the RSM and much to my surprise, the imperious figure of Sergeant Bellringer. Next to him was a tall, barrel-chested sergeant with a neatly trimmed brown moustache and a pockmarked face.

'Hey, Porky,' I heard Spider mutter, 'that geezer next to Ding-Dong looks a bit of a bastard. I wonder what he be taking us for.'

'Cannibalism, probably,' sniggered Porky.

The colonel and those next to him had discarded their smocks and wore battledress and green berets.

The RSM told us to stand at ease. The CO cleared his throat, pursed his lips and immediately launched into his address. 'With luck, perseverance and sheer bloody guts, you are about to join the most elite section of the British army, the commandos.' His accent surprised me. Instead of the usual public school accent, his was straight from London's East End.

'Your course is six 'ard weeks.' His dark eyes narrowed as he stared at us, raised his voice and went on. 'You're all volunteers and I want to impress upon all of you that the only reason you are 'ere is to learn to *kill* the enemy, be they German, Italian or Japanese. In order to achieve that your training will be the toughest you 'ave ever 'ad.' He dropped his voice to a slightly lower key and continued, 'I've got the best commando instructors. Learn all you can from them and remember, they will never ask you to do anything that they cannot do themselves. This also applies to the officers who will always lead you from the front.' He paused and with a glint in his eyes, raised his voice once more. 'And when the time comes for you to face the 'un and he sees the determined look in your eye, 'e'll drop 'is bloody rifle and run like 'ell.' He then turned to the RSM and said, 'Carry on please,' returned the RSM's salute and left the hut.

When the colonel had gone, the RSM, grasping his pace-stick firmly under his left armpit, faced us. 'My name is RSM Jimmy James,' he said, his sharp eyes staring along the ranks. 'There are three training commando groups here. "Keys", "Haydon" and "Sturges" named after men who pioneered the commandos. You lot will be part of "Keys" commando. Tomorrow you do your first speed march around the camp. We call it the Dark Mile and will be completed in one hour. Fall in at 0700. This will be first of many speed marches you will do over the next six weeks, all in FSO and each one quicker than the last.' He paused slightly before continuing. 'If any of your mates crack up, help him out because it's teamwork that'll eventually get you through.'

The RSM stopped talking and the officer took over.

'My name is Lieutenant Grayson,' he said in a plummy public school voice. Each training commando is in four troops. You will be X troop. And I am your troop commander. Sergeant Bullringer and Sergent Leaman here are your DIs.' (Drill

Instructors.) He then turned to the sergeants and said, 'Carry on, please,' and marched smartly out of the hut.

'Right, bonnie lads,' said Ding-Dong eyeing us up. 'I want you to get to know each other as quickly as possible.' He paused and looked along the line. 'I believe we have a few Americans.'

'Sure thing, sarg,' called out someone.

'You will be joining troops containing your fellow countrymen,' said Ding-Dong.

'What a pity,' piped a marine, 'we would 'ave been all right fer a few packets o' them Camels.'

'I'll trade you a carton of them for your wife, buddy,' chimed an American soldier further along the line.

'Forget it, Yank,' cried someone else, 'I've seen her. She looks like a bloody camel, so she does.'

'And smells like one, too,' added another voice.

This brought forth peels of raucous laughter from everyone except Sergeant Leaman, who stood hand behind his back, staring coldly at everyone. He waited until the laughter had subsided, then in a rich North Country voice, said, 'Right, pay attention. I will be taking you on the march tomorrow. If anyone's late on parade I won't be very happy. OK?'

'Told yer he was a tough bugger, didn't I?' muttered Spider.

Back in the mess someone suggested we go to the NAAFI. This was inside one of the larger Nissen huts sparsely furnished with wooden tables and chairs. At the far end were a small kitchen and a counter from which two plump girls, seemingly oblivious to the constant chat up lines from sex-starved soldiers, served beer, rock cakes, corn beef sandwiches and weak tea.

Including myself there were twenty-five marines in our troop. With the exception of a few regulars, the rest were HO's (Hostilities Only.)

'What made you volunteer fer this mad lot, Doc?' asked Taffy Ball, a young fair-haired, muscular ex-rugby player from Cardiff. 'Don't tell me yer didn't like the rum?'

'Got seasick too often,' I replied with a grin. 'Just like Nelson.'

Billy Stone was a tall, heavy-set marine with dark sad eyes and a pale complexion. He was from Doncaster and had been in the service for four years.

'What made you volunteer, Billy?' asked Taffy, 'I bet you 'ad a cushy number in barracks.'

Billy shrugged his broad shoulders. 'Cushy number be buggered,' he replied, 'after Dunkirk I was sent to Malta.' He paused and lit a cigarette. 'Lost a few good mates there wot with the bombing an' all. Then they were gonna send me to some fuckin' battleship. By that time I'd 'ad enough, so I volunteered for this lot. Besides,' he added with a sigh, 'me missus is expectin' our third, so I need the extra six and eight pence a day pay.' From a wallet he showed us photographs of two small children and an attractive brunette.

'Nice family you've got there, Billy,' I remarked handing the photographs back to him.

Jim Wade a tall, lanky Yorkshire lad told us in civvy street he was a rat-catcher. 'Now I'm gonna catch some o' them Nazi rats,' he said, his grey eyes narrowing into angry-looking slits, 'and cut off a few of their fuckin' heads.'

Then there was big Jock Forbes, an ex-policeman from Glasgow with thick, wiry ginger hair and dark, deep-set brown eyes. Paddy Malone an ex-docker from Belfast was remarkably small for a marine. He had humorous blue eyes, a deep barrel chest and arms like Tarzan. Wacker Williamson was a slightly built, sallow-faced, butcher's assistant from Bootle. When I told him I was from Wallasey, he said, 'I met a judy from Wallasey in the Grafton (a well-known dance-hall in Liverpool) once. I offered to get her a pound of rump steak if she'd let me fuck her.'

'And did she?' I asked.

Wacker's face broke into a wide grin. 'She told me the only pound of steak she wanted was between me legs.' After taking a deep gulp of beer he burbled, 'Nice judies in Wallasey, Doc.'

Pete Cronin, a tall, fair-haired lad hailed from Truro; Nutty Slack a lanky, ex bantam-weight boxer was a typical 'Brummie'. There were many others whose names would soon become as familiar to me as my own.

The canteen was crowded. The air was thick with cigarette smoke, sweat and beer. Suddenly my ears pricked up. Among the various dialects I overheard a group of soldiers speaking French. Thoughts of Adele immediately flooded my mind. Lately I had been so preoccupied with what was happening I hadn't thought of her. It had been over a year since Emile, her brother, had visited mum. My hand automatically went to my neck and touched the medallion chain under the thickness of my shirt. I closed my eyes and saw her dark beautiful face staring at me and prayed she was safe. One day I hoped to find out.

CHAPTER TWENTY-THREE

At precisely 0700 next morning everyone in FSMO mustered on the parade ground. Besides our troop there were half a dozen or so others from the Commonwealth, America and all over Europe. Naturally, there was some fierce rivalry between each group, especially between soldiers and royal marines.

After spending an uncomfortable night lying on my so-called mattress, my neck was stiff and my back ached. For a while I felt somewhat helpless, noticing how everyone, with soldierly ease, slipped on their Bergens and handled their rifles. Thankfully Spider and Porky came to my rescue.

'Always make sure your rifle sling is good and tight, Pete,' said Spider, 'and keep it on yer left shoulder like this,' He then slipped his left thumb through the sling of his own rifle and added, 'OK?'

I nodded and did as he said.

'And whatever you do, don't drop the bloody thing,' added Porky.

Dawn was gradually breaking and a pallid moon hovered above in grey clouds. Luckily it had stopped raining but a fierce icy December wind cut through the thick material of my denim battledress. With sleeves rolled up, battledress blouse opened at the neck and cap comforter firmly fixed on my head, I slipped my fingers through the rifle sling, stood to attention and shivered like a jelly.

Sergeant Leaman was waiting outside the hut. Lieutenant Grayson stood next to him. Oblivious to the bitterly cold wind

Sergeant Leaman walked, bolt upright, along the line. 'Don't worry, Doc,' he said as I he passed me. 'You'll soon warm up.'

Our troop was in front of the army group.

Sergeant Leaman turned and in a deep, grating voice, called everyone to attention. He then added, 'Normally you would have PT but today we're going to warm you up a different way. Without intervals, right dress.'

Remembering my basic drill, my head snapped to the right and like the rest, shuffled into line. As I did so I lost my grip on my rifle and to my horror it clattered to the ground.

Soldiers sanding in front of us turned around, some grinning.

'What's up mate,' said one of them, 'is yer rifle too heavy for you then?'

'Face the front,' came a sharp retort from Sergeant Leaman.

Spider standing next to me let out a hollow groan. I quickly bent down to pick up the weapon. As I straightened up I was met by Sergeant Leaman's hypnotic stare. 'Half a dozen press-ups,' he snapped, 'pronto.'

Normally I could have easily done this. But with the weight of a full Bergen pressing down on me I collapsed after four. 'Grab hold of 'im, somebody,' I heard the sergeant growl, 'or we'll be here all day.'

'I warned you not to drop the bloody thing, didn't I?' mumbled Porky as he and Spider helped me up. 'If yer drop it again he'll 'ave yer doublin' round the square till Domesday.'

We marched in single file past the guardroom. I watched as the pale light of dawn cast an eerie glow on the surrounding hillside making the leaves on the fir and pine trees glisten like silver. My observations were abruptly interrupted by the crunching noise of boots as we strode out of camp.

Spider, who was behind me muttered, 'Maybe we'll meet the ghost of old Charlie, Ding-Dong told us about.'

'If we do,' said Wacker, 'the Doc can drop his rifle again and run like fuck.'

'And I'll be right behind him, so I will,' I heard Paddy Malone say.

We came to a steep hill with a line of telegraph poles spaced twenty yards apart. Upon reaching the first one Lieutenant Grayson ordered us to double march.

'Come on, come. Keep going!' bellowed Sergeant Leaman. *'If the officers can do it, so can you.'*

However my lack of fitness soon began to tell. As we started up another steep hill I began to slow down. My chest felt tight and I had difficulty in breathing. My legs weakened and clutching my rifle, I began to stumble.

'Come on, Doc,' I heard Wacker say as he removed my rifle from my shoulder. He then placed an arm under my left armpit. At the same time Jock Forbes arrived and grabbing me under my other armpit, supported me around the waist.

'Thanks lads,' I managed to mumble, 'I'm all in.'

'Steady, Doc,' Jock gasped, 'we've got yer now mon. You can make it.'

However, I wasn't the only one to fall by the wayside. I later heard Billy Stone and Pete Cronin were also being helped along.

After being dragged along for some distance I began to feel better. My breathing became easier and my legs felt stronger.

About a mile from camp Sergeant Leaman seemingly unaffected by the march, stopped the troop. 'Right,' he barked. 'Some of you helped your mates. We calls it the 'me and my pal' act. Remember, we never leave anyone behind.'

Suddenly, I realised what Jimmy James, the RSM, meant by teamwork.

We arrived back just before 0900.

'Jesus Christ,' I gasped, collapsing onto my bed. 'I could sleep for a week.'

'Some hope, you've got, Doc,' cried Spider, throwing me a cigarette, 'we've got weapons instruction in half an hour.'

'Just think, Doc,' said Porky, grinning at me. 'You'll get to fire your rifle instead of dropping it.'

For once it wasn't raining. Ding-Dong marched us to an open field behind Iris, the multi-purpose Nissen hut. Gone were the traditional bulls-eyes and concentric scoring rings. Instead, at various intervals, life-size models of enemy soldiers dotted the area. Some were quite close; others bobbed up and down or swayed awkwardly from side to side. Clearly this was no ordinary firing range.

Waiting there was a team of five instructors and a tall, lean officer with leathery features. An array of deadly looking firearms lay in front of them, one of which was a Vickers machine gun.

'All of you except our medical friend here,' said the officer, 'will be familiar with the Lee Enfield rifle and some of the weapons you see before you.' As he spoke his pale blue eyes flicked into a smile, 'So we're not going to show you how to suck eggs, as it were. However...' He paused, accepted a rifle from an instructor, knelt down, turned, and fired at a small rock about a hundred yards away. Keeping his rifle firmly tucked against his shoulder he worked the bolt so quickly the empty cartridges flew up in the air in one continual stream. Each round was fired so rapidly it sounded like a machine gun. As each shot hit home yellow sparks flew in the air. He never missed.

'Bloody hell, mon, talk aboot Dead eyed-Dick,' I heard Jock say, 'I thought I was a good shot, but that takes the cake.'

A buzz of appreciation went around.

When he had finished the officer stood up. 'My name is Captain Wallbridge,' he said sternly, 'you can improve your rate of fire by keeping the thumb and first finger around the bolt head like this.' He paused, placed the rifle in front of him and demonstrated the movement, then added, 'And use the second finger on the trigger. This will speed up the bolt action. Practise this constantly, and before we've finished with you, you'll all be firing your rifle as quickly as I just did.' He stopped talking, allowing his words to sink, then continued. 'A cup discharger can be fitted to the rifle enabling you to fire a 36 grenade. Each day you will receive instruction on the weapons you see before you with the object of improving your skill and accuracy.' He then handed the rifle to the sergeant and picked up a lethal looking short-barrelled gun. 'You'll be using this little beauty. Looks familiar doesn't it?' He paused again. 'It ought to. It's the Thompson Sub Machine Gun commonly known as the Tommy Gun used by James Cagney in the American gangster films.'

A ripple of laughter immediately echoed around.

The officer waited until the laughter had died down then continued. 'You will also be shown how to use the M1 and M3 American carbines and also the German Schmeisser, Spandau and Luger. In fact, some of you may prefer them to your own.' The officer stopped talking and looked around. 'Any questions?'

'When do we start, sir?' said Pete Cronin behind me.

'Right now,' replied the officer firmly.

For the next two hours everyone, under close supervision, fired at the targets from behind rocks, logs, and even over the inert body of an instructor, acting as a corpse. A small stocky Scots sergeant named McIntyre showed me how to load and use the rifle. Much to my delight I eventually managed to hit a tree some fifteen yards away.

'There, laddie,' he said, beaming with pleasure, 'if that'd been a Jerry, you'd hae hit the bugger right between the eyes.'

For a while I watched as men practised firing the Bren from the hip whilst moving forward. (The name BREN is derived from 'B' for Bruno, designed in Czechoslovakia, 'RE' for Royal Enfield, the manufacturers, and 'N' for Lord Nuffield who financed it.)

'Bloody hell, sarg!' I exclaimed, watching Porky and the others firing from the hip as they ran towards the targets. 'Will I have to do that?'

Sergeant McIntyre threw back his head and laughed. 'No Doc,' he said, 'you'll hae ta pick up the pieces.'

Still laughing, the sergeant took me to one side and picked up a brown canvas belt and holster. Unbuttoning the holster flap he took out what looked like a small revolver. The weapon was about eight and a half inches long with a snub nosed barrel. Holding the barrel he passed it to me. The handle fitted snugly in my hand and felt surprisingly light.

'Now this is more like it,' I said enthusiastically.

Keeping my finger away from the trigger, I raised it to eye level and looked along the barrel, pursed my lips and let out a small explosive noise.

'This is a .45 Colt pistol,' said the sergeant. 'It fires seven .45 ACP (Automatic Colt Pistol) cartridges and has an effective range of some 75 yards.'

As he spoke the sharp rat-tat-tat of gunfire rent the air. I looked across and saw Spider and then others in various positions firing the Bren. Spider, who was kneeling down, glanced up, grinned and gave me a thumbs-up, then let off a quick burst of fire.

Under Sergeant McIntyre's stern gaze I took the pistol apart and with his help, re-assembled it. After doing this a dozen times, he folded a first aid sling and blindfolded me. 'Now let's see you assemble the thing.'

Much to my surprise I managed to do it.

'Now let's see how good a shot yee are,' he said, 'see if you can hit yon tree over there.'

Using my right hand I unclipped the safety catch and gripped the handle. I looked along the barrel, sighted the tree and gently squeezed the trigger. The loud retort that followed startled me. The pistol jerked in my hand and I almost dropped it. With the acrid smell of gunpowder invading my nostrils I looked to see if I had hit the tree.

'Well,' said Jock with a slight laugh, 'yee missed it, but I think ye may have hit a rabbit. Try again.'

I did – after a dozen attempts I saw bits fly from the tree trunk as my shot finally hit home.

In groups of five everyone, except me, were blindfolded and practised assembling their rifles. Shortly afterwards I heard Spider's frustrated voice yelling, 'This fucking barrel just won't go in, sarg.'

'Try turning it around,' laughed Ding-Dong. 'You'll find it easier that way.'

After a welcome dinner of roast beef and Yorkshire pudding I felt shattered. Despite the hardness of my mattress I lay down and closed my eyes. I was just about to doze off when Wacker woke me up telling me it was time to fall.

'Come on, Doc,' he cried, shaking me by the shoulder, 'more weapons training.'

'Not rifles again.' I yawned.

'No,' replied Wacker. 'I 'eard Ding-Dong mention summat about a PIAT.'

The PIAT (Projector Infantry Ant-Tank) turned out to be an odd, tubular steel weapon two feet long ending in a cage-like aperture from which a 2.5lb projector was fired. The shoulder butt was a padded block and under the barrel was a large trigger and the whole supported on a steel stand resting on metal plates.

'It's quite light,' said Ding-Dong, lifting the weapon off the ground. The troop was grouped around Ding-Dong behind the Iris hut. The area resembled a miniature battlefield. In a dugout on the far side soldiers were firing mortar bombs into a dense forest of fir trees about 300 yards away. A flash of yellow and a flurry of falling leaves and branches followed each explosion. To this cacophony was added the intermittent crack of rifle fire. Suddenly, a group nearby opened up with a machine gun. The close proximity of the ear-splitting rat-tat-tat startled everyone who instinctively ducked, clasping their hands over his ears.

'Bloody noisy thing those Vickers are,' yelled Ding-Dong, laughing at us. 'But you'll get used to it.'

The noise died down and still holding the PIAT, Ding-Dong continued. 'Its maximum range is about 100 yards. But the only trouble is the projectile that it fires weighs two and a half pounds.' He paused as another burst of machine gun fire interrupted him. 'However, when you go to HOC (Holding Operational Commando, Wrexham) you'll form Heavy Weapons Groups that will include machine gunners, Bren gun teams and Mortar men.'

Each of us lay down and tried our luck, aiming at a tree some distance away. Many had already used this weapon before and hit the target. When my turn came Ding-Dong grinned, and said, 'I bet you never thought you'd be doing this when you volunteered, Doc?'

'Does anyone ever get hurt on this course, sarg?' I asked.

Furrowing his brow, Ding-Dong replied, 'It happens, Doc. Once in a while it happens…'

CHAPTER TWENTY-FOUR

The next morning we were introduced to physical training, commando style. As it wasn't raining this took place on the parade ground. Wearing denims, boots and gaiters with no headdress, everyone stripped to the waist and fell in. Lying nearby was five heavy-looking dirty brown logs about eight feet long.

'Bloodyn hell, mon,' I heard Jock mumble, 'dinna tell we're gonna toss a few cabers.'

'I don't know about you, Jock,' replied Taffy Ball, 'I'm that fuckin' cold I couldn't toss meself off.'

Facing us were two tough looking army instructors. Both were stripped to the waist. The tallest of them, a lean, wiry soldier gave us a sickly smile.

'Me name's CSMI (Company Sergeant Major Infantry) Frickleton,' he said in a sharp, Yorkshire accent. Then nodding to one side, added, 'And this here is Sergeant Bissell. '

'Now don't worry, lads,' said Sergeant Bissell, a stocky, stern-faced Irishman with a black hairy chest. 'We'll soon get the blood poundin' around yer veins, so we will.'

How right he was. After sprinting around the parade ground, we were placed into groups of five. A log raising competition followed this. These were hefty tree trunks about 15 feet long. On most the rough bark remained. The group I was in consisted of Spider, Porky, Jim Wade, Jock and myself. With the instructors yelling we heaved, lifted and caught the logs. In a short while beads of sweat rolled down my face and my arms ached. This lasted about fifteen minutes after which the CSMI led everyone in single file out of the camp up a steep hill and into a dense forest of pine and fir trees. Soon our boots were sinking into wet bracken as we leapt over rocks, jumped over muddy pools and unsuccessfully tried to avoid the backlash of low lying branches.

'Keep it going, me lucky lads,' cried Sergeant Bissell, 'not long to go now.'

Half an hour later we staggered back into the mess, covered in mud, and collapsed on our beds.

'Christ Almighty,' I heard Spider groan, 'it's only half-past nine and I'm fuckin' knackered.' He spoke for all of us.

After a canteen break Sergeant Bissell came into the mess dressed in FSMO. For a few seconds he stood, hands on hips, surveying us with a sickly grin.

'Right, you lot,' he said, 'get yer gear on, grab yer rifles and fall in. To be sure I have a little surprise fer yer.'

A bitterly cold December wind fanned a misty drizzle into our faces as we marched out of the camp along a muddy pathway. Despite the inclement weather the unmistakable sharp smell of bracken, gorse and pine filled the air.

Accompanied by CSMI Frickleton and 'Sony' Bissell (as he came to be known), Ding-Dong led us through a cluster of beech and pine trees. Away to our left an ancient looking humped-back bridge spanned a narrow part of the river Arkaig whose waters glistened like silver in the morning sunlight. We finally arrived at a line of beech trees from which dangled lines of soggy ropes. Further along I could see part of an obstacle course with high log walls and scrambling nets. More ropes, taut and dripping with morning dew stretched between a series of trees. However, what caught everyone's eyes was a thick hawser stretching down at a steep angle from a platform at the top of tall pine tree across the river.

'What the hell's that?' cried someone as we stared upwards.

'We call that the Death Slide,' I heard the CSMI say. 'We'll get to that in due course.'

'Christ Almighty!' exploded Spider. 'Maybe I shudda joined the parachute regiment.'

The CSMI overheard Paddy and shooting him a sly grin, said, 'The para course comes later.'

We carried on to the riverbank and saw what looked like a rope bridge. This consisted of two side ropes joined together by a third bottom rope to which was attached foot toggles. Slung from tree to tree this crossover spanned a narrow part of the river Akraig. As I watched it a gust of wind caught the ropes making them swing precariously.

'Bloody hell, Ding-Dong!' I exclaimed, 'Do we actually have to walk across that?'

Ding-Dong grinned at Sony, then at me. 'We calls that the Toggle Bridge,' he said sarcastically, 'now don't tell me a big lad like you is frightened of a little height?'

'It's not the height that worries me,' I replied, 'it's the falling down.'

'So this was your little surprise, eh Ding-Dong?' said Spider gazing around. 'A man could do 'imsell an injury just looking at this lot.'

'Never mind, Spider,' replied Ding-Dong, 'if yer land on yer 'ead you'll do no damage.'

The CSMI ordered us to halt.

'This,' he said, bayoneting us with an icy glare, 'is the Tarzan Course. Pay attention to your instructors and there'll be no accidents.'

'I wonder where the apes are,' muttered Spider who was next to me.

'Fuck the apes, where's Jane?' said Porky who was standing by Spider. 'I haven't had a good jump for ages.'

Looking around I muttered, 'I've a feeling you're gonna get more jumps than you bargained for.'

For the next hour Ding-Dong and Sony showed us the technique of climbing up the simple upright ropes. By using the correct grip with hands we soon got the hang of it. Then using a rope slung about six feet off the ground between two trees Sony, with one leg hanging down as a 'keel' and the other leg pushing on the rope, with consummate ease pulled himself across. Of course, at first when we tried it most of us fell off. This forced us to practise a 'regain' by hooking our leg up again over the rope. In due course, even wearing FSMO, most of us managed to slide our bodies to the other side. The only exception was Billy Stone. Even after several attempts he continued to fall off the rope. After failing for the seventh time he threw his rife down, and in an exasperated rage, cried, 'I'll never make it, sarg. I'm too fuckin' clumsy.'

'Calm down, Billy,' replied Ding-Dong quietly, 'and I'll show you again.'

Words of encouragement flowed from the others. 'You can do it, mon,' said Jock, 'just tak yer time, laddie and yerl, be OK.'

Meanwhile the rest of us swarmed through netting, jumped over walls, swung across trees, crawled under round hollow pipes before stepping carefully across narrow, slippery logs ten feet or so off the ground. Panting and sweating we came to the Toggle Bridge and waited for Billy, who had eventually managed to negotiate the rope crossing.

The Toggle Bridge consisted of three ropes. Two of these served as arm supports, the third was used to walk, or in most cases, lurch across a chasm. The whole was connected by a series of toggles. The river Akraig was roughly fifty yards wide. Twenty-five feet below, the clear, fast-flowing waters eddied over rocks before disappearing round a sharp bend.

'Now crossing over this little beauty is easy providin' yer do as I tell yer,' said Ding- Dong. 'Now watch and I'll show yers how it's done.'

Using footholds, Ding-Dong climbed a tree. He then reached out and began to walk across the bridge. With each step the bottom rope bent and twisted under his weight.

The bridge swayed precariously from side to side and for a fleeting moment I thought he would lose his balance.

'To be sure he's gonna fall in,' cried Paddy.

'Bollocks,' replied Wacker, 'any idiot can see he's done this before.'

'Who are yer callin' an idjit?' replied Paddy indignantly. 'Me ma was a good Protestant, so she was.'

Ding-Dong's progress was slow and deliberate. 'Notice how I keep the rope under me armpits,' he shouted when half way across. 'And see the way I use the toggles fer footholds.' When he reached the other side, he turned and waved. 'Nowt to it, lads,' he grinned. 'Now you lot 'ave a go.'

We crossed over in threes and fours. Spider, Porky and me were the first to go.

'Jesus Christ,' muttered Porky, 'I can't swim. If I fall in I'll bloody-well drown.'

'Try not to look down, then,' replied Spider, 'and whatever yer do, don't grab hold of me.'

Finally, after a balancing act that would have done any circus proud, we reached the other side of the bank. Paddy, Billy, Jock and Nutty Slack were the last group. The remainder of the troop having succeeded waited on the far side. With each jerky wobble we cheered them on. Suddenly, Paddy seemed to lose his foothold. His foot slipped between the ropes and with a startled cry he tumbled down and splashed into the water. For a few moments everyone was quiet. Then, as Paddy emerged spluttering and soaking wet but apparently unscathed, the outburst of laughter that followed was more out of relief than humour. Ding-Dong threw Paddy a rope and we pulled him up the bank.

'Now who's an idiot!' shouted Spider, handing Paddy a cigarette.

As we marched back to camp I overheard someone ask the CSMI, 'When do we do the Death Slide, sir?'

'When you've 'ad a good dinner, lad,' he replied. 'It'll giver you summat to spew up when you reach the top.'

Shortly after 1400 CSMI Frickleton and Sergeant Leaman led the troop out of the camp. Each was in FSMO and the CSMI carried a walkie-talkie. Ding-Dong and Sony Bissell brought up the rear. By the time we reached the Tarzan Course the rain was pelting down and a bitterly cold wind made my eyes water. Sony Bissell left the troop and we watched as he negotiated his way across the Toggle Bridge dropping down onto the far side of the river Arkaig. After squelching our way past the obstacles we had met earlier the troop stopped near a tall fir tree.

Everyone looked up. The lower branches had been removed. Footholds and handgrips had been cut into the slippery looking tree trunks. At the top was the underside of a small wooden platform. From here a taut rope, dripping beads of rain, stretched down across the river to where Sony stood.

'Bloody hell!' exclaimed Billy Stone. 'Surely we're not gonna climb up there in this weather. It must be fifty feet or more to that platform.'

'At least,' muttered Porky gazing upwards.

From the corner of my eye I saw Sergeant Leaman's pockmarked face break into a lazy grin. 'Thirty-five feet to be precise,' he said. Then still grinning he added, 'Now pay close attention.'

Everyone watched as Ding-Dong put on his FSMO and began to climb the tree. Sergeant Leaman continued. 'Note how he puts one hand at a time into the grips while placing his foot into the holds. Always have one hand in the grips at all times and don't look down.' Sergeant Leaman removed his Bergen and emptied a pile of toggle ropes onto the grass. 'Wrap one of these around your waist. When you get to the platform, take it off and put it over the rope, thread the toggle through the eye and make a hand strap, and when you push off keep your knees bent.' As he spoke he demonstrated every move. 'Now take a toggle each and try it.'

With a pale, anxious expression Billy Stone asked, 'What if it snaps, sarg?'

'Don't worry, Billy,' replied Sergeant Leaman, 'none of 'em have ever snapped believe me.'

'Aye, but there's always a first time,' I heard Billy mumble under his breath.

Everyone watched as Ding-Dong slowly climbed up the tree and stood on the platform. He grinned and gave us a cheery wave. Then, keeping his feet together and slightly bent, he pushed himself off the platform. Leaving a trail of rainwater spurting from the rope, he quickly glided across the narrow strip of river into the waiting arms of the Sony Bissell.

'There,' beamed Sergeant Leaman. 'What did I tell yer. Easy as fallin' off a log.'

'And just as slippery,' grunted Spider standing next to me.

The CSMI, who so far had left the talking to the others, broke his silence.

'Take your time,' he said, staring at us, 'Sergeant Leaman will be waiting to help you when you reach the platform. Do as he says and you'll be all right.'

Sergeant Leamnan grinned, then filled his empty Bergen with several large rocks. He then secured it over his shoulders, grabbed his rifle and stood at the base of the tree. 'See you all at the top,' he said. Then with surprising agility he climbed up the tree, stood on the platform and gave us a cheery wave.

'I always knew there was summat wrong with that feller,' said Paddy, who like the rest of us stood looking up. 'To be sure, the man's half mountain goat.'

We lined up in single file with Jock, Spider, Porky, Wacker and myself in the centre. Keeping my eyes on the bulky backside of Jock I began my ascent. Placing one boot into the foothold, I dug my fingers into the handgrip and pushed myself up. With each step I felt my Bergen and rifle drag me back and become heavier. With painstaking move clouds of vapour poured from my mouth as I gasped for breath.

'How d'yer feel, Doc?' Spider grunted from behind me.

'I think I've shit myself,' I replied.

'I already have,' panted Porky, 'can't yer smell it?'

'Bollocks,' I heard Wacker gasp, 'that's 'ow yer normally smell.'

'I don't like this at all,' I overheard Billy Stone cry. He was well in front of Nutty Slack and Paddy Malone.

'Neither do I,' gasped Nutty, 'but they don't hand out green berets fer nowt.'

My heart thumped against my ribcage as I slowly edged my way up the tree. My fingers felt numb with the cold and the blood pounded in my head. Still looking up I saw the first man to arrive at the platform and slide down the rope into the waiting arms of Sony Bissell. Please God, I muttered to myself, don't let me fall.

What happened next was over in seconds but seemed an age. With my gaze firmly fixed on Jock's rump I suddenly heard a blood-curdling scream as a blurred figure fell past me. This was quickly followed by a dull thud as the body hit the ground. With the sudden realisation of what had happened my mouth went dry and I froze, too shocked to speak.

'Jesus Christ,' yelled Jock, 'some poor bugger's fell down.'

With mounting trepidation I looked down. Some thirty feet below was a denim-clad figure lying in the bracken. His Bergen had fallen forward obscuring his face. He lay quite still with both legs splayed out at an odd angle. Before looking away I caught a glimpse of CSMI Frickleton kneeling by the man's side.

'Keep moving,' yelled Sergeant Leaman from the platform. 'And don't look down.'

'Who is it?' someone yelled.

'I'm not sure,' came a reply.

Once again the sharp voice of Sergeant Leaman shouted down, 'Keep moving and think what yer doing.'

For a fleeting second I felt slightly faint. My body started to tremble and I dug my fingers into the grips and held on for dear life. Pull yourself together, I told myself, or you'll be the next one to fall. Gradually I inched my way upwards until I saw the underside of the platform. I stopped and watched as Jock's burly figure climbed up, disappeared momentarily from view before hurtling downwards.

Then it was my turn.

Anxious and sweating I climbed onto the platform.

'Wh… who was it that fell, sarg?' I gasped.

'Never mind about that now, Doc,' he said in a calm voice, 'clear your head, concentrate, and you'll be all right.'

He removed the toggle rope from around my waist, placed it over the rope, then threaded the toggle through the eye at the other end to make a hanging strap for sliding down.

The rain had eased off but a sharp, bitterly cold wind bit into my face. Below the river appeared a narrow strip of glistening water surrounded by a dense forest. I paid very little attention to the rolling hills and mountains. Instead I grasped the strap, stood at the edge of the platform and fixed my eyes on the rope descending at an acute angle across the river.

'Hold tight and away yer go, Doc,' cried Sergeant Leaman.

Suddenly I felt my stomach contract and my bowels loosen. With my heart bouncing against my ribs I bent my knees and pushed myself off the platform. The toggle bit into my wrist as my body was propelled downwards. I watched transfixed as the riverbank quickly became bigger. Within a few seconds the heels of my boots sank into the grassy verge as Ding-Dong grabbed me around the waist. My whole body was shaking and as I released the toggle strap I thought I would faint.

'There now, Doc,' said Ding-Dong, still holding on to me. 'That wasn't too bad was it?'

I didn't reply. Instead I looked across to where Jock and a few others stood silently smoking. 'Who was it?' I asked, staring at them. 'Who was it that fell down?'

'Pete Cronin,' muttered Nutty Slack, staring vacantly at the ground. 'One minute he were in front of me, the next thing he were gone.' He paused and with his hand trembling took a deep drag of his cigarette. 'I didn't see his foot slip or anything. He just fell...'

For a while we stood around too shocked to speak. I didn't know Pete well but somehow I felt I had lost a close friend.

Suddenly Sergeant Leaman's harsh voice shook us out of our reverie.

'Right you lot,' snapped Sergeant Leaman, 'Pull yersells together. We're gonna march across the bridge a do the bloody thing again.'

'But sarg...' I cried, 'Pete is still...'

'Just do as I say and shut up,' replied Sergeant Leaman, 'these things 'appen. Now fall in.'

By the time we reached the other side of the river we saw an ambulance splash through a muddy track towards the camp.

Everyone, including myself, nervously struggled up the tree again and completed a second slide without incident.

There was no funeral. An inquest was held. Each of us went before Colonel Vaughan and two officers and gave our version of what happened. Pete's body was eventually sent to his next of kin and all that remained was his empty bed-space and locker.

CHAPTER TWENTY-FIVE

At the end of our first week we were marched into a field strewn with rocks and sweet smelling purple heather. Sergeant Leaman carried the ubiquitous 'walkie-talkie'. Ding-Dong and Jock carried a heavy-looking wooden box. We entered a long trench at the end of which was a small dugout. About thirty yards away was a rusting Churchill tank. Its gun was missing and the side was pitted with what looked like small shell holes.

The December rain had stopped but the trench was dank and muddy. We stood around while Ding-Dong opened the box.

'All of you except Doc here will have thrown one of these,' he said taking out a hand grenade. 'The standard 36 Mills hand grenade. As you know, because of its shape and segment casing it's nicknamed the "pineapple".' He paused, smiled and tossed it in the air and caught it. 'Its filled with amatol and has a 7-second fuse which is activated by pulling out the pin, so.' To everyone's horror Ding-Dong jerked out the pin allowing the safety lever to shoot up. He then dropped the grenade onto the ground. With a sudden outburst of startled cries and expletives everyone made a mad scramble over the side of the trench.

'Come back you daft buggers,' laughed Ding-Dong picking up the grenade. 'The bloody thing hasn't got a detonator in it.'

'How the hell were we to know that?' replied Spider. His normal ruddy complexion was ashen and he was shaking like a leaf.

'Sergeant Bellringer did that to keep you on yer toes,' interrupted Sergeant Leaman. 'Now pay attention.' After inserting a small primer into the base of the grenade he removed the pin. Keeping his fingers firmly over the safety lever he stood with legs apart, drew his arm back and lobbed the grenade out of the trench. A metallic click could be clearly heard as the lever sprung up activating the weapon. Everyone instinctively ducked. Shortly afterwards a loud explosion rent the air. We looked over the side of the trench and saw the tank engulfed in black smoke and dust.

'Bullseye,' beamed Sergeant Leaman. 'Now let's see if you can do as good.'

Ding-Dong picked up the box of grenades and carried it to the dugout at the end of the trench. We lined up in single file. I was at the back. As Ding-Dong called each marine we went forward to the dugout. Sergeant Leaman primed a grenade and handed it to them. The rest stood back and cowered down and watched the grenade being thrown. The throw was usually accurate and the marine returned with a satisfied grin on his face.

When it came to be Spider's turn, Porky turned to him and said, 'A pint says yer miss the tank, mate.'

'You're on,' replied Spider.

Spider's name was called out. With his usual cheery grin he threw the grenade and won the bet.

'Nowt to it, pal,' grinned Spider as he passed Porky, 'just like bowlin' an off break at Lords.'

By this time everyone except Billy Stone and me had thrown a grenade. Billy was in front of me. His face was flushed and he was sweating profusely.

'You look nervous, Billy,' I said, 'anything wrong?'

'N… no, Doc,' he replied, licking his lips, 'I'm OK, it's just that at Dunkirk…' Ding-Dong calling his name abruptly interrupted him.

We watched as Billy accepted the grenade from Sergeant Leaman, pulled out the pin and put his right hand over the safety lever. Suddenly, with his arm drawn back he froze. Still holding the grenade he fell against the dugout wall.

'I can't do it, sarg,' he cried, 'I've 'ad enough. I can't do it, I tell yer.' His eyes were glazed and he sounded hysterical.

'For Chisssake, don't let go of the grenade, Billy,' cried Sergeant Leaman.' Then reaching out with a hand, went on, 'Here, let me put my hand over yours, then we can both throw it.'

With both eyes blazing with fear, Billy flattened his back against the wall. 'No, no,' he yelled, 'keep away, keep away from me.'

Suddenly I was gripped with dread.

'Jesus,' I heard someone say, 'if he lets go of that thing he'll blow himself and the rest of us to kingdom come.'

'Everyone out of the trench at the double,' barked Ding-Dong.

The men needed no extra bidding. In a matter of seconds they cleared the trench and took cover behind some rocks. Ding-Dong followed them. I remained behind.

'Come on, Doc,' shouted Ding-Dong, 'you as well.'

However, I didn't move. For some reason as a medic I thought I might help.

Meanwhile, I heard Sergeant Leaman's voice pleading with Billy to throw the grenade. But Billy refused to do so.

Just then I remembered Billy showing me the photographs of his wife and children. 'Let me talk to him, sarg,' I pleaded, 'I think I could help...'

'Get back, Doc,' yelled Ding-Dong, 'for fuck's sake, move yersell.'

I ignored Ding-Dong and went to the dugout entrance.

Sergeant Leaman, his face gleaming with sweat, glanced at me and frantically waved me back.

'Bugger off, Doc and don't come any closer,' he yelled, 'that's an order.'

My mouth felt like sandpaper and I thought my heart would burst. Nevertheless, I paid no attention to the sergeant and looked at Billy. He was standing half-bent a few yards away against the wall. As I approached I noticed his eyes were glazed and the hand in which he held the grenade was shaking.

'Billy,' I said trying to sound calm. 'Remember showing me those photographs of your missus and kids?'

'Don't come any nearer,' cried Billy, glancing at the grenade, 'I'll drop this, I swear I will.'

'Those photos, Billy,' I said, 'have you got them on you?'

'Yes,' he stuttered, 'yes I have, so what?'

With my eyes alternatively focusing on Billy, Sergeant Leaman and the grenade, I ventured a little closer. 'If you don't let the sarg and me help you,' I replied, 'you'll never see them again. You'll blow yourself and us to pieces.'

My words seemed to fall on deaf ears. Billy didn't reply. Instead he stared at me, straightened up and pressed himself harder against the wall.

Sergeant Leaman nervously bit his lip then looked first at me then at Billy. 'Listen to what the Doc says, son, and throw the grenade,' he said. 'If anything happens to you, your family'll be on their own. Your kids will have no dad and you'll never see them or your missus again.'

'You *do* want to see them again, don't you, Billy?' I asked pleadingly.

The words of Sergeant Leaman and myself appeared to have some affect. Billy nodded then shot a hurried glance at both of us. 'Yes,' he gasped, 'I do, but I've 'ad enough. I've just 'ad enough.' He then turned around and hurled the grenade out of the dugout. He then scrambled up the wall in an effort to get out. Sergeant Leaman and myself threw our arms around his waist and dragged him down into the mud.

'Easy does it, Billy,' said the sergeant, 'you'll be OK. Don't worry.'

Ding-Dong and the others appeared, relief written on their faces.

'Anyone hurt?' asked Ding-Dong.

'No,' answered the sergeant, 'we're OK, aren't we Billy?'

Billy didn't answer. Instead he lay on the muddy ground convulsed in tears.

Just then an ambulance arrived with an army doctor and an orderly. After a brief word with Sergeant Leaman, Jock and me helped Billy up. The orderly opened the back door of the ambulance and we helped Billy who was trembling like a leaf, inside.

As the ambulance drove away Wacker made a poignant remark. 'Poor bugger, he said, 'I guess he just reached breaking point.'

'Aye,' answered Porky, 'and if this fuckin' war goes on much longer he won't be the last. Let's get back and 'ave a pint.'

'Talkin' of pints, Porky,' said Spider, 'I think you owe me one.'

We never saw Billy again. We learned later he was RTU then hospitalised.

CHAPTER TWENTY-SIX

The time was 0800 and the date Monday 16 December 1943. Ourselves and several other troops were fallen in on the parade ground. An umbrella of high pressure hung over the region. The temperature fell below zero and when we washed the water almost froze on our faces. A bitter easterly wind swept down across the square blanketing everything in a veneer of frost. Overlooking the camp, forests of pine and fir glittered like diamonds, and the mountains, shrouded in a swirling mist resembled a scene from a Christmas calendar.

Needless to say training continued as normal – with the emphasis on speed marches. The week before our troop had completed a 9-mile march in just over two hours. This didn't please Lieutenant Grayson or the instructors.

'You must do better,' barked the officer. 'This morning we'll be marching to Spean Bridge and back, a distance of just over twelve miles.' As he spoke streams of vapour poured form his mouth and nostrils. He paused, 'And it must be done in less than two hours after which you'll dig defensive positions and prepare to repel a counter attack. On completion CSMI Frickleton and his team will introduce you to the delights of unarmed combat.' He then turned, swapped salutes with the CSMI, and marched off the parade ground.

CSMI Frickleton tucked his pace-stick firmly under his left arm, turned and faced us. 'A troop in front have challenged us,' he said with a slight chuckle. 'They're doing the same march as ourselves. They'll set off a minute before we do. Sergeant Bell ringer and Sergeant Leaman will lead you and it'll be up to you to catch the army lads. Colonel Vaughan will keep time from his office.'

Just then one of the soldiers in A troop turned around, and yelled, 'And the losers buy the beer. OK with you fellas?'

'Have yer money ready, pal, yee'll need it,' replied Jock.

This brought a chorus of sniggers all round that was quickly silenced by the CSMI bringing us to attention.

'A twelve-mile march, 'mumbled Spider, 'what does he think we are, fuckin' gazelles?'

'Stop moanin', will yers,' replied Paddy, 'if those pongos beat us we'll never hear the end of it.'

Despite the bitterly cold weather everyone wore denim battledress, boots and cap comforters. Stamping our feet to keep warm we watched the A troop set off in single file. Standing outside the guardroom the chunky figure of Colonel Vaughan received and returned the salute of each troop as they marched past the guardroom. Passing the line of 'graves' I noticed a cross didn't have a name on it.

'That one's waiting for you,' I said to Spider who was in front of me.

'Many more of these soddin' speed marches,' he grunted, 'and you may be right.'

Keeping our eyes on A troop we marched out the camp, crossed the bridge at Gairlochy and up the long macadam road that wound up a steep hill. On either side stretched hills covered in the frosty glare of the early morning sunlight. Away to our right Achnacarry Castle with its turrets and crenellated walls loomed dark and foreboding against the pallid blueness of the sky.

In front I could see clouds of vaporised breath almost obscuring the line of flushed faces and bobbing cap comforters. The steady chomp of boots echoed around as we maintained a steady pace behind A troop. When they broke into double time so did we. At one point several men almost lost their balance on patches of treacherous ice. When we reached the summit of the hill a panorama of rolling whiteness stretched out before us and in the distance the snowy peak of Ben Nevis poked uninvitingly into the sky.

'Come on, lads,' shouted Ding-Dong, 'sing sing or show us yer ring.' He immediately broke into *Run Rabbit Run,* to which everyone joined in. *Roll Out The Barrel* followed this. Whenever we broke into double time the singing died down as the men caught their breath.

As we crossed the bridge spanning Lake Arkaig, flocks of squawking gannets swooped down, disturbing the placid waters and sending circular ripples eddying towards the riverbank.

'I'm sure they're bloody vultures,' gasped Paddy Malone who was behind me.

'I shouldna worry, Paddy,' I heard Jock say, 'they dinna fancy Irishmen, their skin's too bloody thick.'

On and on I trudged ignoring everything except the bouncing pack of Spider's Bergen in front and the collective crunching noise of boots biting into the road.

'How yer doin back there?' gasped Spider without turning around.

'So far so good, mate,' I muttered.

By this time sweat was pouring down my face and my denim battledress clung to me like a second skin. My rifle, slung over my shoulder, bounced awkwardly against my left hip. The Bergen felt like a ton.

'Come on, the pongos are pullin' away from us,' yelled Sergeant Leaman, 'don't let the Corps down. Double time.'

Sure enough A troop were now about fifty yards in front and going strong. We watched as they reached the summit of the hill that led down to Spean Bridge.

'Let's catch the bastards up,' cried someone, and without being told, everyone picked up the pace.

Suddenly, I sensed a feeling of determination running through everyone. The pace increased. The gasps, grunts and moans became louder as the distance between the two troops shortened.

'Keep it up,' yelled Sergeant Leaman, 'we're catching the buggers up.'

A glance up showed the soldiers some twenty yards in front. However, despite our efforts A troop reached Spean Bridge first and in good order, turned around.

'What's the matter, Royals,' cried a soldier as they passed us. 'Got sore feet?'

'Can't wait fer that pint,' yelled another.

The two sergeants in front of A troop grinned across at Ding-Dong and Sergeant Leaman. 'See you two in the mess,' shouted one of them.

'Not if we see you first,' bellowed Ding-Dong.

At Spean Bridge a few locals muffled against the cold, smiled and waved. The time on the railway clock read 0900. We had covered the first seven miles in an hour. All we had to do now to complete the exercise was to overtake the army lads and clock up a similar time on the way back to camp. With A troop still twenty yards in front, we turned around and set off up the hill.

'Backs into it lads,' yelled Ding-Dong.

The time for wise cracks had finished. Ignoring aching limbs nobody spoke and the pace quickened. Gradually the gap between the two troops lessened.

At the foot of the hill we finally caught the army lads up. For the next few miles we marched side by side. Too tired to speak a few swapped determined glances at one another.

The sergeants of both troops continued to urge their men on. As we approached the banks of the river Arkaig we knew the camp wasn't far away.

'Big push, now, A troop,' bellowed the army sergeant.

'No let up, lads, ' yelled Ding-Dong, 'keep goin', you can do it.'

At that moment the sharp retort of gunfire accompanied by the drone of aircraft attracted everyone's attention. Both troops slowed down as heads turned upwards. Set against a clear blue sky two aircraft dodged about leaving in their wake trails of wispy vapour while emitting deadly bursts of cannon fire. The RAF roundels could be clearly seen on the wings of the plane behind while the one in front displaying black crosses on its pale grey fuselage was obviously a German. Like two huge bats they darted about intent on killing each other.

'It's a bloody dog fight,' cried Porky.

'Look,' shouted one of the soldiers pointing to the sky. 'That's a Spit on the tale of Jerry,' shouted a marine.

'Aye, so it is,' yelled Sergeant Leaman, 'and the Jerry's a Messerschsmitt 109. The bastards shot us up in North Africa.'

The unmistakable elliptical wings of a Spitfire glinted in the sunlight as it swooped towards its prey. In doing so tiny yellow flames of gunfire flickered along both wings. Just as quick the German fighter took evasion action by banking quickly away to its left. But the Spitfire pilot wouldn't be fooled. Quick as lightning he dived after his quarry emitting bursts of fire. This immediately brought loud cheers from both troops.

'Nail the bastard,' yelled Spider jumping up and down like an excited schoolboy.

I was suddenly caught up in the frenzied excitement and along with the rest shouted also. Others took off their cap comforters, and waved them while yelling their heads off.

However, what happened was over so quickly it took everyone by surprise.

The German turned in an arc and for a few seconds seemed to hang in the air, then dived, and with all guns blazing, came straight at us.

'Take cover,' yelled Ding-Dong. 'Everyone into the side of the road.'

For a second I stood transfixed as the wings and the flurry of propellers roared nearer. Just then I felt a pair of strong arms grab me and in a flash I found myself lying in the undergrowth being showered by speckles of frost. I closed my eyes and tried to bury my head in the frozen turf as the ear-splitting thud of bullets rattled close by. Then, it was all over. The whine of the aircraft quickly faded. I opened my eyes and saw Jock's wiry features staring at me. He had both arms around me and was grinning like a Cheshire cat.

'You know, Doc,' he said with a twinkle in his eyes, 'I ken they're using live ammo on the course, but this is carrying things too fuckin' far.'

Except for Spider who had a small splinter wound in his leg, nobody was hurt.

The sergeant decided to call off the race. Instead we marched back to camp together. As we passed the line of 'graves' next to the guardroom, Spider tapped me on the shoulder. 'If one o' them bullets had been any closer,' he said dryly, 'that cross really would've 'ad my name on it.'

After dinner we fell ready for unarmed combat instruction.

We were in Iris grouped around Lieutenant Grayson. 'This lethal-looking weapon I'm holding in my hand is the commando knife you've no doubt heard about.' In his hand was a sharp-pointed, six-inch, double-edged knife with a small handle and cross guard. As he spoke the blade caught the rays of the sun momentarily turning its dark metal into dazzling silver. The officer continued, 'This knife was designed by Captains Fairbarin and Sykes. It is also the shoulder symbol worn by all commandos. These two officers also introduced their special form of unarmed you are about to learn. The two instructors by my side will introduce you to the delights of using both.' He then handed the knife to one of the sergeants and left the hut.

Both sergeants looked tanned and fit. One was medium height, lean and wiry with weather-beaten features, the other was nearly six feet tall, stocky, with a black moustache. The taller of the two grinned and pointing the knife at us waved it slowly from side to side. In a voice straight from the Highlands, he began, 'My name is Staff Sergeant Davie Davidson and this,' he paused and glanced at his colleague, 'is Sergeant Archie McClelland. Now, afore we show yer how to kill wee this thing, yee'll need to know a few little tricks o' the trade.' He then placed the knife in a small leather sheath which he wore on a belt and he glanced at Archie who took over.

'Forget any nice judo moves yer may have seen in the pictures,' said Archie. As he spoke his dark eyes narrowed. 'Yer dealing with a ruthless enemy and yer job is ta kill the buggers any way yee can.'

For half an hour Archie and Davie demonstrated how to deliver killer blows to the body, how to get free from grasps, holds and throws. We then paired off and with a series of loud grunts and groans, tried them out on one another.

'Don't worry, Jock,' I said trying to get a grip on him, 'remember I'm a medic. If I do you any damage I'll give you first aid.'

Like a typical Scott he replied, 'I dinna mind what yer do, laddie so long as yee dinna damage me wallet.' At which point he turned and threw me to the ground.

The last session concentrated on the use of the commando knife.

'You can keep it in a sheath behind your left shoulder, or by your side. When you go to the holding station at Wrexham you'll be issued with one.'

Without calling for a volunteer, Davie hauled Wacker to his feet. Standing behind him he used one hand to pull back Wacker's head. With his other hand he raised the knife as if to plunge it into the side of Wacker's neck.

'Sever the jugular vein,' said Davie, 'and he'll bleed to death in minutes.' He then lowered the knife to Wacker's side. 'Alternatively you can shove it up hard into his liver and kidneys.'

Wacker's face paled and his eyes widened. 'Fuck off, Staff,' came his muffled cry, 'I'm an only son and me mam 'asn't got me insured.'

The knife was passed around. It was surprisingly light. I grasped the handle wondering if I would have the courage to use it.

On Christmas Day many lads received parcels from home. Mum sent me woollen socks, gloves and a pullover. But the best present of all was news of Adele. Mum's letter contained one written in English to her by Emile. My hand shook as I sat on my bed reading over and over again Emile's words telling me Adele was safe and sound. He also wrote saying Adele loved me and would wait for me forever.

I could hardly contain my excitement.

'She's safe, she's safe,' I cried to nobody in particular.

The lads in the troop all knew about Adele. I had even showed some of them her medallion.

'Lucky you,' groaned Porky, 'my missus says she's got a pair of nylons from a friend.' With a curious expression on his face, he added, 'I wonder who her friend is…'

The news about Adele sustained me over the Festive Season. The excellent Christmas dinner followed by beer and whisky increased my state of euphoria, so much so Spider had to hold me up outside the mess while I vomited my guts up.

With only three weeks to go before the end of the course the training intensified. Live bullets whizzed over our heads as we continued to negotiate the assault course, dig foxholes and zoom down the Death Slide. We learnt the art of camouflage, how to bake a hedgehog and live off the land.

'When you're in the field and your rations run out,' said Ding-Dong, 'believe you me you'll eat anything.'

'Even rats?' chimed in Jim Wade.

Ding-Dong laughed. 'Aye,' he replied, 'and very tasty they are too.'

Using an old LCA (Landing Craft Assault) mock landings became a regular evolution. Splashing through the freezing waters of the river Arkaig we stormed ashore yelling obscenities at an imaginary enemy. To this was added night exercises using small, collapsible canvas Goatley boats (named after the man who designed them).

Despite the January snow, speed marches increased to fifteen miles. Our level of physical fitness had obviously improved as we managed to cover this distance in less than three hours.

With less than two weeks to go CSMI Sammy Leach and Sergeant Spike Pike, two stocky, no-nonsense climbing instructors introduced us to mountain climbing. We learned that Sammy had been a steeplejack before the war. Spike was an ex-paratrooper who had climbed Snowdonia.

Armed with a Neil Robertson stretcher and several large coils of rope we marched out of the camp.

'Bloody hell!' exclaimed Wacker, when we arrived at an outcrop of snow-covered rocks. 'You'd 'ave to be super human to climb that lot.'

'Och away wee yer,' replied Jock, 'where I live in the Highlands that's only a wee ant hill.'

Between them Sammy and Spike showed us the basic skills of roping up, scrambling, boulder climbing and most dangerous of all, abseiling.

Our first attempt at this was from a rock face ten feet high. Spike secured a long stretch of rope around the base of a fir tree and allowed the rest to fall over the rock face. He then took out a leather gauntlet and slipped it to the crook of his right arm. 'This is to prevent rope burns, now pay close attention to what I do,' he said. He then placed part of the rope between his legs, up around his right thigh and through the crook of his right elbow. After taking up the front part of the rope with his left hand he walked to the edge of the rock.

'When I do this,' he paused and bent his elbow, 'the rope is checked and I can't move.' He lent forward to demonstrate the point. 'When I release it watch how I'm able to almost walk horizontal to the ground.' In a series of small jumps he bounded down the rock face onto the frost-covered grass below, unravelled the rope and grinned. 'Come on,' he yelled from below, 'let's see you how you shape up.'

My first attempt was a disaster. I failed to check the rope properly and tumbled onto the slippery ground. However, I wasn't the only one. Spider, Porky and a few others all made clumsy descents. After several successful attempts we moved to higher ground and managed to abseil relatively easy without breaking any bones.

The culmination of the course was what Ding-Dong called the 'Opposed Landing'.

'This is a full-scale night exercise,' said Ding-Dong addressing the X troop outside the hut. The time was 1600. Ding-Dong continued, 'All weapons will be checked and double-checked. Faces will be blackened, pockets turned out to ensure no incriminating items could be used in case you're captured. Each man will be issued with a shell dressing.' He paused, glanced ominously around then added, 'As usual live ammunition will be used so keep yer 'eads down. Two lads were unfortunately killed last year.'

'I don't like the sound of that, mate,' I muttered, casting a wary glance at Spider. 'Whose side are they on anyway?'

'Relax Doc,' replied Spider. 'Just think after this we'll get our green berets and maybe a bit of leave.'

'That's if we're still alive,' added Porky who was standing next to Spider.

After supper three trainee troops marched out of the camp under the eagle eyes of Colonel Vaughan. Ding-Dong and Sergeant Leaman led the way. Everyone except me carried a rifle. Earlier I had been issued with a Colt 45 and medical valise containing amongst other items, monoject ampoules of morphia.

'I only hope I won't need this, sarg,' I said to Ding-Dong slipping the valise straps over my shoulder.

'Don't worry, Doc,' he replied confidently, 'you won't.'

Shining through the darkness a bright full moon illuminated the frost on the fir trees. An icy cold northern wind stung my face numbing my cheeks. We arrived at Bunarkaig on the banks of Loch Lochy and embarked in the small Goatley canvas boats and paddled line ahead towards the centre of the loch. All was deadly quiet. Shafts of moonlight filtered through the trees casting an eerie glow on the placid waters. All that could be heard was the dull plod of paddles and the occasional cry of wildlife.

Nutty Slack nudged me with his elbow. 'Piece of piss,' he whispered.

At that moment all bedlam broke loose. Like a scene from Bonfire Night yellow and orange light from flares burst above the invading party. For a while the blackened faces of our party looked more like travelling minstrels than commandos. Heads instinctively cowered down as a Vickers machine-gun spat out a lethal welcome. Jets of water from mock mortar fire rocked the boat (we learned later these and the other pyrotechnics were pre-arranged). The light from the flares slowly faded to be replaced by white, green and red lines of tracers.

'Fuck me,' came the voice of Spider, 'it they fire any lower, they'll blow our heads off.'

I glanced up and saw pearly arcs of coloured tracer bullets whizzing uncomfortably close. To the cacophony was added multi-coloured detonations of thunder flashes.

'Bloody hell, mon,' screamed Jock, 'are they tryin' ta kill us or frighten us ta death?'

'Both,' cried someone.

Then came another surprise. As the boats bumped ashore the awesome whine of Stuka dive-bombers filled the night air.

'Cor Blimey,' yelled someone as we scrambled onto the muddy bank, 'don't tell me we're bein' bombed as well.'

As we scrambled ashore Ding-Dong, who was in front, kept yelling, 'Fast as you can, lads. Get off the beach.'

Just then the intermittent sound of Bren gun fire added to the mind-boggling din. My boots were sinking into the soft sand making progress off the beach difficult. Many marines had the same problem and moved slowly. I turned and saw Ding-Dong waving us forward. Then, quite abruptly he collapsed into the sand clutching his right leg. 'I've been hit,' he cried, 'for Chrisake, I've been hit...'

Straight away I stopped and kneeled down beside him. 'What's up, sarg?' I cried.

His face, outlined in the moonlight, was contorted with pain.

'It's me leg,' he gasped, 'a bullet must have ricocheted off a tree or summat,' he gasped.

Thinking the accident was an exercise the others glanced at us and carried on up the bank into the woods. Meanwhile the sound of 'battle' continued. Bullets buzzed through the trees amidst the flashes of fireworks and the sickening scream of the Stukas.

Ding-Dong lay on the ground his hand over the lower part of his leg. Thin lines of blood oozed through his fingers. I quickly took out a shell dressing from my trouser pocket and bound it over the wound.

'Lie back, sarg,' I said, 'I'm gonna give you summat that'll ease the pain.' With difficulty I opened the top of his Denison smock and shirt and managed to administer a shot morphia into the upper part of his shoulder.

Meanwhile the raiding party with fixed bayonets disappeared into the undergrowth yelling obscenities. Sergeant Leaman and two other instructors suddenly appeared, and stood silhouetted against the grey sky. 'Is he pulling your leg, Doc?' asked Sergeant Leaman staring down at Ding-Dong.

'Fuck off,' retorted Ding-Dong, 'one of them so-called marksmen of yours can't aim straight.'

The sergeant's voice took on a serious note. 'Sorry, mate,' he replied, 'how bad is he, Doc?'

'He's been hit in the leg,' I replied, placing another shell dressing over the other one. 'Better get him to camp sharpish.'

One of the instructors radioed for a jeep and a doctor. The others went away and reappeared with two army medics carrying a Neil Robertson stretcher.

'It's only a scratch, said Ding-Dong trying unsuccessfully to stand up.

Despite Ding-Dong's protestations, we managed to strap him into the stretcher and carry him to Goatley boat. On the other side of the river a jeep and a medical team was waiting. I quickly explained to the army doctor what had happened. With the help of Sergeant Leaman and two army medics we lifted Ding-Dong onto the jeep and drove off. As we drove into the camp, I looked at Ding-Dong who was smoking a cigarette, grinned and said, 'Now what was that you said about not wanting the medical valise?'

By the time I arrived in the mess everyone had returned from the exercise. I told them what had happened and that Ding-Dong's injury was not serious. That evening everyone including the instructors celebrated the end of the course.

'Remember,' said CSMI Frickleton, raising his glass of beer, 'you're now a commando, the most elite band of fighting men in the British Army.'

Next morning, nursing hangovers, we piled kit bags and packs into trucks. Those members of what was once X Troop were being transferred to HOC (Holding Operational Commando) in Wrexham for specialist training. I would join them after being granted a fortnight's leave.

'Lucky bugger,' quipped Wacker, 'you'll be gettin' yer leg over with judies from the Grafton, while we're floggin' our guts out.'

'Us medics need time to rest our brains,' I jokingly replied shaking his hand and those of Spider and the others.

We had now been issued with the coveted green berets. I was also given a full battle dress, khaki shirts that itched like hell and a pair of black SV (Silent Venture) boots. On each shoulder flash, written in white on a blue background, were the words ROYAL NAVY COMMANDO. With a feeling of immense pride I touched one of them and felt ten feet tall.

CHAPTER TWENTY-SEVEN

By the time mum and dad had become used to me in khaki my leave was almost over. However, when I told them about being posted to some place near Wrexham, their eyes lit up.

'That's wonderful, love,' said mum, 'Wrexham's only forty miles away in North Wales. Maybe we'll see more of you.'

With a pensive expression on his face dad replied, 'Aye, but fer how long. I see we've broke out from Anzio, the Americans 'ave landed in them islands in the Pacific and the Ruskies 'ave knocked the Jerries back at Stalingrad. Now there's lots of talk about a second front, what with all these Yanks here an' all…'

At the pictures newsreels showing masses of GIs and material being landed from American Liberty boats were a common feature. The *Liverpool Echo* printed photographs of Commonwealth troops giving a cheery thumbs-up while disembarking from liners previously used by the rich and famous.

'Yes,' added mum, 'on the wireless anyone who had holiday photographs or postcards of the continent was asked to send them to the war office. I sent those you took in Normandy, I don't suppose they'll be much use though.'

The mention of Normandy immediately made me think of Adele. It had been four years since I last saw her. Some nights I saw her in my dreams. The dreams were always the same. Dressed in a shimmering white gown she would reach out for me, her beguiling brown eyes wet with tears. On each occasion I would frantically run towards her only to see her gradually fade away. When I woke up my face was always wet with perspiration. Then, gently touching her medallion around my neck, I would close my eyes and pray she was safe.

In a perverse way I was glad when my leave was over. Gordon was still away in the army, and although I became friendly with several service lads I met in the pub, I couldn't help thinking about Spider and the rest of the troop.

I arrived at the Holding Operational Commando base on 4 March 1944. Mounds of barbed wire surrounded an area officially known as Hightown Barracks. This consisted of numerous Nissen huts and wooden barrack rooms dotted around a large concrete parade ground. Several squads of marine and army commandos were being drilled and the familiar sound of small arms and machine gun fire echoed from the hills outside the camp.

At the guardroom a tall, fresh-faced young marine officer met me. Glancing at a clipboard his blue pale eyes broke into a boyish grin. 'You've been posted to 41 Commando, Doc,' he said in a plumy posh voice, then added, 'my name's Lieutenant Borrett and you'll be in P Troop.' He then ordered a small stocky marine commando to show me where to go.

On the way to the hut the marine introduced himself. 'Me name's Pete Nightingale,' he said. Then with a toothy grin added, 'Don't laugh but the lads call me Tweety, can't think why.'

Needless to say I did laugh.

There was nobody in the hut and except for two stovepipe fires it looked the same as those in Achnacarry.

No sooner had I slung my gear onto a vacant bunk than the door burst open and in poured a crowd of marine commandos. I instantly recognised the cheeky grin of Spider. Behind him came Wacker, Paddy and Nutty Slack and several others from

Achnacarry. Their sunburnt faces were streaked with sweat and they were talking loudly.

'Bugger me,' cried Spider, seeing me, 'look wot the wind's blown in!'

The bulky figure of Jock Forbes, plus Porky Saunders and Taffy Ball joined him. By the time I had shaken their hands my arms ached.

'What's it like here?' I asked looking at them. 'I've been told I'm P Troop, 41 Commando. How about you lot?'

'Same as us,' answered Porky, touching the pink strip covering his left shoulder epaulet. 'Ding-Dong and Sergeant Leaman are some of P Troop's senior NCOs.'

'Sit down, Doc,' said Spider passing me a cigarette and lighting it, 'and I'll put yer in the picture.'

I did so and took a deep drag of my cigarette. Spider went on. 'There's roughly five 'undred in the commando,' he said. 'Each troop has fifty men. This includes three officers.' He paused and exhaled a steam of blue cigarette smoke. 'P Troop's officers are Lieutenant Grayson, who was at Achnacarry and Lieutenant Dieze from South Africa who drinks like a fish, and Lieutenant Borrett, an ex Oxford Don.'

'Och and dinna ferget old RSM Grundy,' interrupted Jock.

'Shut up yer haggis yaffler,' cried Spider, 'one man, one song. RSM Grundy is an old-timer and has seen service in Africa and Italy so watch yer step. Then there's six junior NCOs and us lot. The officer in charge of P Troop is Captain Slolay, and the CO is Lieutenant Colonel Gray. He's as tough as teak but a bloody good officer.'

'Who are the other commandos here?' I asked.

'There's 45, and several army commandos,' replied Spider.

'What do you do all day?'

'Train, thats what we do,' answered Spider, 'me, Wacker and Nutty are in a Bren gun team. Paddy, Jock and the others make up the Vickers and mortar men.'

'And snipers,' interrupted Taffy Ball, 'don't forget us snipers.'

'Some fuckin' sniper,' laughed Tweety, 'he fell out of a tree and almost knocked Ding-Dong out.'

'What's it like in Wrexham?' I asked.

'Not too bad,' replied Nutty, 'but the Yanks stationed in a camp near ours get all the girls.'

Just then a heavily built officer with dark features and a moustache came in. Everyone immediately sprung to attention. 'Stand easy. Which one of you is LSBA Robertson?' he asked looking around. As he spoke his brown moustache twitched slightly. 'I am, sir,' I replied.

'Right, 'replied the officer. 'The CO wants to see you chop right away. Follow me, and by the way,' he added, 'I'm Lieutenant Slolay your Troop Leader.'

The CO's office was located in a Nissen hut close to an old Victorian building that was used to house the officers. Lieutenant Slolay knocked on a door and we went inside.

Lieutenant Colonel Gray was sat behind a desk cluttered with papers. He was broad-shouldered with dark hair greying at each temple. As I entered he looked up from a paper he was studying. He casually returned my salute and told me to stand easy. His eyes were startling blue under black eyebrows, in a hawk-like face tanned the colour of mahogany, and on the left breast of his uniform were two rows of medal ribbons.

'Glad to see you, Robertson,' he said in a clear, well-modulated voice. 'With the exception of 45 and 41 Commando the medics are all from the RAMC (Royal Army Medical Corps).' He paused and gave a quick smile revealing a small set of even white teeth, 'But I'm sure you won't hold that against them. They're all good men. Any problems come and see me.' He then glanced at Lieutenant Slolay and said, 'Carry on, please.'

The next morning P Troop fell in outside their hut. Waiting for us was RSM 'Growler' Grundy, a small, pugnacious-looking man with a leathery countenance and pair of sharp, dark eyes that didn't miss a thing.

'Heavy weapons, Bren and mortar teams will fall in at 0900.' His rich Yorkshire accent sounded as if he gargled with gravel. He then bayoneted me with a steely glare. 'You are to report to the army doctor for a two-week course on how to treat battlefield injuries,' he paused, patting his right thigh with his swagger, then added, 'When the firing starts, me laddo, you'll be on yer own, so pay close attention.'

Ten minutes later I reported to a young army RAMC captain in a Nissen hut on the far side of the camp. I looked around and couldn't help noticing the green beret of a Royal Navy commando medic among the khaki forage caps of the RAMC orderlies. I sat down on a bench and listened to the captain.

'Each troop will have its own medic.' His manner was firm but quiet. 'Upon landing on a foreign shore his job will be to render first aid, administer morphia, apply a tag if possible stating the time this was given and move on. The main medical team will follow up and give further treatment to the wounded.' (On D-Day this was provided by the 8th, 9th and 223rd Field Ambulances.) The hut was darkened and we were shown a variety of bullet and shrapnel wounds. Afterwards we found a partner and practised dressing imaginary injuries.

I teamed up with the Royal Navy commando medic, a tall and thin-faced lad with a shock of untidy brown hair. As we shook hands there was something about his appearance that looked familiar.

'Me name's Billy Ward,' he said, 'Sharky to you.'

As we shook hands I felt a shockwave run through me. The lad grasping my hand was the brother of Joe Ward one of the bandsmen killed in the *Uganda.*

327

'Are you all right, mate?' he asked, letting go of my hand. 'You look a little pale, like.'

I didn't answer.

However, Sharky's next question made me feel more nervous.

'I hear you were on the *Uganda,*' he said averting his eyes, 'is that right?'

'Yes,' I replied, feeling my mouth go dry.

'So was my brother,' he replied, then quietly added, 'he was killed.'

'I know,' I answered. 'I knew him.' I hesitated, licked my lips and went on. 'He... he was a smashing feller...'

Young Sharky frowned and looked up at me. Tears welled in his eyes and I instinctively knew his next question. 'How did he...?' His voice trailed off.

'A bomb,' I said, taking hold of his arm. 'It... it was quick...'

'Thanks, Pete,' he muttered, 'at least that's summat I can tell me mum and dad.'

At the end of my course I was granted five days' leave.

'Make the most of it, Doc,' said Sergeant Leaman, handing me my pass, 'it may be some time before you get anymore.'

Luckily Gordon was also on leave and we spent most of the time with our parents in the Nelson.

After sipping his pint dad said, 'According to the news the RAF have dropped over 3,600 tons of bombs on Germany in a single raid.'

'How lovely,' replied mum, 'if we keep that up they'll be no need to invade Germany. They'll just surrender.'

'Wishful thinking, mum,' I replied, 'what do you say, Gord?'

'I agree,' replied Gordon, 'us in the South Lancs 'ave been told to make out our wills, so it looks like the big push won't be long.'

'I bet that cheered you up no end,' I grinned, pushing my empty glass towards him. 'Your round I think.'

Throughout March and into April the build up for the invasion across the English Channel gradually gained momentum. The newsreels and daily papers reported England was fast becoming one great military fortress. All coastal areas were off limits to visitors and overseas travel by foreign diplomats forbidden. Some villages in Dorset and Devon were evacuated to allow manoeuvres to secretly take place. At Slapton Sands it was rumoured many men had lost their lives during an exercise. Of course, it was only a rumour...

During this time 41 Commando practised beach landings along the coast of North Wales. Each LSIS (Landing Craft Infantry Small) was 41 feet long, made mainly of wood with two 20mm Oerlikons either side of the bridge. It had a ramp at the front and could hold about a hundred men. Over and over again we hit the beach and deployed as ordered. It was cold, wet, monotonous work. On one occasion the ramp splashed and Spider standing next to me gave a yell, leapt off and almost disappeared under the sea.

'If this keeps up any longer,' he spluttered as I dragged him up, 'I'll be sproutin' gills and swimming across the channel.'

Growler impressed upon us the importance of getting off the beach as quickly as possible. 'Remember,' he yelled, 'when you land you'll be at your most vulnerable.'

'To be sure, sir,' asked Paddy Malone, 'but on what beach might that be then?'

'How the 'ell should I know,' replied Growler, 'why don't you ask Eisenhower. I hear he's touring the bases all over England.'

'Maybe I'll do just dat,' mumbled Paddy gingerly touching the point of his Fairbairn-Sykes knife.

We had been told Erwin Rommel, the German General in charge of defending a 1,200 mile coastline stretching from Norway to France, had placed masses of mines and obstacles on the beaches. This was Hitler's Atlantic Wall but it was anyone's guess where the Allies would eventually land.

Little did we know at that time that large-scale military exercises were taking place all over England with fake concentrations of troops and dummy ships to keep the enemy guessing. Nobody knew where and when the invasion would take place and as time went by I could feel the tension mounting in P Troop.

This pressure came to a head one Saturday evening during the second week in May. Spider, Jock, Paddy and Wacker and myself were lounging against the bar in the Raglan Arms, a small, Edwardian pub in Wrexham's high street. The place was full of cigarette smoke and service personnel. The melodious voice of Gracie Fields singing *Sally, Pride of Our Alley* was barely audible over the noise and the beer tasted like maiden's water.

'Let's give the Doughnut Dugout a go,' suggested Nutty, 'that's where the Yanks and all the girls are, I bet.'

'A good idea mon,' burbled Jock, 'I might be able ta get mysell a drop o' decent whisky.'

'Or catch a dose from one of them judies,' said Wacker.

'To be sure,' quipped Paddy shrugging his shoulders, 'I don't care if I do. I might be kickin' up the daisies this time next year anyway.'

The Doughnut Dugout turned out to be a dingy pub situated down a small, cobbled lane off the main street. A small flight of dark steps led to a closed door and from behind a curtain-drawn window came the steady beat of drums accompanied by the wail of a trumpet. As we went inside, the blare of music, and the smell of perfume mingled with alcohol and cigarette smoke, made my eyes water. Strips of neon lighting attached to a low ceiling bathed everything in a sickly yellow light. A few tables occupied by couples receded into the dark background. A stout, unshaven man in a white shirt and an equally stout woman in a red blouse stood behind the bar. Lounging against the bar, American soldiers, their jackets carelessly undone, stood with their arms around girls wearing thick make-up and tight-fitting skirts.

On a small dance floor a husky, flaxen-haired soldier was doing the jitterbug with a brunette. With each twirl the girls displayed a pair of shapely legs clad in dark stockings and suspenders. A loud cheer followed this as he tossed the girl over his shoulder. In doing so the girl's dress flew over her head showing off a pair of gleaming white thighs and pink knickers.

'Bloody hell,' I cried, 'these buggers certainly have got it made.'

'Aye,' muttered Wacker, with more than a hint of jealousy, 'an' all the talent by the looks of it.'

Jock led the way and elbowed himself past a tall, heavy-set American and a girl to reach the bar.

'Say, buddy,' grunted the American, 'who the hell are you pushin'?'

The American and Jock were about the same size. 'Just tryin' ta get a wee dram fer me am ma mates, mon,' replied Jock, glaring at him.

'Well try some Goddamn place else,' replied the American, 'they're aint no room here, just like there was no room fer you at Dunkirk.'

'What do yer mean by that smart arse,' replied Jock, looking angrier by the second.

'You were licked then,' said the American, 'and that's why we're here again to bail you Limeys out.' He then pushed Jock in the chest.

331

Jock's instant reaction was to butt the American on the bridge of his nose knocking him back against the bar. The American's nose immediately poured with blood.

'You bastard,' yelled the American clutching his face. 'I'll fuckin' kill you fer that,' and he removed a blood-soaked hand and aimed a punch at Jock. Jock evaded the American's fist and sent him sprawling on the floor.

Mayhem immediately broke out.

Voices were raised and girls screamed. Two burly Americans seized Jock and tried to pull him away. I shot a quick glance at Spider and the others who were busy unbuckling their belts and wrapping them around their hands. In a matter of seconds marines and Americans were grappling with one another accompanied by louder screams. Tables, chairs and glasses crashed to the ground. I was suddenly hit on the side of the face by a fist. The last thing I remember before I blacked out was the sound of a Glen Miller record playing *Moonlight Serenade*. When I came too I had a splitting headache and Jock and Spider were lifting me into the back of a tilly. Jock had a stream of blood oozing from a cut over his left eye and Spider's nose looked out of shape.

'What happened?' I gasped. 'Where are we?'

'Relax, Doc,' said Spider, 'you missed all the fun. The Yankee patrol came and sorted it out. They even sent for a tilly to take us back to camp. Nice lot those Yanks.'

Growler Grundy wasn't quite so forthcoming. The next morning we were fell in outside the hut. He slowly walked along the line glaring at each of us. 'Two Yanks and two of our lads are in Wrexham General with head injuries,' he growled.

'To be sure, sir,' muttered Paddy as Growler reached him, 'that makes it equal, don't it, sir?'

Growler stopped and placed his face close to Paddy. 'Where the fuck d' yer think yer are?' he yelled, 'the back streets of Belfast or Liverpool. Look at yer – black eyes, broken teeth, and God knows what.' He then stopped, patted his pace stick impatiently against his thigh then glared at me. 'You're supposed to save lives not take 'em.' He then lowered his voice, and with the hint of a smile, asked, 'Those bruises on yer face Doc, nowt broken I hope?'

'No, sir,' I replied, trying to keep a straight face.

The RSM placed his swagger stick firmly under his left armpit. 'Yer all confined to camp till further notice,' he snapped. 'Now double around the parade ground ten times.'

The following week the whole unit was confined to camp – only this time for a vastly different reason...

CHAPTER TWENTY-EIGHT

On the evening of 24 May Ding-Dong entered the hut and ordered everyone to pack up and be ready to leave early next morning.

'Where we goin' sarg?' someone asked. It was a question on all our lips.

He shook his head and gave his broad shoulders a quick shrug. 'Don't ask me,' he replied, 'I'm just as wise as you lot are.'

After an early breakfast 41 Commando together with units of 45 boarded trucks and left camp.

'Well, we're going south,' said Tweety Nightingale who was sitting on the cramped bench opposite me. 'And that means the coast.'

'Looks like the invasion's on, then,' added Pete Cutting, a tall, thickset lad from Doncaster, who before the war had been a champion sprinter.

'And about bloody time too,' added Tansey Lee, 'if I have to clean that Vickers machine gun anymore, I'll wear the barrel away.'

The journey was long and monotonous punctuated by brew-ups, corned beef sandwiches and calls of nature. After bypassing London we finally arrived at a large concentration of grassland situated on a main avenue leading out of Southampton.

The whole area was heavily ringed with barbed wire with armed sentries posted at various intervals. In the centre was a canvas mess hall beside a makeshift cookhouse. By the time we rigged up our tents the time was just after four o'clock in the afternoon.

'All leave is cancelled,' said Sergeant Leaman, 'if anyone is seen trying to break camp the sentries have orders to shoot to kill.'

'Charming,' muttered Jack Sharp, 'now we're likely to be bumped off by our own lads. Whose fuckin' side are they on anyway.'

An hour later as we lined up for supper Spider looked around and exclaimed, 'Holy Smoke, it's like the League of bloody Nations in here.'

As well as us there were Americans, Polish Dutch and Belgians. (There was also a strong contingent of Free French Commandos who, led by Captain Kieffer, would, as a courtesy, be allowed to be the first to land on French soil.)

On 30 May Brigadier 'Jumbo' Leicester addressed the ten troops that comprised 41 Commando. He was a medium-sized man with broad shoulders and heavily tanned features. His eyes had a steady, quiet look of alert readiness about them that narrowed whenever he paused to make a point. Alongside Colonel Gray stood Lieutenant Slolay, Lieutenant Grayson and several high-ranking officers.

The CO's speech was short but effective. 'You are now part of Number Four Special Service Brigade and will shortly do what you have been trained to do and that's kill the enemy.' He paused momentarily then added, 'The world is watching, waiting and praying for us. We will not let them down. For most of you this will be the most memorable event of your lives. In a hundred years people will say, "They must have been giants in those days." Good luck and God Speed to all of you.'

At 0600 on 5 June Ding-Dong entered the tent. 'Right, you lot,' he barked. 'Pack up. We're leaving. Fall in at 0800.'

'Where to, sarge?' yelled Paddy.

'A small port just outside Southampton, called Warsash,' replied Ding-Dong, 'and from there it's anybody's guess.'

'I bet we'll be landin' at the Pas de Calais,' said Spider.

'Rubbish, mon,' replied Jock, 'my guess it's Dieppe. They'd never expect us to land there again.'

'How about Norway or Denmark,' said Paddy. 'To be sure they believe in free love there, don't they?'

'That's Sweden, you dumb bugger,' cried Wacker, 'and they're neutral.'

'You're all wrong,' stated Tweety, 'my money's on France.'

The mention of France made me think of Adele. I stopped packing my Bergen and for a moment was lost in thought. Spider abruptly interrupted my reverie. 'Come on, Doc,' he said, nudging me in the ribs, 'no time for daydreaming.'

Much to our consternation, everything was delayed for twenty-four hours due, we were told by Lieutenant Slolay, to rain and rough seas on the Channel.

'Thank fuck fer that,' said Wacker, 'I get seasick on the Mersey Ferry.'

At noon we boarded one of a dozen open trucks and left camp. The roads leading out of Southampton were crammed with military vehicles of all shapes and sizes. Heavy and light tanks, SP (Self Propelled) guns and troop carriers formed part of a long convoy stretching for miles. Military Police were constantly moving up and down sorting the many traffic jams. A few cheers greeted us but most onlookers stood in thoughtful silence. Perhaps, like us, they were wondering exactly where we were going.

We arrived at Warsash shortly after three o'clock in the afternoon. 'Bloody hell!' I heard someone exclaim. 'Look at all them LSIs.'

Sure enough, as far as the eye could see were rows of LSIs tied to the jetties jutting out into the river.

We clambered out of the trucks and watched as Lord Lovat's 1st Special Service Commandos boarded the five leading landing craft.

'I suppose they'll be the first on the beaches,' I said to nobody in particular. At that moment I heard the unmistakable skirl of bagpipes echoing around.

'Bloody hell, mon,' yelled Jock. 'I bet that's Piper Millin. If he plays them bagpipes on the beach he'll frighten the life outta the Jerries.'

Then it was our turn to climb onboard. The time was just after 1500. My medical valise and Bergen were strapped on my back. I also carried a large pack of shell and field dressings and from a belt around the waist of my Denison smock hung a canvas holster containing my Colt 45 pistol. I looked at the weapons being carried by my comrades: rifles, grenades, automatic weapons, mortars and Bren guns, all the paraphernalia of war. Suddenly, as I watched them, I couldn't help but wonder how many of us would return.

I made my way to the bottom of the craft where most of the lads were crammed together like sardines. Lieutenant Slolay clambered up by the bridge and stood near one of the 20mm Oerlikons. Next to him stood Lieutenants Borrett and Deize.

'This is what you've all been waiting for,' he said, unrolling a large map of the French coast. As he spoke his moustache twitched more than usual. Suddenly he had everyone's undivided attention. The only sounds were the drone of the engines as the craft gently rolled through the water. All eyes were glued on the map.

After quickly surveying our faces, the officer quietly announced, 'The invasion forces are heading for the beaches of Normandy. Here.' At which point he stabbed a finger at an area along the French Coast.

My God! I gasped, *Normandy!* The name rang like a bell in my ears. *We're going to land in Normandy!* I could hardly

337

believe his words. I immediately thought of Adele. My mind raced. Suddenly I lost track of what the officer was saying. Would she still be there, I asked myself. I quickly dismissed this idea as being foolish. After all before we landed the whole area would be pulverised by shot, shell and bombs. But what if, after all these years, she *was* still there stranded in the middle of the greatest invasion the world has ever seen. And if so how could I possibly get to see her...?

Just then Spider nudged me in the ribs, 'Isn't that where that girl you told us about lives, Pete?' I heard him say.

'Yeah,' I replied. 'But...' my voice trailed away as Lieutenant Slolay continued his address. He had passed the map to Lieutenant Grayson and was using his swagger stick as an indicator.

'The landing area stretches roughly fifty miles,' he was saying. 'We will form part of the British Third Infantry Division commanded by Major General Rennie. The Americans will land at the western beaches designated Utah and Omaha. The Canadians will land on Juno and the British to the east at Gold and Sword. 41 Commando and army units will land on Sword. Lord Lovat's First Special Brigade will make for Ouistreham, push inland and link inland with paratroopers holding a bridge across the River Orne.

Ouistreham! Once again Adele's lovely face flashed before my eyes. My thoughts were interrupted as Lieutenant Slolay went on, 'Earlier American paratroopers will have been dropped behind Utah beach to capture the approaches to the beach and batteries. British airborne units will have done a similar task on the eastern side.'

At that moment the ear-splitting noise of aircraft drowned out his voice. The officer stopped talking and like the rest of us peered upwards as dozens of Lancaster bombers accompanied by fighter escorts flew passed, high in the sky. All had three identification white stripes on their wings and fuselage. These were followed by other large groups of bombers almost blotting out the early morning sunshine.

Suddenly a loud cheer echoed around. Everyone knew where the bombers were heading (5,112 sorties were flown by Allied aircraft on D-Day.)

'If this keeps up,' I heard Taffy Ball say, 'there'll be no Jerries left on those beaches.'

'I wouldn't count on it, Taffy, my son,' replied Nutty who was crammed next to him.

When the last aircraft passed over, Lieutenant Slolay carried on talking. 'The RAF have complete control of the air. H-hour will be 0700. 41 Commando will form part of Force S and land at Queen White Beach, here.' He paused and indicated with his swagger stick a stretch of coastline. 'The South Lancs will land first enabling 41 to thrust forward to Lion-sur-Mer, and capture a German battery, code-named "Trout", here.' Once again he tapped the map with his swagger-stick. 'If all goes well we will move west to link up with 48 Commando advancing from the Canadian landings at Juno.'

Lion-sur-Mer! I gasped, the town where Adele lived. I could hardly believe my luck. I nervously clenched my fists and teeth; somehow I *had* to find out where she was. I also remembered that South Lancs was Gordon's regiment and prayed he'd be all right.

For the next four hours we sat nervously chattering, anxious to get under way. I handed out tiny tablets of seasick tablets (Hyocine Hydrobromide) to anyone who wanted them.

'Remember Nelson was seasick every time he went to sea,' I said, passing one to Jock.

'Och, aye,' he replied, throwing the pill down his throat, 'but look what happened ta him at Trafalgar.'

Finally, to everyone's relief, the engines spluttered into action and we slipped our moorings. Cruising in line ahead our five small craft edged downriver past the Isle of Wight and into the English Channel. Here the flotilla was met by a three destroyer escort. The time was 2130 and dusk was slowly falling. A pale moon darted in between clusters of angry-looking grey clouds occasionally dappling the sea with shafts of anaemic light. Suddenly the swell of the open sea rocked the tiny vessel. Our LSI(S) started to dip and roll uncomfortably. I was sure the other five craft were suffering a similar fate. Each motion was met with a dull thud as the bows rose and slapped into the sea sending a sickening vibration throughout the vessel.

The air was thick with swirling clouds of cigarette smoke. I looked around and saw Jock vomiting into a paper bag. After he had finished, he looked at me glassy eyed, 'So much fer those wee pills ye gave us,' he spluttered and sank back against the bulkhead.

A commando was being sick in the doorless toilet situated aft. He was lying on the deck retching for all he was worth. The smell of vomit was heavy and overpowering.

However, Spider, Paddy and Wacker didn't seem to be affected by the dreaded *Mal de Mare.* They had started a card game. As I stood up and squeezed beside them I could hear the clink of pennies dropping into a green beret. Some men busied themselves cleaning their weapons; others smoked or strained their eyes trying to read novels or letters in the dim moonlight.

The lanky figure of Nutty Slack stumbled from the toilet and yelled, 'I wish this fuckin' boat would sink and put us out of our misery.'

Even old timers like Ding-Dong suffered. 'I don't care how many bloody Jerries are waiting fer us,' he moaned, 'the sooner we get off this soddin' thing the better.'

I eased myself up and looked over the side. What met my eyes took my breath away. In every direction sailing in perfect lines was the biggest armada I was ever likely to see. I could clearly make out the white, frothy bow waves and silhouettes of battleships, cruisers and destroyers ploughing through the choppy sea. Close behind our line of landing craft were rows of larger LCTs carrying tanks and heavy equipment. Others I knew carried deadly rockets. Behind them I could just make out several heavy transports, with landing craft slung outboard on davits.

To this awe-inspiring scene was added the constant drone of aircraft passing above – many flashing DOT-DOT-DASH, the famous Morse code signal meaning V for Victory. 'Bloody hell,' I muttered to myself, 'if this doesn't scare the life out of the Jerries, nothing will.'

Buffeted unmercifully by the rough sea our small craft battled its way towards the shore. On and on we went, plunging into troughs of waves then somehow wallowing up onto the crests.

When I sat down, Spider and the others were still playing cards. I closed my eyes and must have dozed off. Suddenly I was woken by the *whoosh* of shells passing overhead. This was accompanied by tremendous, ear-splitting detonations as every warship opened fire. The night sky almost turned to day as salvo after salvo hurtled towards the French coast. To the cacophony was added the deafening roar as flaming red rockets looking like something out of science fiction, streaked overhead towards the enemy coast. The landing craft rocked even more as I felt a warm blast fan my face. The time by my watch was 0535. With each pitch and roll of the craft I caught a glimpse of the dark line of the Normandy shore.

Gradually dusk changed to a pale dawn allowing me to see masses of black-shaped obstacles poking out of the water close to the beach. Features I remembered such as the spire of Saint Pierre's church in Ouistreham and lighthouse came into view. All this became a cloudy blur as rows of yellow and red explosions rippled along the beach. Suddenly I broke out in a cold sweat. My God I thought, in just over two hours I could be dead!

'Not long to go now Doc,' said Nutty, adjusting the straps of his Bergen. 'Thank fuck I didn't join the navy.'

As if by magic, the pale dawn suddenly gave way to the cold light of day. Grey clouds raced across the sky as the LSI continued to plunge through the choppy sea.

The tall figure of Lieutenant Grayson stood up near the ramp. Grasping a stanchion he yelled, 'Remember, get off the beach as soon as possible. Keep your eyes on the senior NCOs, RSM Grundy and me.' Just as he finished an explosion nearby rocked the craft sending a tall plume of water in the air.

'The buggers seem to have our range,' I overhead RSM Grundy say. 'So keep yer 'eads down.'

'Ten minutes,' cried Sergeant Leaman, 'check weapons and Bergens.'

His words sent my heart racing. The built-up tension inside me immediately turned to fear. My mouth felt dry and I thought my bladder would burst. I looked around and saw faces I had come to know so well, pale and strained. Paddy's hand shook as he tried to smoke a cigarette. Wacker blinked and stared glassily in front of him. Jock nudged Nutty and passed him a cigarette. Spider gave me a reassuring wink, his normal cheery demeanour now quiet and solemn. I nervously licked my lips, grinned weakly and moved towards the front of the craft.

The barrage from the warships was lifted from the beaches and aimed inland. The enemy gunfire coming from the coast was very accurate. Large spouts of water were shooting up around the landing craft. To our right a LSI had received a direct hit and was burning fiercely. Everyone, including myself, was silently staring ahead as our craft drew closer to the beach. Suddenly there was a violent shudder followed by the ramp splashing down into the water.

'Everybody OUT!' yelled Lieutenant Grayson leaping knee deep into the water.

Growler Grundy was the first to be killed.

Just as he turned to say something he was hit and fell backwards, his face a mass of bones and blood. I pushed past someone to see if I could help. 'Leave him,' barked Lieutenant Slolay, 'get off and move quickly.'

'Come on, Doc,' cried Spider, poking me in the back,' I'm right behind yer. Get goin' mate.'

There appeared to be about a hundred yards of water between the landing craft and the beach. Machine gun nests and batteries had replaced the coloured wooden chalets I remembered from 1939.

As I jumped off the ramp all thoughts of Adele and anyone else immediately vanished from my mind. My boots sunk into the soft sand. The noise was deafening. I splashed through the water and was overcome by sheer panic. To my horror I saw several bodies lolling back and forth with the movement of the crimson-stained surf. 'Please God!' I screamed. 'Please don't let me die. Please... please...'

The beach was crammed with barbed wire and masses of sharp-pointed, hexagonal-shaped obstacles. Out of the haze of smoke I caught sight of a DD tank (short for Duplex Drive) crushing everything and thus paving a way for us to go through. (These tanks we learnt, having seen some of General Percy Hobbart's 'funnies', were driven by twin propellers fed off the engine). Further along stretched mounds of undulating sand dunes from which came ripples of gunfire.

'Remember those obstacles have teller mines on 'em,' yelled Ding-Dong, who, along with many other marines, was in front. 'Get behind that tank and follow me.'

The noise of explosions and gunfire was so continuous it seemed like a siren. Two tanks on the water's edge were on fire and clouds of black smoke were blowing across the dunes. Bullets, sounding like the buzzing of bees, constantly whizzed passed. The deadly *thump, thump* of mortars exploding all around sent mounds of wet sand flying into the air. One commando near me screamed and fell back into the water. Another collapsed clutching his abdomen. I ran past a DD tank engulfed in flames unable to get off the beach. Tanks using flails (another of Hobart's ingenuity) beat their way ashore, exploding mines as they did so. On and on I ran, praying I would survive.

The houses of Lion-sur-Mere, clouded in dense black smoke, gradually became clearer. Then something happened that was surely miraculous. There, some fifty yards away behind the dunes, loomed the undamaged, cream-coloured walls of Chalet Henri. This I knew was close to where Adele and I first made love. Suddenly I knew exactly where I was. I also knew Adele's house was nearby. In a flash I pictured her cowering in some cellar, screaming and frightened.

The thought spurred me on even faster. I finally reached the dunes and threw myself into the sand. 'I've made it!' I cried inwardly, 'Thank God, I've made it.' For a while I lay panting. Digging my fingers into the soft damp sand I lay still and felt a warm trickle of urine run down my legs.

I looked up and saw Lieutenant Slolay waving an arm yelling, 'P Troop over here.'

Jock and Spider carrying a Bren gun arrived, followed by Sergeant Leaman, Ding Ding, Paddy, Wacker and many others. I glanced behind and saw vehicles and tanks bellowing black smoke; landing craft with their ramps down lay at the water's edge engulfed in flames; bodies lay everywhere; heavy concentrations of men, bent with fear while clutching their weapons, advanced across what was effectively 'no man's land'.

I tore my eyes away unable to take in the carnage I was witnessing. Without thinking I moved up as if to leave the dunes. Just then an explosion nearby knocked me backwards almost covering me with sand. This was quickly followed by the cry of 'Medic! Medic!'

I crawled over and saw two commandos lying at the base of the dune. One was Porky Saunders. Blood was oozing through the upper arm of his Denison Smock. His pale face indicated he was in shock. The other casualty was Nutty Slack. His green beret was a mass of matted hair and blood. His ashen face and blank, staring eyes told me he was dead. I checked his pulse to make sure. I quickly gave Porky a shot of morphia, placed a shell dressing over his wounds and put his arm in a sling.

'You'll be all right, Porky,' I yelled over the noise. I lit a cigarette and gave it to him. 'The RAMC lads will be here soon. You've just bought a ticket to Blighty.'

'How's Nutty?' he gasped.

I shook my head. I turned away and loosened Nutty's Denison smock and covered his head with it.

I reported what had happened to Lieutenant Slolay. He was busy talking to Captain Powel, the leader of A Troop. Ding-Dong and Sergeant Leaman lay close by. 'The CO wants us to get off the beach and form an advance party,' I overhead him say to the other officer, 'enemy fire coming down the main road is pinning us down. Somehow we've got to reach the road leading out of Lion-sur-Mer. We'll then be supported by AVRE tanks. Then we'll be able to advance.' (AVRE – Armoured Vehicle Royal Engineers. This was a Churchill tank fitted with a special gun called a Petard for clearing obstacles.)

In a flash I remembered my visits to Adele and the cobble lane by the side of Chalet Henri. 'Excuse me, sir,' I gasped, moving close to the officer, 'but there's a narrow street by the side of that house up there.' I pointed to the chalet. 'It leads into the town.'

'How on earth d' you know that?' asked Lieutenant Slolay, 'it's not shown on the map.'

I quickly explained.

'Very well,' said Lieutenant Slolay, 'stay close to me, though. I only hope you're right.' He gathered up the map and glanced at Ding-Dong. 'Pass the word, Sergeant,' he said, everyone to follow me and Captain Powel.'

345

Ding-Dong crawled towards marines bunched together at the base of the sand dunes. A few minutes later Lieutenant Slolay waved his Colt 45 in the air, and yelled, 'Come on, lads, everyone up. Keep behind and follow me and move quickly. Let's go.'

The enemy fire was now sporadic. With nearly a hundred commandos following on I drew my Colt 45 from its holster and scrambled up behind the two officers. The thought that at any moment a bullet might tear through me made me tremble with fear.

To my relief the lane was still there. But more importantly so was Adele's house. The gate where I once parked my bike was broken and the garden overgrown with weeds. All the windows were boarded up and part of the sloping roof was missing.

As we slowly advanced all I could think of was Adele. I still couldn't believe I was here almost in the exact spot where Adele and I had parted all those years ago. I had the feeling fate had brought me here and that she was waiting…

With the two officers in front, myself followed by the rest of P And A Troop moved along the lane. 'Well done, Doc,' came the voice of Lieutenant Slolay. 'You say there's a turning down there that leads into the town?'

'Yes, sir,' I replied, with my eyes glued to Adele's house. At that moment I felt my stomach contract. Twenty yards away the face of a woman appeared from the side of the house. However, my heart sank, even at this distance I could tell the woman wasn't Adele. She was elderly and frantically waving a small tattered Tricolour shouting excitedly in French.

'I speak French, sir,' I gasped to Lieutenant Slolay, 'let me go and see what she is saying.'

Occasional bursts of gunfire echoed around and mortar bombs were still crashing quite close.

After a quick glance at Captain Powel, he nodded. 'OK, but take Seymour and Malone with you, and for God's sake be careful.'

Clutching their Tommy Guns Spider and Paddy crouched forward.

'To be sure, Doc,' shouted Paddy, 'if yer get me killed I'll never forgive yer.'

'Ten to one that party's on the game,' quipped Spider as we hurried across the lane and into the garden.

The woman's thick grey hair was matted with dirt and her wrinkled face covered in dust. Over a grey dress she wore a dirty white smock and her feet was clad in a pair of well-worn slippers. *'Bonjour, Bonjour,'* she cried still waving her flag. *'Vive la France. Welcome Americans. Liberation! Liberation!'* She then threw her arms around me and gave me a garlic-smelling kiss on both cheeks.

'Play yer cards right and you're on there, Doc,' said Spider.

'We're not Americans,' I replied in French, 'we're British,' then quickly asked, 'does Adele and Madam and Monsieur Michaud still live here?'

The woman shrugged her shoulders. 'No Monsieur,' she answered. 'Monsieur Michaud is away at the war. Madam Michaud was taken by the Boche…'

'But Adele,' I replied impatiently, *'where* is Adele?'

'I do not know, Monsieur,' replied the woman, once more shrugging her shoulders, 'she went away too. I am looking after the house…'

Almost as an afterthought, I asked, 'Are there many Germans in Lion?'

The woman nodded and answered, 'Yes, Monsieur, lots of them and guns in the field next to the church.'

'Thank you, Madame,' I replied, 'more soldiers will be coming along soon. You're safe now.'

By now tears were streaming down the woman's face. She flung her arms around Spider and cried, 'Thank you, thank you...'

'It was Spider she really fancied,' quipped Paddy as we hurried back.

'Bollocks,' answered Spider, 'I wouldn't have turned it down but the smell of all that garlic put me off.'

The woman's information proved useful. Lieutenant Slolay found the coordinates of the church on the map and had them radioed to a warship. He then ordered us to turn right along the lane and advance into town. Just then I saw an AVRE rumble into view at the end of the lane in the main road. We were about to move when the tank exploded in a sheet of flame. Everyone instinctively backed away and ducked. We watched helpless as two men, their uniforms on fire, climbed out of the turret only to collapse as bullets rained onto them.

'Poor buggers,' I heard Lieutenant Slolay cry, 'the bastards must have an 88mm near that church.'

The intense heat from the tank seared our faces as we moved forward. As we did so the *whoosh* of shells passing over made us duck again. This was followed by a series of detonations that shook the ground. Abruptly the enemy gunfire ceased. 'Thank God fer the navy, eh Doc?' said Paddy, nudging me with the butt of his Tommy Gun.

But the Germans were far from finished. The rattle of machine gun and rifle fire continued to rain down on us and casualties began to mount at an alarming rate. Four army medics, a doctor and myself were kept busy attending to injured men lying in doorways and against walls. One of those was Tweety Nightingale. His face, like the others, was a dull grey. He lay on his left side with blood oozing from a bullet hole in the side of his neck. When he saw me he tried to smile. Then his head abruptly lolled to one side and his eyes took on the all too familiar blank expression. I gently brushed his eyelashes down and closed his eyes. Jeeps started to arrive and I helped to place the injured onto stretchers for evacuation to the beach.

Two more AVRE tanks rolled up the road behind which crouched the remainder of the commando. Word got around saying the Canadians at Luc-sue-Mer (Juno beach) had met stiff resistance and could not join up with us. Therefore, our proposed attack on the enemy battery code-named Trout had to be delayed. The time was 1330. One by one the commandos filtered into a nearby orchard, eyes alert, expecting to find the enemy. But they had gone. I kept closely behind Spider and Paddy. 'Nice juicy apples, Paddy,' he said looking at the clusters of ripe apples. 'Good fer the bowels, eh?'

'Who needs bleedin' apples,' replied Paddy, 'I've already shit me sell twice so far.'

'And here's me thinking it was me,' I added with a laugh.

Lieutenant Slolay came up and we overheard him tell Ding-Dong the CO had decided to set up his HQ in the orchard.

Except for occasional shellfire and mortar bombs exploding all was quiet. Nobody had eaten anything for over twelve hours. Spider managed a quick brew while Wacker and Paddy opened a few tins of self-heating stew. Meanwhile I checked on several wounded men waiting to be transferred to the beach. The casualty rate had been high. A head count was taken. Out of the 500 men of 41 Commando who had landed that morning 141 officers and men were killed.

By 2300 it was dark. A warm breeze fanned my face and high above a full moon darted in between banks of grey clouds. I had just finished adjusting the bandages of a wounded marine and was walking back to my foxhole. From out of nowhere came the drone of aircraft. The ground shook as bombs exploded all around. Suddenly, a blinding, yellow flash engulfed me, and a searing pain shot through my body. A cloak of darkness descended upon me and I slowly lost consciousness...

CHAPTER TWENTY-NINE

For what seemed like an eternity I floated in and out of consciousness vaguely hearing voices and seeing faces half hidden by green masks. Whenever I opened my eyes it was as if I was an onlooker in some great drama and my body was part of another person. Oddly enough there was no pain. I simply lay in a world of my own unaware those faces in green masks were surgeons fighting to save my life.

The first thing I felt when I opened my eyes was a roaring thirst. I tried to swallow but my mouth felt like parchment. My cracked lips stuck together like rubber bands. I attempted to speak but my tongue stuck to the roof of my mouth. High above, the grey clouds and sky moved gently from side to side. The thumping waves against a bulkhead and the gentle rolling told me I was onboard a ship. I lay naked on a stretcher covered in coarse army blankets. I tried to remember what happened but my mind was a blank. The numbness in the lower part of my body prevented any movement.

My right arm lay outside the blankets bandaged to a splint. I looked up and saw a half-filled bottle of blood and length of rubber tubing ending in my right arm and realised I was having a transfusion. It was then I remembered Adele's medallion. I closed my eyes and worked my free hand upwards. 'Thank God,' I thought running my fingers over the smoothness of the metal. 'At least I'm still alive.'

'How d' yer feel, mate?'

I opened my eyes and saw the unshaven face of a soldier. Running my tongue over my lips, I tried to speak. The soldier quickly realised what I wanted. With one hand he supported my head and held a cup to my mouth. The water tasted like nectar.

'Take it easy,' said the soldier, 'not too much at once.'

After taking several more sips I lay back feeling weak and tired. I turned and saw lines of wounded men on stretchers being attended to by army medics. Some were swathed in bloodstained bandages. Others, like myself, were receiving blood transfusions. At that moment a tired-looking officer with fair hair and a thick five o'clock shadow, arrived and knelt beside me.

'How are you, old boy,' he said quietly, 'are you in any pain?'

'No, sir,' I answered hoarsely, 'but what happened? I can't remember anything.'

I listened to the doctor while the medic gave me a few sips of water.

'I was told by one of your officers that three Heinkels dropped a stick of ant-personnel bombs on your HQ,' said the doctor. 'An officer and two men were killed and your CO was severely wounded. Like yourself he's being evacuated to England.'

'We were led to believe, there wasn't any Jerry aircraft,' I replied hoarsely.

'So we were told,' answered the doctor, 'anyway the Spitfires eventually shot them down.'

I tried to move my legs but a dagger-like pain shot right through me. I let out a cry and turned my head to one side.

'H... how badly am I hurt?' I gasped.

'It's difficult to say,' replied the doctor, 'but I'm sure you've broken your left shin and thighbone and you've suffered extensive tissue loss. You've also lost a lot of blood. Luckily you're blood group is O, therefore you can receive blood from anyone.'

'*Good God,*' I cried, 'will I lose my leg?'

The doctor sighed, shook his head and said, 'I'm afraid we'll have to wait and see.' He then opened a medical valise and took out a small ampoule. 'I'm going to give you another shot of morphia, it'll kill the pain and help you to sleep.' He then turned to the medic and said, 'Check the dressing regularly and let me know before the blood runs out.'

The effect of the morphia worked almost straight away. When I woke up a warm breeze was fanning my face and I was being lifted into an ambulance.

'You're safe and sound in Blighty, now,' said, an army medic as the ambulance moved off. 'Next stop Southampton General.'

There were three other stretcher cases in the ambulance, two on racks opposite and one above me. An army medic gave each of us a cigarette.

'Lucky sods,' he said, lighting them, 'you'll all be up in no time chasing all them sexy nurses, not to mention some decent scran.'

But I wasn't 'up in no time' as he put it. Neither, I imagined were the others. The ward was full of casualties. Those sexy nurses the medic mentioned never stopped working. One, a pretty little blonde, even found time to write a letter for a soldier in the bed next to me who had both arms bandaged.

'There,' she said, holding the letter so he could read it, 'I've put a few kisses on the bottom, just for luck.'

'What does, BIBAW mean?' he asked.

'Be in Bed And Waiting,' the nurse replied with a giggle.

As I listened to her I touched Adele's medallion and wondered if she was waiting.

On the first day my legs were X-rayed and under a general anaesthetic and my wounds cleaned. In the evening two elderly doctors in white coats accompanied by a stout nursing sister came to my bedside.

The tallest of the doctors was a grey-haired man with a thin face and dark rings around both eyes, 'My name is Mr Griffiths.' He spoke with a Welsh accent and his manner was quiet and reserved. 'I'm a Consultant Surgeon' (Consultants are always referred to as 'Mr'), he paused and shot a quick glance at is colleague, 'and this is Doctor Gerrard who is the hospital's Chief Orthopaedic surgeon.' Mr Griffiths paused again, cleared his throat then continued. 'Your left femur is broken in two places and your left tibia is fractured rather badly. You have also lost a lot of musculature in both your left calf and thigh.' He stopped talking and glanced at Doctor Gerrard.

Dr Gerrard, a white-haired man, smiled at me and spoke. 'You'll have to have the fractured femur reduced and pinned and your wound cleaned.' As he spoke he avoided my eyes. 'Your tibia will have to be reduced and put in plaster.' He then paused, pursed his lips and added, 'I'm afraid you're in for a rough time, my boy.'

I nervously licked my lips, 'When will this happen?' I asked.

'Tonight,' came Doctor Jenkins grave reply, 'or else you could lose your leg.'

The sister, who so far had stood staring at me, an expression of concern fixed on her florid features, then said, 'You'll be going to the theatre in an hour. When did you last eat?' Her manner was brisk and businesslike.

I shook my head and replied, 'I can't remember.'

'I see,' replied the sister thoughtfully. 'Do not eat or drink anything. I shall give you your pre-med (an injection of Omnopon and Scopolmine, a substance that helps a patient to relax and one which dries up the nasal passages) in an hour.' She then reached down, smiled, patted my hand, smiled and quietly said, 'Don't worry young man everything will be all right. But you'll have to remove that charm or whatever it is from around your neck.'

'Oh no,' I replied, touching the medallion, 'it's rather special. You see...'

'Now, now,' said the sister raising a hand, 'it'll be kept in your locker and you can put it back on afterwards.'

The injection made me drowsy. I vaguely remember a strong hand lifting me up onto something soft, the sound of wheels gently rumbling, bright lights, a pair of eyes staring down at me over a surgeon's green mask... then oblivion.

When I finally woke up my mouth felt like sandpaper. My left leg was in a Plaster of Paris cast and was suspended through a circular metal ring resting on a splint. All movements I later discovered were controlled by a series of pulleys and weights. (This contraption was called a Thomas's Splint.)

My left arm was also resting on another splint into which I was receiving a blood transfusion. White screens surrounded my bed and shaded light cast a dull yellow glow over the single sheet covering the rest of me.

I must have fallen asleep again because when I opened my eyes I saw the smiling face of a nurse. 'How do you feel?' she asked.

'Thirsty as hell,' I managed to say, 'and a bit groggy. What time is it?'

'A little after midnight,' replied the nurse, taking hold of my right wrist and checking my pulse. After making a notation on a chart she left only to return shortly afterwards holding a cup. After helping me to take a few welcome sips of water I sank back into the pillows. It was then I remembered the medallion. When I told the nurse, she took it from a drawer in my locker.

'Is it special?' she asked, attaching it around my neck.

'Yes,' I replied, 'Very special. Thanks very much.'

At that moment a small doctor with a pale, drawn face and black-framed spectacles opened a screen and came in and stood at the foot of the bed. In his hand was a small folder. 'How are you feeling Mr Robertson?' he asked while opening the folder and studying its contents.

'Not too bad,' I replied, 'but my left side feels numb.'

'I'm Doctor Donaldson, the Duty House Surgeon,' he said looking up from the folder. 'Your fractured femur has been reduced and a pin placed through your lower leg attached to a weight to provide traction.' He paused, examining the folder again before going on. 'Your shinbone was shattered and parts have been replaced, but I'm afraid this will require further surgery. You also have a drainage tube from the flesh wounds in your thigh.'

'How long do you think I'll be in here, sir?' I asked.

'Quite some time, I'm afraid,' sighed the doctor and closed the folder.

During the next three months I lost count of the operations I had on my thigh and leg. I became adept at balancing on bedpans and using odd-shaped urinal bottles. I even knew how many lights there were on the corridor ceilings leading to the operating theatre. However, there were a few compensations.

On a warm Saturday afternoon in early July I was talking to Tim Hughes, a ginger-headed soldier in the Welsh Fusiliers who had lost a leg on D-Day. He was in a wheelchair by my bedside. We were talking about the war when I looked up and to my amazement, saw my parents coming towards me.

'Mum, dad!' I exclaimed. 'It's great to see you. What a surprise. How did you get here?'

When mum saw me she immediately burst into tears. 'Oh son,' she sobbed, hugging me, 'you didn't tell us in your letters how badly hurt you were.'

Dad stood and smiled, then, with tears in his eyes also, said, 'They've got you trussed up like a chicken. How are you, son?'

I introduced them to Tim and they shook hands. 'In better shape than some of them in here,' I replied, nodding towards Tim, who politely excused himself and left.

'By the way,' said dad, 'your pal Gordon is home on leave and sends his best.'

'That's good to hear,' I replied, 'he must have landed near us with the South Lancs. Tell him he owes me a few pints in the Nelson.'

My parents were staying at a boarding house nearby and came every day for a week before saying a tearful farewell.

'You will try and write and let us know how you're getting on, won't you, love?' said mum, giving me a wet kiss. 'We'll be worried sick about you.'

Meanwhile the Allies continued to advance into Europe. In July an attempt on Hitler's life unfortunately failed. Russian forces occupied Bucharest and Nazi tanks razed Warsaw. Paris was liberated and the American advance in the Pacific gained momentum.

In late September casualties from Arnhem began to arrive. Clad in their Denison smocks they reminded me of Spider and the lads I had left behind.

That same month the pin in my leg was removed. Then complications set in. The bones in my tibia failed to knit properly, and the wounds in my thigh and calf became infected. This meant more operations and injections of the new wonder drug called Penicillin. Thankfully, by December my condition had improved and I was able to walk slightly using crutches.

Depending on what kind of drugs they were on, each patient celebrated Christmas 1945 with two bottles of stout. Someone produced a mouth organ and everyone sung carols. However, it was a muted affair. Naturally, our hearts and minds were elsewhere.

On the afternoon of New Year's Day I was lying on my bed. My eyes were closed and I was lost in thought. I was about to doze off when I heard a familiar voice say, 'Wake up, Jack. You can't sleep here.'

I opened my eyes and there, standing beside my bed, was Spider and Wacker Williamson. Both were in battledress with their green berets tucked neatly under their shoulder straps. For a few seconds I stared at them too surprised to speak. Spider hadn't changed. His cheery face and pale blue eyes wrinkled into that familiar cheeky grin I knew so well. Wacker's sallow features still looked as if he'd spent a year in solitary confinement.

'Well, I'll be…' I finally cried, pushing myself up on my elbows. 'How the hell did you two get here?'

I managed to stand up. 'It really is great to see you,' I said shaking their hands. 'How did you know I was here?' I asked then sat down.

'After D-Day our lot along with the Canadians landed in Walchern,' said Spider, 'that's in Flushing, Belgium.' He paused, handed Wacker and myself a cigarette. 'We came back to Southampton. An army medic told us you'd been sent here.'

'What about Jock and the others?' I asked.

'Ding-Dong bought it in Normandy,' replied Spider sombrely. 'Paddy and Sergeant Leaman were killed in Walchern along with Lieutenant Grayson.'

'What about Jock and Taffy Ball did they…?'

'No,' replied Spider, 'they're OK. They made it.'

I slowly shook my head and for a second the faces of those killed flashed in front of me. 'Bloody hell,' I muttered, 'I can't believe it…'

'Out of the original fifty in P Troop that landed in Normandy,' said Spider, 'less than half returned home.' He paused, gave me a quick grin, 'Anyway, me old cock sparra,' he went on cheerily, ''ow the 'ell are you, then?'

A nurse appeared with a tray of sticky buns and tea. When it was time for them to leave, my throat suddenly felt tight.

'Thanks for coming,' I managed to say.

'Look after yersell, Doc,' said Spider.

'Aye,' added Wacker, 'Good luck, lad. We'll try and see yer again.'

As they reached the ward door Spider turned around, grinned, gave me a thumbs up and left. We never did meet again.

During the second week in January I was transferred by ambulance to the naval hospital at Haslar, Gosport. Saying goodbye to the wonderful staff and fellow patients I had come to know was quite hard. No sooner was I safely ensconced in D1 orthopaedic ward, then the infection in my leg and thigh muscles flared up again. More operations and injections followed. The treatment dragged on. By the middle of February I had recovered sufficiently and was able to walk again using crutches. At the end of April I was discharged and lived in the staff quarters. This enabled me to attended physiotherapy twice a day. VE Day (8 May) saw me unsuccessfully trying to walk using one crutch. Luckily the physiotherapist caught me in time! In July I was fully ambulant, albeit with a pronounced limp. Later that month I went before a survey board and was officially discharged from the navy. I was then sent on a month's terminal leave and celebrated VJ Day, 15 August, in the Nelson.

'Thank God, you won't have to go back, son,' said mum, as we clinked glasses.

'And no more goodbyes,' added dad.

However, deep down I knew there was one more journey I had to make.

EPILOGUE

A hand shaking my shoulder woke me up. I opened my eyes, blinked a few times and saw the face of the elderly gentleman wearing black leather gloves and a dark overcoat, his eyes partly shaded by the rim of a trilby.

'Pardon me, Monsieur,' he said politely tipping his trilby, 'we are due to arrive in Calais shortly. I thought I had better wake you up.'

His English, spoken with a slight accent was perfect.

'Thank you,' I replied, stretching out my arms and yawning. 'I was well away.' I then looked at him closer, and asked, 'Didn't we meet on the train?'

His fleshy features broke into a wide grin. '*Oui*, you speak French very well,' he replied, showing an uneven set of tobacco-stained teeth. 'Permit me to introduce myself. My name is Paul LeBrun.'

I stood up and offered my hand. 'Peter Robertson.' With a deft movement he removed a glove and we shook hands. He told me he was a wine merchant and was travelling to Calais on business.

'As I recall,' he added, 'you said on the train you were going to Ouistreham. You will have to go via Caen. Have you been to France before?'

For a few seconds I was silent. 'Yes,' I replied dryly, 'but it's been a long time…'

I remembered to put my watch on an hour and by the time we got ashore the time was just after five o'clock. My left leg

359

ached and as we walked along the quayside a blustery, Autumnal breeze beat against my overcoat and almost blew my trilby off.

'The railway station is at the end of the quay,' said Paul. He then glanced at his wristwatch. 'If we hurry you'll be in time to catch a train to Caen that leaves in ten minutes.'

From where we were I could see part of the port. Many of the houses still lay in ruins. However, several ships unloading cargo gave a semblance of normality to the docks.

Outside the station we shook hands. '*Au reviour*, Monsieur Robertson,' he said slightly out of breath, 'I hope you find what you are looking for.'

I managed to board the train a few minutes before it pulled away. The journey took a little over two hours and it was seven o'clock when we arrived in Caen. How different everything seemed from that sunny day six years ago when, full of the innocence of youth, I was met by Aunt Matilda and Uncle Claude. Evidence of the war still abounded. The roof was partially missing; part of a platform was in the process of being re-built and the station was dimly lit.

My leg was aching badly. I decided to continue my journey in the morning and booked into a small *pension* opposite the station. The proprietor, a small, rotund man with a red face and an untidy, drooping moustache greeted me, accepted my five francs and showed me to my room.

'It is small but clean Monsieur,' he said, 'and there is a restaurant next door.'

That night I lay in the narrow, uncomfortable bed thinking about Adele and the time she showed me around Caen. Finally, listening to the sound of an occasional car bleeping its horn I fell asleep.

Next morning dawned clear with patchy white clouds and a surprisingly warm October breeze. After breakfast in the restaurant the proprietor directed me to a line of bus stops outside the station. 'Buses to Lion-sur-Mer via Ouistreham leave on the hour, Monsieur,' he said, 'you are visiting friends, yes?'

I nodded and murmured, 'Yes.'

Just after nine o'clock wearing my trilby, overcoat and blue pinstriped suit I left the hotel. I crossed the road and without much difficulty, found the correct bus. The single decker was almost full and avoided much of the city I thought must still lie in ruins. The bus slowly wound its way out of the city and into the countryside. This time there weren't fields of yellow corn stretching away on either side. Only the River Orne and villages such as Herouville, Collville and Benouville served to remind me of happy times before the war.

The bus slowly rumbled up a steep gradient. With every jolt of the bus and bump in the road my excitement mounted. Suddenly my mind was in turmoil. What would I do if Adele wasn't in Lion-sur-Mer? Where, after all these years of waiting could I go? And more important, would I ever find out what had happened to her?

When the bus reached the summit of the hill I caught my breath. Spread out before my eyes stretched a wide ribbon of yellow, sandy coastline and a great sweep of the English Channel sparkling like diamonds under the glare of the early morning sun.

Suddenly, my hands began to tremble and I came out in a cold sweat. This was where Ding-Dong and thousands of others lost their lives on that fateful morning in June two years ago. And somewhere along that same coastline was the spot where I was wounded.

My sombre mood changed to excitement as the house-tops of Ouistreham came into view. Further along the curve of the coast I recognised a dense cluster of houses and thought, *My God, that's the place, that's Lion-sur-Mer.* Straight away my heart leapt into overdrive. 'Please God, please,' I silently begged, 'let her be there.'

A wave of nostalgia swept over me as we entered Ouistreham. People still shopped in the cobbled square and the Church of Saint Pierre looked intact. The narrow street where Aunt Matilda and Uncle Claude once lived also hadn't changed.

The bus stopped and many passengers, chattering loudly, left. 'Riva Bella and La Breche are the next stops,' cried the bus driver, a round-shouldered, dark-haired man who immediately revved the engine.

From the bus window the sand dunes and the beach were much closer. Several German batteries barely visible in the sand still lay in ruins. The chalets, painted gaily in various pastel colours had been rebuilt in an effort to give the coastline its pre-war holiday appearance. Then, just as the bus turned to enter the town I caught a glimpse of Chalet Henri and the narrow road leading up to Adele's house.

Suddenly, the tension was too much. 'Can you stop here, please, driver?' I cried excitedly, first in English then in French.

The driver glanced over his shoulder and must have sensed the urgency in my voice. He braked and to the cries of what few passengers there were, came to a sudden halt. 'Anything to oblige the English,' he said with a toothy grin.

The tall, half-timbered house was till there. For a few minutes I stood staring in silence listening to the pounding of my heart. There was a new fence and gate both painted green and the smell from the roses and bougainvillea in the garden hung in the air like aromatic scent. The shutters and the bay windows were the same and except for a few marks here and there in the cream-coloured brickwork the house hadn't changed. It was almost as if the war had passed it by. Only the small box Ford motorcar resting by the side of the house looked out of place.

With blood pounding in my ears I opened the gate and felt my feet crunch under the gravelled path that led to the arched doorway. Just then a tall, dark man whom I instantly recognised as Emile opened the door. For a few seconds he looked at me, then with both arms raised he cried in French, *'Pierre. Pierre, Mon Dieu, mon ami.* Is it really you? I saw you through the window and hardly believed my eyes.'

I dropped my case as we embraced one another. 'Yes, yes, I replied in French, 'it really is me.' Then, as tears welled up in his eyes, I asked, 'How are you and your parents? How is Adele? Tell me is she here?'

Emile frowned, removed his arms from my sides and stared at the path. 'No, my friend,' he replied in English, 'they are not here. Come inside and I'll explain.'

Through a side door we entered a stone-floored kitchen. A small fire burned in a black iron stove and the spicy smell of coffee lingered in the air.

As we sat down at a large, well-scrubbed wooden table in came a woman carrying a tray of cups. Strands of ginger hair mixed with grey hung down from under a white headscarf. Straight away I recognised her as the woman I met with Spider and Paddy shortly after we landed. For a few seconds she studied me. With a look of surprise her pale blue eyes lit up. *'Mon Dieu,'* she cried excitedly placing the tray on the table, 'you are the British soldier that came here all those years ago. I remember, you asked about Mademoiselle Adele.'

'Yes,' I replied, 'have you still got the Tricolour you waved at us?'

'Folded in my best drawer,' she replied. 'It is good to see you, Monsieur.'

She carefully poured out two cups of steaming hot coffee and with a smile left the room. When she had gone, I lent across the table and took hold of Emile's hand. 'Please, Emile, I implore you,' I said, 'tell me what happened. Where is everybody'

Emile sat back, took out a packet of cigarettes, passed one to me and lit it. After taking a deep drag, he exhaled a steady steam of blur tobacco smoke and quietly said, 'Mama and Papa are dead. Mama was taken by the Gestapo to Auschwitz. We never saw her again. Papa was killed trying to escape from his concentration camp, and Adele…'

'Oh my God,' I cried anxiously, 'don't tell me she's…'

'No,' answered Emile, taking a sip of coffee, 'she's alive but…'

'But *what?*' I gasped. 'For God's sake tell me.'

'As you know she spoke and understood English very well.'

I licked my lips and nodded. Emile stubbed his cigarette out on the floor and with both hands shaking, lit another one. 'In 1943 she and Juliet Delon, who also lives in Lion, went to Paris and obtained posts at Musee de l' Homme, which was part of the National Museum of Arts.'

By now my coffee was cold. Nevertheless I finished it in one gulp. 'Go on, go on,' I cried impatiently. 'What did she do there?'

'The staff at the Musee de l' Homme were all in the French Resistance. She and Juliet joined them as interpreters. But one evening they were betrayed by a collaborator and arrested.'

I clenched my fists till they hurt, then cried, 'Good God, was she…?'

'Yes,' answered Emile hoarsely. 'She and Juliet were taken to Amien prison.' Emile paused, gave a deep sad sigh and sat back in his chair. 'Juliet told me what happened there. Her description of what the Nazis did was so horrendous….' Emile stopped talking, stood up and turned so that his back was to me. He was obviously finding it hard to continue. 'Adele and Juliet were badly tortured,' he murmured, 'she said they placed the electrodes… everywhere,' he paused again. 'Juliet was a very strong girl. Adele broke down completely, but neither of them gave away any secrets. After the RAF bombed the prison in 1944 many inmates managed to escape. Juliet and two prisoners rescued Adele who was unconscious. They were hidden from the

Germans in a house belonging to a Partisan. Here they stayed until the Allies arrived.'

(News reached Churchill that 120 prisoners were to be executed on 15 February, 1944. Operation Jericho, the bombing of Amien prison was carried out on 14 February allowing prisoners to escape.)

'But where is Adele now?' I pleaded. 'How is she?'

'After a long period in hospital,' replied Emile, 'she suffered a complete nervous break down and is now being cared for by nuns in Saint Theresa's Convent outside Caen.'

'A nervous breakdown, you say,' I said, 'what exactly is wrong with her? Is she ill or what?'

'She doesn't appear to be sick,' replied Emile, 'and has only talked a few times during the last year, but she doesn't really recognise anyone, not even me. She just sits in her room staring out the window.'

'I must see her, I must,' I pleaded leaning forward, 'when can I go?'

'This afternoon,' replied Emile, 'I've managed to obtain a little petrol. I'll drive you there after lunch.'

I was unable to eat any food. Thinking of Adele's suffering all these years had taken away my appetite.

We left Lion-sur-Mer at one o'clock. The windows of the car were turned down allowing the fresh breeze to fan my face. A warm sun shone from an unusually clear autumn sky enhancing the various shades of russet browns on the trees spread across the countryside.

'Don't expect too much,' said Emile shooting a quick glance at me. 'She may speak or simply ignore you.'

'Does she know about her mother?' I asked.

'Juliet told me a message was smuggled into the prison,' replied Emile. 'I think that strengthened her resolve and gave her courage.'

I didn't reply. Instead I pursed my lips and nodded. I then sat back, closed my eyes and nervously wondered what the day would bring.

Saint Theresa's Convent is a picturesque seventeenth-century granite building lying in quiet isolation a few miles off the main road to Caen. It was just after two o'clock when we arrived. A high wall prevented entry. Emile stopped the car and opened a set of spiked wrought iron gates. He then climbed back and drove up a narrow pathway flanked by well-kept gardens and parked the car near the arched entrance. A small nun dressed in a black and white habit opened the door. Upon seeing us her round, florid features broke into a warm smile.

'Monsieur Michaud,' she cried, raising her hands, 'welcome to you and your friend.'

'I am Maria, the Mother Superior,' she said as we shook hands.

'This is Monsieur Peter Robertson from England,' said Emile. 'He is a great friend of Adele. With your permission he'd like to see her.'

'Ah, yes, Adele, the poor creature,' she sighed while fingering a white ivory crucifix hanging on a small chain around her neck. 'Please come this way.'

We entered a long corridor smelling faintly of incense and mansion polish. Small chandeliers hung from a high, curved ceiling and as we walked our footsteps echoed on the black and white tiled floor. Religious painting depicting the saints hung on the walls alongside those of Christ on the Cross and Mother Theresa.

'How is she?' asked Emile in hushed tones.

The Mother Superior turned and looked at Emile and shook her head. 'Just the same as your last visit,' she replied, 'sometime when we serve her food I imagine a glimmer of a smile, but, alas, nothing else.'

'What do the doctors say?' I asked the Mother Superior.

'Not a great deal, I'm afraid,' she replied, 'Adele is suffering from what they call post-traumatic shock. They're not sure how long it can last. When did you last meet her?'

'Just before the war,' I replied wistfully, 'it seems such a long time ago…'

Two nuns, heads slightly bowed, clasping both hands in front, passed us without speaking. We followed the Mother Superior through a set of glass-panelled doors onto a balcony. In the distance the Normandy countryside rolled away in an undulating carpet of green fields and small areas of woodland. A set of steps led down and around a well-kept lawn. A few wooden benches rested at the edge of a gravelled pathway close to rows of multi-coloured rose bushes and Bougainvillea. All the benches were empty except one on which sat a nun and a woman. I stopped and felt my heart pound against my ribcage. Even though she had her back to me I instinctively knew the woman sitting next to the nun was Adele.

'That's her, isn't it?' I murmured, moving forward. 'That's Adele sitting with the nun.'

'Yes, but be careful and don't hurry,' replied the Mother Superior placing an arm in front of me. 'Keep your voice down or you'll frighten her. We'll keep close behind you in case we're needed.'

As I walked down the steps towards the bench I held my breath. This, I told myself, was the moment I had dreamt about for years.

The nun sitting next to her looked inquiringly at me as I approached. I raised a hand, smiled and put a finger to my lips. The nun gave an understanding nod and returned my smile. Adele had her back to me and appeared to be staring at the ground. Her hands rested in her lap nervously twisting a pink handkerchief. The shoulder-length dark brown hair I remembered so well looked darker against the white gown she was wearing. I cautiously moved in front of her and gave a start.

She had lost weight and her gown hung loosely on her. She wore no make-up. Her full lips looked anaemic and her oval face, still beautiful, was pale and drawn.

My movement startled her. With one hand she shielded her eyes against the sun and looked up. Those luminous brown eyes I had seen so often in my dreams, stared into mine. Only self-restraint prevented me from throwing my arms around her.

'Adele,' I whispered, 'it's me, Peter.'

To my dismay she turned away and continued staring at the ground. I slowly sat down next to her and placed a hand over hers. Without looking at me she gave a slight whimper and quickly moved her hand away.

'Adele,' I pleaded, gazing longingly at her. 'Don't you remember? Lion-sur-Mer. The beach. Me... us...'

I felt a soft hand on my shoulder. I glanced behind and saw Emile and the Mother Superior. 'I'm sorry, young man,' said the Mother Superior, 'all we can do is pray...' Her voice trailed away.

I felt my throat contract and slowly stood up. This was the woman whose memory had kept me going through the turbulence of war and nights of pain. Now, she looked so pale and helpless. How could I possibly walk away, I asked myself. Surely there must be something I could do. I reached down and gently stroked her hair. She moved her head slightly but didn't look up. Suddenly I too felt helpless.

I was about to walk away when I remembered the medallion.

I quickly undid the clasp and drew the medallion from around my neck. I sat down next to Adele and slowly lifted the medallion in front of her face. At first she simply stared blankly at it. All of a sudden the metal caught the rays of the sun making it glitter like silver. Suddenly, a light that had been dimmed kindled in her eyes and her pallid lips curved into an odd smile. With a slight whimper she reached out a hand and touched the crucifix embedded in the medallion's round shape and murmured, 'Grandmamma, Grandmamma. This was my Grandmamma's.' Her voice was soft and she spoke slowly but with great difficulty.

From behind I hear Mother Superior gasp.

'Adele. Adele,' I cried, staring into her eyes, 'it's me, Peter. You remember? Peter, the man you met a long time ago in Lion-sur-Mer.'

She looked away from the medallion at my face. 'Is it really you,' she said, touching my face with a finger, 'or am I dreaming?'

'No, no,' I replied reaching out and placing my hands on her shoulders, 'it really is me. I told you I'd come back. That wish I made all those years ago has finally come true. I've waited so long for this moment...' My voice trailed away and I felt warm tears running down my cheek. At that moment we were both overcome with emotion. Still holding the medallion she placed a hand on my arm. 'So much has happened to me,' she sobbed, 'so much... Please tell me you'll never leave me again.'

'I'll always be with you,' I gasped, 'now and forever.'

I remained in France for a further month visiting Adele every day. Three months later we were married in the Church of Saint Pierre in Lion-sur-Mer. Mum and dad, smiling and crying at the same time, were there. Emile gave Adele away and Gordon was Best Man.

We now live in Adele's parents' house. I teach English at the local secondary school. Adele eventually recovered and obtained a post with the local council. From the window of our bedroom we can see what was once Sword Beach and on balmy nights, walk hand in hand along the path where we first met during those halcyon days in the summer of '39.